I AM I

I AM I

JAMES LATHAM

ARPress
45 Dan Road Suite 5
Canton MA 02021
Hotline: 1(888) 821-0229
Fax: 1(508) 545-7580

Ordering Information:
Quantity sales. Special discounts are available on quantity purchases by corporations, associations, and others. For details, contact the publisher at the address above.

Printed in the United States of America.

ISBN-13:   Softcover   979-8-89356-002-2
            Hardcover   979-8-89356-003-9
            eBook   979-8-89356-004-6

Library of Congress Control Number: 2024902559

BRINGER OF PEACE

The sun rose quickly into a beautiful summer blue sky. Cotton white clouds drifted across an endless ocean of air. And those on solid ground enjoyed a sun's loving care. As a young boy, Jim looked to the skies and dreamed of soaring endlessly over tall buildings and snow covered mountain tops. Jim craved to behold all from high above. Patiently Jim waited for the day when the wings of flight would lift him into the endless skies.

Days and years flew by as Jim watched and dreamed. Dreaming, he flew the mighty jets so flawlessly through the ocean of blue skies. Many, many years later Jim, a man in his late thirties, worked as an aircraft jet engineer and designer. Day to day Jim helped to improve the jets' performance and speed. He was thrilled to hear the pilots describe their flights from high above the clouds. The feeling of flight became a great sound of excitemet. One day, as Jim was observing engineers piece together an aircraft engine, an image began to form within his mind. An engine without fuel of any kind. A craft never having to refuel. That would be a craft as free as a bird, Jim thought. Keeping his idea to himself, Jim felt he may have found a way to fly the skies of his boyhood dreams. To soar high above the clouds and dance into the endless skies. An idea that sounded like wishful thinking, Jim still felt he had to try. To bring to reality the flight of a bird and power of a jet, Jim experimented feverishly. Experiment after experiment proved to be very successful. Eager to bring his dreams to reality, Jim began to think much bigger. Needing more room to expand, Jim moved his experiments to his two-car garage. With plenty of room to expand, Jim went to work immediately. Weeks flew by as Jim slowly pieced together his device. Every day was a day of progress in the right direction. After four exciting months of piecing together a strange-looking device, Jim felt confident a day for testing was in sight. Anxious to finish, Jim stayed up late and installed the last few

pieces. Tired, Jim stood back from his device and admired his hard work. "Soon we'll see what you can do", Jim says aloud looking at his creation. Turning, Jim steps to the door that entered into the house. Turning out the light Jim enters the house and heads to his bedroom. Once inside his bedroom Jim heads straight to the bed. Lying upon the bed Jim falls asleep without a struggle. The darkness within Jim's mind quickly becomes a dream of flying high above the clouds, so high above the planet he loved so much that the land began to curve. Only large bodies of land and water pictured within Jim's mind. So real and yet a dream, what did it mean? Hours passed as Jim flew the skies of his dreams. Awakened by the soft touch of the morning sun, Jim found a bright warm sun high in the sky. A bright clear sky warmed by a summer sun invited Jim outside. Deciding to enjoy his weekend outside, Jim neglected his chores and even his well-kept secret. Having been cooped-up inside his home and work, Jim realized how much he had missed being outside under a yellow warm sun. How life of many kinds and nature in its ever growing struggle to survive existed under a glowing yellow sun:a sun that gave life to a planet of many kinds. The green of trees and colors of flowers attracted many forms of life. Watching the birds fly about and land made Jim realize how birds were enjoying the freedom of flight. Being able to land and take off at any moment impressed Jim of their abilities. Flight to a bird was natural, Jim thought. Flight to a human was beyond words of excitement. Continuing to watch the birds of many sizes land and fly, Jim imagined one day he'd fly the sky's himself. To land and take off as freely as the birds. To see the wonders of Earth as he has never seen before. Looking up past the trees, Jim scans the skies only to see a mighty jet quietly passing through the skies. Too high to hear a sound, the jet flew freely high above the drifting clouds. Seeing only a blue summer sky with peaceful chirping birds flying back and forth, Jim knew it would take more than the wings of a bird to fly in or above the clouds. Stepping outside, Jim rests in a lawn chair watching the peacefulness of the day. After many hours under the sun, Jim decides to return to the quietness of his house. Finding the plans of his device, Jim beings to examine every page, every line, and every detail. Sitting within his living room, Jim stares out the glass sliding doors. Birds of many kinds flew about enticing Jim's mind of the gracefulness of flight. It has to work, Jim thought to himself. The day of sun and warmth, of blue skies and drifting white clouds, followed its path across the sky disappearing at Earth's distant horizon. As Jim watched the sun slowly dip into the horizon, he knew somehow, some way, he would reach his dreams. To Jim the sun was not saying goodbye, it was saying "Follow me." Now the sun was gone and another day of sunlight came to an end. Darkness came with all the glitter of the distant stars. What would tomorrow bring? Jim thought. Calling it a day, Jim left his chair and went to bed early. With a sky full of stars outside his window, Jim slept soundly. The next day began with a sunrise as beautiful as the sunset. Chirping birds began the day as a subtle sound of music waking all. Ready for the first test run, Jim had high expectations for success. But first thing's first, Jim thought. Breakfast was first in line to quell the growing growl within his stomach. Sitting down to a light breakfast, Jim found himself empty of thought. There were too many pros and cons to think about. Finishing breakfast, Jim makes his way to the garage. With his hand on the door knob, Jim pushes the door open and steps into the garage. A few feet into the garage Jim sees his device as if it was waiting for him. Silent and still the device waited to churn the power it possessed. Checking the device one last time, Jim felt confident all was in order. Now the moment of success or failure was at hand. Reaching for the start switch, Jim held his breath. Months of work and only a few seconds to find the moment of truth. Turning the switch, Jim watched with great anxiety. Second after second Jim watched and to his surprise and dismay, nothing happened. Time after time Jim turned the switch back and forth with the same result, nothing. A feeling of great failure and confusion grabbed Jim. "What is wrong, why didn't it work?" Jim asked himself. Struggling to find the problem, Jim re-checked every inch of the device. Lost in his efforts to succeed, Jim continued to search for the eluding problem. Knowing there would be days like this, days when disappointment would test his inner strength, Jim knew it only meant he had to try harder and learn more. Even a bird has to learn to fly. To practice over and over till the wings of flight lift him into the air, Jim thought. Feeling a bit less disappointed, Jim knew not to give-up. Flight is for those that see an endless sky.

Days drifted by and Jim, unable to find the problem, grew frustrated and very impatient. The answer came to Jim from the mailman. A very colorful advertisement was in Jim's mailbox. Pulling it out of the mailbox Jim holds it with both hands and reads the advertisement. Tonight at 7:00 o'clock we welcome all too thrilling rides, exciting games, and wonderful eatable treats. Come join the fun and win prizes. It looked like a fun time to be had and a time to clear his troubled mind. Needing a few items from town, Jim decided to pick-up the items first then go the carnival. Wasting no time Jim dresses in a nice shirt, blue jeans, and shoes. Out the house Jim dashes and into his truck. Down the road Jim drives, headed to town a few miles away. It didn't

take long and Jim was in town. Driving down the town's main street Jim finds a parking place and parks. Stepping out of his truck Jim sees a large colorful picture taped to the store's glass. It was the carnival's poster with far more to see than his small mailbox advertisement. As Jim read the poster, others gathered around to also read. Excitement was in the air and Jim could feel it. Aroused with the carnivals arrival, people in town hurried to attend. Finding the items he needed, Jim found his way back to his truck. Nearing six o'clock Jim decided to head to the carnival. On a road outside of town, Jim knew he was on the correct road. Bumper to bumper, trucks and cars lined the road like a long snake slowly slithering. Off in the distance a large wheel slowly circled within the sky and in the far horizon the sun was saying farewell. With sunset quickly approaching, the carnival turned on their lights and illuminated the grounds and sky with brilliant colorful lights. Finally, Jim reaches the parking area and finds a place to park. Out of his truck, Jim follows a steady stream of people into the carnival's entrance way. Once inside Jim is amazed at so many rides of various kinds. Excited and fascinated, people rode swirling rides round and round and rides that quickly turned up-side down with cheers and smiles upon excited faces. Side by side game booths lined the walkways inviting people to play and win. As people tried their luck at winning prizes, others gathered around to watch. The smell of food cooking floated freely through the air enticing many to stop and satiate their aroused appetites. For the first time since starting his project, Jim had completely forgotten his worry about his project. Free of problems and failures, Jim was enjoying the carnival's exciting atmosphere. Just to be among so many people having a great time put a smile on Jim's face. Moving past the numerous booths and food venders, Jim found himself in front of the carnival's main attraction. Startled by its size and glow of brightness, Jim could only stare. Tall and round, the carnival's main attraction stood as a giant wheel glowing brightly with colorful lights. A one hundred foot-tall Ferris wheel filled with people slowly turned as riders smiled and watchers stood in awe. A long line of people stood waiting to ride the glowing wheel. So Jim decided to see more of the rides. Crowded with people exploring with excitement, Jim worked his way through the crowd enjoying the excitement. As Jim enjoyed the excitement, he noticed a ride that grabbed his immediate attention. Like arms of an octopus, six long poles branched out holding one-seated saucers. Round and round the saucers flew, up and down without a sound. Children riding inside smiled from ear to ear. But Jim's mind raced back to his secret project. Drifting from the carnival's excitement and returning to his childhood days, Jim finds himself standing alone watching the jets of his youth roaring across a blue sky. "Could it be possible? Could I put together such a ship with my device and make my dreams come true?" Jim whispers to himself. Continuing his sightseeing, Jim enjoyed the carnival just watching others having fun. Still deep in his mind Jim held tight to the saucer ride. Hours later after Jim had toured and enjoyed the carnival's excitement, Jim left the carnival with ideas and a very vigorous appetite to reach the skies. Back at home Jim laid in bed and began dreaming of soaring from one planet to another. Meeting beings of different planets and learning the universe's hidden secrets. The next day Jim awoke with a clear mind and was very excited to find the problems that ached his mind. Restudying his plans, Jim decides to make a few changes that could spark life into his device. Hopeful for a spark of needed success, Jim worked with a refreshed mind. Hour after hour Jim worked with the feeling that this time success would triumph over his defeats. Not realizing the time of day , Jim had worked most of the day only to see the sun slowly fading away. Still feeling that success was near Jim put his tools down and called it a day. Leaving his garage Jim returns to his bedroom. Setting his alarm clock for eight o'clock he lay down. Staring out the window, his eyes gazed at the star-filled sky never knowing what his future would bring. Never to know he would fly more than the skies above the clouds. To use his knowledge and gain knowledge far beyond his wishful thinking. As the hours of sleep crept by, Jim slept soundly. Within the confines of his mind, the skies of space were limitless as Jim roamed the stars, planets, and galaxies. Their wonders were far too many for one to explore. Still Jim's thoughts were faster than the speed of light as he reached across the galaxies to find new wonders. After eight long hours of sound sleep, a sudden fast metallic tapping noise awakes Jim. Pulling himself back to Earth, Jim sits up drowsy with eyes unfocused. Realizing the irritating commotion was the alarm clock. Jim grabs the clock and stops the clamoring noise. Bringing his eyes into focus, Jim realizes another day awaited. Another day and another chance to succeed. Springing to his feet, Jim dresses and makes his way to the kitchen. Sitting down to a breakfast of eggs, toast, butter, bacon, hash browns, and coffee, Jim wanted to make sure he started his day on a full stomach. While Jim enjoyed his breakfast, he pondered if the day would bring joy or sorrow. After breakfast Jim was determined to try and start his device again. Leaving the kitchen Jim enters the garage again. Silent and still his device lingered lifeless. Staring at the device, Jim says to himself, "I haven't given up yet." Success or failure Jim knew he had to try again. Crossing his fingers, Jim turns the switch. Anticipating better success than days before. Jim watched and hoped for the best. Still and silent the device

rested lifeless. "Not another defeat," Jim said to himself. The long hours of work once again became fruitless. Success was not to be, and great disappointment began to settle within Jim's mind. Sitting down and crushed with defeat, Jim was ready to give up. Months of work and a lifetime of dreams disappeared into the mist of frustration. Lost in his thoughts of defeat, Jim reaches out to turn the device off. As if the device said no, a small movement budged the wheel of power forward. Slowly the lifeless wheel showed signs of life. More and more the wheel turned as Jim looks on with amazed eyes. Standing, Jim watches as the seconds of movement grow into minutes. Continuing to move and increase in speed Jim was happy but not satisfied. With only the speed of a slow-moving ceiling fan the wheel turned. The power of life was in the device, but not the life of power it needed to be great. To be great the device would need much more power to fly a ship high in the sky. Still Jim was relieved and gives a smile of satisfaction. Now Jim was able to throw the heavy weight of defeat from his mind. To have stayed defeated, Jim would have had a lifetime of many regrets to carry. To look into the sky and see the mighty jets year after year divide the blue sky with long white tails of smoke. To know only what others have seen and the feel of flight they experience. Never to know the true feeling of flying high in the clouds. Needing more improvements, Jim still felt satisfied he was headed in the right direction. To see the device moving gave Jim the motivation he needed to continue. The long road of uncertainty became the road of success. Jim was glad success had finally shone a glimmer of light upon him. Having found his way out of the maze of confusion, Jim learned a valuable lesson, never give up on your dreams. Dreams can be one's life ambitions. With a smile of relief, Jim turns the switch off. Slowly the life of the device came to a halt. For the first time Jim walked away content and no longer followed by the shadow of failure. Jim knew more improvements would increase overall speed and power. Stepping out from the garage, Jim looks into the day's sky. Somehow, some way, Jim knew he would soar among the many drifting clouds. To be one with jets he watched when he was a boy. Off to work Jim hurried with his secrets locked within his mind. At work Jim found the day to be long. His mind was still at home studying his device, determined to find the ailing problem. Watching the many jet engines being tested, Jim could only imagine his device being tested. To see his device at full power running beyond all scales of power. To hear its roar of power echo throughout the building as a lion protecting its territory. To give notice to all that heard and saw, a new power was born. Torn between work and home Jim was unable to focus at work. The hours slowly rolled by while Jim remained deep in thought of his secret at home. How to improve and increase power were now problems soon to solve. The day of work finally came to an end. Driving home Jim's thoughts were still the same. Stay focused and succeed. Back at home Jim gazed into the night's sky. The moon and stars seemed to speak a language of their own. Their distant glow summoned a stare of wonder Jim couldn't interpret. Feeling a sense of being called, Jim could only wonder why. A strange feeling so far away touching him deep to his core of feelings. Back in his bedroom, Jim decides not to set the alarm. Laying down Jim falls into a deep sleep. Morning returned and the sun's warm rays fell upon Jim as a friendly hand gently waking him. Jim awakes with only one issue on his mind. Improving the device's speed. Hurriedly Jim dresses and heads to the kitchen. Sitting down to a small and simple breakfast, Jim ate slowly. Listening to the radio, Jim, for the first time since starting his project, found himself relaxed and full of confidence. Ready to take on the next challenge that led to the gateway of endless skies. The skies were only the beginning for Jim. For Jim would see skies far beyond the skies of Earth. Finishing a short cereal breakfast Jim felt certain today would be a day of great improvements. Leaving the kitchen, Jim heads to the garage. Turning the doorknob, Jim enters the garage. Full of confidence Jim was ready to start a new day. In silence the device sat poised in the middle of the garage. Jim approaches and stares at the lifeless device. "How great and powerful can you be? Can you power a craft as large as the jets of today? Can you touch the stars that light our night? Be the power I dreamed of so many years ago," Jim said to the device. Reaching to the control switch, Jim turns the switch on. Full of confidence Jim watches as the device began to slowly budge. Like a slow moving train wheel, the wheel of power rotated as if pulling a heavy load. Round and round the wheel slowly turned. With no more power than the day before the speed was not to be seen. After a few minutes of watching, Jim decides to approach the problem a different way.

Turning the device off, all motion of the wheel slowly came to a halt. Jim had an idea what the problem was. Adding another part to the device Jim stands back and restarts the device. Quickly the wheel started spinning faster and faster. A small gust of wind blew from the bottom of the device to all directions of the room. The device was alive and powerful. Seemingly the device must have heard Jim's outward thoughts. It was a power Jim had watched when he was young. A power that could achieve every demand that was requested of it. Spinning faster, the device yearned to escape its bonds that held it in place. A high pitched noise began to climb above the noise

of wind and blades. Faster and faster with no end in sight, the device spun causing a strong gust of air to erupt. Checking the power level, Jim noticed the meter had plenty of room to increase power. Only a very small portion of the device's power was being displayed. Far too powerful to display all its power. Satisfied for the time being, a dream of Jim's was coming true. A smile of great satisfaction replaced a worried stare of failing. On and on the blades turned harnessing raw power with no fuel. As Jim stared, he knew there was no place to go but up. To move forward and reach for the skies. To drift quietly with the clouds and see all from high above. Jim's mind was already in the sky of dreams. As Jim watched, his mind drifted to the time he visited the county fair. Remembering the saucer ride, he imagined the saucer without the support pole.

"Could I do it, could I really make it work?" With his mind fixed upon the skies, the desire to fly overwhelmed all his other thoughts. To take his place among the clouds so high above all and soar was a desire Jim craved from boyhood. "Yes, I can do it," Jim said quietly to himself. Bracing himself for yet another uphill task. Jim accepted his new challenge with great eagerness. Turning the device off, Jim watches as the fast moving blades slowly lose their momentum. The high pitched piercing noise with its swirling gust of air slowly faded away. Now all was quiet and still once more. Exhilarated with the day's accomplishments, Jim's mind was back in the sky soaring high. Higher than the birds and clouds, Jim soared with great satisfaction. Now to give this great power a body worthy of soaring high. Like the jets that adorned the blue skies. A body sleek and curved with the ability to cut through the sky like a knife. A shape that can withstand high speeds and flights beyond Earth's atmosphere if possible. Big enough for two or three people and most of all, a ship with the ability to land and take off from anywhere. Definitely a ship very similar to the fair's flying ride ships, Jim thought. Gathering the much needed information within his mind Jim was ready for his new challenge. Ready for the wings of flight to take him high. Wasting no time Jim immediately began his new project. Days drifted into weeks of drawing and redrawing plans. Jim had learned his lesson well, never give up. The sun will rise and shine brightly and all will become clear. After three weeks of drawing, Jim had finally settled upon a basic set of plans. Plans that would meet all his specifications. Plans that others would call crazy or impossible. Jim would bring them to reality, and soar the blue skies like none before him had ever soared. With a great power source and ship design, Jim needed someone to build his ship. Not just any builder, a very good builder.

One with years of experience and know how. One that would listen and give ideas. One that took pride in his work. Using the phone book, Jim finds a list of welders. Many companies and many welders. Knowing he had to keep his ship a secret Jim couldn't use a company to weld his ship. They would insist the project be built in their shop. Jim knew that would be impossible. The world would end up knowing his secret. Calling the independent welders, Jim learned many were booked-up for months or welded only in their own shops. Not a listed welder seemed to be available. Remembering what he had learned, "never give up", Jim still had a few more calls to make. Within Jim's calls, an unlisted name continued to arise. Left with only this one person to call, Jim had little choice. Considered to be an excellent welder as told by other welders Mr. Joe Simmons came highly recommended and highly cautioned about his bad habit. Skeptical of even calling Mr. Simmons, Jim had little choice. Reluctantly Jim calls Mr. Simmons. "Simmons welder's shop," a voice said. "Mr. Simmons?" Jim asks. "Yes this is Mr. Simmons," Mr. Simmons said. "My name is Jim and I've been looking for a welder. Everyone I've called is booked-up. But a few of the welders have recommend you. Would you be interested in a welding job?"

"What do you need welded" Mr. Simmons asked. "I have a project that will take a few months to complete. If you're interested I'll give you my address," Jim said. "I'll come over and take a look, and I'll let you know then," Mr. Simmons said.

Deciding to meet the coming Saturday, which was two days away, Jim was grateful for the lesson he had learned, "never give-up." Knowing he had to be ready Jim rechecks every inch of the ship's blueprints. To design a ship was not as hard as inventing a zero fuel device. But to design a ship never seen before was a challenge. Realizing that Mr. Simmons would have a few questions to ask, Jim prepared himself with a believable story to tell Mr. Simmons. I'm sure Mr. Simmons would think something was not right, Jim thought. As the day continued, Jim made ready to meet Mr. Simmons. The next day arrived and Jim felt comfortable with his plans and concealed story. Knowing the blue prints showed no power source. Jim felt his story would be enough cover to hide the unexplained hole. Deciding to spend the day away from his project Jim relied on his job to amuse himself. The new jets tested roared with power. Slicker and more bullet-shaped, the future jets would dominate the skies above the clouds. And how would my ship of the sky, fair against the new jets? Jim wondered. Designing a ship far from bullet shaped, how would its speed match or beat the future jets. The future

for Jim was not far away and his questions would all be answered. Jim knew his ship would have the ability to turn in seconds. To rise and decline in one place. And a speed that would frighten its pilot. That day Jim studied many ship designs and worked with engineers. Listening to the roar of new jet engines being tested made Jim wonder what his device would sound like at full power. Another day of work ended, finding Jim driving home from work feeling anxiety building within his thoughts. What could go wrong tomorrow? What do I do if Mr. Simmons says no? There is no one else to build the ship, Jim thought. Arriving home, Jim still managed to see a day of sky and sunshine. A day full of warmth and beauty. As the day ended with a glow of light in the distant horizon stars and a glowing moon lit the night and all rested waiting for another day of sunlight. Saturday arrived bringing a bright sunny day. With very few clouds, the sun's scorching hot rays gave notice to all that summer was here. Finishing breakfast, Jim decides to wait for Mr. Simmons outside under a large shade tree. A short walk from the house Jim reaches the tree. A tree over a hundred years old stood with wide branches and wide leaves. Giving shade to all seeking relief from a pouring rain or a burning sun as it has done many, many years. Sitting down at the base of the tree, Jim leans back and rests against the tree's trunk. Enjoying the cool gentle breeze under the tree Jim dozes off as time lingered by. Waking to a large truck passing by, Jim glances at his watch. Noticing the meeting time had passed, Jim wondered if Mr. Simmons had changed his mind. Deciding to wait a bit longer, Jim stares across a blue sun-lit sky. Clouds float calmly giving shade as they pass over and birds fly freely from place to place. A sky touched only by mankind's powerful jets. Leaving the skies free for one to close his or her eyes and dream of flying the skies. And that's just what Jim had been doing. High in the sky Jim flew fulfilling his boyhood dreams, with a sky wondering adventure. As Jim waited for a jet to pierce and divide the unbroken sky. He scanned a tranquil sky only to see blue upon blue miles of peaceful serenity. So he imagined his ship speeding quietly across a calm sky without a trail of white smoke. With only a reflection of sunlight, his shiny ship flew the skies freely.

Hold me not, for I fly so high High above all that I see. Hold me not, for all that I see. I see in awe and wonder,

Jim thought to himself as he looked into a world of sky. Suddenly the sound of a pickup broke Jim's daydreaming. Grabbed from the sky of endless dreams, Jim found himself back on solid ground. Looking toward the road, an old red pickup needing a paint job slowly headed toward his house. Behind the driver's cab was a large welding machine. On one side of the pickup door a sign read, "Joe Simmons Welding."

Slowly the pickup reached the house and rolled to a stop as if it ran out of gas. The driver's door opens and a man in his late forties gets out and starts walking toward the house. Quickly Jim gets up and briskly walks toward Mr. Simmons. Before Mr. Simmons reaches the house. Jim calls out, "Hello I'm Jim, I called you two days ago." Stopping, Mr. Simmons looks toward Jim. Not waiting for Jim to reach him, Mr. Simmons starts walking toward Jim. "Sorry I'm late, it took me a while to find your address," Mr. Simmons said. Walking toward each other, they meet and shake hands. While they shake hands, Mr. Simmons asks Jim to call him Joe. Inviting Joe into his house, both men casually talked about the hot weather. Once inside, Jim and Joe settle down at the kitchen table. Jim offers Joe a cold drink. While Joe drinks his drink, Jim gets out the four-page plans of the ship. Laying the plans on the table Jim sits down and waits for Joe to examine the plans. Setting down his drink Joe, unaware of what he was to see, looks down at the plans. Frozen with surprise Joe's eyes widen as if he had seen a ghost. Turning to another page Joe still sat in shock. Page by page Joe studies the plans carefully. It was obvious Joe had never seen a project like this. A project so far from the little welding jobs he's completed. A project that stirred the inner core of Joe's thinking into endless questions planted across his face. Continuing to study the plans, Joe's eyes moved over the plans as a painter studies every detail. After a few minutes of mind-shattering contemplating, Joe looks up with a very puzzled look upon his face. Having welded for many years Joe had never seen a project like this. Far more complicated than welding farm machinery or pipe fences, Joe was faced with a project that challenged the best of his metal fabricating and welding skills. Looking at Jim still with a puzzled face he asks, "What's this exactly for?"

Now came the time for Jim to see how believable his made-up story would settle Joe's puzzle mind. "I consider it an educational project for young scientific minds," Jim said. Joe, still puzzled, felt he still needed more of an explanation for such a project. Feeling Jim was pulling his leg he said, "Would you put that in English, so I can get a better picture of your project in my mind?."

"It's to give young minds in school that are studying space, or would like to, the feeling of being in space," Jim said. "So you're going to take this ship to a school and let the students use it," Joe said still with a look of bewilderment upon his face 'Yes' Jim said. Joe came to the conclusion it was

a job unlike any he'd ever done. A job that would not lose interest. "Well this project will take some time and cost some money," Joe said.

Smiling at Joe, Jim said, "You build it Joe, and I'll take care of the bills."

"Fair enough," Joe said. With that, Jim holds out his hand and Joe having lost his puzzled look smiles and shakes Jim's hand. As they shake hands, Jim was relieved that Joe had taken the job and the plans would become reality. Jim had a feeling that Joe was the best pick for the job. Still the thought of Joe's drinking problems floated wildly in Jim's mind. Would Joe's problem arise during the ship's construction? If so, Jim would have more problems and headaches than he could truly imagine. So much hung on Joe's stability. Jim would learn weeks later how right he was. For Joe would take the project to heart and build the ship to perfection. A ship able to travel far beyond Earth's solar system, into a solar system even Jim would find hard to believe. The lives of many upon many who looked to the stars for their answer, waited. Parting hands, the feeling of uncertainty had disappeared and replaced with smiles of a great friendship to be. Having made their agreement, Joe informs Jim. "I'll also need an assistant,"

"Do you have someone in mind?" Jim asked. "Yes I do, and he's a good worker," Joe said. "If he wants the job, bring him with you," Jim said smiling. "Give me a week and I'll be back with my tools and assistant," Joe said. Shaking hands once again Jim and Joe said their goodbyes. Walking Joe to the front door, Jim stood and watched Joe get into his truck. Starting his truck up, Joe smiles and waves good-bye. Slowly the truck drives away out of sight. As Jim watched the truck disappear he hoped everything would work out. So much was at stake. Time, money, and a lifetime of dreams were quickly racing to a sudden impact. Spending the week getting ready time seemed to fly by. Daily, Jim checked his device and marveled at its power. No more slow dragging starts. The device was a burst of energy equal or better than the metal birds that ruled the skies. Daily Jim dreamed of soaring through the endless skies. Through clouds and above the clouds, he felt the same delight so many pilots felt. Living on the outskirts of town and surrounded by ten acres of trees Jim's privacy was intact from any inquisitive eyes. Only the eyes high in the sky would know of Jim's intentions. But hidden within the trees even the eyes in the sky would have to look very hard. It was Sunday night—the day before Joe would arrive. Jim found himself unable to rest but managed to lie down a few hours. As Jim gazed out the bedroom star-filled window he felt a feeling of urgency, a feeling of great need, a feeling of being whispered to. "Who are you, where are you?" Jim asks quietly. Somewhere in the distant mist of shining stars, cries of help echoed through the endless depths of space. "How can I help? I am so far away," Jim says quietly. As Jim stares into the distant stars, his eyes close and darkness takes over. The next day arrived with another hot summer day. Up early and having finished breakfast, Jim finds himself waiting for Joe to arrive. As if waiting for a school bus Jim stares down the long road, across the open fields and into the distant horizon. No red pickup, only others coming and going. The day was still early so Jim steps back inside his house and waits. The sun was rising fast, bringing light and life to a new day. A day that would put in motion a new and unexpected way of life for Jim and others. Occasionally staring out his front window. Jim would check to see if Joe's red pickup was in sight. Almost ten o' clock and the sun beamed a steady glow of light and heat. Jim noticed a truck in the far distance. Closer it came and Jim could see it was a red pick-up. As the truck neared, Jim noticed another man with Joe. Jim guessed it was Joe's assistant. Slowly the truck reached the house. Stopping as if rolling to a stop Joe and his friend step out of the truck and walk to meet Jim. Shaking hands with Joe and his friend, Joe introduces his friend, to Jim. "Jim this is my good friend, Sam. We have known each other for many years. We first met years ago in the army. We have been friends ever since. Sam is skillful with metal and electrical devices," Joe said. "Great, we can use a good electrician. Our project will be filled with electrical devices," Jim said shaking Sam's hand with a smile. "I guess you've been informed of our project?" Jim asks. With a big smile on his face Sam says, "Yes. Joe and I have talked about the project. It sounds very exciting and very different from what I've ever done." Sam, a man about the same age as Joe, was of normal build and also stood as tall as Joe. Short cut blond hair and dressed neat, Sam showed signs of the military still ran within his veins. After greeting each other Jim suggested they walk to the back of the house and decide on a suitable site to build the ship.

Walking into a cluster of tall trees they search for a suitable site. "Over here," Joe calls. Joe had found a site of tall trees with an area large enough for the ship and materials. Being only a few hundred feet from Jim's house the sight was excellent. With all agreeing to the site Joe returns to his pickup. Turning his truck, Joe backs the truck to the site. Unloading the metal and supplies upon the ground site Joe took charge and was very meticulous about where everything was placed. Following Joe's lead, Sam and Jim placed everything as Joe instructed. Jim was glad Joe was taking charge. Without Joe, the project would stay on paper. So Jim decides to follow Joe and help wherever needed. After unloading, Joe informs Jim more metal was

needed before they could get started. "Sam and I will get metal today and be back early tomorrow morning," Joe said. "Then I'll see you two tomorrow morning," Jim said. Without a word Joe and Sam smiled at Jim, waved good-bye, and departed. Off Joe and Sam go driving down the long road and out of sight. Things seemed to be going in the right direction. Joe had stayed sober, on time, and in full control. The construction of the ship would soon be getting under way. And once it did, the builders would feverishly continue till they finished. That night Jim stared into the star lit sky. What amazing wonders occur within the stars? One will never know unless they are there, Jim thought. The stars and calmness of space revealed nothing by staring at them. They shined and twinkled and brought to all a calmness of peace within the heavens. And yet a strange feeling seemed to be felt. Like a whisper in the wind calling Jim over and over. The feeling of someone being so close and yet it was only a feeling. Lying in bed Jim stares at the glow of stars till he falls asleep. Bright and early as Joe had said, he and Sam returned and began unloading a large load of metal. Joe and Sam worked well together and seemed to be enjoying the project. It was their private project they kept hidden. Like three boys building a tree house in a secret hiding place. Joe seemed to be everywhere. Taking control and guiding the ship's construction. Joe gave the orders and Sam and Jim obeyed. All three seemed to be enjoying the very unusual project. Working side by side they worked as if they had known each other for years. As the weeks passed, the ship's frame took shape. It was far more than a diagram on paper. There it sat in midst of the trees. A frame of metal, shaped like two plates facing each other. Only a frame and yet it caught one's eyes, attention, and curiosity. A boyhood dream slowly coming to life. Weeks slowly turned into a month and the ship's frame, a wonder to behold, waited to be finished. Precise in his measurements and welding Joe constructed a frame that caught one's eyes and imagination. Within the thickness of trees rested the unknown to one that would happen upon the mysterious object. As only a frame, the ship's shape would raise many questions and send one's mind racing faster than one's legs could run. Joe examined and re-examined every weld and every measurement leaving nothing to question. The stories from other welders Jim had heard were true. When Joe sets his mind to a project he did it right. Perfection guided every weld Joe made. Resting on the ground a true work of art gave credit to Joe's abilities. An unfinished frame, it still sparkled of great ingenuity. The smiles worn by Joe and Sam told Jim all was going as planned. Two months had swiftly passed and a very unusual object rested among the trees. An object one would not have guessed to find hidden in a cluster of trees. Finished with the framework Sam ran a few feet of wire for lights and controls. "All we need is the outside covering," Joe says with a proud smile. Jim knew the power source had to be next, before any outside covering. What will Joe and Sam say when they see the device resting in the garage? Jim thought. The connection of the device was a must and Jim knew it. They had worked very hard that day. So they planned to start the outside covering the next day. Jim smiled and agreed with the guys. Off Joe and Sam drove waving their hands outside the truck windows. The next day Joe and Sam were back bright and early. Both were so excited to begin covering the ship. Before Joe and Sam could get tools and the welding machine ready Jim told Joe and Sam he had something to add to the ship's frame. Looking at Jim a bit puzzled Joe and Sam followed Jim without a word. Off to the garage they walked in complete wonder. Entering the side garage door, something large rested in the center of the room. Covered with black plastic, its true identity was concealed only revealing its shape. Approaching slowly, all three stood next to the unknown covered object. Large and round Joe and Sam were both mystified by Jim's covered secret. Standing with puzzled looks upon their faces they waited for Jim to reveal what laid underneath. Jim knew he couldn't keep his secret a total secret, there was no other way. Finishing the project by himself was impossible. Jim could only hope for the best. Staring at Joe and Sam, Jim could see their curiosity was getting the best of both. Without a word, Jim grabs the plastic and gives a good pull. Without blinking Joe and Sam stare in absolute wonder. Off slid the sheet of black plastic, revealing its unknown secret. Standing like statues, Joe and Sam just stare. Their eyes and facial expressions could only express their bafflement. After a few minutes of staring, "What is it?" Joe asked. "Whatever it is, it's big," Sam said. With a big smile Jim extinguishes Joe's and Sam's bewildered curiosity. "It's a device that will produce a small amount of electricity to run the ship's controls."

Not wanting to show the true potential of the device Jim covers a demonstration with a cover story. "It still needs a few more adjustments before it can be fully operational. But I can get that done once the device has been adjusted to the ship's frame," Jim said. Still with roaming eyes coving the device, Joe and Sam consent to Jim's story and merely stare with curiosity. The device rested on a metal frame built around it with wheels attached to the metal frame. Jim felt the three of them could roll the device to the ship. Raising the large garage door all grab hold of the device and slowly push the device out of the garage. Across the yard they fight a battle of pushing and

tugging. Reaching the trees they found the trees to be a maze of left and right turns. Finally they reach the clearing and the ship. Rolling the device under the ship, all three dripping of sweat collapse from exhaustion. Tired and sweating heavily, Jim cried out, "Let's take a break."

"I second that," Sam said lying on the ground. "I can't move another muscle. How in the world did the Egyptians push all those large stones and build the pyramids?" Joe asked while lying on the ground.

"I'll tell you Joe, they used trucks, chains, and cranes," Sam said. Looking at each other, the remark was ridiculous for the time, but pictured in one's mind it sure looked funny. Breaking out into a wild laugh the three of them forgot about being tired. Not realizing the moment, the three of them were building more than a ship. They were building a friendship that would span across the reaches of deep space. After a long laugh and acting as if they were using trucks and operating cranes to build the pyramids they regained their strength and returned to work. The work continued for hours with very little said. By the end of the day the hook-up of the device was complete. Hungry, tired, and needing a bath all were too tired to see a demonstration. Before leaving the ship, as if leaving a friend, they stood a few yards from the ship and stare in silence. They knew they were building something very special. Something they would keep to themselves as theirs. Calling it a day, they said their goodbyes. Off Joe and Sam drive disappearing into a distant horizon. A horizon filled with a day's achievements, a horizon saying goodbye to another day. Dipping lower into the horizon, the light of the day slowly gave way to the shadows of the night. After a well-earned shower, Jim went straight to bed and floated into his dreams. The next day Joe and Sam arrived wide-eyed. Like two little boys wanting to play. Joe and Sam stood anxious to see the device work. Checking the device, Jim was satisfied all was ready to go. Turning the switch to on, the blades began to turn. Revolution after revolution the blades spun faster and faster. A gust of air blew up from the bottom of the ship, followed by a soft hum that danced in the air. By the sound of the hum, Jim knew all was running perfectly. Stone stiff, Joe and Sam stared wide-eyed with pure astonishment. Not seeing a motor or fuel tank, Joe was extremely curious. "What's powering the device to run?" Joe asks as he continues to look for a hidden power source. Jim with a smile upon Joe's curiosity pointed to outer edges of the device. Astonished at what he saw, Joe just stared at the cleverness of how the device was made. Jim's spur of the moment thought had not only created a powerhouse of power. It had also paralyzed two minds that had seen many powerful military machinery.

Now to see a device moving by its own power was a leap to new technology. Unbeknownst to Joe and Sam, Jim had created a powerful turbine jet engine. "I see, I see that's very ingenious," Joe said wide eyed. "We're the only ones that know of this device, call it top secret," Jim said smiling. The ship's great design and ingenious power source was all the inspiration Joe and Sam needed. Realizing they were building more than just a show-off ship for school children to play in Joe and Sam give each other a silent stare. Turning the device off, all three continued to watch as the blade's slowed and gusts of air disappeared. Still speechless, Joe and Sam stood in absolute amazement. "Well, are we going to finish this ship or just stand and stare all day?" Jim said with a smile. Without a word Joe and Sam broke free of their hypnotic spell and continued to work feverishly. Over the next few days the ship took on a look even its builders were amazed to see. With the exterior almost finished, the ship was a fascinating sight to behold. Adorned with a glow of brightness and straight smooth welds, the ship glistened of radiant beauty and wonder. Joe turned out to be an excellent welder. Employing the best of his welding talents, Joe put together a ship truly far beyond his wildest dreams. Standing back and staring at the ship the three of them merely give a smile of their approval to each other. Three with the same plan in mind, worked as one driving force, bringing a dream and ship to life. As one that fashions forms for the eye to behold, Joe like a sculptor, stared. Determined to build the ship as perfect as possible Joe took a special eye to every detail. Every measurement, every cut of metal was made by Joe. Joe's meticulous eye for perfection created a three dimensional wonder. Making the ship strong and airtight the ship could even float on water, Joe had said. "Today we finish the exterior," Joe proclaimed proudly. With welding rods in one hand and the welding torch in his other hand. Joe pulls his welding shield over his face. Weld after weld Joe raced the setting sun. Lower and lower the sun began its subtle setting. With only the thought of finishing, Joe never looked up. Minutes before the sun set, the shadow of darkness began to spread and Joe finished his welding. Standing back from the finished ship's exterior Joe took off his welding shield and stares. The imagination and talent of the three men rested under a setting sun. Admiring its beauty, its smooth curbs, its size and its out-of-this-world appearance it was a ship far ahead of its time. A ship that was made to fly high above the clouds. High above the many snow-covered mountain tops. And maybe to reach out and touch the stars.

Among the tall, green trees, the ship rested silently. No breath of life spun its mighty power. Only the eyes of her builders gazed upon her. Joe and

Sam never dreamed the ship they built could fly the endless blue skies. Or seek other distant destinations far beyond mankind's ability to reach. Nor would their ship change a nation to view the skies in wonder or fear. And Jim only wanted to achieve his boyhood dreams. To fly above the clouds and mountain tops. To see a world in its awe and glory. While admiring the ship, the sun vanished once again. Now the light of moon cast its subtle gleam of visual light. The glow of the ship appeared like a shiny nickel under the moon light. Round and shiny the ship stood out of place among its surroundings. It belongs in the sky like the powerful jets that fly freely among the roaming clouds, Jim thought. Once again Joe and Sam tired of work called it a day. But this day had begun a new page in all three of their lives. For the world they lived in would change as night changes to day and day changes to night. Their thoughts their plans would be tested and questioned by so many. To possess the power to sore the endless skies carried a price known only to those that dreamed. The next day, all three stood side by side staring silently. Wondering about the ships true potential, each dreamed his own dream. Thinking out loud, "What are you going to name the ship," Sam said. "Name it?" Joe said. "Yeah, name it, it's a ship. All ships that journey the skies or seas have names," Sam said. "You two name it, you built it," Jim said. Looking at each other they excitedly proceed by voicing names of vehicles, buildings, and people past and present. The list of names was becoming endless. As Jim watched Joe and Sam trade names back and forth, he realized time was ticking. "Okay," Jim says with a bit of frustration. "We'll get a name later, let's get to work."

Entering the ship, they spend many hours filling the emptiness. Control seats and compartments began to bring life to the ship's interior. As they worked, the thought of their lives changing by their actions never entered their minds. They were too busy, absorbed by the excitement of the moment, the ship's completion was a must. As three boys building a tree house they were three men building a ship. Just as exciting and unique to create and explore their wildest imaginations. And unknown to Joe and Sam the ship would rise them far above the ground, far higher than a tree house. And live an experience they would never forget. Once again a day of great progress had come to an end. A day that had made more than a ship. A day that brought three men closer to their destiny. A destiny each would face by themselves. And in the end, each would touch the lives of many. Tired but in good spirits, Joe and Sam worked another day of great progress. With no set schedule of when to finish the day of completion neared quickly. So much done in so small of time. Waving goodbye, "Tomorrow," Joe says with a smile. Jim waves to both. As Joe and Sam walked past the ship, they slid their hands across the ship's smooth surface. Both smiled proudly at each other. Jim stares with a grateful smile. Reaching the truck Joe and Sam slid into the pickup and slowly drive away. Jim watches as the truck's tail lights disappear into the dark of night. The three of them were boys with a secret. Keeping it well hidden and well-guarded. A very unearthly shiny secret. That week their efforts were diligently focused on finishing the ship's interior. Sam turned out to be an excellent electrician. His soft spoken orders were followed without question. For the first time Joe was not the boss of the ship's construction. Still Joe was in the midst of all the work. Following Sam's orders Joe was determined not to be left out of any part of the ship's construction. Nearing the end of the week Joe and Sam finally agreed upon a name for the ship. "Jim, Sam and I have a name for the ship."

"I've been wondering when you two would come up with a name," Jim said.

"We want to name her the Shining Star," Joe said with a proud smile. Before Jim could say a word. "She'll shine like a bright star in the night's sky," Sam said and Jim had to admit, the ship's silver exterior shined brightly when the moonlight struck it. "Very well," Jim said looking at Joe and Sam. "Put your hands on the ship as I do." All three stood with their hands on the ship. "We the makers of this ship christen this ship, 'The Shining Star.' May she fly swiftly and bring our greatest imaginations to life," Jim said. Smiling from ear to ear, Joe and Sam give a nod of approval. Staring at the ship, Joe and Sam still didn't know the true greatness of the ship's awesome power. "All the controls are set and wired. We should be finished with the interior by the end of this week," Sam said. "That's great news to hear, Sam. The ship looks great, you and Joe have done a fantastic job," Jim said. The day faded away as another day of progress, and so did the week. By the end of the week, the interior was completely finished as Sam had said. Jim enters the ship and feels his boyhood dreams coming to life. Even within the quiet and stillness of the ship a great power awaited to be awoken. Stepping back out of the ship, Jim gives Joe and Sam a big smile. "Great work guys, great work," Jim said. Tired and exhausted, Joe and Sam decided to take a few days off and get some much needed rest. Completely finished, the rush to finish the ship was over. That night, Jim laid in bed staring out the window. Remembering his boyhood dreams, the powerful jets and the feeling of seeing all from so high above pictured in his mind so clearly. The waiting to fly didn't seem as

long as the years he dreamed. Waking early, Jim dresses and finds his way to the kitchen. After breakfast Jim began to feel the urge to sit within the ship. Fighting the urge Jim decides now was not the time. The urge in daylight would only lead to trouble. The morning seemed long without Joe or Sam. Their company brought much excitement and gave much excitement to both. Now the morning was quietly filled with only the birds chirping to each other. As the day moves on Jim finds himself at work. Unable to focus Jim managed to endure a day of many thoughts. Driving home, Jim again felt the feeling of urgency as if someone or something was calling him again. Once at home, Jim heads straight to the ship. Walking into the dense green trees Jim sees a sparkle of light. Coming into the large clearing of trees, an object of brightness stood proudly. Lowering the ship's door, Jim enters and sits in the captain's chair. Looking at the control panel Jim pushes power on. A spin of noise begins and control lights faintly flicker on. Continuing to brighten and glow, all lights and control panels glowed with power. The ship was alive, and slowly charging to full power. A soft hum Jim recognized filled the ship. Seated in the captain's chair the morning urges returned far greater than Jim could bear. With hands on the ship's controls, Jim fought the urge to touch the skies. Closing the entrance door, Jim sat alone with only a soft hum keeping him company. Pushing the front window shield button, the shields slid open revealing a cloudless sky. Moon light softly shinned in faintly lighting the ships interior. The stars one after another lined the night's sky as a road map leading to unknown destinations.

Still with his hands on the ship's controls, Jim continued to fight the urge to fly. To fly would answer Jim's many questions and satisfy his impulsive emotional urges. Gazing at the ship's control panel, Jim could see the ship was at full power. The urge to fly slowly began to die away as Jim's logical reasoning overcame his urges. Tonight was not the night, Jim concluded. A few more tests still had to be performed before the ship's grand flight. "Another day," Jim thought. Turning the power off, all became still and silent as the stars that lit the night. Opening the exit door, Jim steps out. Turning around Jim closes the door. Putting his hand on the ship like a good friend, "Another day, another day," Jim says. Turning from the ship, Jim walks away into the surrounding trees and heads to his house. Still with much on his mind, Jim decides to stay away from the ship. It was Friday and Jim needed to clear his mind and focus his thoughts and go to work. Off to work Jim goes with a much clearer mind. The day at work transpired into a day of great progress. Finding a problem within a ship's inner functions, Jim is treated as a hero. The stalemate with the ship's problem was over putting many back to work. The work day ended with many handshakes and many grateful workers. Reaching home Jim enters his house untroubled by his many thoughts. Knowing that Joe and Sam would return Saturday, Jim decides to go to bed early. Sleeping without his many problems Jim slept peacefully. The sun rose early and so did Jim. After breakfast Jim walks to the front window and looks out. Noticing a truck coming, his guess was Joe's truck. Joe and Sam both had woken early and were anxious to test the ship. Driving to the usual parking area the truck stops. Joe and Sam step out and Jim walks toward them. "Good morning," Joe said. "Good morning Joe, Sam," Jim replies. Stepping toward Jim, "Well how did she perform?" Sam said with a smile. Sam and Joe knew Jim would test the ship. Jim, with a curious smile, said "She performed without a flaw. She's a marvelous piece of machinery."

Smiling at Jim, "We have a present for you," Joe said. Sam and Joe walk to the back of the truck. Letting down the tailgate they grab a big box. The box didn't seem to be too heavy as they lifted it. Gently carrying the box to Jim they set it down next to Jim. "We imagined you might need this one day," Sam said. Not knowing what was in the box, Jim pulls back the box flaps. To Jim's great surprise, Jim stares speechless. Slowly grabbing a large and very expensive helmet, Jim pulls it out of the box. Holding the helmet high, Jim stares in great disbelief. Looking at Sam and Joe once again they just smile. Still without a word, Jim sets the helmet on the ground and looks back in the box. Pulling out a large white bulky suit, Jim holds the suit by its shoulders. Jim knew who the owner was. The suit's owner was powerful enough to send a ship into space with men in space suits like this. Resting the suit by the helmet Jim once again looks into the box. At the bottom of the box rested a pair of large shoes. Not a pair of shoes one would find at a shoe store. A pair of shoes specially made for a very special place.

Jim looks at Sam and Joe again, trying to find words to say. Before Jim could say a word, "Don't ask and we won't tell," Joe said. Looking at each other they couldn't help but smile and burst into laughter. Jim knew very little of Joe and Sam, only that they met in the army years ago and have been good friends ever since. As the laughing subsided, "Now you can teach the school students how to wear a space suit," Joe said with a big smile. With that said laughter broke out again. The three knew the suit could never be shown. It was all within the excitement of the ship. Joe and Sam felt the suit belonged with the ship, not hanging on a display. Now the display sat empty drawing dust of past memories. The suit was a few years old but in great

shape. It could have been used for military space training or maybe a backup suit. No insignias on it, other than a patch on the front that read U.S.A. Taking the space equipment to the ship, Joe and Sam follow Jim. Hiding the suit, helmet, and shoes within a floor compartment. Jim realized he now had more than one secret to hide.

Turning back to Joe and Sam, Jim smiles and says, "thank you guys, I hope it's my size." The three break out laughing. "One size fits all," Joe says laughing. Never giving it a thought to using the suit, Jim felt he'd seen the suit for the last time. Turning his attention back to the ship, Jim asks, "What is left to complete the ship?"

"The interior is finished, I just need to recheck the controls and make sure they work properly. I'll be finished in an hour or so," Sam said. "Then we can take her out for a test run," Joe said. Shocked by Joe's comment, Jim fires back quickly, "Test run!"

Joe and Sam had built the ship. They knew the ship inside out. Not having the expertise to build a power engine device, they did know how to make it work. And make it work they did. Giving Jim a look of "we know better" on their faces, the look on their faces told Jim they knew far more than he thought they knew. Standing with a silent stare, Jim realized he had to share his secret with two others. Jim could only hope that Joe and Sam would keep his secret. "We know the power is real and we know the ship has the power to really fly. The ship is air tight and can float on water. This ship is far more than a ship for training school students. It is the sole one of its kind on Earth. From the beginning I saw a grand opportunity to make something worthwhile. More than sticking two pieces of metal together. I made a flying ship that challenged my abilities and ingenuity. I wanted to complete this project so badly, I haven't had a drink in three months. That's how dedicated I've been," Joe said. Joe was right; he never had the hint of liquor on his breath. He never missed a day and his work was superb. Joe had found a project that excited his building abilities. Looking at Jim very sincerely, "Your secret is our secret Jim" Joe said. Jim looks at Sam. Standing with his arms folded in front. Sam nods his head up and down with the same serious face as Joe. For the first time all three were without a smile and silence filled the air. Now the truth was known and Jim's secret was now shared by two more. Jim had to make a decision and make it fast, for two stood silently waiting for an answer. Still searching his thoughts, Jim realized he didn't have much of a choice. Joe and Sam were the builders and Jim felt they would protect the ship as he would. Joe and Sam even risked getting in trouble stealing the space suit. Realizing it would be best to reveal his secret, Jim concedes to their wishes and surrenders his secret. "You're right Joe, I never intended this ship to be a learning tool or to display it. I truly wanted to soar the skies. To be one with the sky, to see all from high above. But many years ago to my disappointment, I failed the pilot's sight test. My dreams of flying the skies faded away. Now I have found a way to bring my dreams to reality," Jim said. There was a moment of silence between the three of them. For the first time in three months they were not building, they were at the moment of truth. To fly the ship they built and see all from high above. Breaking the silence "Why don't we take the 'o-girl' out for a ride tonight?" Jim said with a smile. The looks of uncertainty disappeared and smiles of their friendship reappeared quickly. Excited to be part of a once in a lifetime adventure. Joe jumped with cheers of excitement as if he had won a million dollars. As Joe jumped, Sam danced a jubilant dance around the ship. Watching Joe and Sam, Jim smiles from ear to ear, just as happy himself. After a few minutes of overjoyed dancing and cheering Joe and Sam filled with the moment, calmed down. Knowing they couldn't fly in broad daylight they waited for the sun to disappear beyond the horizon. As three boys in their secret tree house, they gathered around and planned their trip. After a while of planning, a decision was made to take the ship no further than a few miles from home base. If all went well, they were to circle the town. With excitement in their eyes and silent smiles, they waited for the day to end silently watching the sun gleam a picturesque horizon. A different suddenness of light appeared upon a land also ready to shine its moment of the night before the sun began another day. The light of the moon now stood high in a quiet sky. With only moonlight visibility, Jim hoped they would only be a shadow in the sky. The time had come and one by one all three lined-up to enter the shiny ship. Giving the builder of the ship the honorary privilege to enter first. Jim and Sam watch as Joe enters the ship. Stepping next into the ship, Jim began to fulfill his boyhood dreams. To fly the skies, to follow the clouds, to be as free as a bird. Once inside the ship, Joe was waiting for Jim. "Jim you belong here, she's your ship to fly," Joe said. Sitting in the captain's chair, Jim felt a rush of feelings never felt before. The feeling of wings lifting him and guiding him across and endless sky. As Jim feels the rush of feelings. Sam enters last with looks of silent wonder. Joe sits to Jim's left and straps himself tightly to his chair. "Close the door Sam," Joe calls out to Sam. Jim having strapped himself tightly to his chair waited for Sam to be seated. Closing and locking the door, Sam quickly takes the seat on Jim's right side. Grabbing his chair straps, Sam fastens his straps tightly. A quiet and silent moment took the thoughts of all

three. No longer plans on paper, no longer a shiny powerless ship. Now a ship that would soon hum its might and lift the ship to unknown heights. Taking its builders to wherever they commanded. Seeing that all were ready, Jim turns the power switch on. A slow churning sound spun around and around quickly increasing its speed and building power. Eyes of all three watched waiting for the moment of truth. Controls dimly lit-up and small inside lights lit the ships darkness. Continuously increasing power, a soft hum from below the ship filled the builder's ears. Having heard the whirling sound of power before, Jim wasn't surprised. But Jim hadn't heard the ship's full power to lift the ship. A power that longed to prove itself. A power that possessed the strength of an angry wind twisting and turning like a ravaging tornado. Combined with a ship, the power would break the chains of gravity. Freeing a bird to soar high into the drifting clouds. Without a feather to guide its course the ship would fly leaving only a humming sound far behind. And far below, those on the ground would never know a bird flew so high in the sky. As the ship powered-up, the three occupants stared out the ship's window. Looking as astronaut's ready for blast off their hopes of success were only moments away. "Full power, all controls ready to go," uttered Sam. "Keep your fingers crossed," Jim said. Having no idea what would happen only what should happen. All held tightly to their seats. A steady, powerful hum and a tremendous burst of air lifted the ship. Slowly the ship broke Earth's mighty grip, raising the ship off the ground. With excitement expanding their hearts second after second the ship rose higher and higher as they dared for more. Like a good friend, the ship's peaceful hum gave assurance all was working flawlessly. Stopping a few hundred feet in midair the ship hovered like a cloud. All within the ship had become one with the sky. Looking into the sky, the openness of the night revealed a vastness of stars. Stars that covered an endless view. Rising once again Jim felt the time was now. Now to take the first step into his dreams of yesterday and bring them to reality. Like a winged stallion, the ship was ready to soar. Slowly moving forward, the ship made a steady trip around their home base. As if sliding on ice the ride was tremendously smooth. Back to their starting point in only minutes all were mentally and physically stomping their feet with ecstatic excitement. The short trip was smooth and exhilarating. Wanting more, Sam bursts out, "Let's take her out over the town." With smiles upon their faces Jim aims the ship at the town. Shooting across the sky they head for a trip around the town. Wide-eyed and smiles, all looked forward for more, as they rushed through the empty sky. Jim realized he flew the carnival's space ship without the support pole. Smoothly the ship slid across the night's sky with only a small hum from below. Over glowing scattered lights, under all the stars that shined above, they flew. Excited with the ship's performance, all realized the moment. In mere seconds they had reached the outskirts of the night-lit town. Around the town they flew in a wide circle. Street lights and house lights lit the area in an un-systematical form. Through the night's sky the ship carried its makers like a magical carpet ride. Before the end of the first time around, the three began planning a new test for the ship to perform. Having passed all tests effortlessly, agility, power, and speed all were qualities the ship carried in abundance. "What's next?" Sam said. "The clouds, we're headed for the clouds," Jim said. Looking at Jim, Joe and Sam smiled from ear to ear. Immediately the ship began to pierce into the night's sky and flew higher and higher above the town. Swiftly sliding through the sky like sliding across a frozen lake, the ship flew trouble free. Once inside the clouds a moment of peacefulness existed. One ever-changing cloud after another drifted the skies. Slowing the ship's speed, they drifted along with the clouds. Following the clouds as a flock of birds would. The freedom of the sky was a bird's endless paradise. Becoming hypnotized by the tranquility of the sky and clouds all continued their carpet ride daring the unknown. Riding the night's sky, lit by the stars and moon Jim and crew had found their unlimited fantasy. Into the endless clouds they soared without a worry of stop signs or getting lost. They sailed the oceans of the sky boldly. Resting his eyes upon each floating cloud, Jim flew the soft transparent clouds as if they were waves of the ocean. Out of the blue Sam's excited voice cries out loud in panic, "Plane, plane, a plane Jim," Jim, not realizing he'd been hypnotized by the clouds and sky, was suddenly awoken to the dangers of the sky. Grabbing Jim by the arm Joe brings Jim back to reality. "To your left, Jim," Joe said. Quickly looking to his left Jim almost goes into shock. A large passenger airliner was headed right for their ship. Frantically Jim dips the ship downward and barely misses the bottom of the airliner. Shaken out of wits, Jim's heart was now surging violently with fear. Realizing even the skies were filled with hidden dangers, dangers that one learned if they were to soar the skies safely. Free of danger, they try desperately to shake off the fear of a near collision. Wide-eyed and stiff of a near miss, they stared out the viewing window fear-minded of another plane. Not knowing what would suddenly appear. All eyes continued to stare into the moonlit sky. Calmed down, Jim steers the ship back under the drifting clouds. Quietness had replaced their excitement as all stared. Back into safer air space they roamed the endless skies. Regaining their wits, the three of them agreed they'd had enough for the night. The ship was a dream come true. It passed all the tests of the night.

It had taken its makers from the ground into a star-filled sky. It had fulfilled Jim's boyhood dreams. And gave two others an excitement they would never forget. The thrill of the night was over, a night ride all three would never forget. Homeward they flew, passed the lights of the towns and back to the nest of trees they called home base. Before the ship floated down to its nesting ground. Joe asks, "What would the pilots of the airliner say? Would they report the near miss incident? Or did they ever see us?"

"Oh, they saw us visually and on radar, Joe". Sam said. "Don't worry Joe, the pilots careers hang on being stable and sane. Reporting U.F.O.'s would only raise eyebrows. If they do report anything, believe me, it'll be a fabricated story." Jim said. Still with a bit of worry upon his face, Joe smiles a bit showing he was alright. Setting the ship down in the midst of trees, they were once again safely resting back on the ground. The experience that night was unforgettable for the three. The ship performed without a flaw and was a marvel to control. Turning the power off, the steady hum that gave the ship power and its crew company, slowly died down and faded away to a slow gust of wind that disappeared into silence. Staring at each other with the same silence as the ship, they began to smile a wide and wider smile. The wonder of the ride had overridden the scare of the night. Breaking into a joyful laugh, they laughed away the airliner's near miss scare. Realizing they had built a ship that could fly and land anywhere, their imaginative destinations soared. Congratulating each other over their success, they hadn't realized the problems that would follow. Unknowing to all three they would become separated, three men to face the long arm of the law. Turning to Joe and Sam, Jim expresses his thoughts. "I could never have reached my dreams without you two. Whatever becomes of this moment, I will never forget you two," Jim said. As the congratulating simmered down, the moment and feelings of friendship stayed strong. Becoming serious once more, Jim looks at Joe and Sam. "You two have helped bring a boyhood dream to life. I have soared the clouds and become one with the sky. I cannot put the feeling of flying into words. The feeling lies within me and the joy on my face. I have reached my dreams of yesterday. Thank you, Joe, Sam, you two have given me a moment I will never forget," Jim said. Faces of gratitude smiled at each other. "I have done many things in my life. But this project will be the one I will never forget," Sam said nodding his head up and down with a smile. "Life for me has been a bore since I left the army. One welding job after the next and I had no real goals or ambitions. I spent my life's earnings on booze and slept late. Now I want to live to see another day and meet people like you, Jim,"

Joe said smiling a grateful smile. "We have only begun to learn the ship's true potential. There are more tests to be performed," Jim said with a smile. Sam gets up and opens the door. Exiting the ship, all walked a bit wobbly until they regained the feel of being back on solid ground. Smiling at each other, like little mischievous boys guarding a secret, they knew they were the first to fly a non-winged ship. The 'Shining Star's' maiden voyage was a brilliant success. A ship like a bird that could land and take off anywhere. A ship like no other on Earth. Built to explore one's wildest dreams. Agreeing to meet the next day Joe and Sam, having shaken the near miss from their minds, walked to the truck reenacting the moment and laughing. The moment of fear had turned into the moment of laughter, and both laughed together. Once inside the truck Joe, without a word, looks at Jim and smiles a smile of sincerity. Joe's life had changed for the better. Thrilled to have met Jim and changed by building the ship. Jim knew what Joe was saying and Jim felt the same way smiling back at Joe. Jim nods his head slightly as he smiles. Joe turns, starts the truck and drives away into the night and disappears. Staring into the night's sky Jim once again feels a breeze as if one were reaching out and calling him in great need from a calm sky of friendly stars so far away. Jim stared and wondered what was this mystic awareness. Where was it coming from and who was sending it? Jim could only stare and wonder how to communicate. The stars stood still, lined in every direction. Silent and peaceful they revealed nothing. Only a dark blanket of glowing stars testing the minds that gazed the universe. The next day arrived sunny and warm. The sky was filled with birds chirping and bees busy leaping from flower to flower. A day to be outside to enjoy the beauty. Remembering to check the News stations, Jim turns on the television. Station after station, all reported the same. No near air collisions and no U.F.O. sightings. It was just another day of business. The pilots most likely feared repercussions of reporting U.F.O's and decided not to say a word. Safe for now, Jim knew they needed a plan to safely protect the ship. The eyes in the sky never slept, they were always watching. Joe and Sam had learned this very well. The military watches day and night. Arriving at noon Joe and Sam were still jumping with excitement. Relieved of the night's scare, Joe and Sam relived every exciting moment with a smile. Finally settling down the three of them discussed the ship's safety within the trees. Working out details to keep the ship safe and out of dangerous hands. They made planes to readjust the ships controls, to be started only by themselves, agreeing upon code words known only by themselves. The safety of the ship laid in their hands. Discussing the ship's abilities they agreed the ship performed brilliantly. Within the short

distance the ship had traveled, the 'Shining Star' passed all her tests. Only a long distance test would finalize the ship's worthy powers and abilities, to fly with the metal eagles of the sky. A test they knew the eyes of the sky would see. Still they would never know without testing. It was a gamble to take that could bring many problems. And still the need to know loomed in the minds of all three. The ship could have internal problems, crash, or be shot down. Knowing full well the hazards of a long distance test, all three still had their minds made-up. Even before the eyes that watched the skies, all were determined to find the ship's potential. The 'Shining Star's maiden voyage had only incited their inner emotions for more. Agreeing with Joe and Sam, Jim felt there was no other way. The 'Shining Star' was a bird needing to be set free, to fly the open skies in complete freedom. The time was growing nearer as the ship's makers planned an incredible journey. A journey that would eventually take each other in different directions, leaving only memories of a fantastic journey within their minds. A journey that would only be the beginning of a very long journey. "What would be a good long distance test and when?" Jim asked Joe and Sam. Knowing a long distance test was hard to take without letting so many know the three of them agreed not to rush and make a hasty decision. Using an old military net Joe had purchased at an army surplus store, Joe covered the ship completely. Safe for now the ship blended into the tall trees and disappeared. Days went by and the three of them communicated only by phone. After four days, Joe arrives and passes his usual parking spot. Driving straight to the ship Joe stops. Strange for Joe to park there, thought Jim. Jim walks from the house and meets Joe. Finding Joe in good spirits with his usual smile, Joe moved his attention from Jim to the back of his pick-up truck.

"What's up Joe?" Jim said. "I've got my hands on something the ship really needs," Joe said. Pulling back a dark green canvas, underneath lay a metal device about the size of a small television set. "What in the world is that?" Jim asks. "Well if we had this on our first test run. We would never have come close to that airliner," Joes said. "I give up Joe, I have no idea what it could be," Jim said. Smiling from ear to ear, "It's an early warning device. This little device will inform a pilot of an object at least six miles away," Joe said. "You mean a radar," Jim says with an astonished voice. Stunned, Jim fights the many thoughts in his mind. "I don't want to know where the device came from," Jim said. "I buy all kinds of things at that surplus store. I have good connections that owe me," Joe says still smiling. Grabbing the device, Joe picks it up without another word and walks to the ship and enters with the device. Following slowly behind, Jim enters the ship and assists Joe. It didn't take long for Joe to install the warning device. "Sam said it was easy to connect," Joe said to Jim. Sam was right. Joe installed the warning device in less than thirty minutes. Making sure the device worked, Joe turns on the ship's power. Slowly the majestic wheel of power turned. Faster and faster the power source spins. In just minutes a rapid whirl of power turns into a strong steady hum. A round screen on the device lit up with a thin line of light turning round and round. Jim stares at the device as Joe begins to explain how the device worked. "We are in the center of the circle. When an object approaches, a beeping dot will show up on the screen. We'll know from which way and how fast our pursuers are advancing," Joe said. Listening to Joe, Jim realized Joe had finally found a project that kept him sober and very motivated. Joe no longer lived a boring, dull life. With each day Joe's drinking days were growing further behind him. Turning the power off the hum of power slowly disappeared and the radar screen went blank. Stepping out of the ship, Joe and Jim continued talking about the radar. As Joe and Jim talked, a car drives up and parks at the usual parking area. It was Sam paying a visit and checking on Joe's installation job. Greeting Sam as he approached, Jim could see a glow of excitement in Sam's eyes. "Well, does it work?" Sam asks Joe. "I attached it just as you said, turned the ship's power on, and it worked," Joe said smiling. The near miss justified a radar. A radar and its origin known only by Joe and Sam. Now a part of the ship, the radar gave the ship eyes and knowledge of incoming objects far beyond human sight. "We won't have another airliner come close to us again," Sam said. "No, we won't, but that airliner sure woke me up," Joe said, breaking into a laugh, that Jim and Sam also joined. It was a night they would never forget. A flight they would cherish forever. Sam had not only come to check on the warning device, he also needed Joe to help him move his new refrigerator into his house. Saying their goodbyes to Jim, Joe and Sam leave quickly. Left alone, Jim stares at the ship. Months ago it seemed like a dream. And now the dream was real. Resting on the ground, the ship waited to be powered up. Waiting to surge its power and climb into the endless sky. With a warning device the ship could fly higher and further than the ship's first limited testing. Jim felt satisfied with the ship's abilities and knew deep down the last test would be a success. The next day at noon Joe and Sam returned. Once again Jim, Sam, and Joe regrouped near the ship. Having a few days to ponder the ship's last test, they knew with the radar they could fly the open skies without fear. "Your thoughts of the ship's last test are open for debate. Where and when speak your minds," Jim said. Wasting no time Sam spoke up. "I've always

wanted to visit California." Sam says emphatically while Joe laughs. "Why not?" Sam said while looking at Joe with a serious face. Smiling at Sam, Joe suddenly loses his smile. "Are you really serious?" Joe asks Sam. Before Sam could reply Jim says, "Why not? It'll be a great test. We can fly straight across Texas, New Mexico, Arizona, Nevada, and then California. Turn around and head back. A great trip to test the ship's overall speed and endurance."

Silently staring at each other, they began to smile with their mischievous daring smiles. "California here we come," Jim sang out. Agreeing to fly to California and back to Texas, the three made a list of items to take with them and initiated a complete inspection of the ship. While Jim and Joe began their inspection of the ship's exterior, "Even a small crack needs to be re-welded. We can't have our ship falling apart in mid-air," Joe said. Painful as it was, every weld that held the ship together was followed from top to bottom, from left to right. After a few hours of inspecting. Sam and Jim finished, informing Joe they couldn't find even a hair line crack. Staring at Joe, Sam and Jim realized the big smile Joe wore was letting both know he did the welding. Smiling at each other, Jim tells Sam and Joe, "Bring what we'll need tomorrow and be ready to leave at sunset."

Agreeing to meet Jim the next day, Joe and Sam leave and wave goodbye. As Joe and Sam were leaving, Jim could hear Joe say, "You didn't find not one small crack or bad weld, Sam?"

"Okay, okay, you're a good welder," Sam said. Joe laughs as the truck drives away. Once again the 'Shining Star' would journey into the night. A night the moon would hang high in the sky as a new moon. Completely dark, the moon would rest with the night. And still the eyes of the night would be watching. For the 'Shining Star' would be known only by those that watched the open skies over the trees, over the roof tops, over the barren deserts and over the towering mountains. The 'Shining Star' would fly with a gust of wind and a hum of power burning the skies at record speeds. A speed that many on the ground would watch with great wonder. Hours later, the day ended with dreams and ideas waiting to become reality. Having checked the ship from top to bottom, the ship stood ready to touch the sky once more. Catching himself once again staring into the night's sky, Jim wondered about the feelings he'd been having. Were they just in his mind or were they real? "So many stars so far away, how do you see such a small planet as Earth?" Jim asks himself. The next day arrived with a soft light to start a new day. Meeting each other at noon the three of them spent the day enjoying each other's company. As they waited for the hours of the day to pass, they talked about their lives, places, and achievements they'd incurred. It seemed like a very exciting time. Getting to know each other and building a friendship. While they talked, the radiant sun dipped hour after hour yielding to a peaceful night. The waiting was over and the time to fly was now. Walking to the ship, Jim reaches out and pulls on the ship's camouflage netting. The netting smoothly slides off the shiny ship. There it stood: the ship that held their hopes, dreams, and hard work. The sleek, shiny ship beckoned the three to enter. Stepping forward Joe lowers the ship's door and enters. Sam eagerly follows and enters next. Entering the ship last, Jim steps in and leaves the ground for an experience of a life time. Closing the door and locking it tightly, Jim turns around to see his friends waiting, staring at Jim with great admiration.

"She's your ship, Captain," Joe said. Taking the captain's seat Jim gave out his first order. "Take you stations men." Joe sits to Jim's left at radar and Sam sits to Jim's right at the ship's vital controls. Seated in the ship as if in a church, the three of them sat quietly. Jim starts the journey by turning the power on. A quiet night awakens with the sound of a high-pitched whistling swirl. Feeling the time to depart was near, all three sat nervous and a bit excited. As the whistling sound turned into a friendly hum, Sam opens the ship's window shields letting in a soft starlight. Seconds later, "Full-power," Sam sounds out. This time braced and ready to go, Jim without hesitation raises the ship far above the surrounding tree tops.

"We've reached two hundred feet," Sam says. That was all Jim needed to hear. Aiming the ship westward Jim slices through the night sky like a cannonball speeding toward its target. Pressed to their seats, all were headed for an adventure they would never forget. Across a starlit sky they flew with only a friendly hum to hear. Increasing their speed to six hundred, they flew into a calm night, guided by stars lighting their way. Smoothly coasting upon the night's sky, Jim begins to test the ship's abilities by dipping the ship downward and rising slowly. The ship gave all the feeling of a very fast roller coaster ride. Next Jim slightly weaves the ship from left to right and finds the ship responding smoothly. Satisfied with ship's abilities, Jim continues their journey slowly increasing the ship's speed. Over towns and cities they fly, looking down, they see lights gathered close together resembling fire flies. The ship and crew flew unbothered and Jim smiled a smile of great satisfaction. His dreams of yesterdays were now his reality. Keeping the crew company the ship spoke to all with a soft hum. Crossing Texas the ship was a mere whisper in the night sky. Nearing west Texas the ship flew over as a gust

of wind. Here, there, and gone the ship flew into another state. Into New Mexico the ship flew knowing no boundaries in the sky. Paving a worthy sky path, the ship flew romancing the New Mexico sky. Across the ground, a blend of trailing lights laid upon a dark sheet of night. Following the trail of lights as pioneers followed each other, the ship continued to fly westward. Time passed quickly as patterns of ground lights guided the ship through an ocean of darkness. Feeling comfortable with the ship's abilities and speed, the thought of uncertainty faded away. After seemingly minutes of reaching New Mexico, Joe grabs Jim and Sam's attention. "We've been traveling over New Mexico very quickly. Soon Arizona will be beneath us." The time seemed like long minutes and the miles traveled seemed like large steps over water puddles. Keeping his eyes on radar, Joe watched intensely as the glowing line circled the screen. Alone in the sky they flew freely as they raced time on the ground and in the air. Mile after mile they flew, over glowing cities lighting the night or glowing stars lighting the sky. Stars in the sky and lights on the ground resembled each other as the ship sailed into the night. Upon a speeding star they flew, within their minds they grew and together they shared the wonders of the sky. Miles upon miles they logged into their minds, views only thoughts could describe. The curve of the land and protruding hills dazzled the eyes in the sky's night. With towns and cities enjoying the night, no one knew of a ship piercing the sky high above. Breaking the calmness all were enjoying, Joe speaks out with urgent news. "Company is coming our way fast," he says looking at Jim and Sam in a very concerned manner. "Sam, it looks like we'll have to delay our visit to California," Jim said. "Well, I've been expecting company. And I'm a bit surprised we got this far. The eyes of the sky have been watching us," Jim said. "And now they're coming to greet us. It looks like our visit to California will have to be another day," Joe said. Jim notices Sam's quiet and worried stare. "Don't worry Sam, the 'Shining Star' has plenty of speed we haven't touched yet," Jim said. "Who is approaching us Joe?" Sam asks. "At the speed they're approaching. I would say fighter jets coming to investigate. They must be coming from an air base in California, they mean business," Joe said. "I definitely agree, they mean business," Jim said. "Let's head up to New York, let's give them a chase across the good o' U.S.A.," Joe said smiling. "New York?" Sam said with a bit of shock in his voice. "We can't go back to Texas, they'll just follow us," Joe said. "Joe's right, Sam, New York will give us a chance to really test this ship's abilities, and test the fuel levels of the planes following us," Jim said. "New York State or New York City?" Sam asks. "Whichever comes first," Joe said with a smile. To Joe, the best part of the trip seemed to be the chase. Joe was excited and ready to play a game of chase. Looking at Sam, Sam had a bit of worry upon his face, but still managed to stay in control. As Joe stared at the radar he shouted, "We need to go faster Jim…a lot faster!"

What would happen if we get caught? The thought filled the minds of Jim, Joe, and Sam. If they could not out run the jets, they would surely be blown out of the sky. Joe was right, they needed to go faster, a lot faster. Now within the calm of the night, ships raced across the sky testing their powers against each other. A power and speed only metal birds of prey could fly. Round and round the lit line rotated around the radar screen. And each time the two bleeping dots drew closer and closer. Staring at the radar, Joe gets a bit nervous. "They're getting closer Jim, a few more minutes and we'll be waving at each other," Joe said. By now Joe was getting very edgy. Realizing Joe's uneasiness, Jim decides to ease Joe's worries. "We didn't come this far to be caught or shot down. Let's show our curious chasers what this ship can really do," Jim said. Accelerating to a speed of one thousand, the 'Shining Star' shoots across the sky like a raging bullet. Immediately a great distance separates the chasers. "We're doing it Jim, we're pulling away," Joe said. Stuck to his chair, Joe shows a smile of relief. With his eyes glued to the radar, Joe continues to watch with a subtle feeling of relief. Gone from the radar screen, the two jets were miles away. The skies were theirs once more to dance upon the clouds. Continuing to watch the radar screen, Joe waited for another bleep to appear. It didn't take long for the two bleeps to return and Joe knew the two bleeps were the same two jets. "They're back and getting closer. We need to go faster Jim," Joe said with great urgency in his voice. Already with their backs pressed to their chairs, the need for more speed found the crew wondering if their ship could escape its pursuers.

"Hold on to your seats," Jim said, shooting across the sky at a speed far beyond any speed they had flown. All three found it hard to move, pressed to their seats. Once again they find themselves alone. Alone to a sky of seemingly hanging stars. The ship's friendly hum had turned into a roar as they shot across a moonless sky. "We've pulled away again, our pursuers are giving up their chase," Joe said. Slowing the ship's speed, they traveled once again as travelers exploring and enjoying an endless sky. Calmer and relaxed the three began to share their thoughts.

"That radar sure came in handy," Jim said. "I knew it would, but it's no match against ground radar or satellite. Someone is still watching us, Jim," Joe said. By this time the pursuers were nowhere to be found on radar or anyone else. Still Joe kept his eyes glued to the radar. The feeling of another

pursuer haunted Joe's mind. Keeping his eyes fixed upon the radar, Joe was right. Someone was still watching the skies and ground's highways. One can run from a satellite but one can never escape, Jim thought. As they continued their journey, Sam, having said so little during the whole chase, finally unlocked his inner thoughts. I feel as if I've been dreaming. Dreaming a dream others would never believe no matter how I told the dream. Looking at Jim and Joe with wonder upon his face, Sam had lived an awake dream. Finding it hard to believe all that had happened, Sam sat speechless. Looking at Sam, Jim smiles and feels in many ways the same as Sam. For, if it were a dream, they were all dreaming the same dream. A dream of hair raising adventure with pursuers becoming flying lions hungry for a kill. Yet today the lions would not make a kill. For today the lions were no match against a winged stallion. A stallion that flew the endless skies. The 'Shining Star' flew as the winged stallion, unmatched in power and speed. Bred to fly the mighty sky, the 'Shining Star' still had more to prove. Limited only by one's thoughts, the 'Shining Star' would prove one can dream while they are awake, making their dreams and reality the same. "Tell us your dream, Sam, I'm sure we'll believe you," Jim said. All three laughed. "The great thing about it, Sam, is you're not dreaming and we're not finished yet. Not by a long shot," Jim said. Having shot across an open sky and freed themselves of their pursuers, the crew of the 'Shining Star' had lost all track of their ground location. Once again they find themselves flying by the lights of the ground. Scanning into the darkness of the night they search for a recognizable site. Over many lights they fly until the lights disappear. Puzzled, they look at each other without a word.

"Where are we?" Jim asks puzzled. Still staring at each other, Jim and Joe turn to Sam. Sam had already figured out the disappearance of the lights and their location. "Below us lies one the great lakes. I'm guessing we're at the bottom of Lake Michigan," Sam said. Surprised they had traveled so far in seemingly such a short time, they had not realized the need to go faster turned miles of distance into seconds of time. Slowing the ship's speed to nine hundred, they were themselves once again. Smiling and voicing their fears of the recent events they laughed and laughed as if they had ridden a runaway roller coaster ride. The look upon their faces said they were ready to ride again. The ship continued to live up to its builders' expectations and more. It had passed all the tests they could impose upon it. All but one test, Jim thought. The test of flying beyond Earth. If she couldn't, she would be just another Earth-bound ship, soaring across the blue skies. Calm and relaxed again, all three had no idea what the next few moments would bring. Speeding across the dark waters, they waited to see another glow of lights. Lights that would indicate land and their position to their destination. Before the lights appeared, Joe again breaks the calmness and warns of trouble approaching.

"Heads up, two more visitors headed right for us,"Joe cries out. "Joe, if we're fired upon, inform me immediately," Jim said. "Will do, Cap," Joe said. Time seemed to stand still as they flew. "Here they come," Joe said again. In no time two blinking lights came at them so close they barely missed having a collision. Gone in the blink of an eye, the two ships were gone out of sight. Not diverting from their destination, Jim and crew continued their journey to New York. It didn't take long and Joe was once again warning of approaching visitors. "The jets have turned around and are back on our trail," Joe said. Watching the radar Joe spots another blinking object. "Jim there's another object a few miles in front of us," Joe said excitedly. "Is it another jet fighter?" Jim asks. "It's larger than a jet fighter and its flying slower than a jet fighter. We can catch it in a few minutes or less if we increase our speed." With a smile of excitement and a hidden idea brewing behind his smile, Jim increases the ship's speed and a burst of power sends all three pressed to their seats. Closer they drew, while lights coming from something very broad, blinks lights off and on. With two great wings and a tall tail the airliner, this time, was a blessing in disguise in Jim's eyes. "It's a passenger airliner," Joe said. Remembering the first airliner, Joe and Sam wanted to stay clear of the plane. "Jim, we need to get away from the airliner," Joe said. "I agree, Jim, the sooner the better," Sam said. With a plan in mind, Jim ignores Joe's and Sam's pleas. "Hold tight, we're going to hitch a ride," Jim said. Both Joe and Sam look at Jim with a very puzzled stare. "What in the world are you going to do," Joe asked. "Watch this maneuver, Joe," Jim said. Knowing full well the danger of maneuvering close to an airliner, Jim felt he could make it work. The eyes of the sky knew he was there, and Jim had a plan to disappear. Catching up to the airliner, Jim flies to the plane's tail and stares with a smile. As Joe and Sam, unknowing of Jim's plan, stare in fear. Jim dips the ship under the airliner's tail, then flies to the belly of the airliner. Holding the 'Shining Star's' position, Joe and Sam sat as stiff as statues frozen in time. Looking at Joe and Sam, "What do you think? Will that make those pilots wonder where we disappeared to?" Jim said. Sitting wide-eyed, Joe and Sam were speechless. "Where's those two jets?" Jim asked. Regaining their senses, Joe and Sam return to their controls. Studying the radar, Joe looks up. "The two jets should be catching up to us any minute." Close to the airliner's

belly, the three watched as the two jets roared swiftly by. "There they go," Sam said smiling. Deep into the darkness of the sky the two fighter planes flew. Hungry to catch their prey, they flew like winged lions searching deep into the night. With happy faces, Joe and Sam couldn't believe what had just happened. "It worked, they just flew by us," Joe said smiling. "They're following their radars and now there's nothing on their radars, except an airliner heading for New York," Jim said. Smiling from ear to ear, all three were ecstatic with joy. A small roar of victory lived within the ship. For the moment they were free to travel the skies unhampered by minds of curiosity. Having flown a splendid trip across America, out-ran and out-foxed four fighter jets, Jim and crew proved their ship was worthy to fly Earth's skies. Now the tree house secret was known. Known to all that watched the skies and ground. The only secret left was who flew the incredible craft. And where did it come from? Following below the airliner, they entered New York State. Leaving the airliner, they fly freely and unnoticed. In a matter of minutes, they fly over a splendidly lit array of tall buildings. Glued to the viewing window, they were amazed of so many sky-touching buildings. One after another, buildings covered a sky-lit city. Flying straight through New York State then into New York City, they fly like a bullet racing to the coast line. Turning to Jim, Joe with a look of concern, said "Jim, the ship has passed her test. We couldn't keep pressing our luck."

Looking at Joe, then Sam, both agreed only by facial expression. Jim knew they were both right. The 'Shining Star' had passed all her tests. And yes, Jim thought, they were pressing their luck. They had rolled the dice in the sky and won many times. Without a word, Jim turns the ship south and puts the ship back into high speed. Across a coastline they fly viewing land and ocean. Even without a moonlit night, the ship reflected light from stars and buildings. Heading south along the coast a beautiful view of ocean displayed its calmness while it slept. Remembering what Joe had said, "One way or another someone is following us." Joe was right. By satellite or ground radar someone is still following them like their own shadow. To fly straight home would only show those following us where our secret hideout was located. Then it wouldn't take long before many would come to investigate the ship's resting ground. We must continue and lead the eyes of the night in another direction, Jim thought. Knowing the night would surrender to the sun, Jim needed a new plan. As they flew south along the coast line, Jim remembers the ship's last test. The test that would end all the ship's tests. The ability to be space-worthy. To escape the eye high in the sky, one had to escape the Earth's grip and pierce into space, Jim thought. And that was Jim's last desire. To take the 'Shining Star' into space. Knowing the dangers were real, the temptations overran all logical thinking. Jim was determined to escape the satellite's watchful eyes and fly in space. Once again Joe and Sam stare at Jim; they knew what was stirring within Jim's mind.

Moving the ship upward they fly into a place only reserved for rockets. Higher and higher they flew out of sight. Pressed to their seats, they spoke no words. Only a wide stare into emptiness as they climb higher. The ship roared with power, not showing any signs of weakness. If one had wanted to turn back, it was too late. Jim was determined to reach the top of his mountain. Not knowing how high they had risen, their backs were no longer pressed to their seats. Jim levels the ship and flies without resistance. Looking through the viewing window, the Earth was a round ball of land and water circled in a pocket of oxygen. Glowing brightly the Earth was a candle in the night. "Jim we're not being pulled by Earth's gravity any longer. We're in space, we've left Earth completely," Joe said excitedly. No longer in Earth's atmosphere or pull of gravity, they were now under the rules of space. Eyes of wonder looked at each other in silence. Staring down at Earth, they knew it was the only planet they called home. Speechless they breathed slowly as they watched. To see Earth from space was a breathtaking experience. An experience they would never forget. They had reached their highest level of achievement: "Space". So close to the stars, Jim felt he could reach out and touch them. With the help from Joe and Sam, Jim achieved his boyhood dreams and more. He had flown the skies he so dreamed of so many years ago. And now he and his friends gazed upon Earth like children looking through a school bus window. To look at the three of their faces one could see stunned amazement over and over. As they stared at Earth, only the water and land could be seen. Mankind and his doings were over shadowed by Earth's vastness of water and land. While admiring Earth, Jim realized they had a ship anyone or any nation would love to have. Knowing this could create a problem, Jim and the ship's builders would need more than a camouflage netting. Eyes would be everywhere now, making it hard to keep the ship. Having traveled less than an hour in space, Jim knew the darkness of time was ending. Bracing themselves for re-entry, Jim dips the ship downward. Feeling the pull of Earth's gravity, the ship began to shake. Once again all inside were silent as they held tight to their chairs. Shaking and pitching from side to side the ship fought her way back to Earth. Heat began to rise from the ship's outer hull creeping into the ship. All began to sweat nervously. Readjusting the ship's descent, Jim regains

control over the ship's erratic behavior. Back in control, Jim guides the ship lower and lower. Humming a steady hum the ship's overwhelming power had not been effected by leaving Earth or returning to Earth. The hum of the ship reassured its builders power was not a problem. Flying lower and lower the dangers of crashing or burning disappeared from their worried faces. Tired of such a long trip, the three of them sat with smiles of relief. The danger was over as they flew once more into the skies of Earth. Checking their position on radar, Joe began to recognize land patterns.

Before Joe could give an answer Sam gives the answer. "I've been here before, I know this area. We're in the Pacific Ocean," Sam said. "You're right, Sam, that's exactly where we're at." With darkness still in full control, the lay of land and water was hard to focus. Far in the distance a faint glow of light glowed upon the water. Heading toward the light, it rose from the waters and stood atop a tall mountain. Closer they came only to see more lights around the mountain glowing brightly. Larger the lights grew as excitement grew within the ship. With excitement on his face Sam bursts out, "It's Hawaii, the glows of light are coming from Hawaii," Sam said. The urge to stop and pay Hawaii a visit was strong. Still the need to get back home and hide the ship was stronger. Swiftly flying across the water, they pass Hawaii as they race home. The land of enchantment, Jim thought with a smile. "One day we'll get our chance to visit Hawaii and see all Hawaii's wonders in daylight," Jim said. Flying low to evade radar, Jim and crew quickly pass all of Hawaii's Islands. Heading north, the ocean seemed to be a world of its own. Like sand in a desert, water was everywhere. Ripples in the water moved slowly as sand ripples on the desert moved by the wind. Passing an occasional ship liner headed to Hawaii reassured Jim he was headed north. Miles of seemingly endless water waved kindly as the 'Shining Star' flew daringly near the ocean surface. Again, Jim was pushing the 'Shining Star' to perform to her best. And not to be let down, the 'Shining Star' performed flawlessly with a hum of power.

Scanning the landless body of water, all eyes watched endlessly for land. Over the ocean they flew with only the ship's reassuring hum of power building their passions. "What's that?" Joe asked. Pointing to the left side of the viewing window, all three looked at a darkness upon the water. A dark shadow covered the calm water in the far distance. As they approached, they realized it was a larger fishing ship with no lights on. Flying close to the lightless ship the 'Shining Star' blew a strong gust of wind rocking the ship.

Flying a steady course, more fishing ships were spotted, smaller in size with fishing nets combing the shallow waters.

"Land can't be far away," Sam said. "The smaller ships don't fish that far out." Not far in the distance, a glow of faint light lit the land. Glowing brighter as they neared, they knew the land was called "Mexico", the land of the Aztec warrior. Moving quickly closer, more lights came in to focus. Now only minutes away the land near the sea glowed an inviting light. The waiting was over. Leaving the sea the 'Shining Star' zoomed across the land and city, leaving many looking to the sky in wonder. As an uninvited guest in Mexico, Jim knew not to slow down. Gambling their speed and low flight clearance would keep the military from enforcing evasive action. Jim continued their course as fast as the 'Shining Star' could fly. Over cities, mountains, and deserts they flew leaving only a sound in the air. The day was slowly coming alive with rays of light pushing the dark of night away. Now the 'Shining Star' was no longer protected by the cover of night. Soon many would see the flash of light high in the sky. "Water," cries Joe, "It's the Gulf of Mexico." Smiles of joy embraced all three faces. "At the speed the ship is flying, we'll be home in minutes," Jim said. Over ships and over scattered oil rigs, the 'Shining Star' flies. Passing many ships as they calmly float, the 'Shining Star' leaves not a shadow, only a sound. Now the sun was beginning to peep above the horizon and more and more people awake to a new day. Reaching land, the 'Shining Star' entered Texas. Smiles and cheers broke the quietness within the ship. Staying away from the cities, Jim flies over small, populated areas. Flying low to the tree tops, the trees sway back and forth resembling winds of a hurricane. Now the sun had pushed away all the darkness of the night. And in the sky all was visible to the open eye. With only minutes away from reaching the ship's cover of trees, the 'Shining Star' was only something that went by very fast in the sky. Reminiscing of the night, Jim had flown into the clouds and touched the sky of dreams and dared to see the path of stars that Earth followed. Three who had dreams higher than the skies were on a course of a new future. For they would find a life and sunset far from the one they had seen all their lives. Recognizing the lay of the land, they fly over homes, streets, and farmlands they've known for years. They flew until they reached the long road that led to Jim's house. Down the road they fly, then over Jim's house. There they find the large cluster of trees that guarded and protected the ship. Hovering above the tall trees vigorously swaying back and forth from the ship's mighty power, Jim reduces the ship's power and the ship slowly descends to its resting ground. By now the sun was in full bloom

and so many people were busy about their daily chores. No one even noticed a ship of fantastic abilities in their own back yard. Home once again and safe among the tall trees, the ship and crew were back on solid ground. Turning the power off, the steady hum they had grown so fond of slowly became silent. Jim looks at Sam and Joe with a silent smile.

"We make a great team. I couldn't have brought to life my dreams without you two. Thank you for helping me reach the clouds," Jim said. Smiles of great friendship hung on their faces replacing words of great feelings. "Go home and get a few days' rest. We'll talk when you two are ready," Jim said. Still sitting in his chair, "I must admit, I'm tired but I had a time like no other in my life. And I look forward to another flight." Stretching his arms out wide, "I've never worked so hard sitting down," Joe says with a laugh. Shaking Jim's hand, Joe gave his usual big smile. "I'm glad I took this job. It opened my eyes to a new life and world," Joe said. Joe stands up and exits the ship. Stepping on the ground Joe's legs wobble a bit. Before Sam exits the ship he turns to Jim, "We did it, didn't we?" Sam said.

"Yes Sam, we did it. We flew the skies and more. And it wasn't a dream," Jim said. Wearing a big smile, Sam holds out his hand and shakes Jim's hand. Sam was right, we did it, Jim thought to himself. Following Joe, Sam exits the ship. Standing outside the ship, Sam shakes Joe's hand. They had a friendship that would last many years. Before Jim exits the ship he puts his hands on the captain's chair. "We did it, we really did it," Jim says to himself. Exiting the ship Jim sees Joe and Sam starting to drive away. Both wave to Jim and disappear down the long road. The day was beginning and unknown to Jim a new time was beginning. A time when Jim would find out why the stars were so mystic. A time that would test his meaning of life and death. And a time to find the peace he would seek. Closing the ship's door Jim finds the camouflage netting and covers the ship. Staring at the shiny ship, "Rest well my friend, you were superb last night," Jim said. Leaving the ship to rest, Jim exits the shady cluster of trees. Tired but not sleepy, Jim lays down and looks out the bedroom window. As the light of the day shined in, Jim's mind was heavy with thought. There is an answer to the problem, I just need to find it, Jim thought. Pondering over the ship's ability to fly so easily from Earth's atmosphere, Jim knew any nation with such a power would dominate other nations or start a war. It should be for all the world to have. I couldn't live with myself to see nations fighting over such a power. Do I destroy the ship, give it to the world, or fly away, never to return? Jim thought. Trying not to let the weight of his decision become a great burden, Jim felt time would give him an answer. As Jim looked to the sky, he could see another beautiful, bright shining day busy at work. Rays of sunlight reached out in all directions. And under the sunlight a new day bloomed its many colors of life. After a few hours of rest, Jim turns on his television. News was everywhere. On every news media one could see or hear. "U.F.O. flies at will across the United States. Reported public sightings across Mexico and Texas were only of something flying very fast leaving a whistling noise." Blurred pictures of sightings covered the newspapers with much discussion. Repeated News reports caused a great scare and almost panic in some places. Gun sales jumped to an all-time high as people armed themselves , guarding against their fears. Jim knew, news of the U.F.O would continue until other news more exciting replaced it. Jim frowns. With no one to help Jim decide what to do with the ship, Jim carried the weight of the problem for days. By the third day Jim was expecting to hear from Joe or Sam. The phone rang early that morning, it was Joe. Sounding very troubled, "They're on to me Jim, they're coming for you. Let the bird out of the cage." Jim knew Joe was in trouble. Joe had released one of their coded warnings. Joe's tone of voice was very serious and Jim knew Joe wasn't joking. Before Jim could say a word, the phone went dead. Putting down the phone, Jim took Joe's advice and headed for the back door. Exiting the house, Jim walks briskly across the backyard. While walking, Jim turns his head to take a look. Down the long road Jim notices three black cars one behind the other headed straight to his house. Time was very critical and Jim knew it. Realizing the time was at hand to make his decision, Jim has his final thought. Joe would not have called unless he wanted me to take the ship. 'Let the bird out of the cage,' were Joe's last words. Joe had spent his last moments thinking of Jim and the ship. Joe felt the ship was the best and most exciting project he had ever accomplished. 'Yes', Joe, Sam, we'll fly again. Even if it's only in our minds. Reaching the tall trees. Jim dashes quickly to the ship. With no time to waste, Jim pulls off the camouflage. Staring at the ship, it seemed different. It was a ship that was missing two of its crew and builders. And though the ship couldn't feel the missing elements, Jim could. A feeling of deep regret filled his mind. Still Jim longed to explore the open skies. Opening the ship's door, Jim enters and locks the door behind him. Quiet and still, the ship was lifeless. And still Jim could hear the voices of Joe and Sam. All the memories and moments echoed inside the ship. A ship full of friendship and dreams. Sitting in the captain's chair, Jim straps himself tightly to the chair, looking to his left then his right. Both chairs were filled with only memories. Memories of their daring flights, Jim would not forget. "We're still a team, we're still a team,"

Jim says to himself. Turning the power on, a slow rotation begins. Waking from its long sleep, the ship's power increases and a friendly hum begins. While the ship powered up, Jim opens the ships window shields. Glancing out, Jim could see through the trees, two men in black clothes were running to the back of his house. With their hands on the sides of their faces, they peep into the house's windows. Jim knew they were looking for him. Why, was it the space suit or the radar they were after? Maybe the ship had been spotted by satellite three days ago. Joe did say that 'you can run, but you can't outrun a satellite'. Suddenly the two men were distracted by the ship's soft humming. Turning their attention to the cluster of trees they briskly walk across the yard and into the cover of trees. Reaching the clearing within the trees, the two men find a silver disk-shaped ship of unknown origin. No more than thirty feet from the ship, they stood stiff. With no idea where to fly, Jim knew the moment of truth was only minutes away. Reaching full power, the ship was ready to depart. A swirl of power filled the air as the ship braced itself upon the ground. Once more, Jim looks out the window. Now the pair of men were four men dressed in black suits. Stiff in their tracks they were not expecting to see a U.F.O. Out matched by the power of the ship, their abilities to apprehend Jim were useless. While the four men stared, Jim takes the opportunity to pick from the many thoughts that filled his mind. Knowing this was no longer his home. Home where he lived for so many years. The place he'd ruled and called his castle. Where Joe, Sam, and he'd built their ship. All good memories filled his mind. Now it was time to find a new home and a new way of life, Jim thought. Not realizing the very ship he helped build would soon take him to his new home. A home unlike any on Earth. "I take with me what you cannot have. My memories, my memories, my fond memories and friendships I've held so close. The rising suns that began every day. A moonlit sky that calmed a restless night. The peaceful chirping of a bird calling his mate. Buzzing bees flying from flower to flower. These memories are mine to take."

Slowly the ship rose from its resting ground blowing strong threatening winds at the four men watching. Protecting themselves, they covered their faces as they desperately tried to watch the ship rise. Hovering above the tall swaying trees, Jim sadly looks down at his house. With his ship and memories intact Jim had more than one could ask for. In a blaze of wind, Jim and ship were gone. Heading south with no place in mind, Jim suddenly remembers the land surrounded by water, Hawaii. Remembering he said he would return, Jim continued forward never looking back. Knowing he was a hunted man, Jim's stay in Hawaii would be short. Still Jim pressed on to Hawaii. Through a clear sky, the ship blazed a speed any jet pilot would envy. To the eyes that caught a glimpse or the ears that heard a scream of sound, all knew something had flown by fast. Features along the way became little more than shapes and lines on the ground. As Jim neared the Texas border he knew he'd be heading back into Mexico. Once again Jim stayed low avoiding radar. Flying over trees and unpopulated areas, Jim continues to challenge the ship's awesome speed and power. As a beam of shining light, the ship passed safely over Mexico. Reaching Mexico's border, the blue ocean to Hawaii danced of glittering light. Mile after mile Jim flew pondering over the day's events. It all seemed to have happened so fast. To lose so much in one day seemed like a bad dream. A dream Jim had to live with every day. Dotting the blue ocean like bread crumbs laid out, a line of ships sailed to Hawaii. Following the steady stream of tourist ships, Jim blazed a remarkable trail, only birds of prey could ever fly. Jim had lived a life time of excitement in just mere days. Hopeful for a place to land, Jim focused his mind on high mountains. Flying pass ship after ship the trip of incredible speed saw only the reflected gleaming of ocean mirrors. Hour after hour and mile after mile the sea and distant ships were all that existed. An imaginary land of blue water reflected the calmness of the sky. Far in the distance, Jim could see a small protruding figure surrounded by an endless blue ocean. Growing closer, mountains and hills of unrelenting beauty protruded high in the sky. A paradise of land stood within the ocean's vastness. Slowly coming into view, Jim knew it was the Hawaiian Islands. Jim had kept his promise, he had returned to see the flower of the ocean. Slowing the ship's speed, Jim approaches the Island making a wide circle around the second Island. Finding an isolated ridge high on a mountain, Jim sets the ship down in an area thick with foliage. Covered by tall trees and thick foliage the ship was safe from curious eyes. Turning the power off, the whirl of power faded into quietness beneath the tall trees. Hours before the frantic day's end, Jim sat alone within the ship. Tired and confused, Jim closes his eyes and doses off to sleep. Many hours later, Jim awakes to see a new day. Far in the horizon a bright yellow sun rose from a blue bed of calmness. Rays of subtle sunshine floated up on a gentle water. A new day had begun giving light to plants and creatures. Gently blowing through the trees a cool breeze touched the birds which began to chirp to each other. Longing to stretch his legs and stand on solid ground, Jim moves to the ship's door. Unlocking the door, Jim pushes the door open and steps out of the ship unto solid ground. The feel of solid ground and the breeze of cool fresh air awoke Jim and started his new day. Looking about,

Jim could see nature was flourishing everywhere. Fertile soil and plenty of rain and sunshine nourished all to grow abundantly. Looking over a cliff, blue water softly clashed against large rocks. Slowly the ocean retreated back only to softly splash again. It was a pleasant romance of land and sea. That day, Jim walked along the green hills unhampered by human beings. Admiring an endless view of beauty with sounds from colorful birds, Jim rested his thoughts as he looked upon the ocean that seemed to stand still in time. Built by Earth and managed by many creatures, the beauty of the hill top stood as a beautiful picture. Continuing his walk, a day of peace followed Jim closely. The sun shined brightly with a continuous soft breeze cleansing Jim's mind of recent events. Drifting across a lazy sky, the sun warmed and gave light to the islands of Hawaii while an ocean of water gently splashed against its escalating cliffs and calmly settled upon its sandy beaches. Becoming late of day, Jim decides to return to the ship. As the day began to end, Jim found himself watching a brilliant sun slowly settling into a calm blue sea. A picturesque scenery strikingly beautiful, seen from high atop a mountain, designed and crafted to capture one's conception of beauty. Standing within the picturesque scenery of land, water and sky, Jim found the worries of his life drift away with the setting sun. The night of the day was once more a white moon and twinkling stars glowing abundantly in the dark sky. Not far from the ship, Jim finds a group of palm trees. Lying under one of the tall palm trees surrounded by lush flora, Jim looks up into the greeting sky. An ocean of space full of stars and planets slowly pull Jim in. Closing his eyes, he steps into the endless wonders of space. Traveling the wonders of space, Jim leaps from galaxy to galaxy, fascinated by the unknown. Spending his night under the stars and mentally in space, Jim slept as one with the stars. Waking many hours later to a thunder in the sky, Jim knew exactly what was making the angry thunder. A sound he's heard many times before. Above the mountain tops, two fighter jets fly side by side circling the island. High and low, the jets fly scanning every foot of the island below. Jim knew exactly what they were looking for, 'him'. Knowing it wouldn't be long before the two jets found him. Jim decides to depart the land of paradise. Where to go, another island like Hawaii or a place far away from society? With a ship worthy of fulfilling his dreams other unexplored places were possible. Maybe unknown planets not yet found in the near universe, Jim chuckles to himself. Jim did realize the gold of space was the knowledge of space. Deciding to travel to a place he'd gazed from a distance, a place visited by only a few, Jim chose to follow and pay the moon a visit. Not just to fly by but to land on the moon. Feeling rested and under control, Jim felt the day of rest had healed his worried mind. With his mind restored and full of confidence, Jim was ready for the challenge. Quickly climbing back into the ship, Jim closes the door and locks it tightly. Returning to his chair, he straps himself tightly to the chair. Turning the power on, the ship also awoke from its rest. The sound of power broke the tranquil sound of nature. An unknown roar of energy vibrated through the morning trees and foliage, causing a great alarm among its inhabitants. Faster and faster the wheel of power turned. The sound of wind whirling quickly disappeared replaced by a soft hum. Lights and controls lit up brightly. Once again the ship was alive and ready to fly another journey. And Jim once again was ready for the thrill of excitement. Slowly Jim rose the ship like a hot air balloon. Perched high in the sky, Jim gazed upon the beauty of the island. Having the feeling he could have lived there many years, Jim looked upon the island with good thoughts. Suddenly Jim's thoughts were distracted by the two jets. Swiftly the two jets fly by so close Jim could see the pilots. Away the two jets roared with streaks of white smoke trailing behind like two run away trains side by side. Not to give the pilots a second look, Jim flies higher, higher, and even higher. Reaching an altitude just under the clouds, Jim looks down just in time to see two distant jets streaking across a blue sky. Now Jim was at his moment of truth. To leave Earth and follow his dreams, or continue to play chase with the jets. Realizing he had to follow his dreams. To go where so few had gone. Raising the ship above the clouds Jim embraced his new challenge, 'the moon'. Gone from the roaring jets and mother Earth's mighty grip, Jim left Earth, called by the unknown of space. Now beyond all earthly authority, the 'Shining Star' drifts away from the blue planet of land and water. A planet Jim has known as Earth and home. Focusing his thoughts on the distant moon, Jim doesn't look back. Leaving Earth further and further behind, Jim followed the great unknown as others had. Feeling he had nothing to lose and everything to gain, Jim disregards the dangers that lied ahead. Heading to the moon eagerly, Jim felt this was his answer to the unexplained feelings he was getting from the stars. To explore and find the many hidden wonders of space. Wishing Sam and Joe were with him, Jim sat alone and flew a lonely adventure. Flying among the inviting stars, stars that filled his eyes with wonder and curiosity, Jim felt like a guest among friends. The trip turned into many long hours, then into a day. And the moon was still far away. The excitement of space and the distant moon couldn't relieve Jim of his lack of rest. Needing to close his eyes and rest within the darkness of his mind. Jim continued his trip listening to the steady humming of the ship's power. The powerful hum gave companionship to Jim but also gave a hypnotizing effect. Finding it impossible

to resist closing his eyes, Jim sets the ship's controls for a straight course to the moon. Free of flying the ship, Jim dozes off and begins to drift into the darkness of his mind. Dreaming of his life, as if watching a movie, Jim's childhood and life flash through his mind. Within his dreams, Jim finds the 'Shining Star'. And the many unknown cries for help. Not knowing where the feelings came from, Jim was touched with the feeling of many in need. Within his dreams, Jim doesn't realize his greatest moments of his life were to be of his future. Hours upon hours, Jim sleeps and dreams. Awakening after many hours of sleep, Jim finds a much larger moon waiting. Bringing his sleepy eyes into focus, Jim looks about wondering his whereabouts. Drowsy but awake, Jim continued to revive his mind with every blink of his eyes. Closer and closer the ship approached the moon. A moon full of wonder and unexplored sights, invited Jim to explore with his wildest desires. Still far away and still drowsy, Jim still held the urge to fulfill his dream, staring at the moon with its glow of innocence and wonder. The moon drifted slowly in space following Earth as a quiet companion. Still tired and drowsy, Jim once again lets the ship fly itself. Still exhausted and needing more rest, Jim returns to his darkness of sleep. Floating within the darkness of space and the darkness of his mind, Jim existed only as a thought in time and space. Many hours later, Jim awakes to find the moon stunningly large. As if seen from Earth by a powerful telescope, the moon reviewed far more than its glow and roundness. The smoothness of the moon began to disappear with ridges cascading deep and mountains protruding high above the surface. Covered with large round indentions, the true character of the moon reviewed its distant anomalies. Mere hours away, Jim scans the largeness of the moon for a place most inviting. As the ship closed the gap of distance, the time to land also diminished. At least three days had passed since leaving Earth. And still the feeling of Earth was strong. The love for Earth was the same as the love for a person. It hurt to say goodbye or give a stare one last time. Now Jim was at the point of entering the realm of the moon. Circling the moon's outer realm, Jim finds a suitable place to land. Flat with high mountains in the near distance Jim begins to make his landing approach. Down the ship went with very little gravitational pull. Minutes passed and Jim finds himself over the landing site. Jim lowers the ship's landing legs. Reducing power, the ship hovers above its resting ground. Slowly the ship descends blowing a cloud of moon dust out from under the ship. As the ship settles to the moon, so does the disrupted moon dust, adorning the ship with a cluster of gray dust. Turning the ship's power off, the hum of great power disappeared into the quietness of the moon. Now the 'Shining Star' rested quietly as the moon.

Leaning back in his seat, Jim is relieved to have come so far without problems. Looking out the viewing window, Jim could already see a view of the moon's mystic curiosity. As if the moon was expecting company, it displayed its own enticing blanket of space and shining stars. Like an excited boy eager to go out and play. Jim hurried to put on the space suit Joe and Sam risked so much to get. Up from his chair, Jim kneels to the floor behind the chairs. Grabbing a handle Jim opens a floor panel. To Jim's surprise, two air tanks hooked together rested on top of the suit. When had Joe and Sam found time to bring the air tanks? Jim wondered. Fixed in a harness, the two air tanks were to be worn on one's back. Putting the air tanks aside, Jim pulls out the helmet, suit, and shoes. Standing up Jim grabs the bulky suit and slides in one leg at a time, then one arm at a time. Now in the suit completely, Jim found it very comfortable and warm. Grabbing a shoe, Jim slides his left foot into the left shoe. Then slides his right foot into the right shoe. Locking the suit legs to the shoes, Jim was ready to put on the air tanks. Grabbing the air tank arm strap, Jim slowly slides his left arm through the strap. Reaching back with his right arm Jim manages to slide his right hand into the arm strap. Resting on his back, Jim locks together the front straps. An airline hung from the side of the air tanks. Grabbing the airline, Jim hooks it to the side of his suit. "Not bad for the first time suiting-up," Jim says as if talking to someone. Only needing the helmet, Jim looks down at the faceless helmet. Bending over, Jim grabs the helmet and slides it over his head. Turning the helmet to his right a bit then back to his left. The helmet locked itself air tight. Looking down at the airline, Jim turns the air valve to on. Air begins to fill the suit and helmet and Jim takes a deep breath. Smiling Jim says within the suit. "I'm ready to explore." Stepping to the ship's door, Jim slowly unlocks the door and pushes the door open. Before Jim steps out of the ship he stares at a silent moon. A planet touched only by footprints. Unlike any place Jim had ever seen, the moon was a planet without time or life. Merely following Earth as a companion in space. Turning around Jim backs out and steps out of the ship. Landing softly on the moon, moon dust pushes upward and coats around his space shoes. Stepping away from the ship, Jim takes a quick look around. Beautiful in its own way with craters, rocky mountains, and meteorite pits covering the face of the moon, the moon was a planet of scenery built by space and distant meteors. Deciding to explore as much as he could, Jim takes out across the still vacant moon with big broad leaps. Leap after leap Jim finds himself enjoying the moon like a child on a playground. Setting his sights on a tall pointed mountain, Jim leaps straight for it. Reaching the mountain in only a few flying leaps, Jim begins to climb

the mountain. Step by step Jim rises higher and higher. Space shoes and low gravity make climbing very easy. A mountain unlike any on Earth, he found it very special. Fifty feet up, Jim clings to the mountain. Untouched for so many ages, the moon was more than unique in so many ways. Believed to be a goddess years ago and also evil. Superstitions of various kinds filled the minds of many upon Earth. Of all these claims, the natural unique beauty of the moon was quite innocent of all charges. With every turn, Jim saw a new stunning view. Stopped by the view Jim would never forget. Staring as if he were watching a beauty contest. There she was, slowly spinning around in all her beauty. Like a beauty queen wearing a gown of sparkling diamonds. Mother Earth stood for all to see. Was this the reason no one lived on the moon? Jim asks himself. Getting caught in Earth's visual pull made it hard for Jim to climb down. Climb down he did, back to the surface back on the moon's playground. Continuing to fascinate himself with the moon's low gravity, Jim lifted large rocks and made running leaps that could have been world records on Earth. Exploring and having a great time, Jim had the moon's playground to himself. Checking his oxygen level, Jim noticed it was getting low. Reluctantly Jim decides to return to the ship. Across the moon Jim leaps leaving dust floating in the sky like a galloping horse. Back in the ship Jim refills the ship with oxygen and immediately sheds himself of the helmet and air tanks. Turning on the ship's power, Jim waits for the ship to power up. As Jim waits, the view of Earth was pictured within the ship's window. Earth, the most beautiful sight in the universe, slowly spun around showing her true colors. With her north and south poles painted white with ice and snow. And her oceans a scenic dark sky blue. Earth was a beauty to behold as she danced around and around adorned by glittering stars. By now the ship was at full power and Jim was back in the captain's chair ready to fly.

Grabbing the ship's controls Jim lifts the ship slowly until it reached fifty feet above the moon's surface. With a high view of the moon, Jim moves the ship over the moon's devoid surface. A surface that so many on Earth have gazed upon from far away. Slowly gliding across the moon, Jim imprints many moon features within his mind. A moon of many wonders seemed like a book of post cards, filled with mesmerizing pictures, each one exciting to see. Across the moon Jim flies, over hills, over dry valleys and land that dated further back than mankind's first arrival. Simple in complexity, the moon existed as dirt and rocks. And still mankind gazed upon the moon for many reasons. After a few hours of curious wandering across the moon's surface, Jim felt it was time to say goodbye and depart. Staring at the moon,

Jim promises to be back as one would a friend. Jim leaves with a silent smile. Deciding to return to Earth, Jim raises the ship high and easily breaks the moon's grip without straining the ship's power. As the ship parted from the moon, Jim begins to have feelings to travel further out. A feeling he could only relate to as a whisper in his mind. A strong feeling or urge overriding his better judgment. Knowing just the planet to settle his curiosity, Jim sets his course for a closer look at Mars. As Jim speeds to Mars he realizes the vastness of space was overwhelming. The sun's majestic size, the Earth and all the planets that circle the sun. It all painted a picture far larger than any mind could hold. Watching intensely as the small round planet of Mars grew larger, Jim's logic became entranced by a force Jim could not comprehend. His need to know pulled him into the unknown of space. Continuing his journey, the traffic jams of Earth were not of space. Endless miles of space unfolded into more untouched miles of space. While the grandness of stars and planets never failed to get a breathless stare. Still Jim traveled hoping to get a better glimpse of Mars. With Mars in sight a glow of rustic red burned in the sky of space. With the excitement of space and the ship's space worthiness, Jim found himself glowing with great satisfaction. Not realizing how far he had traveled, Jim slows the ship and takes a look at Earth. Appearing smaller, Earth follows its course unhampered by the thoughts and actions of existing life. Realizing he had traveled far enough, Jim decides to return to Earth. Taking one last look at Mars and seeing how it glowed of red, the same red Romans saw so many years ago, it was a sight Jim would never forget. Turning the ship around, Jim plans a course of return to view the Earth, moon, and sun all at once. Starting his return to Earth, memories of boyhood dreams, powerful jets and friends begun to surface within his mind. As the ship flew effortlessly through space a sudden jerk of the ship startles Jim. Looking quickly throughout the ship then through the viewing window a calm space of stars reviewed only a stillness of time. Feeling it to be an oddity Jim continued his return trip home. Caught by surprise once again, Jim began to fear the worst. As if pulled by a giant hand the ship began to drift in the opposite direction. Immediately closing the ship's window shields, space debris began to pelt the entire ship. Helpless to escape the unknown pull, the ship's great power fell defenseless. Jim decides the best action to take was to turn off the ship's power. Flying wildly within the invisible pull. The ship headed away from Earth deep into the unknown of space. Faster and faster the ship flew leaving behind the world that Jim knew. Flying like the stars that streaked through the unknown of space. The ship flew at speeds even light couldn't catch. Following the calls from the deepest of space, Jim would

answer in person. Stars and planets were streaks of light swiftly disappearing. Pinned to his seat, Jim could barely breathe. Helpless to resist, Jim slowly begins to lose consciousness. Closing his eyes, Jim falls into a deep sleep. Unknown to Jim, he and the ship were pulled by a great force deep into another solar system far, far away from Earth. Seated in the captain's chair Jim sleeps in his deepest dream of darkness. As Jim sleeps, the forces of space carry the ship into another star-filled area of space. To a place untouched and unknown by mankind. Finally the unknown power releases the ship and the ship drifts aimlessly to the calls of space. Slowly Jim opens his eyes and begins to examine his surroundings. Weak from the strain of the flight, Jim could barely move. Not sure what had happened or even where he was. Jim had the feeling he was very far from Earth. Struggling to turn on the ship's power, Jim manages to reach out his right hand and push the power switch on. The sound of power surged through the ship and Jim knew the ship was still able to fly. Lights and controls dimly lit up as the ship powered up. Cold and stiff Jim begins to move his arms and legs. Weak but regaining control of himself, Jim decides to open the ship's window shields. Slowly the shields slid back completely open, and Jim beheld a sight he could not comprehend. Out beyond the ship's window, stars sparkled upon a background of almost emptiness. Two moons floated in the distance, one like Earth's moon and the other red in color. Realizing he was beyond his solar system, Jim's mind ran wild with many thoughts. With no one to turn to for an answer, Jim could only stare. While staring out the window, Jim is shocked to see what he hadn't noticed. How could I have missed an object that big?, Jim said to himself. A planet larger than Earth covered in a haze of slow moving black clouds was right in front of him. So dark were the clouds that light wouldn't reflect. "I know this isn't my solar system, not the solar system I learned and lived in," Jim whispers to himself. Realizing he was far away from Earth, the cry for help was only in his mind. With only a few days of food and oxygen. Jim knew to survive he had to replenish his supplies. Deciding to give the dark planet a closer look. Jim begins to circle the planet in hopes of seeing bodies of land or water. Unable to see through the thickness of clouds. Jim decides to fly a little closer. Angling the ship downward the ship quickly begins to fly blindly into the planet's darkness. Gambling the thick haze would soon vanish once the ship had penetrated deep within the planet's dark clouds. Jim continued to fly using his radar as his eyes. The pull of gravity was much like Earth's gravity. Having learned not to dive too steeply, Jim decides to circle the planet and slowly descend as he flew. Mile after mile Jim flew with his radar guiding his downward approach. Not knowing what to expect, Jim continues his downward descent. After many hours of flying blindly into the haze the ship breaks through the thick haze into a lighter sky. Still hazed but visible to maneuver without radar, Jim is amazed to see what was hidden below the dark clouds. Scattered across the planet's surface, were many large rock mountains covering an endless body of land. Cautious not to fly too low, Jim slows his speed and stays alert. Passing over many mountains of solid rock, the view seemed to never end.

Disappointed not to find signs of life, Jim continues to fly until he passes over a very large rock mountain. So impressed, Jim turns around to get a second look. Flying passed the mountain in silent awe. A prolonged mountain of solid rock towered high in the sky above all other mountains. On a clear day the mountain could be seen from very far away. Breath taking at any angle the mountain was a tower of strength. Deciding to land near the large mountain, Jim searches for a suitable place to land. Visibility low due to the lack of sunlight and rock mountain shadows covering a barren land cautioned Jim to look twice. Scattered across one side of the mountain were tall monolithic columns protruding from the ground. Aroused by the shape and position of the columns, Jim found the columns to be the first signs of intelligent life. Speculating that maybe life once lived on this planet of rock mountains. Jim's curiosity dared him to take a closer look. Flying lower, Jim could see many more columns over ten feet tall, arranged in grouped patterns. Finding a place to land, Jim lowers the ship's landing legs. Gently lowering the ship, the ship touches the planet's surface with its full weight. Turning the power off, the hum of power disappeared leaving Jim alone in silence. Sitting within the darkness of the ship on an unknown planet, Jim realized how much the hum of the ship's power gave him company. As a friend the ship's hum filled the empty space of silence and protected Jim's sanity. Now the hum of company and assurance was gone leaving Jim once again alone to his thoughts and safety. Staring through the ship's window into the haze of the planet, Jim could only think of his friends. This would have been a great discovery had Joe and Sam been here. To be the first humans placing footprints upon the surface of an unknown planet. And place a name upon the planet to last an eternity, Jim thought. As Jim sat pondering, Jim had no idea how far he had traveled. No idea how far away from Earth his friends were. Had Jim known his whereabouts, Jim's sanity would have disappeared in a wave of shock. Within his many thoughts, a smile arose upon his face. Maybe one day I'll meet Joe and Sam and then I'll have a story to tell them. A story of adventure and excitement within the stars of space. Having made up

his mind to explore, Jim ignores the unknown dangers that awaited outside the ship. The feeling of the unknown that would have sent chills through others. Only encouraged Jim to explore and satisfy his curiosity. Unbuckling his chair straps, Jim stands and moves toward the floor compartment that held the suit's helmet. Opening the floor compartment door Jim stares at the helmet. Remembering the day Joe and Sam gave him the space suit, Jim smiles a smile of thankfulness.

"I never would have believed I would have ever used this suit. Now I will use it a second time," Jim said to himself. Pulling out the helmet Jim sets the helmet on the floor. Looking back down into the compartment, Jim bends over and grabs the air tanks by the harness. Sliding his arms back through the straps, the air tanks hang on his back. Connecting the straps in front, Jim then reconnects the airline to the suit. Reaching back down Jim picks up the helmet and holds the helmet high. Remembering the first time he held the helmet, he saw his face. Now his face would be on the inside looking out. Sliding the helmet over his head Jim connects the helmet to the suit. Reaching to his side, Jim turns on the air. Swiftly flowing into the suit air fills the suit. Full of air once more Jim took a deep breath. Once again, Jim was ready to explore the unknown. To be the first to step upon the unknown planet. To imprint upon the ground mankind's arrival. Facing the ship's door, Jim stood and just stared at the door. What am I getting myself into? What is on the other side of the door? Jim asks himself. As was on the moon, Jim could only see another place to explore. Smiling, Jim knew the adventure overwhelmed his fears. Slowly moving toward the door, Jim suddenly stops. The unknown of the mysterious planet finally grabbed Jim's adventurous mind. I might need some protection, Jim thought. Turning around, Jim bends down and opens a small floor compartment. Reaching in the compartment Jim pulls out a hand gun. Making sure the gun was loaded, Jim gently puts the gun and a few extra bullets into the suit's pocket. Feeling a bit safer, Jim returns to the door. Unlocking the door with great caution Jim pushes the door open. Gazing upon a hazed unknown planet. With no seeable life of any kind, it was as Earth's moon, a planet of dirt and rocks. Still Jim's curiosity was pushing him to get out of the ship and explore. Stepping out of the ship onto the dark planet. Jim had no idea he was stepping onto a planet that was far from being uninhabited. A planet all knew as Rou, would challenge his very existence. A challenge that would change his life forever. Not knowing the planet was once a planet of plush lustful beauty with skies of transparency. Now existed only as days of haze and cold darkness. Standing on the planet's surface Jim gets a better view of the surrounding area. A completely different planet than Earth. No life, very little sunlight and a surface as bare as Earth's moon. Taking a few steps, Jim quickly hears a dry crunching sound. Looking down a totally black ground lay covered and untouched. Curious to know what he was stepping on, Jim bends over and grabs a handful of the black substance. Staring at the substance in his hand, Jim finds the substance to be that of ash. The ground as far as he could see was covered with the black substance. Confused in wonder, many thoughts ran through Jim's mind. Looking down at his shoes he noticed both were covered with a dark coating. Emptying his glove it too was coated black. Unable to smell the substance, Jim was sure the ground had been burnt. Was the whole planet the same? How could one burn a whole planet? Deciding to continue his exploring, Jim moves closer to the mysterious protruding monolith columns. Reaching the columns Jim puts his gloved hand on a column, Jim's suspicions are confirmed. Intelligent life did live here and they made these columns. Many questions raced through Jim's mind, as Jim drifted from column to column. Smooth and cut to precision with hieroglyphics embedded into the columns. Jim could only wonder what the hieroglyphics meant. Putting his glove where other beings once put an extension of their body, Jim could feel the excitement of another being surging through him. Looking into the hazed sky, Jim realized he would never meet beings of the planet. Never to know each other or trade the secrets of intelligent life. A deserted planet in the mist of space continued its slow journey around its sun with unanswered questions. A planet marked by the existence of life, life journeyed silently day by day aided by a yellow sun. Turning his attention to the great rock mountain, Jim looks straight up. Tall and very impressive, Jim thought. An impossible climb for anyone straight up, stunningly long, it stretched into the thickness of haze. Deciding to return to the ship and refill his oxygen tanks. Jim suddenly hears a faint noise. Closer and closer the noise grew. Standing still Jim looks around, only a land and sky of haze existed. Once again Jim hears the noise. Closer and louder, Jim knew the noise wasn't something in his mind, it was real. Looking to his left high in the hazed sky, a small glow of blue-green light moves in the sky. Now Jim knew he wasn't alone on the dark and lonely planet. Taking cover behind a protruding column, Jim keeps his hand firmly resting on his gun as he watched. Out of the haze a ship the likes he's never seen before slowly skimmed across the hazed sky and lands about a hundred feet from his ship. Almost twice the size of his ship with a bronze color, the ship rested on the ground. Slowly the noise of its power faded away. The blue-green lights blinked off and on for a few seconds. Still and breathing slowly, Jim stood

quietly and stared. Quickly a door slides open, then another door triangle in shape slides open. Nervously waiting to see what would step out. Jim stood as stiff as the column. What stepped out was something that scared Jim stiff with fear. A being at least seven feet tall with a light brown outer shell and a face that was similar to Earth's planet eating grasshoppers' steps out. With two arms and pincers on each and two long slim legs with claws for feet it walked with a forward tilt and carried a device that looked like a large round pipe about four feet long. At one end of the device a clear bulb existed. At the other end was a rectangular-shaped box. Carrying the device at its side the being kept both its pincers on the round part of the device. Realized the device was a weapon Jim stood still, hesitant to make a move. So taken by the being, Jim hadn't noticed a second being like the first to exit the ship. While Jim watched the first being search the area, the second being circled around the other side of Jim. Having no idea he was surrounded, Jim continued to watch the being silently. Hearing a small sound to the far side of him, Jim quickly turns to see a second being that looked the same as the first being holding the same device. The being stood and stared curiously at Jim. Stricken with fear and physically frozen stiff, Jim merely stared at the being. Staring at Jim the being hadn't made a move either.

Not sure what Jim was, the being stared at Jim daringly waiting for Jim to make a sudden move. Curious of Jim, the being began to take a small step closer. Jim stood still as a rock. Slowly the being took another small step then another small step. Still frozen with fear, Jim found it hard to move. Feeling the moment of life and death, Jim began to tighten his grip around the gun. Knowing he had to defend himself or die, Jim knew the time was now to act. Not reacting to his mental commands, Jim's body stood stiff of fear. Closer and closer the being approached. Now Jim's mind was in panic sending message after message to protect himself. Still Jim stood as stiff as a rock. Before Jim's mind could persuade his body to pull his gun, a flash of burning light passes Jim and hits the being squarely in the chest area. The being staggers as if drunk. Then another blast of flashing light hits the being almost exactly in the same area. This time the being is pushed back a good ten feet and falls to the ground. Lying still without a sound, Jim's body reacts to his mental commands. Quickly Jim moves to the being pointing his gun. A large burned out hole burned within the being's chest area. Who fired the weapon that protected me? Jim asks himself. Grateful for having his life spared, Jim had not forgotten about the other being searching. Quickly Jim turns around pointing his gun in the direction of the other being. By now the other being had seen Jim and was heading toward him. Seeing the other being Jim aims his gun at the charging being. Feeling his heart beating out of control. Jim's mind tells him to protect himself or die. Without hesitating Jim pulls the gun's trigger until all six bullets were fired. True to Jim's aim, each bullet found its target. Stopping from its charge, the being stares at Jim as if in a daze. Still pounding heavily within his chest, Jim's heart could beat no faster. Staring at each other without a sound the being falls backwards losing its weapon. Collapsing into a dark cloud of dust the frightful moment of life and death had found its victims. Slowly the floating dust settled to the ground. Quickly reloading his gun, Jim runs to the being. Pointing his gun at the being, Jim waits for it to move. Showing no signs of life Jim lowers his gun. With his shoe Jim nudges the being to be sure the life of the being was no more. Staring at the being, Jim found it ugly by human standards. Even with the danger over, Jim's heart was still racing. Having never killed anything in his life, Jim had killed an alien being. Killing for food, Jim could understand. But killing another being tested the best of Jim's nerves. Even killing a being with hostile intentions to save his own life. Jim wasn't sure if he or the being represented goodness or evil of life. In all the excitement Jim had forgotten about the one that saved his life. The one that watched over him and protected him. Sweating within his suit and breathing heavy, Jim nervously looks around for the hidden protector. Within the stillness, Jim was startled by a very unfamiliar sound. A sound unlike any sound he had ever heard before. Like someone vibrating their tongue in their mouth.

Quickly Jim looks toward the sight of the sound. Seeing only emptiness, Jim continues to look. Again Jim hears the unusual sound and again Jim looks quickly to where the sound originated from. Feeling a bit stressed, Jim felt maybe it was just his nerves weighing heavily upon his mind. A lot had just transpired and Jim felt he was a bit shaken. Shaken enough to hear unusual sounds? But Jim questions his thoughts, who killed the other being? Looking toward the first being that was killed, it laid still upon the ground. And its ship was in sight. It's not my imagination, someone killed that being. Again the unusual sound is heard and again Jim looks to the direction of the noise. Looking lower Jim is startled to see a little head-to-toe whitish being. At least four feet tall, the little being looked at Jim from a distance. Realizing the little being meant no harm and was trying to communicate, Jim puts his gun back in his pocket. Showing the little being he meant no harm, Jim holds out his hands. Looking down at the being, Jim felt it was really cute. But Jim did realize it did kill the other being. Seemingly not afraid the little

being walks to the dead being Jim had shot. Looking down at the dead being, the little being nods his head quickly and made a short vibrating sound. As if to say, I'm glad you're dead. Then the little being walks to the dead being's weapon, picks it up, and carries it to Jim. Looking up at Jim, the little being vibrates something to Jim. Then he hands the weapon to Jim. Not sure what the being meant Jim takes the weapon and holds it by his side. Then the little being points his little hand at Jim and again makes a vibrating sound. Looking a bit confused, Jim wasn't sure what he wanted. Does he want to know my name? Jim asks himself. Not sure what the little being was saying, Jim tried to communicate the best he could. Pointing his hand to his chest Jim speaks. "I…" and before Jim could say another word the little being went wild with his vibrating. Trying again, Jim points at himself again and slowly tries to communicate. " I…" and again the little being held both his hands high above his head and continued his vibrating. Content with being the little being's friend and not being killed, Jim held the dead being's weapon and wondered what to do next.

Suddenly the ground begins to tremble like a small quake. Not knowing what was happening, Jim looks at the little being who stood unafraid. Staring with great pride the little being stood facing the great rock mountain. Jim sees a large doorway pulling open. Wider and wider the hewed out opening opened until a very large cavity spanned open across the mountain's side. From the darkness of the opening, came dozens of little white beings and headed for both of the ships. Surrounding the two ships they point strange looking hand devices at the ships. As Jim watched, both ships began to rise a few inches from the ground. Having a hard time believing what he was seeing, Jim stood and watched in amazement. Slowly the little beings walked the two ships to the mountain. As Jim watches in amazement, Jim sees his ship float by like a floating balloon. "Hey, that's my ship!" Jim cries out loudly. Having little effect upon the little beings, Jim's ship floated by. And to Jim's surprise the little beings made a vibrating noise. "What did that mean?!" Jim says out loud. To see his ship collected with the other ship, Jim knew he was powerless to leave. That will definitely change my travel arrangements, Jim thought. Without a ship Jim had no idea what to do next. Not knowing low amounts of oxygen existed on the planet, Jim keeps his helmet and suit on slowly consuming his oxygen to dangerous levels. As the ships disappeared into the rock mountain, the little being looked at Jim and pointed to the rock mountain. While holding the enemies' weapons they follow the beings and ships into the mountain's entrance.

Once inside, the ground began to rumble and the rock door slowly began to close. Closer and closer the rock door rumbled till it finally extended across the opening. Completely shut, the door cut off all light from shining in. Inside the mountain, darkness was everywhere. Suddenly lights began to light the inside of the mountain. Lights not from light bulbs high on the ceiling but from lights floating in the air. A marvel of grandness, Jim could only stand and stare. Continuing his walk inside the mountain, Jim was amazed at the mountain's inside hugeness. Technology far beyond all that Earth's best minds could invent, dressed the cave's interior. Jim couldn't help but wonder why these beings with such great minds were hiding from other beings. Realizing the fight that had transpired outside, Jim knew a life and death struggle was being fought. Free to walk among the many little beings, Jim quickly became the main attraction. Word spread of Jim and a rush of little beings came to investigate. Gazing at the tall being in the strange suit, the little beings gathered closely to touch the suit. As Jim walked among the friendly beings he checks his oxygen level. Seeing that he had only a few more precious minutes of oxygen left Jim quickly looks for his ship. Turning completely around Jim saw no ship. With no way of refilling his air tanks, Jim realized his time had come. Feeling his air beginning to thin, a feeling of light headedness and weakness pulled his body downward. Unable to hold his own body weight up, Jim falls to the floor. Into the darkness of his mind Jim falls. Silently lying among his new friends, time and darkness stood still in Jim's mind, as time in space stood still unmoved by the living Jim's new life, unknown to him, was just beginning. Time passes and Jim awakens to find himself floating over a long flat table now surrounded by strange looking medical devices. Jim knew he was at the mercy of the little beings. Knowing considerably little of the beings, Jim did know his life had been saved twice. As Jim becomes aware of all his senses the aches and pains of years ago were no more. For the first time in many years Jim felt great. What have these beings done to me? Jim asks himself. Stepping to the side of Jim, a being looks at Jim with a serious expression. Vibrating from the mouth, the little being stares at Jim. Staring back with wide eyes Jim was speechless, every vibration was understood as words. The little being asks Jim again, "How are you feeling? We've been waiting for you to awaken." Looking at the little being, Jim was still dazed in his thoughts. How could this be, how could I understand? Jim asks himself with a puzzled look on his face. Still without an answer, the little being that saved his life steps up and looks deep into Jim's eyes as an eye doctor would. "How are you feeling 'I', do you feel well? Many have labored to fix you. It took much time to learn your anatomy."

Still floating above the table, Jim got the nerve to speak. "I feel great." Smiles filled the many faces that surrounded Jim. Their work was a success. They had saved the human and given him their most precious technology. By now more of the little beings had gathered around to see the awakened giant. Looking at the little beings, Jim asks, "How did you fix me?"

The being with the serious look upon his face, looks at Jim. "Your body is not able to survive in our atmosphere, easy to fix."

"How?" Jim asks. "We put into your body," saying a word so long it sounded like groups of words run together. Explaining to Jim the word simply meant microscopic organisms with mechanical abilities designed to keep the organism that they dwelled within alive. Using the first letter 'M', of the very long word, Jim spoke to the serious looking being. "How do the 'M's' keep me alive?"

Explaining to Jim, "The M's will heal you from within. A main 'M' is placed at the back of your brain that will control millions of individual 'M's'. They will reattach you bones, heal lacerations and prevent illness. Not only keeping you healthy, they will keep you alive on our or any low oxygen planet. The main 'M' will also translate many languages and provides knowledge that spans our known universe."

"There are many languages on this planet?" Jim asks. "There is only one language and one race on 'Rou'. The other languages are from many other planets," said the being. Looking at the little being, Jim was silent for a moment. "Where am I?" Jim asks. "You are on the planet 'Rou'. In the heart of what you call the Milky Way. We are called E-tuc's," said the little being. "How did you know I knew of the Milky Way?" Jim asks. "We know all you know 'I', and soon you will know all we know. Over time the main 'M' will bond with your brain giving you information we have lived to learn. You are the host to the 'M's'. To protect you means their survival. The 'M's' will protect you or die with you," the being said. Jim found it hard to believe all that was said yet he was alive, breathing, and understanding every word said. "You said other being's languages," Jim inquired.

Leaning toward Jim the little being looks eye to eye at Jim. "Yes 'I' many other languages. Some of the many different beings visit us, some we visit. But now that has come to an end. Many of what you call years, we have been relentlessly attacked by hostile beings killing and destroying our way of life and planet. Forcing us to take refuge within these rock mountains. We call these beings, 'Repssa's'. We have no knowledge of them or where they come from. They are ruthless, they live to destroy, to eradicate all by complete genocide. We have been unable to leave our planet since the 'Repssa's' invaded. Now our once beautiful planet is ash upon the ground. The 'Repssa's' have destroyed our planet and soon our very will to live. "The rock mountains for many have become their graves. One day the last of us will leave the rock mountain, look upon the sky we so cherished, then die. We shall vanish from this planet as if we never existed." With eyes of great sadness he stares at Jim. "Time will show no trace of us, for there will be no one left."

Silence grabs the little beings as they stared at Jim. The look on their faces was more than Jim could bear. Continuing to talk, the little being told Jim they were unable to communicate beyond their planet. With no visitors to help and no ships to depart, they were isolated from all and doomed. Lowering Jim down to the table, Jim is helped back to his feet. Standing on his feet Jim feels better than he has ever felt in his life. With no aches or pains Jim's body is overflowing with an abundance of energy. Stepping up to Jim, a little being holding a shiny suit in both his hands presents it to Jim. Taking the suit, Jim holds it out in front of him. Looking at the oversized shiny suit, it reminded Jim of a jump suit. With no pockets no collar and no zipper in front. Looking at the little beings they urge Jim to put it on. Stepping into the suit Jim finds the suit to be very flexible and soft to his skin. As Jim stands with the suit on he finds the suit to be about two sizes too large. Suddenly Jim feels the suit moving. Looking down, the suit automatically seals together in front. Slowly the suit begins to shrink and shrink till it fits Jim perfectly. Covered from his upper neck to ankles and arms. Jim stands admiring the body-shaped suit. Given a pair of shiny gloves and shoes made of the same material, Jim puts on the gloves and watches as the gloves shrink to fit his hands. Skin tight but very flexible, Jim could only smile as he makes a fist so easily. With his new hands Jim grabs the block looking shoes and slides his left foot in one shoe then his right foot. Staring at his new shiny metal looking shoes they also began to shrink to fit his feet. Covered from upper neck to feet Jim's face and head were all that remained uncovered. Looking like a metal human robot, Jim was unknowingly the E-tuc's new giant leader. As Jim was admiring his new suit, the serious-looking being looked up to Jim and uttered," The suit will obey your every thought."

Stunned to hear what the serious one had said, Jim looks at him puzzled. "When in danger the suit will assemble and harden for combat. It will protect you in every way. It will help you to move faster, jump higher, and give you strength of many. There is more but that is for 'SI' to tell you."

"You mean the 'M's inside me can communicate with me?" Jim asks. "Only the master 'M' can communicate with you. In time 'SI' will speak to you. Test your suit 'I'," the being said. "How?" Jim asked. "Think of danger 'I'," the being said. Thinking of the moment the 'Repssa' caught him off guard, the suit began to take on a life of its own. Rising from Jim's upper neck, the suit covered Jim's face and head completely. While Jim's head was being covered, the suit formed shoulder, arm, chest, back, and leg plates. Jim's entire body was ready for battle. Stunning to view, Jim could see an armor similar in many ways to Earth's middle ages. Light and easy to move in Jim realized the suit was far beyond his rational reasoning. "I just don't believe this," Jim says in amazement. Looking forward Jim could see the smallest item so far away. Why? Jim asks himself. Why so much for so little I have done? Within Jim's thoughts a voice or thought within his mind interrupted his thinking. "They gave you so much because they are depending on you 'I'. They need you to help them free themselves of the 'Repssa's'," the voice said. Who said that? Jim said to himself, looking around the large room filled with only little E-tuc's surrounding him. "Who is speaking to me? Is someone speaking to me telepathically?" Jim asks. Jim was unprepared for his new world. In every way or thought, Jim was in a world far above his or Earth's technology. A world he had to learn and learn fast. 'SI' introduces himself. "It is I, the master 'M' within your head. I am called 'SI'. I am now fully activated and can deliver all information you will need or want," 'SI' said. "What are you, a computer chip or some sort of E-tuc-made hi-tech advanced device?" Jim asks. "Neither, I am as you are, a living organism. Taken from a creature of little or no intelligence and enhanced as you are with E-tuc technology. I do not miss my former body as you will learn not to miss yours. We are both better off as enhanced beings. I have been given the E-tuc knowledge which will date back thousands of E-tuc years on 'Rou'. I will supply you with all the information, you will need. To acquire this knowledge, raise a thought and information will fill your mind as fast as you can think. I am to control the 'M's' as you say and help keep you alive by directing the millions of 'M's inside you. "You are the host 'I', there is no transferring us out of you. If you die we will die. We will not permit that to happen to you 'I'. You are the warrior that has come from the furthest of stars to lead the E-tuc's to freedom. To right what has been wronged. To rid 'Rou' of those that bring war and destruction upon her. To save the E-tuc race and bring stability to the planet of 'Rou'. All have been waiting for you 'I'. Lead and many will follow," 'SI' said. "Me? I'm just a guy from another planet. I'm not a great warrior to lead these E-tuc's into battle or anyone else," Jim said. "You are what you want to be 'I'. A warrior and leader is one that can learn to do what must be done. To know who to attack and when to attack. To protect and guide, you can learn 'I'," 'SI' said. "Why are you calling me 'I'? Why am I being called 'I'? My name is Jim. I'm from the planet Earth. I am a human. I AM A HUMAN," Jim says almost screaming within his head. "You are 'I'. As we are who we are. You will forever be 'I', the first grand warrior leader of 'Rou'. Make your decision 'I', be the warrior leader of 'Rou' and help so many. Or be stripped of all that the E-tuc's have given to you. And then you will die on this low oxygen planet beside the E-tuc's," 'SI' said. Standing and displaying the full-armored suit. Jim gazed upon so many little sad and wandering eyes. With hopes and dreams of returning to the surface, the little E-tuc's stood gazing at 'I'. "Their trust and best technology were given to you 'I'. You are their last hope of living. A race that is doomed to die, to disappear from time can only live in peace for many of what you call years, if only a warrior such as you protects them," 'SI' said. Realizing he couldn't return to Earth, life expectancy was only minutes without the suit, and most of all the E-tuc's had already saved his life twice, staring at many little E-tucs, Jim speaks to 'SI'. "I accept the offer 'SI'. I will lead the E-tucs and help reclaim their once greatness among the stars that shined upon 'Rou'. What must I do 'SI'?" 'I' said.

"Speak to the E-tucs. Let them know you desire what they desire. That victory and peace can and will be once more," 'SI' said. Staring at so many within the great rock mountain, 'I' addresses the massive mass of E-tucs that had gathered. In a strong and loud voice 'I' spoke. "I am with all, to a new and bright beginning that has just begun. We shall triumph, we shall see a new sunrise filled with our hopes and dreams of a better life for all. Together we shall find a way to triumph, and together peace will be our guiding light," 'I' said. The cries of freedom broke the silence and echoed the length of the mountain. Hearts were filled and minds clung to hope. Slowly walking through the mass of little white beings, they relentlessly cheered in their own way. The moment filled 'I' assuring him he had made the right choice. But how long would it last? Would it last days, weeks, months or would the rock mountains be my grave also, 'I' thought. Continuing to walk through the cheering E-tucs, 'I' realized he needed a plan and 'SI' would be the one to help him. As the cheering subsided, one of the leaders revealed their underground world to 'I'. Lead through many floor levels 'I' began to understand the feeling of being a prisoner. Even with miles and miles of tunnels, 'I' found the E-tucs longing for the planet's surface. To walk within

the sunlight, to feel the warmth of day and gaze upon the stars at night. Having never seen a human, the E-tucs followed the E-tuc leader and 'I' like a giant parade, slowly growing larger. Gathering in a very large room, 'I' and the leader walk up steps to a platform about ten feet high. As they stand and wait, thousands of E-tucs gather and wait for all the leaders to arrive. Parting at the entrance doorway, three distinguished looking E-tucs walked through. Walking to the center of the room they step up each step until they reach the top of the platform. Once at the top of the platform, the filled room grew quiet. As the leaders greet each other, they turn to the many that waited. Standing tall for all to see, 'I' gazed down at the massive crowd of E-tucs. To have so much knowledge and hide from aggressors, 'I", could not understand. "The E-tucs are known far and wide as beings of intellect, not harvesters of war," 'SI' said. "Can they learn to fight?" 'I' asks 'SI'. "One has, and he stands a few feet from you," 'SI' said. 'I' looks to his right, and there stood the little E-tuc that saved his life. He seemed different from the others, he knew how to fight back. Still 'I', found it amazing to be with such intelligent beings not wanting to defend themselves. "The E-tucs have lived to learn not to kill. Their weapons are almost nonexistent. Learning to defend themselves and kill will be a whole new learning experience for the E-tucs," 'SI' said. As the leaders began to speak, 'I' noticed his little friend holding a 'Repssa' weapon by his side. A weapon of great prize for all to see, a weapon to show one's great bravery. Poised as if ready to take command he listens in earnest. There was something different about this E-tuc than the other E-tucs, 'I' thought. An E-tuc by himself that stalked and killed 'Repssa's'. Was it a burning desire to retaliate, or did he kill the 'Repssa's' as a kind of sport? 'I' wondered. Whatever the reason, 'I' knew he had one E-tuc that would fight. As the meeting continued it seemed dreadful. The E-tuc situation continued to decline in resources and the living. 'I' was mentioned as one from far away that would help fight the 'Repssa's'. As 'I' listened he knew he had to first raise the E-tuc's spirits then he could raise a fighting force. 'I' began to wonder about ways to fight back with such a limited amount of weapons and resources. Conversing with 'SI', 'I' learns more of the war-minded 'Repssas'. "The 'Repssa's are conquerors of many planets in our solar system. They spread their destruction killing and burning planets to the ground. With an overwhelming force the 'Repssa's' fear no one. Their spread of destruction and death is a warning to other planets, death is soon to arrive. The 'Repssas' live to fight and destroy. You have already seen two 'Repssas' close-up. The 'Repssa's' circle 'Rou' with one warship. They investigate any movement upon 'Rou' with their fighter ships. As they did when you entered 'Rou's' orbit and landed. After they investigate they return to the warship. Having destroyed all of 'Rou's' space worthy ships all on 'Rou' are doomed to certain death. The 'Repssas' are very confident and fear no attacks. This could be their downfall," 'SI' said.

Together 'I' and 'SI' devise a daring and very dangerous plan. As the meeting came to an end, 'I' descends from the platform and mingles with a jubilant crowd of E-tucs. After meeting so many, 'I' is given living quarters. Lying down, 'I' retraces his moments of arrival. A new planet, death, and near death. Living day to day. Jim felt he was being chased once more and not given a chance to live in peace. Interrupting 'I's' thinking, "'I', you need your rest. I will help induce your rest by clearing your mind and relaxing your body," 'SI' said. 'I' falls asleep soundly. The next day 'I' returns to the great room to hear another meeting of tragedy. More lives were lost from attacks by the 'Repssa's'. 'I' could not bear to hear the deaths of more E-tucs unable to fight back. Finding the steps to the platform 'I' climbs the steps to the top of the platform. 'I' gives a bow of respect. "O great leaders of 'Rou', I have a plan, may I tell all that want to hear." As the four leaders stare at 'I' a leader steps forward close to 'I'. "Many plans have been given 'I', and many have failed. All plans that pass must be agreed by the many over the few."

Bowing once more to the leader, 'I' stands before the many of 'Rou' and reveals his daring plan. A room of many stood quiet and listened. After a portion of time 'I' finishes and the great room stood speechlessly silent. Having caught the leaders and all those that heard by surprise. It seemed that no one was as daring as 'I'. No one rallied together to attack the 'Repssa's'. 'I' was disappointed. Looking at the leaders, they too were silent. A moment of silence filled the uncomfortable moment. Once again a leader steps forward and speaks to 'I'. "'I' your plan is very daring and too daring for many to follow. We only intended to use the captured 'Repssa' fighter to seek help from our closest neighbor, 'Sis'," the leader said. Before the leader could say another work 'I' speaks. "They are but one war ship. We can use their ship and attack by disguise," 'I' said. Standing dazed at 'I's' daring plan the leaders once again were silent. A great murmur erupts in the room. 'I' stands with eyes staring at the massive mass of little beings. Frantically they whisper their private thoughts to each other. 'I' knew it would take much more than a daring plan to motivate many to agree. Having heard enough murmuring, 'I' steps forward and raises his hands high in the air to quiet the uneasy thoughts. Staring at the many undecided, 'I' speaks. "If we are not willing to die for our freedom, we will definitely die hiding. To live in fear is not to live

at all. There is no guarantee of life or another day while the 'Repssas' orbit 'Rou'. The 'Repssa's' will guarantee you death as they have so many. It's time to fight back, time to live once more under the sun. The door of opportunity has opened. We must take that opportunity and regain our freedom. Choose to live or die, choose to live under the sun or stay hidden underground. The time for running is over. As for me I choose to fight, I will hide no more," 'I' said. Looking at the filled room of E-tucs, all stood quiet, not a sound. Years of living in peace had disabled the E-tuc's from arming themselves. Unarmed and unwilling to fight, the E-tucs were lost in their moment of life. As 'I' waits for an answer, another leader steps forward and speaks. "It will be very hard to find many, if any, for your bold plan, 'I'". "I can't do it all by myself, but I will show the 'Repssas' I do not fear them," 'I' said. 'I' stands alone staring at the massive gathering of E-tucs. 'I' was on the verge of giving up his risky plan. With only seconds from stepping down from the platform, 'I' stares once more hoping for a miracle to happen. Far in the distant room 'I' notices a 'Repssa' weapon winding its way through the large crowd. In and around it made its way closer to the platform. Standing at the bottom of the steps the little E-tuc stares up holding his 'Repssa' weapon. It was his friend that had saved his life. Once again his little friend was watching and protecting. Step by step he reaches the top and stands looking up at 'I'. Proudly and bravely the E-tuc said for all to hear, "I'll fight the 'Repssa's' with you 'I'." Like a gust of wind blowing a grass fire, the crowded room of E-tucs blazed with volunteers ready to fight. Standing a few feet away the four powerful leaders of 'Rou' stood wide-eyed at what had just happened. Never had so many agreed to a plan and never were so many excited to fight. The little E-tuc had not only found a friend, but he was now making him a leader. A leader that would regain greatness for 'Rou' far beyond her greatest days. Standing beside 'I' the little E-tuc held his 'Repssa' weapon as high in the air as he could. Encouraged by the E-tuc teaming up with 'I', the crowd of E-tucs swarmed around the leaders' platform. Cheers of unity were loud and deafening. Not sure of 'I' as a leader yet, they were very sure of their E-tuc friend who had proved his bravery and carried the enemy's weapon. A weapon that all E-tucs longed to hold. Satisfied minds were ready to follow their friend who was ready to follow his friend, 'I'. Having made up their minds to fight and live, they knew the time was now. Leaving the room hurriedly they realized there was no time to lose. The time to strike was now. 'I' and his friend step down from the platform leaving the four leaders alone. As 'I' and his little friend walk out of the great room, many E-tucs were already arming themselves and boarding the two ships. Walking to the ships, E-tucs lined the walk ways giving a hero's praise. The moment and time seemed right. Though it was another plan from so many before, the fight for freedom still burned in the hearts of all. And 'I' had to prove to all his leadership and bravery. For some reason 'I' felt no fear. His confidence was soaring as he walked to the two ships. Reaching the 'Repssa' ship, the room was filled with praising E-tucs. 'I' felt there was no need to say another word, only the need to back his words. 'I' walks to the ship's ramp and stops. Staring into the ship's open doors 'I' could see many armed E-tucs lined up to the ship's doorway. Entering into the 'Repssa' ship, 'I' and his friend became the last two to enter. 'I' knew he would be the first out, and that was what he wanted. Looking at the many E-tucs waiting to fight, answered 'I's' wondering question. Would the E-tucs fight back if given the chance? Inside 'I' stood with his friend who held tight to the only 'Repssa' weapon by his side. Many eyes stared upon the 'Repssa' weapon with great admiration. A sign of true bravery against a superior force. "So many 'SI', so many willing to risk their lives," 'I' said. "They want their freedom and now is the time. They are proud to follow the brave that will lead. So proud, they're willing to give their lives if need be. They have found a leader in you 'I'. E-tucs have never followed another being, you're the first. They see leadership in you. Be victorious, be the leader that can lead and learn," 'SI' said. By the fighter ship's own instruments, the 'Repssa' warship was located circling 'Rou'. 'I' breaks the silent stillness that kept all in suspense. "Close the ship's doors," 'I' said. The doors slide shut. Then the sound of the ship's engines vibrate throughout the ship. All knew the time to fight was near.

Slowly the rock door rumbled open revealing a very wide opening. Easing a few feet off the ground the many surrounding the ship hurriedly moved to safety. Slowly the ship inched forward passing through the rock mountain. Clearing the mountain's doorway the ship was free once more. But this time it carried the thunder of an advancing storm. Slowly the ship rose higher and higher. Moving forward with increased speed, the "Repssa' ship flew high above "Rou'. Having learned the ship's controls, E-tuc pilots flew the fighter ship as well as any 'Repssa' could. Their flying ability made it hard to believe "Repssa's' weren't flying the ship themselves. Silence again covered all like a large blanket. Tension began to grip all tightly as the ship flew into orbit. Within the darkness of space, "I' and crew gazed at the countless amount of stars. A sight one could barely see from "Rou'. A sight only remembered within one's mind. Cautiously flying to the warship's signal, another "Repssa' fighter ship was spotted heading the same direction. 'I' immediately orders

the pilots to follow behind the fighter ship. Reducing speed all cautiously watched as they flew behind the fighter ship. Not a sound was made, only wondering eyes fed their minds. As seconds and heartbeats, ticked and beat. 'I' wondered if the E-tucs worried as he did. Trying not to think of all the things that could go wrong, 'I' did his best to show confidence as a leader. Within 'I's' mind, "I'm preparing your body and mind for battle," 'SI' said. Puzzled how 'SI' could do that, 'I' asks, "How?"

"I'm easing your mind of worry, to help you focus and see with a clear mind. For a mind of worry will surely lead in unsure directions. Forward your thoughts to achieve your goals. I am also charging your body with energy to fulfill your task. You will be ready in every way," 'SI' said. Moments passed without sight of the warship. The time was near and 'SI' was right. 'I's' mind was as a lion roaring over his domain. Letting all know he ruled as far as one could hear his roar. And with the added armor 'I' could defend his domain against all. Continuing to follow the fighter ship they find the warship. Like a shadow lurking in the dark one could see but not be sure. Cloaked in darkness and dangerous as a killer with a cold dagger. The warship boldly drifted in the darkness of space around 'Rou'. Quickly alerting the other ship in waiting to follow, 'I' and the E-tucs continued to follow the fighter ship. Nearing the warship, lights were spotted at one end of the warship. Into the lit opening the first fighter ship flew and then 'I' and crew followed. Entering into a wide landing bay, 'I' instructs the pilot to land close to the landing bay control room. Maneuvering the fighter ship, the pilots fly easing the ship close to the control room. Slowly the fighter ship lands about fifty feet away from the control room.

Looking at 'I', 'I' gives the E-tucs his most unshakeable look of confidence. It was the look the E-tucs wanted to see. The look matched the feelings the E-tucs held deep inside. "We shall be victorious today," 'I' said. Armed and ready to fight 'I' felt extremely anxious. Like a lion waiting to leap upon its prey. 'I' stares into the eyes of the E-tucs. 'I' was ready to put fear into 'Repssas' within their own ship. Now it was the 'Repssas' time to defend themselves. To know the feeling of life and death. 'I' nods his head to the pilots. Doors unlock and slide back like a lion's cage letting out angry lions. The taste of blood and revenge swirled within the attackers' minds. To plunge the dagger of death deep into the 'Repssas' heart then twist it, still fell short of satisfaction. Stepping out quickly 'I' aims his side arm stunner immediately at a 'Repssa' nearby. Firing without hesitation, the 'Repssa' falls to the floor. The next 'Repssa' raises his weapon but 'I' was quicker. Firing his weapon over and over the 'Repssa' falls backward and lies motionless. Bursting from the ship the little E-tucs fanned out in all directions. The fight had started and all knew it would end with only victory. But which side would proclaim victory, and rule the skies of space and 'Rou'? Fighting became fast and fierce and death spread throughout the landing bay. Many 'Repssas' fell by being surprised and many seemed to replace them as quickly. Hit a few times 'I' knew his plan had to work. There was no retreating and 'Repssas' took no prisoners. To take the ship meant freedom for all of 'Rou'. Even if only for a while. Having never seen a being like 'I' fight stunned the 'Repssas' to see a being as fierce as or fiercer than they. Feeling invincible 'I' fought with the strength of many. One 'Repssa' after another fell at the hands of 'I'. As the fighting continued it was obvious the 'Repssas' were not giving up. Grouping and regrouping the 'Repssa' fought back relentlessly. Through heavy weapons' fire and growing smoke the two forces fought back and forth. Fires broke out in many places and smoke began to darken the landing bay. Exploding, a fighter ship sends parts of the ship and near bystanders in all directions. Still the fighting continued back and forth. Flashes of light cut through the smoke finding their targets, while other weapons fire wildly hit ghosts in the smoke. The little E-tucs fought bravely. Quick and precise they gave the 'Repssas' no second chance. Fighting in pairs the madly driven E-tucs attacked the 'Repssa' expiring them quickly. As the 'Repssas' fell so did their weapons. Quickly the weapons were grabbed and very effectively used against the 'Repssas'. With no end in sight the sounds of weapons firing and cries of the wounded or dying echoed within the landing bay walls. Noticing a clear path between the fighting and control room, 'I' decides to charge the control room. Dashing as fast as he could, 'I' fires a blast from his weapon at the door. A loud metal crashing noise grabs the attention of all. The door to the control room was severely damaged. Half of the door was bent inward, exposing the control room. Quickly 'I' dashes into the control room. Only a few feet into the room, 'I' is hit by a qualton weapon's blast. Knocked to the floor, 'I' regains his balance and continues to fire back. Aided by two E-tucs, the control room soon became a flash of light. Back and forth beams of light flashed. The 'Repssas' were determined to keep the control room under their control. Firing back and forth the fight continued without a takeover. 'I' knew he had to take the control room and stop other fighter ships from landing. A sacrifice had to be made. Knowing his armor could take a blast and regenerate back, 'I' motions for the E-tucs to ready. Stepping out from hiding, two 'Repssas' quickly step out and fire at 'I'. As 'I' falls backward, the two E-tucs quickly fire back and hit the 'Repssas'. Down fell the 'Repssas'

enabling the E-tucs to move forward. Back to his feet, 'I' continues with the E-tucs.

One by one control room 'Repssas' fall. With nowhere to hide or back-up to, 'Repssas' charge into the line of fire. Death came to the last of the control room 'Repssa's'. As 'I' looked at them, strangely 'I' thought, the 'Repssa's' life was only to fight, to kill or die trying. The control room was finally theirs. Approaching the landing bay's entrance, the second ship came sliding across the floor overtaking attacking 'Repssas'. Exiting the ship E-tucs were ready to fight. Now the E-tucs had the upper hand and the 'Repssas' knew it. Rushing the control room, 'Repssas' became easy targets. Not knowing what defeat was, the 'Repssas' continued aggressively to attack. Regrouping their forces, another wave of attack was about to begin. Greatly out-numbered, the 'Repssas' disregarded their grave situation. Moving forward the 'Repssas' attacked the heart of the E-tucs. Lights flashed in many different angles and many fell smoking of burned bodies. The end of the 'Repssas' had come, death with no mercy. The landing bay had grown quiet and not a 'Repssa' was standing. Caught by surprise and defeated, the 'Repssas' no longer controlled the landing bay. Now with full control of the landing bay 'I' orders the bay doors closed. Gazing across the landing bay, bodies laid motionless. 'I' had no feelings for the 'Repssa' dead, only for the small brave 'E-tucs' that gave their lives. The battle held no guarantee, still they fought on, in their greatest moment of life. Never to know their bravery won victory that day. Now their bodies were loaded into a fighter ship to be returned to 'Rou'. 'I' hoped the dead would be received as brave heroes and never forgotten. Regrouping his thoughts 'I's' heart leaps to see his new friend approaching. Carrying his 'Repssa' weapon he walks before 'I' and stops. Looking up at 'I' with a serious face. "We fought well today," the E-tuc said.

"Yes we fought well today," 'I' said. Even in the mist of death, 'I' thought of his new friend. And now the battle is over and his friend lives. Now the beginning of freedom had begun. Having captured the ship's landing bay, 'I' knew the rest of the ship had been alerted to the landing bay attack. Leaving a small group to guard and control the landing bay. 'I' and the remaining E-tucs readied to head upward to the ship's control room. Knowing a fight awaited, 'I' and his eager group of E-tucs were ready to take the ship. Leading the way 'I' and the E-tucs found the rest of the landing bay deserted. Every room and hallway gave no surprises. Up the stairs they ascend, reaching the third floor 'Repssas' begin to spring from hiding and attacked. Too few to stop the large group of E-tucs. Not wanting to be pinned down by hard to reach 'Repssas'

'I' charged and took many weapon blasts. Continuing to move forward, fighting became savage and brutal on both sides. Bodies began covering the floors like a trail of bread crumbs. Killing became a back and forth struggle. Wounded 'Repssas' struggling to fight on were beaten to death with their own weapons. And many 'Repssas' were blown to pieces by vengeful E-tucs. The 'Repssas' had truly made a true enemy of the E-tucs. Unforgotten in E-tuc's minds were the deeds of the 'Repssas'. Out for more than blood, the E-tucs hunted the hidden 'Repssas' like an angry mob. A sudden noise or movement quickly drew the attention of every E-tuc holding a weapon. Entering a large room a 'Repssa appears from a dark corner. Unknown to the following E-tucs, 'I' had only a split second to react. Quickly aiming, 'I' sends a blast blazing to the 'Repssa'. Moving forward with a watchful eye, 'I' once again spots a figure aiming his deadly weapon. Quickly 'I' fires a full blast from his arm stunner. A flash of light and a glow of fire encompasses the hidden 'Repssa'. Onto the floor the burning 'Repssa' falls, only to be attacked again by vengeful E-tucs. The eye of gratefulness looks at 'I' in the dimly lit room. Words could not convey the thoughts that ran through the E-tuc's mind. Only what the future would bring by the E-tuc's help. Continuing to move forward, close quarter fighting continued as shadows leaping from the walls. Dim rooms and walkways gave the 'Repssas' a great advantage. But the 'Repssas' were tall and clumsy. A lumbering giant with a lumbering shadow. 'I' had the strange wondering feeling. "Why hasn't the warship called for help?"

"They are beings that fight to the end, they are arrogant in every way. Fear is something they haven't learned yet," 'SI' said. "Then we will teach the 'Repssa' fear. For it means death follows close behind," 'I' said. Nevertheless, the 'Repssa' ship was still in space, hidden within the dark curtains of space. Determined to win and keep the ship, 'Repssas' fought on. And the E-tucs fought back determined to win and take the ship. Advancing to the end of the second floor, 'Repssas' were spotted darting to the top floor. A cheer erupted from E-tucs. Fear had been struck into the minds of the 'Repssas'. The grave feeling of dying or being conquered concealed their arrogant ways. To see the 'Repssa' run only encouraged the E-tucs to move forward, to know that victory was not far away. 'I' knew not to be overly confidant, not to accept victory until victory is made. Turning to E-tucs 'I' quickly informs them a trap may be waiting. "Don't get overconfident, let's move very cautiously," 'I' whispers. Advancing across the second floor without a fight seemed too easy. What was waiting upstairs? 'I' thought. Slowly moving to the top floor 'I's'

nerves began to jump. "There must be a trap waiting," 'I' says to 'SI'. "Stay calm and cautious 'I', victory comes to those that can see through the eyes of the enemy." So much ran through 'I's' mind and only one phrase stood true in his mind. Caution comes before victory. Cautiously making every step upward, the moment of surprise waited at the top floor. Step by step carried a look of great uncertainty. Knowing the moment of truth waited only moments away. "'I' your armor is dangerously low on power. The numerous attacks upon your armor have greatly weakened you armor's ability to protect you. Your armor cannot maintain itself or protect you from another direct blow," 'SI' said. "I trust you to protect me; I have not ventured this far and dared life and death and witnessed many bravely sacrificing their lives. To shun from my position and let others take my place. If the moment of death befalls me, we will both join the many brave within the darkness of eternal space," 'I' said. "Life is existing and exploring the wonders of reality. Death is the other side of enlightenment. If I can't protect you I will gladly join you in the darkness of space. Be brave and cautious," 'SI' said. "Together 'SI', we will face life and death and learn how precious life is." Slowly the remainder of 'I's' forces made their way up the winding stairs. Clearing the last step, all stood aiming their weapons down the hallway leading to the control room. The quietness became a feeling of eeriness. The darkness held shadows of unknown shapes. And to 'I', his moment of darkness waited for him to lead the final assault. Where are they hiding? 'I' thought. Standing on the top floor, only darkness knew the truth. With only an empty hallway leading straight to the control room 'I' found it hard to believe the top floor was theirs without a fight. Still feeling there was one last battle to be fought, 'I' and the E-tucs crept down the hallway expecting a surprise at any moment. Reaching the control room doors, all were surprised no attacks befell them. 'I' could only wonder what waited for them on the other side. The cost to capture the ship was already high. At least half of 'I's' force was dead or badly wounded. And the ship was still in the claws of the enemy. The sacrifice of lives was not over yet. To gain control of the ship would cost more precious lives, 'I' said to himself. "Take the control room and the ship, is yours," 'SI' said. "Yes 'SI', take the control room and the ship is ours to command," 'I' confirms. Standing back a safe distance, two armed E-tucs aim their 'Repssa' weapons at the doors. Firing upon the doors a loud crashing noise filled the quiet hallway. As the smoke slowly cleared, two twisted and bent doors hung open, slowly smoking. Now a large pathway opened into a dark room. Smoke and darkness filled a quiet control room. Standing at both sides of the doors. All waited for the smoke to settle. Quietly at the edges of the doorway,

'I' peeks into the dark smoke filled room. Strange, 'I' felt the eerie feeling again crawling over his skin. Hidden within the smoke filled room, life or eternal death waited. The stillness and smoke gave the room a graveyard effect. "Where are the 'Repssas' 'SI'? I've been expecting a battle to the death, where have the 'Repssas' gone? Is this the room many will die in?" 'I' asks 'SI'. 'SI' was silent unable to answer the 'Repssa's' ways. Slowly the smoke cleared and objects became visible in the dark. Still feeling uncertain, "'SI' is there a way to know how many are in the room?" 'I' asks. "'I' your armor sensors are only picking up the E-tuc's life signals. There are no other signals of life within this area," 'SI' said. "Then how are 'Repssas' covering up their life signals? To enter into a trap would mean death for many," 'I' said. "There is only one way to know, we must enter the room," 'SI' said. The thought of losing more E-tucs greatly saddened 'I' but 'SI' was right, they had to enter to be certain and take control of the ship. Slowly and cautiously 'I' and the E-tucs enter the control room expecting a fight to begin at any moment. Quiet and dark, the room stood still in time. A large control room filled with 'Repssa' technology was now in the E-tuc hands. Tense and eyeful of his surrounding, 'I' kept his guard up. Still feeling the last battle to be a life and death struggle 'I' took nothing for granted, anything that moved would be confronted. The prize that so many gave their lives for became a silent victory. No last battle to be fought. And no more lives to be lost. 'I' was relieved the fighting was over. At least for the 'Repssa' warship. Reaching the captain's chair, four 'Repssas' were found grouped closely around a 'Repssa' seated in the captain's chair. All were dead by self-infliction. 'I' realized that even a 'Repssa' knew fear. "Did they fear the E-tucs or fear the consequences of losing the ship?" 'I' asks 'SI'.

"They had failed and that was enough," 'SI' said. It seemed that failure had only one price, death. Pointing to the seated 'Repssa'. "He must be the ship's captain. We put the fear of death and defeat into their minds. Now the 'Repssas' have escaped into the endlessness of space," 'I' said. Staring down at the E-tucs, 'I' proclaims proudly, "The warship is ours." A cheer of victory vibrated within the ship's control room.

As 'I' had said, victory is ours today, and so it was. Not far from 'I', stood his brave little friend. 'I' walks to him and kneels on one knee and looks eye to eye. "It is good to see you alive my friend. Life is short in the struggles of living. And even shorter in the struggles of war. 'I am grateful for your confidence in me," 'I' said. "We are warriors 'I', we must stay alive to keep the peace, yes," the little E-tuc said. "Yes, together we will keep the

peace," 'I' said with a small smile. Grabbing 'I's' 'Repssa' weapon 'I' stares and understands what he was saying. 'I' also grabs his friend's weapon and stares eye to eye. Having found a new home and new friends in a faraway solar system seemed more like a wild dream than reality. Yet two beings of distant galaxies began a friendship that would change a galaxy of lives for thousands of years. Their friendship became binding as distant stars shining a glow of light at each other. Victory aboard the ship didn't last long. The celebration and togetherness suddenly came to an abrupt end. A loud excited cry alerted everyone. Out a port window a glow of light lit the darkness of space. Folding back the dark curtains of space a 'Repssa' warship of the same design emerged from the cold depths of deep space. Staring out small port windows the investigating warship drifted closer. The chill of fear froze the cheers of victory. 'I' and the E-tucs were not ready for a battle. Drifting closer it neared to investigate. Not knowing it was too late to help, it drifted closer. "The 'Repssa's' warship must have received a distress call from this ship."

"Yes 'I', right before they killed themselves. Now we will have to answer for a victory," 'SI' said. Now life and death will mingle once again, 'I' thought. With no power and darkness within the control room, all desperately searched for the power source.

"'I' scan around the captain's chair."

Quickly removing the 'Repssa' bodies, 'I' scans as 'SI' had requested. "Where could it be?" 'I' asks 'SI'. "There," 'SI' said. 'I' stops scanning at the back of the captain's chair. One foot off the floor was a small glass-like orb, about three inches in diameter. "Touch the orb 'I', "'SI" said. Touching the small orb, lights quickly lit the room. Controls lit up and the control room became operational. Notifying the landing bay crew to ready themselves for an attack. The E-tucs in the control room began studying the controls feverishly. Time was of the essence to control the ship. Frantically trying to comprehend 'Repssa' language and controls the E-tucs quietly grouped around the largest control panel studying the many symbols. Suddenly a beeping noise began then stopped. Standing still all looked around in wonder. Again a beeping noise began and stopped holding all in stunned wonder. "What's making that noise 'SI'?" 'I' asks. "It's the approaching warship trying to communicate," 'SI' said unable to control the capture warship. "Just as soon as we understand these controls and their language. I'll personally give them a space to space call back," 'I' said to 'SI'. The control room was almost in a panic. All knew what would happen if communications were not established. Even for another 'Repssa' warship, death would be quick. Dashing to the other controls, the

E-tucs had managed to solve some of the confusing 'Repssa' language. Now the new crew began to operate the controls.

"Through your eyes, I have learned some of the defensive controls," 'SI' said. "We haven't a moment to lose 'SI', we must know our defenses. Our plans and all the lives aboard this ship will all be in vain if we fail. We are but a moment away from living or dying," 'I' said. By now the approaching warship had stopped and was staring as an enemy. The thought of firing upon a ship of their own must have made the warship hesitate. Still the warship readied for an all-out attack. Again a beeping sound is heard and again all within the control room became paralyzed. It must be our last warning, 'I' thought. Staring at the many symbols upon the control screen only became a headache and then panic. Knowing all within the warship only had seconds to live. "'I', I understand some of the symbols on the defensive control panel," 'SI' said. "Excellent, what defenses do we use?" 'I' asked. "Arm the ship with the reflective pulser field," 'SI' said guiding 'I' to touch a symbol upon the screen. The symbol glowed bright and outside the ship a light fog coated around the ship. The protective field came none too soon. Two glowing objects raced each other to kill and destroy. The sight of the glowing object froze all as they watched in fear. The feeling of helplessness paralyzed the minds off all as the moment of death approached. Slamming against the protective field the objects of death spiraled wildly into space. The reflective pulser field had worked. With a look of relief all quickly returned to their screens. Safe for now with a ship they knew little of and only minutes to learn.

"'SI', we need to know more," 'I' said. "Repssa war ships are equipped with ten large qualtron cannons and ten Fron Cor type of missile. All can be operated from the control room," 'SI' said.

"What is a Fron Cor missile?" 'I' asked. "A Fron Cor missile is a missile designed to penetrate a ship's hull. The missile will then become extremely hot then explode. Sending melted fluid in all directions," 'SI' said. Breaking 'I's' concentration a cry rings out loudly. We've been fired upon again. Two bright glows once again catch the eyes of all. With nowhere to run all stood and watched. "

'SI', will our repulse field repulse the incoming missiles?"

"Yes, they're testing the reflective pulser field. And our knowledge to control the ship," 'SI' said. 'SI' was correct, the two glowing missiles hit the reflective pulser field and spun wildly into space. Again all were relieved and went back to work. By now 'I' had grown frustrated, aching to fight back.

Giving out the order to attack with two fighter ships. 'I' was determined to destroy the attacking warship. Ordering a Fron Cor missile to be readied 'I' was hoping to weaken the warship's pulser field then attack with a Fron Cor missile. Moments passed, then suddenly two fighter ships flew by and headed to the 'Repssa' warship. As the fighter ships approached the warship, they circle the warship like angry bees. Firing upon the warship the two fighter ships kept the warship busy while 'I' and crew readied their attack. As the two warships approached each other, a flash of light lit the darkness of space. Back and forth the two ships fired upon each other displaying a brilliant glow of light. Ten large qualtron cannons on each ship continued to bombard each other feverishly. At close range the two ships resembled Earth's sea warships firing upon each other. And yet the massive display of light gave no damage to either ship. Protected by their reflective pulser fields, both ships drifted past each other unharmed. Watching through the small control room window the two fighter ships circle the 'Repssa' warship, firing upon the warship at will.

Still 'I' waited for the moment to use the Fron Cor missile. As 'I' waited the two warships recircle and head toward each other. Ready once again, the fight would continue as the fire in each other's minds burned hot. The darkness of space glowed between the two ships. Blast upon blast the 'Repssa' warships reflected each other's attacks. A quick death to the warship, if the protecting field failed even momentarily. On and on the warships continued their onslaught of blasts. From the control room the view looked as if a meteor shower was pounding both 'Repssa' warships. As 'I' watched a fighter ship was hit sending it wildly spiraling into space. Inflamed to see another E-tuc lose their life. 'I' became more determined to defeat the 'Repssas'. "'SI', how long can their fields of protection hold up to this bombardment?"

"Just as long as our ship can," 'SI' said. Turning to the E-tucs in the control room, 'I' orders all large qualtron weapons to aim at the warship's control room. Reaiming all qualtrons, the attack continued relentlessly. A glow of angry light looked as if a new star was being born. A star that would soon find its resting place once the anger of the warships died away. Informing the last fighter ship to also attack the control room, 'I' cries aloud. "Stand ready with a Fron Cor missile. 'SI' is there a chance a Fron Cor missile can penetrate their field?" 'I' asks. "We know so little of the 'Repssa's' technology. Their protective fields are as strong or as weak as ours," 'SI' said. Still 'I' was unsure to fire a missile. But not to try meant not to know. "The 'Repssa's' ship had to be destroyed," 'I' whispers to himself. Staring back at the 'Repssa' warship 'I' calls out like a lion roaring, "Fire a Fron Cor missile!"

Seconds later a deadly missile streaked out as a bright light. In seconds the missile attack answered 'I's' unanswered question. Watching as the missile spiraled out of control, 'I' could only give a frown of frustration. Disappointed, 'I' stares at the ship as anger builds inside him. "'I', you must stay calm to think clearly," 'SI' said. Before 'SI' could say another thought to 'I', 'I' ordered two Fron Cor missiles to be loaded. While the missiles were being loaded, the fight continued without any let-up. Blast after blast the two ships pounded each other's fields of protection relentlessly. Suddenly 'I' feels the ship rocked by the massive blast attacks. "Our field of protection are getting weaker, 'I' thought. "Then so are theirs," 'SI' said. "Yes 'SI', so are theirs," 'I' said with a grin that meant death to the 'Repssas'. Minutes later the gunner speaks out, "Missiles loaded and ready to fire."

"Aim at the control room," 'I' ordered. As 'I' watched the madden bombardment both ships inflicted on each other. 'I' again roars out the order. "Fire both missiles." Again both missiles blaze from the ship one behind the other. In seconds the first missile reaches its target only to be pushed away deep into the darkness of space. Right behind the first missile the second missile struck. To everyone's surprise the second missile penetrated the ship's weakened fields of protection. Into the control room the missile disappeared. Seconds later the continuous rapid firing ceased, recalling the sole remaining fighter ship to safety. 'I' orders all weapons to cease firing. Drifting apart the two warships were silent as space itself. All stare at the wounded warship's last moments. Space was once more quiet and peaceful. Only distant stars twinkled their light of peace. Quietly floating in space the control room of the wounded warship began to glow bright. Glowing red from within the missile was a ticking time bomb one could not run from in space. While the 'Repssa' warship spent her last few moments of peace among the stars. 'I' and the E-tucs watched waiting for the moment the missile's ticking would stop. Soon the missile would spread its touch of death and the warship and crew would be no more. Before one could blink another eyelid the ship blew from within and shattered itself into thousands of red hot melting pieces. Flying in all directions of space the warship was gone and so was the enemy inside. The ship that helped kill millions of lives on 'Rou', found its final resting place where it began its evil. Destroyed by one of its own weapons the warship and crew received no mercy. The touch of death reached into space.

'I's' crew was beyond joy as they congratulated each other. The battle was over and so was the 'Repssa's' deadly grip on 'Rou'. For the first time in years the E-tucs were free beings. Once more masters of themselves and their planet. The plan had worked far beyond even 'I's' imagination. 'I' had proved his worth and the E-tucs would follow undoubting him. As the sun rose to shine on 'Rou', a new leader rose to protect and oversee 'Rou'. 'I' had become 'Rou's' protector. A new and grand beginning had begun for 'I' and the E-tucs. Informing 'Rou' of their great victories E-tucs on 'Rou' rushed out of their rock mountains by the thousands. Standing on the land they stood many years ago they viewed a land not of ruin and haze but of freedom and a new beginning of prosperity. The once beautiful land now burned to the ground and the everlasting stars blocked by a hazed sky projected the feeling that the E-tucs felt they were on another planet. Still they felt they could overcome the destruction and rebuild. For freedom was in the air once more. And life would continue as a flower struggling to survive between rocks of no value. Rebuilding the land and planet would take years. But first they would start by making 'Rou' a planet that could defend itself. And to do that 'I' would lead and safeguard 'Rou' and her inhabitants. 'I' was now the answer the stars had given to 'Rou'. And Jim had found his answer from the stars that gazed upon him while on Earth. 'I' was to lead the E-tucs safely into a new era, a new beginning of peace and prosperity. Returning to 'Rou' by fighter ship found the E-tucs more than grateful. Not realizing how many hid within the many rock mountains 'I' and fellow crew members were greeted by more E-tucs than had ever gathered on 'Rou' since the 'Repssas' had arrived. Word had spread far and wide of the dangerous mission and the spectacular victory. The being from the distant stars was now known by all of 'Rou'. As 'I' was greeted by 'Rou's' leaders their gratefulness was shared by all. Within the leaders' chambers, 'I' discusses plans of seeking help from their closest neighbor, 'Sis'. This time 'I' found no disappointing stares. Agreeing unanimously with 'I's' plan. Supplies were loaded within the warship and warship repairs began. Also needing repairs, 'I' was taken to a very familiar place. The same place he awoke days ago to find his new way of life. Still clinging to his past, 'I' remembered Earth and his closest friends. Lying over the table once more 'I' falls into a deep sleep. Dreaming of his friends, Sam and Joe. The need to know of their situation weighed heavily within his mind. Awakened, 'I' had no idea how long he had slept. Feeling as if he had been pulled out of Earth's reality 'I' once again finds himself back within his new reality. With memories of space and warship battles, 'I' slowly regained his most recent memories. "Welcome back 'I', your memories of your past trouble you," 'SI' said. "Yes 'SI', my friends I hold dearest to me. They are part of me as I am part of them. Our situation became uncontrollable and now only memories exist." As 'I' sits-up and focuses his sight, 'I' could see he was once again in a very familiar place. Standing on his feet 'I' felt rested and very energized. Surrounded by many E-tucs, 'I' noticed they all had 'Repssa' weapons. Realizing they were his warriors who had fought and won the warship, they stood with pride as they held the enemies' weapons. Standing closes to 'I' was his little friend looking up at him. "O 'great 'I', you have been fully energized and are much better than before. You have also been given a new suit of armor to protect you and help guide us," he said. Looking down, 'I' was astonished to see a new suit fitting the same as his first suit and feeling much lighter. 'I' admired the suit and its color which was as black as night. The suit itself flowed with many decorative designs covering the entire suit. Made with the most guarded E-tuc technology 'I' wore a suit like no other. Made to protect its wearer from the most brutal attacks. 'I' could only hope the days of battle were over. But to the E-tucs and the devastation inflicted upon them they were taking no chances with their defenses. Having found their grand warrior, the E-tucs were determined to keep 'I' at all costs. As 'I' stood and stared at the many little beings. he realized, had it not been for them, he would surely be dead. The road home was unknown and life beyond 'Rou' was unknown. To help the E-tucs meant they lived and he lived. And life would continue within their universe. 'I' had no choice but to accept his new life and live. Once again 'I' was ready to protect his new friends. "'I', let's see your new armor," 'I's' little friend says to him. Looking down at the little beings staring at him with great excitement. With only a thought, 'I' imagined danger. True to the ingenuity of the suit and 'I's' thoughts the suit quickly began to transfigure itself. As if seeing moving water, the suit unfolded and grew larger around 'I' Cloaking 'I' the same as the first suit. 'I' was totally concealed from head to toe. In only mere seconds the suit was ready for battle. Stunned and amazed to see the shaping armor morphism effect, all gazed at its gleaming power. Standing in silence and wide-eyed, all knew a new warrior was born. Staring at the armor himself, 'I' knew his new armor far surpassed his first armor. Looking at the amazed E-tucs, 'I' bows his head in gratitude. "I will use my new armor and its great power to protect 'Rou' and others in need of help," 'I' said to the awed E-tucs. A new time had dawned bringing a new freedom to rebuild lives and a damaged world. Having defeated the 'Repssas' and regained control of 'Rou' once again, the E-tucs were determined to keep what they fought so hard for. As the bonding between 'I' and the E-tuc warriors became their word, their word would

reach deep within their hearts and minds. Moving with the E-tuc warriors to the leader's council room 'I' spoke with great respect and gratitude pointing out there was much work to be done. "If we are to stay free, we must learn to protect ourselves. We must arm ourselves and never let the hand of death rise again."

All listened to 'I' in earnest. For his words were heard as one that cared for many. His bravery and great leadership proved his worth. In word as in battle 'I' stood on solid ground. Agreeing with 'I' to immediately arm as many as they could. Plans were drawn up to arm the massive area around the rock mountains.

Finishing his thoughts and plans, 'I' is informed communication with 'Sis' did not exist. The E-tucs warn 'I' to be careful, the journey could be dangerous. 'I' bows and informs the leaders the mission to 'Sis' will be successful. Staring at 'I', a leader speaks. "Let our strength, knowledge and technology guide you. Complete your mission with peace in mind. And prosperity will follow all."

'I' understood the words and thoughts. Bowing his head in respect, 'I' turns and exits the room. Followed close behind were his many warriors. Preparing to leave immediately 'I' and warriors return to the warship. Only days after battling the 'Repssas', 'I' and ship crew were readying to leave the once 'Repssa' patrolled orbit of 'Rou'. No time to waste, 'I' thought. Lives depended on reaching 'Sis' for help. With ship repairs finished and a new type of weapon added to the ship's arsenal the warship was ready to seek help. Rested and ready to journey, I' and crew leave the once 'Repssa' dominated orbit of 'Rou'. Having lost a battle but not the war. 'I' knew the 'Repssas' would be back in larger numbers, there was no time to lose. Knowing the 'Repssas' still lurked behind the curtains of space. Far out of 'Rou's' orbit the captured 'Repssa' ship flew. Streaking across space the 'Repssa' ship now carried its new masters. Viewing 'Rou' as they parted, 'I' felt he was leaving home once again. Small and smaller 'Rou' shrank till it mingled with the stars. As the ship raced to 'Sis', 'I' felt it wise to learn as much of the ship's inner workings as possible. Now with lit rooms 'I' drifted from one room to another. It all seemed so different when we fought and captured the ship. The ship was dark and eerie. Now it was a ship that opened up and revealed itself, 'I' thought. Learning much of the ship and added improvements 'I' felt he now had a ship worthy of traveling space. In 'I's' search to learn the ship, 'I' finds a room, with a large viewing glass. Looking through the glass, 'I' felt as if he were floating in space. The vastness of stars and space could not be described with one word or even a sentence. Space was just too vast. "'I', this is a war room of planning and strategy. I'm sure all their warships are equipped with a room like this," 'SI' said. 'I' sits down and stares out the view glass seeing Earth within his mind. 'I' knew he was a long, long way from home. The feeling of leaving so unexpectedly was still a shock he hadn't recovered from, yet. As 'I' looked out upon space his heart began to beat faster. It was his past he thought of so much. His heart and mind together melted in sadness.

What has happened, where has my world disappeared to? 'I' asks himself. "I sympathize with your feelings. We are both without, but we are alive to see another day with free will. Look and go forward 'I' and your days of loneliness will fade away," 'SI' said. "I still have unfinished business on Earth. My friendship with others runs deep." Interrupting 'I's' thoughts, 'I's' little friend comes into the room. Holding his 'Repssa' weapon by his side he stands a few feet from 'I'. Noticing 'I' was in deep thought he wanted to know what bothered him. "'I', do you miss your planet?"

Looking at his little friend, "Yes, I miss my planet very much," 'I' said. "What kind of planet did you live on?" he asks. 'I', told his friend about the many people that lived on his planet. Their many languages they spoke. Their many different customs they lived by. Their clothes they wore and the many different types of shelters they lived in. With a sad look and frown upon his brow, 'I' also told his friend of the many atrocities humans so mindlessly inflicted upon each other. "The scaring of a beautiful planet. And the feelings of hate that humans would endure for generations. War seemed to follow humans like an angry shadow. Their love and glory of war, their might and power of weapons, their readiness to fight and sorrow of death. Looking at his little friend. War and dying is everywhere, it's universal. Shedding his frown 'I' begins to smile. Still as a whole, humans live in peace with great humanity toward each other. As humans, there are many animals upon Earth. Some on land, some in the water and some in the air. Many are friendly and many are very dangerous."

Looking at 'I' without blinking his eyes the little being didn't miss a sound. His eyes stared with great interest and great admiration and wonder. 'I' continues his description of Earth. "Upon the land many different kinds of plants gave our planet the oxygen we live by. Some plants were edible and some were for shelter and some we just call beautiful."

Looking at 'I' with a curious blank look upon his face. The word 'beautiful' seemed to catch his interest as 'I' stops and smiles. "Our skies are endlessly blue with sunshine from a yellow sun. White clouds of happiness and dark clouds of anger float in the skies. And vast bodies of water connect great bodies of land." Suddenly 'I' stops talking. A sign of sadness settled upon his face. That was the only life 'I' knew. "Our planet was very similar until the 'Repssas' attacked. Millions died for no reason. And our planet of life was burned to the ground," the E-tuc said. Silence fell between the two of them, as they shared the same pain of loss. Looking at 'I', the E-tuc asks, "Will you return to Earth one day?"

Before 'I' could get his thoughts together and answer. The E-tuc said, "We need you to lead us and help maintain the peace. Many will scatter without a great leader. And our planet is on the verge of dying without the warmth and light of the sun. To lose you is to lose all that clings to life," Still without a word, 'I' looks out the viewing glass into the vastness of space. The stars, planets and distant sun gave an ever changing picture. "Home is where one is happy where one can watch a new day unfold into a day of peace. To know that even beyond what one can't see is more of what one can imagine. I long for that place and time. To have the power of peace as the sun has the power of light and warmth. Show me the place that when the day ends and sun shines no more I can rest my heart with the ones I love. Show me that place and time and I will live there." With sadness in his eyes, the little being is speechless. "The universe isn't big enough for a place to live in peace. What I knew and had on Earth, I couldn't be a free man. I am only existing day by day as does the universe my friend. For the time being, I will stay and fight the 'Repssas'. I will look for that place and time of peace. And when I find it, I will rest in peace. I will not forsake those that have given me life. Knowing they are in their time of life and death. I will stay and help regain the peace we all seek." Staring into each other's eyes. "If I die fighting the 'Repssas', I die for a good and worthy cause. For peace glows within the hearts of many that live in peace," 'I' said. "Yes 'I', peace is a worthy cause. If that day comes for you, then we both will die for a worthy cause."

Staring at each other, the ship traveled the endless miles of space filled with stars that lit their way. A friendship and bond from distant stars glowed brightly that day. Not knowing one day, the two would be the most loved, admired and enemy feared team of beings that traveled the known stars. Silently enjoying each other's company, the two peacefully watched an endless array of stars. The time of peace and friendship didn't last long. A loud warning alert sounded, bringing 'I' and his friend to their feet. As those on board ran to their stations, 'I' and his friend ran to the control room. Entering the control room, 'I' could see two blimps upon the long distance warning screens. Two 'Repssa' warships were spotted slowly circling 'Sis'. As they circle 'Sis' they scanned the planet. Giving the order to prepare for battle a crew ready for revenge and another kill waited. Still a great distance away from 'Sis' 'I' knew he couldn't afford a mistake. Too many lives depended on a successful mission. The distance began to close fast with rising tension. Flying a 'Repssa' warship would be the cover they needed to get close. But had the 'Repssas' been warned of the defeat at 'Rou'? If they had, a battle of two warships to one would occur with a very questionable outcome. An outcome with the lives of many disappearing into time, into the darkness of space. "Missiles are loaded and all on board are ready," 'I's' little friend reported. "Thank-you my friend," 'I' said. Silent within the control room, only the ship's powerful thrusters would be heard. After long moments of flying in silence 'Sis' was visually in sight. Unaware of being stalked by a ship of their own. The 'Repssa' warships continued scanning 'Sis'. High in the dark of space the stalker readied for a kill. E-tucs in the control room sat quiet as cats staring at their monitors. Hungry for another 'Repssa' kill, the E-tucs waited for 'I's' command. They watched one of the 'Repssa' warships slowly circling 'Sis'. "Target the warship," 'I' orders. Seconds passed. "Ship on target," called out gunner. As the warship unknowing its danger slowly drifted around 'Sis', 'I' calls out. "Fire both Fron Cor missiles. Out shot two missiles side by side."

Like two runaway stars, they chased the unsuspecting warship with vengeance and death. In seconds the bright glowing missiles slammed into the side of the warship and disappeared. Knowing the warship would explode wreckage in all directions, 'I' orders reflective pulser fields on. Holding their position, all watch as the wounded 'Repssa' warship slowly stops orbiting 'Sis'. All seemed normal until the ship began glowing bright red. Burning from within, the ship and crew had no avenue of escape. Certain death awaited the ship and crew. Not forgetting the catastrophe attack the 'Repssas' dealt 'Rou', the E-tucs watched and waited. With nowhere to run, 'Repssas' within the ship, could only wait for the moment of death. A moment they all knew would end their lives. Seconds later the 'Repssa' ship bursts into a red ball of flames sending large flaming chunks of melting metal racing in all directions. Protected by the ship reflective pulser fields melting chunks of the shattered ship danced away from the ship. Moments later only the dark of

space remained, leaving the 'Repssa's killing ways within the E-tuc's minds. Another dreaded 'Repssa' warship was gone. A very easy kill by deception, 'I' thought. "My burden of problems just became one 'Repssa' ship less," 'I' says to 'SI'.

"'I', be very careful, the second ship will be waiting for us," 'SI' said. 'I' noticed something was different. The control room was still quiet. No sounds of victory for a destroyed 'Repssa' warship, as the previous warship received. To 'I's' amazement, all E-tucs had stayed at their controls. Surprised not to hear E-tucs rejoicing with loud cheers. 'I' inquisitively looks completely around the room and is stared at. All E-tucs within the control room had focused their eyes upon 'I'. Realizing the hunted had become the hunter, the E-tucs were now looking for another kill. 'I' immediately gives orders to reload missiles and search for the other 'Repssa' warship. Not a sound was made by the E-tucs. Using their monitors and controls they searched 'Sis's' orbit thoroughly. "Will the other 'Repssa' warship know of the attack 'SI'?" 'I' asks. "The two warships are not able to see or communicate from opposite sides of the planet. They have been communicating by orbital probes circling 'Sis'. Once they lose communications they will know something has gone wrong. Time is short 'I', act quickly and wisely," 'SI' said. "We must attack before they realize what has occurred," 'I' said to 'SI'. Looking at 'I', 'I's' little friend asks, "'I', what are we to do?"

Looking down at his friend, "To follow the 'Repssas' and attack would give the 'Repssas' the opportunity to set a trap. We must fight a different way," 'I' said. As 'I' stared at his friend, a question ran through 'I's' mind. How would the 'Repssas' react if they saw a ship of their own heading straight at them? Yes, 'I' thought, a few seconds of hesitation is all the cat needed to catch the bird, 'I' thought. Without another thought, "Turn the ship around, let's fly head on into the 'Repssa' ship and attack," 'I' orders. Without a doubtful stare or question of uncertainty. The two E-tucs guiding the ship follow 'I's' orders. Slowly the ship turns around and heads in the opposite direction. Turning to the gunner, "Target the 'Repssa' warship at the first sight," 'I' said. With a look of vengeance in his eyes the gunner nods his head. Silence fell over all, as eyes and ship's scanners scanned the orbit of 'Sis'. Waiting for the first sight of the 'Repssa' warship all stood and held their breaths in silence. 'I' knew the first missile attack was no good unless one could hit the target. Knowing the gunner was hungry for another kill, 'I' knew he would not miss. Confidence spread throughout the ship like an infectious disease. Whatever it took, all wanted another kill. As all waited, poised and eager to fight, time seemed to stand still. So much ran through 'I's' mind. And still life for all depended on ending the enemy's life. If the approaching 'Repssa' warship also had its pulser fields on the struggle for life and death would most likely be a lucky missile piercing the reflective pulser fields, 'I' thought. Loaded and ready to lock onto the approaching 'Repssa' ship time ticked by without a sound. Circling 'Sis' like two birds high in the sky the two ships flew unnoticed. Breaking the silence, scanner operators cry out, "The enemy is near." Giving the gunner the enemy's location the gunner zeros in on the target. Suddenly a reflection of light is seen in the far distance. "That's them," 'I' shouts out in excitement. The moment to fight was nearing quickly. "Locked on to target," cried the gunner. Without hesitation, 'I' gives the order, "Fire." Off the two missiles of death raced. Glowing a path of light straight to the drifting 'Repssa' warship. All waited once again in silence. Quickly the missiles find their target. Just as quick as the missiles find their target the missiles dance into the unknown of space. The 'Repssas' had been waiting for an attack. Their reflective pulser fields were up and protecting their ship. Ready to attack themselves, two missiles were fired and true to their gunner's targeting the missiles slammed into the reflective pulser field. Pushed away into the open fields of space the ship for the moment was free of danger. Knowing the other 'Repssa' warship had been destroyed the 'Repssas' fury for revenge made hunters of the 'Repssas' also. Now was the moment for each ship's crew to decide who was to live or die. Experienced in battle and eager to fight both beings hunted each other. Now each had to find a way into each other's defenses and destroy the other. Knowing missiles were useless against each other's defenses the two ships slowly come in sight of each other. Passing each other like killer sharks in the high seas they cunningly stare at each other and plan their next move. 'I' immediately orders the ship to turn around and ready for battle. Not a second was wasted as the ship turned around. Missiles were loaded and all ship weapons were ready. All knew this battle would be another clash of cunning wits. Silence held 'I' as he thought of the next move. "Load energy sphere weapon," 'I' orders. Let's see how their reflective pulser fields cope with an energy sphere, 'I' thought to himself. "Loaded and targeted," cried the gunner. All watched as the 'Repssa' warship gradually began to turn around. As the warship turned, the planet of 'Sis' hung behind the ship making a very large background exposing a deadly moving target. "'SI', this new weapon, will it work?", 'I' asks. The minds that created the weapon were very confident the weapon will succeed. Instead of reflecting away from the ship the weapon will cover their reflective pulser field. Then it will drain its power until the ship is powerless. Eager to see

the weapon work 'I' couldn't resist the chance to catch the enemy off guard. Seeing the 'Repssa' warship' broadsided 'I' cries, "Fire!"

Out of the ship, two E-tuc energy spheres headed to the turning 'Repssa' ship. All watched two glowing balls of electrical bands expanding in size, heading toward its victim. Before the ship was completely turned around both energy spheres struck the ship's reflective pulser field. Covering the ship with continuously moving electricity bands all on board viewed a truly amazing spectacular sight, never seen before. Bands of overlapping electricity moved around and around the 'Repssa' ship. A glow of moving light lit the darkness of space. Trapped within a spider's web of electricity all watched and waited for the spider to attack. What seemed like an hour was only about thirty minutes of electrical wonder draining the 'Repssa' warship. Slowly the bands of electricity faded away. Floating in space neither advancing nor retreating, the ship appeared lifeless. To everyone's great and happy surprise, the ship started to drift lifelessly toward 'Sis'. Smaller and smaller the warship appeared in space. Pulled by the gravitational pull of 'Sis' the warship drifted closer to 'Sis'. Like a spider pulling in its victim, the ship had no chance of escape. Too close to 'Sis' to fly away the ship was now in the inescapable grip of 'Sis'. Small to the size of the planet, the warship exploded into a great ball of fire. Shock waves rushed in all directions. As all watched, large pieces of ship rained down on 'Sis' becoming balls of glowing red fire. The terrors in the orbit of 'SIS were no more. A just reward for the death and destruction caused by the 'Repssas'. Destroyed by beings that only wanted to live in peace, the E-tucs were now the hunters. Hunting the 'Repssas' to extinction to regain the peace they had enjoyed for thousands of years. Now the once mighty warship laid on the surface of 'Sis'. Scattered across the surface of 'Sis', the warship found her resting ground, the same planet she helped to destroy. A grim reminder to 'Repssas' they too can be killed. Once again the E-tucs laid their eyes upon 'I'. Looking at the E-tucs with a look of satisfaction.

"We have met the enemy and now they are no more. Now we must meet the victims of 'Sis' and render aid to all in their most critical time of need," 'I" said. Circling 'Sis', 'I' gazed at the planet and knew what the darkness of the planet meant. "Why 'SI", why?" 'I' asks. "Wars are fought with anger. With difference of opinions and needs. Gains and eliminations of the other become the spoils of war. This battle of life and death is no different than the wars on your planet. It's just a different time and place. Destruction and war only cease the wonders of life. Whatever the 'Repssas' want, they will sacrifice all to acquire their gain. The 'Repssas' wanted 'Rou', they killed millions and burned 'Rou' to the ground. Now the 'Repssas' have done the same to 'Sis'. What the 'Repssas' want no one knows. They were succeeding until you arrived. You, 'I', have changed the course of life. 'Rou' and 'Sis' now have a fighting chance to live," 'SI' said. "I am but one 'SI', a lone wolf crying deep in the woods at night. My time I left and the time I live in now are two different times," 'I' said. "And still you live, and your cries have been heard. For those you lead stand and cry with you a mighty voice," 'SI' said. "Still I'm no match for the entire 'Repssa' forces," 'I' said. "Your victories have proved you are a great warrior. You are and always will be a great leader. You are not alone ,'I', you are many upon many. Lead 'I' and many will follow," 'SI' said. 'I' immediately gives orders to circle 'Sis' and destroy all 'Repssa' probes. As the ship circles 'Sis', four orbiting probes were found orbiting 'Sis'. "I'm sure the second ship knew of our attacking its sister ship," 'I' said. "Yes, 'I', we overcame the odds against us and conquered our enemies and our fears. Our biggest advantage is using a 'Repssa' warship against the 'Repssas'. We have the ability to approach deceptively. Our quick thinking has kept us alive and given us many victories," 'SI' said. 'I' looks at a monitor and sees 'Sis' close up. A planet the size of Earth slowly rotating as it circled its great sun. Still silent the control crew stares at 'I' for orders. 'I' knew the crew was well aware of 'Sis's' condition. "The help we have so desperately needed is not here," 'I' tells the crew. "Nevertheless we must land and search for survivors. We will take two fighter ships and only volunteers."

Leaving the ships two navigators in charge 'I' heads to the ship's landing bay. Through the ship 'I' walks and many began to follow. 'I' had proved his leadership abilities and the E-tucs were more than ready to follow. Entering the landing bay, more E-tucs carrying 'Repssa' weapons stood ready to join. Looking across the landing bay two 'Repssa' fighter ships and his own ship remained close by. His ship battered but still flyable, rested idle and alone. Realizing so much had happened in such a short time, memories faded away as new events happened. Stepping to the 'Repssa' fighter ship, 'SI' informed 'I', "'I', the level of breathable oxygen on 'Sis' is much like 'Rou's'. You will need your full armor to survive. Without a word 'I' responds by arming himself with only a thought. Into the ship 'I' disappears, followed by ten E-tuc volunteers. Doors slide shut and the ship readies to leave. Seconds later the fighter ship rises and out the warship two fighter ships fly. Viewed by warship monitors the crew watches as the fighter ships enter into 'Sis's' atmosphere. Into the hazed sky the two fighter ships flew as 'I' continued to view as much of 'Sis' as he could. Unlike Earth, 'Sis' had no icecaps, no high

mountains, only endless stretches of land. A once thriving planet of beings as 'SI' had told 'I', now had little evidence of life that had existed. A lifeless planet much like 'Rou' existed only for the strongest of will to live on. After circling 'Sis' once, the fighter ships began to descend lower and lower. Amazed how the E-tucs managed to fly so calmly through the thick haze 'I' sat and waited patiently for the ship to land. Slowing in speed, the pilots had found a landing site. Brought to an area that was once populated by millions of the once thriving planet the fighter ship softly touches ground and rests its full weight on 'Sis'. Now on 'Sis' the ship engines rest in silence. Holding their 'Repssa' weapons the E-tucs gazed out the small windows. As 'Rou', 'Sis' was hazed to the ground with a strange dead silence. A silence only breakable by the living. Nothing moved, not even a slow breeze. An eerie feeling crept within the haze that cloaked the view of 'Sis'. While waiting for the ship's scanners to scan the surrounding area all readied their weapons. Questions began to run through 'I's' mind. Would the beings of this planet welcome us? Can they be trusted? Are they armed? Knowing the description of a 'Repssa', 'I' wanted a mental description of the beings on 'Sis'. Abiding 'I's' thoughts 'SI' implants a description within 'I's' mind. In the blink of an eye, 'I' was facially frozen. By 'I's' facial expression he was more than surprised. He was mentally stunned and speechless. "'I', you are not functioning properly. I will scan your brain for injury," 'SI' said. "No 'SI', there is no injury to my brain. I find it hard to believe, so far away from Earth that beings could resemble humans," 'I' said. "You have much to learn 'I', much to learn. The Sislens are able to communicate verbally and telepathically. I will translate their language to you. Like the beings of your planet the Sislens are proud beings also. They have great honor and respect for each other. Their achievements are great wonders of their race and their expectations of each other are high. Their word is their bond. Seek their bond and add an ally. The seed of peace that has spread throughout this part of the galaxy has enabled all to prosper and flourish. Wars haven't existed for thousands of years. Now death and despair lay upon 'Sis' as 'Rou'. The 'Repssas' must be stopped before the deadly germ of war and death spread to other planets. We must preserve peace at all cost, 'SI' said. "Yes 'SI', peace is only a word without the effort to keep it. The history of my planet has seen many wars. Many nations fought against each other with killing that spread around the planet. Yes 'SI', peace must be maintained at all cost," 'I' said. Turning to 'I', one of the pilots informs 'I' all was clear. 'I' gives the nod to exit. Doors quickly slide back and the moment of visual reality made all stand still. Not a sound stirred within the air. Only stillness existed, awakening one's deepest thoughts. What waited in the shadows of the hazed planet had all holding their weapons tightly. 'I' had longed to see a living planet and breathe fresh air. To see a planet like Earth and feel the sun's warmth. As 'I' continued, 'I' was as ready as he could be for any sudden attack. Fog and smoke thick enough to cut hung in the 'Sis' air. Unable to see no more than fifteen feet in any direction 'I' stepped onto the uninviting ground. The first step made a sound of dried cracking leaves. Every step there after erupted into a loud cracking noise letting anyone near know where they were. From what 'I' could see, 'Sis' was no better off than 'Rou'. Attacked and burned as 'Rou', 'Sis' suffered the same fate. Now in hiding, the Sislens trusted no one. Not knowing if 'I' and the E-tucs were with friendly intentions. The Sislens watched through the thick atmosphere. Stepping cautiously 'I' searched for the inhabitants if any, with great difficulty. Followed by twenty E-tucs fully armed, all were ready for a sudden attack. Using his suit's technology, 'I' scans through the thick haze from left to right. Deeper and deeper they move into the thick haze. Looking back toward the fighter ships, both ships had disappeared into the haze. The thickness of haze had covered everything completely. 'I' and the E-tucs continued to move forward, with weapons pointed in all directions. The eeriness of haze, the crunching noise of the ground and the feeling being watched kept all breathing slowly. The glowing sun gave only enough light and heat to keep the planet from darkness and freezing. "This was once a planet of many beings and vegetation. Now it's a planet of darkness and complete disarray," 'SI' said. "War and death will reveal the deepest and darkest thoughts of demented minds," 'I' said to 'SI'. "The right of a being to live is universal. We can solve our differences and give hope and prosperity to all. For one to kill another is to take away the freedom of life and damage the lives of many," 'SI' said. "Yes 'SI' you are right," 'I' said. Through the haze laid twisted debris of a once thriving civilization. Darkness and lifelessness processed every step they took. Forging ahead 'I' and his warriors who had become fighters in every sense of the word, looked for signs of life. Flanked on both sides 'I' continued to move cautiously forward. Having been dealt a horrible blow to lives and planet the Sislens continued to watch in hidden silence. The searching was starting to make the E-tucs very nervous. Occasionally they would aim their weapons at anything that made a noise. Even shadows that walked with every step they made. Surrounded by an unbreakable wall of haze 'I' felt helpless to the feeling of being watched. "We need to find the inhabitants of 'Sis'." 'I' said to 'SI'. "They are here 'I', they have been watching us since we landed," 'SI' said. "Why do they not show themselves?" 'I' asks 'SI'. "They do not know you and caution is their only protection," 'SI' said.

"Time is running out for the both of us. I feel strong feelings of a presence of many very nearby," 'I' said. "Yes 'I' the Sislens are very near," 'SI' said. Seconds later 'SI' replies. "You are correct 'I', movement is estimated at one hundred yards straight ahead," 'SI' said. "Then we shall greet them or fight them be they friend or foe," 'I' said. Informing the E-tucs of life forms ahead, 'I' and the E-tucs move closer to the destination. Still out of sight the unknown kept all moving cautiously. With weapons pointed in all directions many brave E-tucs followed 'I' expecting a surprise attack. Nearing the sight of inhabitants, a very large clearing could be seen. Step by step all watched for a sudden attack. Reaching the clearing 'I' and E-tucs step out of the thick haze. Within the center of the clearing stood ten beings almost as tall as 'I'. Dressed in long dark robes and wearing metal helmets covering their heads and face. 'I' immediately orders the E-tucs to lower their weapons. "They are not our enemy, if they were we would not have gotten this far," 'I' said to following E-tucs. Continuing to move forward, 'I' and E-tucs approach as friends. "Why are they standing in an unprotected area?" 'I' asks 'SI'. "There once stood a great structure on this area. A structure that all the leaders of 'Sis' congregated in. The laws of the planet were all made here. Even without the structure the laws of the land are still made here," 'SI' said. "I understand 'SI', we shall greet them with great respect and dignity," 'I' said. Reaching the unknown beings, 'I' and the E-tucs stood mere yards away. Recognizing the E-tucs the tall beings bowed their heads slightly as did the E-tucs in return. Realizing the beings had known of the E-tucs arrival 'I' knew their intentions were not hostile. Looking at 'I', the leaders could only stare and wonder who or what this fully armored being was. An armor they've never seen before. Staring at each other, 'I' wanted to break the uneasiness of their first meeting. Before 'I' could speak, a familiar sound broke the silent stares of curiosity. It was 'I's' little friend stepping forward to speak. "This is 'I'. 'I' has traveled from a very distant planet. He has led us in many victories against the Repssas'. 'I' has been appointed grand leader of all planet and orbital forces on 'Rou'. I' answers only to the high council on 'Rou'." Bowing his head slightly the E-tuc steps back in place. Once again silence lingers in the air as 'I' stares at the leaders. "'I', these are the leaders of 'Sis'. 'I recognize the one in the middle as E-tik-norc. Standing by him are E-cal-law, Ru-fe-fas and Wa-korb."

'I' knew he had to speak. To cross the bridge of friendship and trust each other. "Your planets orbit and darkened skies are clear of your enemy. Friends orbit your planet with peace in mind. We have traveled to 'Sis' to ask for help, now we see a planet in great need of help," 'I' said. 'I' stood silent and waited patiently for a response. Staring back at 'I', they knew 'I' spoke the truth. They had seen the flashes of lights in the sky. The balls of fire burning down to the ground. They also knew the E-tucs had lived in peace and now they were arming themselves to fight an enemy. Realizing they must do the same, their only question was who would lead them? Without a sound the Sislens continued to stare. As they stared they used their mental abilities to communicate and decide their fate. 'I' now fought the battle of trust. Would the Sislens trust him with their lives as the E-tucs have? Hanging in the balance of life and death the Sislens knew they had little choice. Their planet was destroyed completely and millions of lives had disappeared. Those that lived, only lived another day to starve to death. 'I' had proved himself to the E-tucs. Now he had to prove himself to Sislens.

Deciding to remove their helmets, the Sislens revealed themselves. A feeling of relief and friendship glowed within all that stared. 'I' had won one battle only to start another battle. To prove himself worthy of their trust, having revealed themselves, 'I' felt it fitting to reveal himself. With only a thought in his mind 'I's' face and head protection retracted swiftly revealing himself. Glued upon each other's likeness, 'I' and Sislens were stunned at their many similarities. Without a word, the unknowing stare of tension began to disappear.

"We have come in peace, we are here to help. And the enemy that orbited your planet is no more. They have answered for their deeds with their lives. Your problem is our problem. We both share the same enemy, they know us both. We can fight the 'Repssas' together or separately. Look at the destruction on 'Sis' and you will see the same on 'Rou'," 'I' said. Within silence the 'Sis' leaders' eyes moved about looking at an endless destruction of their planet. "If we fight separately we may lose all. Standing together freedom and life will not disappear. The E-tucs of 'Rou' will hide no more. They will fight and I will fight with them. We choose to live, we choose to fight. The 'Repssas' want what's not theirs. They will have to fight and kill us to get it. We will not disappear as if we never existed," the Sis leader says. "We have captured one of their warships. Now we have used it to destroy a few of their warships. We will continue until the warship fights no more. The E-tucs carry the enemy's weapon of choice, the 'Repssa' qualtron weapon. A powerful weapon the 'Repssa' will only surrender if dead. We have and will use the weapon against our enemy until peace is regained." 'I' stops for a brief moment and stares strongly at the 'Sis' leaders. "Join us and regain your freedom. Rebuild

your world and together we'll share the peace we all seek." As 'I' finished speaking, a 'Sis' leader steps forward and begins to describe the tragedy that befell 'Sis'. "A calm sky broke into a fierce storm of fire. A fire that glowed red with angry balls of burning death. Down upon the ground the balls of death hit and destroyed everything. I heard cries of despair, of pain, of suffering vibrating intensely in the air. Many ran helplessly, disappearing into a blaze of fire. The world around me changed so violently as if to say, 'this was not to be.' I reached out to help, only to find I was too far away. The day turned into night and yet the sun still shined with its gleaming light so far away. So many gasped for life as the precious breeze of life was swept away by the breeze of death. I'll never relinquish within my mind the horrors of death served so savagely and mercilessly. The lives of many came to an end too tragically so early in life. And when the sky cleared of fire ships the same as those you arrived in clouded the sky and attacked continuously until all laid dead. Death was upon our once peaceful planet. The day was short for living and long on sorrow. So many perished before the sun laid to rest. A planet we have loved and cherished had quickly died before our eyes. How many have survived, we can only guess. We live and die, day by day. Our planet is now a dark cold uninhabitable graveyard in space." Bowing his head, he looks down in sadness. Looking with a stern and powerful stare. "Life has a way of surviving. As long as there is hope the seed of life can grow. We are proof life will find a way and many will follow," 'I' said. The sorrow and pain embraced their faces as they bowed their heads. "We can't bring back those that have perished. But we can protect those that are living," 'I' said. The tall being in the middle of the group looks at 'I'. "Your words are the strength of many. Even in the time of death, you speak of life moving forward. Yes 'I', as long as there is hope, the seed of life can grow." Staring at 'I' and E-tucs with a very commanding stare he said, "We are the last leaders of 'Sis'."

A silence of sadness hung in the air. "The 'Repssas' had almost won their battle on 'Sis'. Only a small handful of leaders exist. Leaders that rule a crumbling existence on 'Sis'." Looking at 'I', the 'Sis' leader invites 'I' and the E-tucs to their safe dwelling. 'I' and the E-tucs were lead through many narrow passage ways. Finally they reach an opening wider than the narrow passage ways. Entering a dark passage way all walked in darkness until a glow of light could be seen. Reaching the distant light 'I' noticed guards posted at the outskirts of the dim light. Seeing company arriving, the guards push the large door open. Standing at the doorway, a huge and bright room awaited. Leading the group, the 'Sis' leaders step into the room and a pathway opens inviting the group. Eyes of the room focus on the visitors. A clashing of many whispers began to fill the room. Having seen E-tucs before, the eyes of wonder fell upon the new being of similar features.

Parting to let the leaders and visitors through, a massive crowd of Sislens began to follow close behind. The image of 'I' had never been seen before. Strikingly similar to the Sislens all wanted to learn more of the being. Amassing shoulder to shoulder, a wave of Sislens gathered close. Reaching a massive carved out rock, the leaders stepped up steps to the top. 'I' and the E-tucs followed close behind. Upon the rock, the leaders and 'I' stood. A growing clamor of noise began to grow. So many questions were being whispered, only to fade away into the growing excitement. It was a day of excitement, a day that would prepare for war and a day to dream of freedom. Staring at so many Sislens, 'I' realized he was staring at one of the Sislens' last few strong holds. Time was short and 'I' had to get the message of their situation to all fast. The urge to speak was great. 'I' could not hold back his impatience. Before the leaders could introduce the visitors 'I' surprises all by stepping forward and raising his hands for silence. A hush of silence began to fill the room. Moments later, the walls of the room were ready to repel a strong echo from 'I's' voice. Seeking 'SI's' wisdom, 'I' speaks to the Sislens in their own language. "You have been dealt a horrendous blow to your lives and planet. Your way of life has changed. And your days of living are also numbered. The day will arrive when the 'Repssas' will return and finish what they had started. Soon, time will show your race never existed if you continue to hide. I and all on 'Rou' will fight the 'Repssas'. Join us today and we will fight together and win our freedom. Regain your planet and your way of life." 'I' stops speaking and stares at the crowd. The noise of the crowd begins to grow. Behind 'I' a 'Sis' leader steps forward only a few feet from 'I'. "How can we fight these savage beings, if they live to fight?"

'I' turns to the leader. "Cling fast to what is true, and you will have no doubt the reason you fight," 'I' said. "We as the E-tucs have lived in peace for thousands of years, we are not fighters," another leader said. "The planet I am from, there is a great beast called a lion. It is very brave, because it will fight all that invade its territory and not run. One doesn't have to be a lion to be brave. One fights an aggressor so they and others can live in peace," 'I' said. Another leader steps forward. "It is impossible to fight such a well-armed enemy."

"Impossible is possible if you change the course of possibilities to your favor," 'I' said. "How does one change the inevitable?" a Sis leader says. "The

'Repssas' are arrogant beings that can be defeated by their own arrogance. We are proof of that. We stand here today because the 'Repssas' feel they cannot be defeated. Their arrogance cost them four warships. With our will to live and willingness to fight we changed the course of possibilities to our favor," 'I' said. "We have no weapons to defend ourselves," a leader said. 'Rou' is arming itself with long range and ground weapons. A great force is growing among the E-tucs. We can bring you the same weapons and install them on 'Sis'. Stand tall and defend what is yours. This will be a battle the 'Repssas' will not walk away from. We will show the 'Repssas' we can fight. Our lives will continue side by side with time. We will not disappear into the dark of night. We will continue to see a new sunrise," 'I' said. As 'I' finished speaking, the Sislens leaders gathered close together and spoke unheard. At the same time the massive crowd of Sislens began sharing their thoughts. I' knew he and the E-tucs couldn't defeat the mighty 'Repssas' alone. The 'Repssas' were too many and too powerful. 'I' once again raises his hands and quiets the crowd. "Give me your brave, your strong, your most daring. And together we'll bring peace and a new ray of sunlight upon 'Sis'. A sunlight that will shine across 'Sis' as long as we stand united. Time will remember us as a voice that roared loudly. Today we are lions ready to defend our territory," 'I' said. 'I' was right, a loud roar burst from the massive crowd. As the walls vibrated of numerous decisions it now became the leaders' time to share their thoughts. 'I' and his friend stare at each other and smile. They knew what the answer would be. 'I' had spoken from the heart, igniting a firestorm of thought. Quickly two of the leaders step forward and hold their arms in the air. The roar of minds was loud and getting louder. Relentlessly trying to quiet the unraveled crowd the leaders were fruitless in their efforts. Tempers were rising within the massive crowd. And only time knew what would happen next. Fearing the worst, the leaders look at 'I'. 'I' steps forward and raises his arms. Slowly the roar begins to diminish and all wait to hear the leaders' decision. Looking across the multitude of determined minds, one of the leaders takes a deep nervous breath. Not knowing how the massive crowd would react, the leader speaks. "We choose to defend our planet. To hide no more, to run no more. To face our aggressors and defend what is ours." Looking at 'I', "We choose to fight alongside of 'I'. Lead, 'I', and all of 'Sis' will follow," the leader said. The leaders of 'Sis' were wise. They knew 'I' was right, the 'Repssas' would be back and all would be lost. Help from 'Rou' and 'I's' leadership may give 'Sis' a fighting chance. The feeling of freedom and unity flowed through the room of excited Sislens. As if the 'Repssas' were already conquered, the walls of the room echoed with excitement and unity. 'I' had only been on 'Sis' a few hours and already he was treated like a hero. A being from far away was now to lead two planets. To victory or to death they would fight to the end. Approving the leaders' decision, the massive crowd of Sislens vibrated the thick walls as thunder would. 'I' and the leaders stood and listened to the delirious crowd gone wild "You have done well 'I'. You have given hope where there was despair. Eased hearts and minds of fear and sadness. And begun a unity of Sislens and E-tucs that has never been done. Now you will lead a mighty force in the struggle for peace. This is your destiny 'I'," 'SI' said. "Is this what the stars have been telling me 'SI'?" 'I' asked. "Yes 'I', and so much more to come. The stars picked you for a reason. There is a reason for all that exist. And your destiny has been written in the stars. Peace is a heavy burden, yet it yields much happiness. You were picked to restore the peace and bring forth a new unity of trust and friendship. Fulfill your destiny and all your thoughts of sadness will find answers," 'SI' said. Unknowing to 'I' and 'SI', the future of 'Sis' and 'Rou' would one day be the gateway into a peaceful galaxy of stars. Wasting no time, 'I' gives orders to the E-tucs to disperse all of the warship's food and medical supplies to the Sislens. Immediately 'I' helps the leaders to organize large populated areas into safe strongholds and greatly encouraged the Sislens to use their technology to defend themselves. 'Sis' like 'Rou' was a highly advanced planet living in peace. Weapons and war were mere stories of the distant past. Still the knowledge to make weapons was strong. Strong enough to give 'Sis' a chance to regain control of 'Sis' and peace. Clinging to unity and hope, the Sislens and E-tucs worked together and began to build a great bridge of trust. Two days later 'I' and crew had transformed 'Sis' into a fighting fortress. Time waited for no one and 'I' could sense danger coming. Gazing over a ravaged land of destruction the feeling of war and death chilled 'I' to his inner most feelings. 'SI' was so right, peace was a heavy burden. As a flower beginning to grow, it must survive in its surroundings. And so must the living. The future was not written for death. It was written for the living to decide their fate. Approached by the 'Sis' leaders, 'I' was asked to take with him females and the very young. Hunger and illness spread wide on 'Sis'. Many women and children suffered daily. Agreeing to take all the ship could carry, the fighter ships traced the skies carrying as many as they could. Hours later, the warship was full and 'I' gives his word to the leaders. Vowing to return, 'I' assures the 'Sis' leaders, only death would prevent his return. Bowing his head to the 'Sis' leaders, 'I's' face and head resumes battle form. Entering into the fighter ship 'I' and crew disappear into the hazed sky. High in the sky the fighter ship flies. 'I', looks down at the dark and hazed planet of 'Sis'. A planet of total destruction as 'Rou' with inhabitants surviving day

by day. 'I' was helpless to help, 'I' would return to 'Rou' empty-handed. As the fighter ship flies to the warship, 'I' asks himself, are these Sislens we take to 'Rou' safe with us or are they in more danger? Still looking down 'I' wondered what 'Sis' looked like before the 'Repssas' attacked. Maybe a planet similar to 'Rou'. Now it didn't matter, 'Sis' was leveled to the ground with no seeable beauty. The only beauty of 'Sis' that remained was in the minds of those that survived.

Entering into orbit, the warship quickly came into view. Seeing the warship eased the minds on board the fighter as they moved closer. Leaving his thoughts, 'I' reminds himself of the task at hand. Slowly drifting in orbit the warship waited to be boarded. Entering the warship's landing bay the fighter ship slowly lowers and touches down softly. Focused and ready, 'I' steps to the exit door. The door slides back quickly and 'I' is surprised to see so many 'Sis' women and children. Greeted with a hero's welcome, 'I' knew he had only proved himself in words of bravery and intentions. Now 'I' knew he must show his bravery in action to back his words. And sadly, 'I' thought, the action may cost him and many others their lives. Stepping out from the fighter ship 'I' was surrounded. Standing in the midst of the excitement 'I' informs all they were safe. "Do not worry, we are headed back to 'Rou' for help. Worry didn't seem to be on their minds, with 'I' they felt safe. Making his way through the elated Sislens 'I' leaves the landing bay and heads to the control room. Close behind 'I', E-tucs follow carrying their 'Repssa' weapons. Every room and hallway 'I' walked, women and children greeted him with great respect. Reaching the control room, the door slides open. 'I' enters and once more 'I' finds the room quiet and all eyes upon him. 'I' knew all within the control room were ready for orders. A warship designed to kill, the E-tucs had learned so very well. Now the ship was theirs to fly. With a crew to manage the ship, they were as deadly as any 'Repssa' warship. Staring back, 'I' knew they were more than ready.

Giving the order to leave orbit and return to 'Rou' the E-tucs at controls immediately programmed their controls to return to 'Rou'. Out of 'Sis's' orbit the warship flies, leaving behind so many in desperate need of help. Heading back to 'Rou empty-handed was not the plan 'I' had in mind. 'I' once again is left with the burden of finding help. The trip back to 'Rou' was a full day, a day to hash his thoughts and find a solution. Seated in the captain's chair, only an occasional beep from a control panel could be heard. Out a view window 'I' could see stars flash by. What are we to do for help? Our closes neighbors also need help and both planets are in the same condition.

'I' was sure the 'Repssas' would send another ship or ships to investigate the sudden stop of warship transmissions. As 'I' ponders, he questions himself. Maybe the 'Sis' leaders were correct. Maybe we can't overcome such a large and well-armed aggressor. Maybe I will end-up leading a grand force to be slaughtered. My will is strong, yet my knowledge of war strategy is weak. I am not fit to lead such brave beings to their deaths. 'I' sits quiet and just stares forward. 'SI' had been listening very carefully. "No 'I', you are amiss in your assumption of your abilities. The E-tucs and Sislens were both defeated. It is only a matter of time before both are totally abolished from their planets and time itself. You have given the E-tucs more than hope. You have restored their pride and will to live. The E-tucs will gladly follow you, no matter how many 'Repssas' attack. Yes 'I', many will lose their lives and many will live for their courage. The struggle to live is not easy. But facing their fears, they can live proud and free of shame. So should you. Face your fears and strike down the evil with great courage. Bring back the day of peace and sunshine. With you, life will find a way to survive. Without you, the hand of death will reach out to all. Lead, 'I', and many will follow," 'SI' said. Looking out the small window, 'I' shuddered at the thought of lives that would perish. There was just no way of avoiding or stopping another attack. Once the 'Repssas' attacked thousands of peaceful years of existence could disappear in the rising and setting of the sun. There must be a way, 'I' thought. Having delivered a great blow upon the 'Repssas', all within the ship were in high spirits. Would the 'Repssas' realize they had lost enough and leave? Were the 'Repssas' that determined to continue their iron grip on both planets? Time would only tell how the 'Repssas' would react once they returned. War was very much in the air. Victories had changed the E-tucs into a fighting force not to be taken lightly. Peace of the past was still far away. Too far to start celebrating. Staying busy within the ship kept all calm. Ship's power source and weapons were improved adding to greater confidence among the crew. Eager to learn more of the Sislens 'I' stands and heads to the control room door. Sliding open, 'I' exits and walks through the hallway. Down to the second floor 'I' walks and finds children playing. 'I' stops and looks down at the children. The thought of seeing the children happy and playing made 'I' smile. Looking up at 'I', the children merely smile and continue playing. Children seem to find time to play even in life's darkest moments, 'I' thought. 'I' continues his journey passing many with grateful smiles. Reaching the landing bay, 'I' enters, finding more children playing and women speaking to each other. They notice 'I' and gathered around to ask many questions, they worried about so much. 'I' tried his best to eased their frightened minds and restore

their confidence. Standing steadfast with a stern expression poised upon his face, he says "We shall prevail and win the day. Peace will be restored and the days of darkness and death will fade deep into the past. And once again all will live in peace." Content for the moment the women give a smile of relief. Once again 'I' had soothed the troubled hearts and minds with mere words. So amazed by the human likeness 'I' didn't feel so alone anymore. Other than the light blue and white mixture of their skin and white hair, 'I' could see very little difference. Spending much time talking and observing, 'I' found the Sislens very much like humans in many ways. Their feelings, thoughts, worries, life and death: The same problems as humans that decided how they lived. Not understanding why beings would kill one another greatly confused so many. War and death were not part of the E-tuc or 'Sislen' way of life. Both were new horrors of living. With the wants and needs of life so easily given to all.

Why would others completely destroy what can be given to them? they asked 'I". This was a question asked of 'I' so many times. A question even 'I' couldn't answer. But 'I' did know the killing wasn't over yet. And the pain of losing so much showed within their eyes. Having lost so much, many aboard the ship were confused and dispirited. 'I' could only comfort them and let them know he and the E-tucs were there to help in any way. While answering questions, 'I' was approached from behind. A soft spoken voice cut through the many voices. Turning around 'I' was caught within a magnetic grip of beauty. With his great powers and strength, 'I' became defenseless at the sight of her. Her beauty sparkled like a diamond reflecting light in all directions. Even within the mist of others she stood alone in absolute splendid beauty. At almost six feet tall she was of perfect proportion. "Who is she?" 'I' asks 'SI'. "She is the daughter of a 'Sis' leader," 'SI' said. "I was not aware, that one of great importance was aboard," 'I' said. "She is the ambassador of 'Sis'. One of great power and influence. One day she will replace one of the aging leaders. Her reasons for being here could be many," 'SI' said. "When time reveals her intentions, we will know," 'I' said. Stunned by her beauty, 'I' was speechless. Still without a response, 'I' could only stare. A rose of beauty lived among death and darkness of 'Sis' surviving the harshness of war. Again she asks, "Why have the 'Repssas attacked us and totally burned our planet?" Looking at her, her beauty glowed like the morning sunrise. A beauty 'I' had never seen before. Stunned and at loss for an answer, 'I' finally collects his thoughts. "I do not know why they have done such a horrible act. I do know they will attack again. This time the 'Repssas' will find a force ready to engage their assault. 'Rou' with all her force will fight with an energy unknown to the 'Repssas'. The E-tucs and Sislens have the right to live as all beings have. This war regretfully will cost many lives to prove my point." Staring into each other's eyes 'I' realized she had seen her share of death. Realizing the talk of war and more war to come scared all that heard 'I' changes the subject. "Have you visited 'Rou' before?" 'I' asked the ambassador. "No, my father has. He was very impressed," she said. "I'm sorry to say, when you see 'Rou', you won't be impressed. 'Rou' and 'Sis' now look the same," 'I' said. The smile on her face disappeared and a saddened displaced look appeared. "'Rou' is the same as 'Sis'?" she stares silently. "Do not be saddened, you will be very impressed with the underground living quarters. I've seen much of it, and marveled at its beauty and splendor," 'I' said. Still looking at 'I', "From what distant star did you voyage from?" she asks. "A planet very far away, deep within the stars," 'I' said. Even 'I' couldn't say for even he didn't know. "Is your planet a peaceful planet?" she asks. "Most of the time it is and at times the inhabitants find it hard to agree with each other," I' said. "I have never seen a war until now. War is a horror I don't want to know or dream of. Many that I have known all my life have perished, never to be seen again. I have been left heartbroken, lost, and lonely without my friends. As the sun rises each new day I look upon 'Sis' and realize the world I knew is gone," she said. "Nothing good comes from a war. Only sorrow and grief of a past tragedy. We have the knowledge to solve our differences. Yet war prevails and many die," 'I' said. Still curious of 'I's' planet, "Is your planet a large planet?" she asks. "It's about the same size as 'Sis'. Covered with blue water and a blue sky. High mountains that reach into the sky with white ice covering the top and bottom of the planet. Tall green trees cover the land giving shade to all. And many beings upon the land breathe an endless supply of oxygen that fills the skies," 'I' said. Her blue eyes enlarged and glowed at the sound of oxygen. "Is there a lot of oxygen on your planet?" she asks. "Yes, all the oxygen one can breathe," 'I' said. Looking into her blue eyes, 'I' was saddened to know that oxygen had excited her so much. A precious element 'Sis' and 'Rou' both lacked, became exciting due to the lack of it. Still 'I' was fascinated by their way of life and their great likeness to humans. "Rou and 'Sis' will one day regain their greatness and there will be plenty of oxygen," 'I' said. Wordless she smiles at 'I'. 'I' couldn't help but look deep into her blue eyes again. Something within her eyes told him what peace and life were all about. How beings could solve their problems and live in peace. The Sislens and E-tucs had lived in peace for thousands of years and flourished. Still the pain of losing so much ran deep within her eyes. 'I' without a word nods his head

and gives a smile. "Peace will find its way back and life will thrive once more," 'I' said. Stepping back a step, 'I' bows slightly, turns and walks away. Returning back to the control room a plan begins to form within 'I's' mind. A plan not of defeating the 'Repssas' with one ship, but of surviving as long as one could. An age-old plan of hit and run used so many times in so many battles on Earth. Would it work and disrupt and cost the 'Repssas' more than they could lose? "'I', you stand as a beacon of light and hope for two planets. To lead many into battle you will have to stand tall and show the way. Do not despair 'I', you are not alone. Many follow your light of leadership. Lead, 'I', for many seek the path of life," 'SI' said. Retracing his route back to the control room. 'I's' deep thoughts were interrupted by the same children playing. Again the children look up at 'I' and give a smile of happiness. Returning to their play 'I' grins. Continuing to the control room 'I' knew he carried the burden of millions, knowing deep inside he needed a miracle to happen. Reaching the control room, 'I' retakes his place at the captain's chair. Slowly adding to his plans, the hours swiftly pass by. Nearing 'Rou', ship sensors blast a continuous loud alert. Ordering a full stop, 'I' orders two probes to investigate. Quickly the probes leave the warship and enter into a wide circle, circling around 'Rou'. 'I' immediately orders all to battle stations. A rush of feet broke the ship's silence. Repulser fields soar up and long range sensors scanned anything that moved. Immediately sensors located traces of another ship's heat particles. "There is another ship in the area," an E-tuc at controls said. War continued to echo within 'I's' mind. Knowing he couldn't afford to take chances with their sole battle ship. 'I' moved very cautiously, as a stalker watching every move. Surviving with the heartbeats of many, 'I' knew that life had a way of surviving as long as there was hope. "The crew is very confident and their ability to fight is without question," 'SI' said. "Yes, 'SI', they have a reason, they want to live. To see and feel all the measures of life. Once the E-tucs were the hunted, now they are eager to kill the hunter," 'I' said. Hidden within the darkness of space 'I' and crew waited for the probes to return or send information. Back at last, the two probes returned like two pigeons returning home revealing a message of a single 'Repssa' ship circling 'Rou'. A ship half the size of a warship, most likely a scout ship searching for clues and answers. "'I', it may be a ship far ahead of an advancing 'Repssa' force. It must not get away," 'SI' said. Continuing its searching the ship gave little notice of being observed. "They haven't given up yet, they're still wanting control of 'Rou', why?" 'I' asked 'SI'. "That will be a question best answered when all of 'Rou' is in the 'Repssa's' claws," 'SI' said. Giving the scout ship their full attention, 'I' begins to devise a plan to trick the 'Repssa' ship. E-tucs at control panel stare at 'I' waiting for orders. Staring at the E-tucs without a word 'I' finally formulates his daring plan. "Send out a distress signal," 'I' orders. All in the control room freeze at 'I's' order. The E-tucs had not yet learned to play the Earth game of opossum. "I do not understand. Why are you letting the enemy know our location?" 'SI' asks. "We fly a ship of their own, a ship that needs help," 'I' told 'SI'. "But our ship is functioning excellently," 'SI' said. "Does the enemy know that?" 'I' asks 'Si'. "So you are pretending our ship is in distress? Giving us the ability to get closer," 'SI' said. "Yes 'SI', that is exactly my intentions," 'I' said. Once again 'I' stares at the E-tucs and repeats his order, "Send out a distress signal."

This time the order is obeyed and the signal is sent out. Over and over the signal was transmitted like a wounded animal calling for help. The signal never stopped. All in the control room nervously waited for a response. Finally the scout ship responded and inquired about the ship's problem. Slowly the scout ship came closer lured by a hungry enemy. By this time both ships were in sight of each other. Again the scout ship requests the ship's problem. "Propulsion problem," 'I' tells the E-tucs at controls. "Send the message," 'I' orders. Off to the other ship the message went. Minutes slowly ticked by as the web of death waited for the scout ship to get closer. Knowing the scout ship was scanning the warship for damages the ship drew closer, close enough to target. Lowering their reflective pulser field, the scout ship became unknowingly helpless to the warship's deadly intentions. Still a distance away 'I' orders the gunner to target the ship and fire when ready. Floating without protection the scout ship drifted closer becoming a target of death. Out of the warship raced a Fron Cor missile heading straight to the scout ship. Seeing the missiles race to them, it was too late to raise reflective pulser fields. Slamming into the broad side of the unsuspecting ship, it was a perfect aim. Tilting to one side, the scout ship tried to escape the warship's hunger. Like a wounded animal glowing blood red, the scout ship retreated slowly toward one of 'Rou's' moons. Drifting behind the moon, the retreat was futile. The taste of another kill was already being swallowed by the warship's crew. Knowing the main body of warships would arrive within days 'I' had very little time to waste. Once again 'I' and crew wait for the crippled ship to meet her end. It wasn't a long wait. Aglow of bright light lit the far side of the moon and disappeared as quickly. Once more the skies above 'Rou' were free of menacing eyes. And 'I' knew that wouldn't last long. The day of 'Repssa' judgment was coming and the skies of 'Rou' would once again be filled with 'Repssa' warships and their killing ways. 'I' knew those on 'Rou' had seen

the burning in the hazed sky appear and disappear. And now the darkness of space covered all once again. The plan of tricking the enemy had worked. And the E-tucs in the control room stared at 'I' in astonishment. "The ways of war are many, so are the ways of life. Today the two ways mingled as one. To fight and kill, to live and give life. You, 'I', have proved to all the seed of life will find a way to live," 'SI' said. "Have we become cold-hearted killers, 'SI'?" 'I' asks. "Yes 'I', we have become the same as those that hunt the E-tucs on 'Rou'. E-tucs have lived in peace for thousands of years. Now they must kill to regain that peace," 'SI' said. As 'I' looks at a monitor screen scanning space, 'I' realizes the coldness of killing was far colder than space itself. "Do not let your mind be troubled. For you fight the evil that comes to take life. Stand strong ,'I', and face the enemy. For the evil the 'Repssas' bring will spread if we don't stop them," 'SI' said. "How will time judge us 'SI'?" 'I' asks. "Those that continue to live, will write the events of time. If everyone is dead, so is time. Time is a concept made by the living. In space, time doesn't exist. Space continues changing and evolving one moment to the next. What happens between two moments is time and yet who records it? Not space. The truth stands with us, 'I', in spirit and in our deeds. WE will record the events of time. From time's beginning to its end, time will not show how one killed another, only how one restored peace from war. How a great leader led many to victory. And helped restore a planet to its beauty once more," 'SI' said. "I stand strong for those on 'Rou' and 'Sis'. I will give all that I am to help restore the peace that once existed," 'I' said. "If we fail in our efforts, we will fail together. We fight a worthy cause against the darkness of evil. You have made me part of a great moment in time. For the moment in time will only be a small span in time. A time that will not be forgotten. It will be a reminder to all. War is the evil of the living. A dark and distant place one goes to in their mind, filled with horrors. You are the light that will lead all. Lead 'O great warrior of 'Rou', and many will follow," 'SI' said.

The E-tucs and 'Si's' loyalty to 'I' was undeniable. 'I's' ability to lead even amazed 'I' himself. I'm amazed I'm still alive. How long will it last? Time only will know, 'I' thought to himself. Once again 'Rou's' orbit was free of the 'Repssa's' watchful eyes. A dark peaceful space illuminated 'Rou' with glittering stars. Down at 'Rou' 'I' looks and wonders if 'Rou' had been invaded. Leaving his most trusted to command the ship 'I' takes a few well-armed E-tucs and flies down to investigate. Descending into 'Rou's' orbit, ship scanners scanned for 'Repssa' fighter ships. Through the hazed sky the E-tucs flew the fighter ship as if a clear sky existed. Over 'Rou' the fighter ship flew viewing only ruins of a once peaceful planet. 'Rou' was as they had left it, dark, lonely and hazed. Once again the fighter ship lands near the great rock mountain. Viewing the hazed and quiet area, 'I' had the same feelings as the first time when he landed on 'Rou'. What am I to see? 'I' thought. Hoping for a grand welcome 'I' felt he had accomplished much in just a few days. The visit to 'Sis' and ship battles made 'I' feel he had been gone more than a few days. Standing at the ship's door, the door slides open and 'I' steps from the ship. Viewing the surrounding area all was quiet and still. Not a sign of life and no hero's welcome. Standing within sight of the great mountain the ground began to shake. It was the great mountain's door opening. Wider and wider the door opened. To 'I's' surprise a long wide row of E-tucs stood shoulder to shoulder. Springing from the doorway they rushed to 'I'. A hero's welcome had begun. Still with a thick sky of haze, spots of sun broke through. The day of celebration had begun. Free of the rock mountain's protection, the E-tucs held their hands high and chattered to the sun. As if dancing, the freedom filled the E-tucs with happiness even under a troubled sky. As 'I' looks on he smiles. "You have changed their lives for the better. You have helped return their freedom and their will to live. You have used your time wisely," 'SI' said. "To see the E-tucs happy makes me happy inside," 'I' said. Now with a 'Repssa' warship circling 'Rou' and controlled by E-tucs. 'Rou' was safe again in E-tuc hands. Free of being attacked the E-tucs continued to celebrate the day. The day was beautiful, even with a hazed sky an occasional ray of light pierced through. "Will it last?" 'I' asks himself. "It must for all to live. The 'Repssas' aren't beings to give up so easily," 'SI' said. "I've a feeling they'll return sooner than we expect," 'I' says. Knowing peace would only be the calm before the storm 'I' knew the storm would arrive and peace would only be a thought of the past. Later that day the sun disappeared and night slowly covered 'Rou'. Re-entering the great room a massive crowd of E-tucs gathered close to hear 'I' speak. Standing high, 'I' looks across a field of wondering minds. Knowing they were expecting help from 'Sis' 'I' had to inform them 'Sis' was worse off than they were. As 'I' described the drastic situation of 'Sis', 'I' could sense the feeling of sadness. Informing the crowd of their many victories robustness began to grow from the crowd. "Attack they will, lose their lives they will, win the battle, win the war we will," 'I' bellows loud and clear. The life and spirit once again flowed within the massive crowd. The next day before the sun lit the horizon. Thousands of E-tucs wake early to save their planet. Blending large assortments of artillery power into the ground and mountain, weapons unimaginable to the 'Repssas' awaited to leap from the ground. The surrounding area and

mountains became a deadly trap. "Will the 'Repssas' walk into our trap?" 'I' asks 'SI'. "In order for the 'Repssas' to walk into our trap they must attack the surface and mountains with troops," 'SI' said. "That day will be the end of 'Rou' or become a new beginning for 'Rou'," 'I' said. The day had awoken and light filled the sky through the haze. 'I' is found standing safely atop a tall mountain. Beholding a vast array of battle installations 'I' is joined by 'Rou's' leaders who also gazed upon the vast installations.

With a look of great concern, "'I', when will the 'Repssas' attack?" a leader asks. "Soon, the 'Repssas' are just gathering their combined forces. This time they know our address," 'I' said. As 'I' looked across the soon-to-be field of battle 'I' envisions a great battle. A battle that would engulf many lives for survival or conquer. "They will attack the great rock mountain and all other known mountains across 'Rou'. Our blood will mingle with theirs on the field of battle. Lives will end where they fall, creating a field of lifeless warriors. This time the 'Repssas' won't leave until all the inhabitants of 'Rou' are dead. Only the strongest of will shall survive. They will be the only ones to tell the horrors of war and how war changed the lives of the living," 'I' said. In 'I's' conversation with the leaders 'I' reviews his bond with the Sislens. "I have given my word to the 'Sis' leaders I would return as quickly as possible with provisions and weapons. I have guaranteed the 'Sis' women and children would be treated the same as all on 'Rou'. My word is my bond with the Sislens. I will return," 'I' said. Looking at 'I' with honor, "Your bond with the Sislens is our bond also. We will supply all that you request. And the women and children will live no different than us on 'Rou'," the leader said. Looking at the leader 'I' smiles and nods his head. "You have given my word great meaning and saved many others. I will leave knowing the Sislens are well cared for and safe. This I will tell the leaders of 'Sis' of their most beloved." The day of light had begun making it the second day since 'I' returned from 'Sis'. With no sight of a 'Repssa' attack the day was busy with flights to the warship and ground installations. The day continued and so did the E-tucs. By the end of the second day 'I' was informed all provisions and weapons were loaded within the war ship. Returning with his friends, 'I' pays a visit to the leaders once more. Standing in front of all 'Rou's' leaders he says "I came to inform you the warship is ready to depart. I leave to honor our bond with the Sislens. To help save a planet in great need. The death of 'Sis' must not be. For 'Sis' like 'Rou' will fight for its existence till the last of them. We must not let 'Sis' fade away into the dark of night, as a voice crying for help, never to be seen again as the sun sets."

Staring at 'I' with a grateful expression, a leader speaks. "Seek peace as your final resolution and knowledge of many will fill your mind. Let death walk with you to remind you how precious life is. And see the next day as better than the day at hand."

'I' and his friend bow without another word said. They turn and exit the room. Down the long hallway 'I' and his friends are greeted by many. A wonderful sendoff but how would their journey end? 'I' thought. Out the great mountain 'I' and his friends exit, only to find many more excited E-tucs gathered. 'I' and his friend step onto a transport vehicle. Slowly parting from the many that had gathered the vehicle heads to the fighter ship. Passing many who stand and stared 'I' could only hope the 'Repssas' would not attack while he was gone. Reaching the fighter ship, 'I' and friend were once again swarmed by well-wishers. To see so many happy faces, 'I' regretted the need to leave. Stepping from the transport, 'I' heads to the fighter ship and doesn't look back. The nightmarish thought of returning and seeing all dead, tormented 'I'. Inside the ship with his friend, both were seated and ready to depart. The sound of the fighter ship's power notified all to stand back. As the fighter ship rises, 'I' tries to guess how many ships and troops the 'Repssas' would bring. The strain of guessing and being defenseless to help clouded 'I's' mind. On 'Rou' and in orbit 'I' knew they had to be ready. Even their sole warship they so gallantly won had to be ready. "Hard to imagine, a 'Repssa' warship which had served so well and embraced by so many would receive the same fate as those she destroyed. To burn brightly in space or streak across 'Rou's' skies like a racing fireball," 'I' pondered. Back to the warship the fighter ship flew. Beyond the dark haze of 'Rou' they flew. Into a new sky of stars and sunlight the fighter ship meets the warship. Entering into the warship with its last load of supplies and the driving force of the E-tucs the fighter ship softly sets down upon the landing bay. Fighter ship's power disappears and all is quiet. 'I's' mind quickly races back to the moment they caught the 'Repssas' off guard and took the ship. The events of life and death seemed to race from heart beat to heart beat. Up from his chair 'I' stands at the fighter ship's door. Sliding back, the door opens to 'I's' surprise. Cheering E-tucs lined the fighter ships doorway. 'I' slowly steps from the ship into two long rows of E-tucs thrilled to see him back. As 'I' walks between the E-tucs, they lay their hands upon him. "'I', it is the act of showing they are with you in life and in death. It is the highest honor an E-tuc can give another."

The two lines stretched almost to the landing bay's entrance door. Reaching the doorway 'I' turns and faces the two long lines of E-tucs. "To

breath the air of freedom one must be brave when life's most challenging moments stare you in the face. We here have met that moment. And we will meet it again and again. Fear not for your life, make your enemy fear for their life." 'I', was in the hearts of every E-tuc warrior. Their approval was in their eyes and undivided attention. 'I' bows his head in great respect. Raising his head, "We have no time to lose. We must reach 'Sis'."

Determined to reach 'Sis' as fast as possible 'I' rushes to the warship's control room. Entering the control room, 'I' greets a welcoming crew. "You have done well my friends. The ship is worthy of flight and ready for battle," 'I' said. "It is good to have you leading us once more. The ship is ready to journey with you in command," an E-tuc said. Staring at 'I' the spirit of trust and loyalty filled the control room. Now with the task of returning to 'Sis' 'I' leaves behind 'Rou' unprotected. To have or not to have? To live or to die? Could both planets be spared or would one perish into the darkness of space? 'I' had the feeling of uneasiness. Lives depended on supplies and weapons and a leader to bring hope for another day. "Do not grieve 'I', you have done all that is expected of you. The greatest we can be is the greatest courage we can possess. Face your enemy with courage then you will know their courage. You have truly united the scattered and battered. Your leadership and courage have bound together a race of beings that face total extinction. Now the E-tucs stand strong like a great rock mountain," 'SI' said. "I am honored to have encouraged and aided beings that seek peace. Now I must do the same for 'Sis'. The Sislens have great courage. Their unity is strong as is their will to live. The help we give may be the help that saves the Sislens. How long at full power till we meet our destination?" 'I' asks 'SI'. "The warship's power has greatly been improved. Our trip to 'Sis' and back will take less than three 'Rou' days. That includes unloading supplies and weapons," 'SI' said. "If 'Rou' is attacked, the 'Repssas' will lose many. This time 'Rou' is ready and willing to fight," 'I' said to 'SI'. The thought of losing the warship and many that couldn't escape troubled 'I'. If returning to 'Rou' and finding 'Rou' being attacked, many on board would surely perish. Filled with concern and gratefulness toward the E-tucs 'I' looks down at the E-tucs. "We are free today and we shall stay free. Together we are many, together we are strong. Today, tomorrow, and forever, time will find us side by side the same as the stars. Victory will be ours," 'I' proclaims. Cheers filled the control room walls. United as one, the E-tucs' hearts and minds were a force as mighty as their adversaries. 'I' leaves the control room and continues the ship's inspection. Finding himself within the cargo bay, 'I' found it full from end to end. The much needed supplies and weapons 'Sis' needed waited to be delivered. And still as 'I' gazed upon the mountain of supplies he knew, as a planet, 'Sis' needed so much more. "You have given 'Sis' a chance to live and protect themselves. If not for you the 'Sislen' of 'Sis' would surely perish within two moments of time," 'SI' said. "I feel I have only briefly extended life for both planets. I have raised their hopes and dreams of peace. And now they await the coming of peace, only to find their orbit and hazed skies filled with an enemy ready to kill all," 'I' said. "And by your thoughts, life is a struggle as a flower growing in between rocks. Struggling to stretch its roots and find nourishment to live," 'SI' said. "I understand 'SI'," 'I' said. Returning to the control room 'I' was followed like a king. A crew overjoyed to have their grand leader back, were ready to battle any warship. Returning to the control room, the door swiftly slides open revealing a crew diligently monitoring the ship's vital controls. Looking up, they see 'I'. 'I' knew they were ready for orders. Deciding to keep only the ship's weapon operators and control room crew 'I' orders the remaining crew to return to 'Rou'. 'I' was sure all left on board could abandon the ship safely when the time came. As 'I' decides his next move, 'SI' reflects his thoughts to 'I'. "You have taught the E-tucs that size in battle does not matter. Courage and bravery can win the day," 'SI' said. "Yes 'SI', courage and bravery can make the greatest of forces. And now 'Rou' has a great force waiting from the 'Repssas' to attack," 'I' said. Silence falls between both as 'I' departs the control room once again and returns to the landing bay. Finding many E-tuc warriors ready to return to 'Rou' 'I' praises their bravery and explains his reasoning for their departure. "I trust you will lead those on 'Rou' with your bravery now and forever," 'I' said. Bowing to the many warriors, the E-tuc warriors return the honor and bow to 'I'. Boarding the two fighter ships the E-tucs were ready to leave. Returning to the control room 'I' sits in silence. Moments later, 'I's' little friend enters the control room. Stopping, he stares at 'I'. The little being knew he had found more than a friend in 'I'. He had found one like him. One not afraid of the 'Repssas' and one willing to risk all for peace. Knowing that 'I' was the leader that would bring 'Rou' back to her greatness, protecting 'I' meant their dreams of peace would become reality. Seated once again in the captain's chair, 'I' assumes full responsibility. Looking on, 'I's' little friend waits for the moment to depart. Lights flash and departure time arrived. Interrupting 'I's' thoughts, the little E-tuc informs 'I' the ship was ready to depart. Out of his deep thoughts, 'I' glances at his little friend and smiles. "Very well my friend," 'I' said. Staring at the control room crew they wait in silence for 'I' to speak. "The time is near to depart, lives on both 'Rou' and

'Sis' depend on us. The evil that has destroyed and killed must be stopped. The light of life must not fade away into the darkness of space. We have one chance to regain the peace we seek. We must not fail our mission. When we return to 'Rou' and find the 'Repssas' attacking. We will not be of fear, for our greatest fears are the fears we fight within our minds. We will attack with the fullness of life and courage. We will show the 'Repssas' they have awoken their worst fears. Death and defeat will come to the 'Repssas'," 'I' said. A roar of cheers and ready eagerness were in their eyes. A unity of great power flowed within the control room. Uncoiling slowly the cheers of unity faded away. "As the 'Repssas' had huddled around the 'Repssa's' captain and died. The E-tucs huddle around you and live. Your victories are for a reason. Go forward and challenge the unknown with vigor. Your destiny and the lives of many await you," 'SI' said. Returning to their stations, controls were set for 'Sis' and all awaited 'I's' orders. Leaving 'Rou' unguarded didn't set well in 'I's' mind. With no choice, 'I's' destiny laid elsewhere. With eyes fastened upon 'I', 'I' gives the awaited command: Depart 'Rou' and head to our new destination, 'Sis'. Gradually the warship parts from 'Rou'. Faster and faster the warship accelerates. Staring at their monitor, 'Rou' becomes a small dot in space. Gone from view, 'Rou' was no more than a memory within one's mind. 'I's' feelings for 'Rou' were becoming the same as of Earth, 'Home'. Returning to 'Sis' 'I' noticed the ship's speed had been greatly improved. Stars became distant twinkles as they disappeared into the darkness of space. Time for 'I' to ponder upon lives of many and his life. Longing for human contact, a thought even 'SI' was unable to answer, and still 'I' envisioned Earth and the life he once lived with pictures flashing within his mind as fast as the stars of space flashed by the ship. "Even with my galaxy knowledge, Earth has been a challenge. Not knowing from which direction or the distance you traveled, the search could be endless. I will continue my search until I succeed," 'SI' said. "Thank you 'SI', I have great confidence in your knowledge. To find Earth is not my most important thought. But I do wish I knew the way home. To defeat the 'Repssas' is foremost in my thoughts. We know the 'Repssas' are arrogant beings willing to march into a burning fire to extinguish it. If we return to 'Rou' and find the 'Repssa' forces attacking 'Rou' they may pay little or no attention to one ship against so many. It is to our advantage to test their arrogance. To attack their outer rim of forces and cause the 'Repssa' to make mistakes. Quickness and speed will be our friend. Darkness of space will cloak us invisible. And bravery will be our impregnable shield. We know they fear and we know they can die. We shall fight the many 'Repssas' until they are no more. We will not fade into the darkness of space and become a silent moment in time. We will rise and shine as the glowing sun itself," 'I' said. Now able to communicate with 'Rou' from the ship 'I' would know the very moment the 'Repssas' made their appearance. With long range and orbital probes, 'Rou' would know friend or foe, if a ship was approaching. Now with eyes in space, 'Rou' wasn't blind to unwelcome guests. "Rest 'I', there is much to be done once we reach 'Sis'," 'SI' said. "Yes 'SI', rest will soothe my mind of so many worries," 'I' said. Taking 'SI's advice, 'I' closes his eyes and falls in to a deep, starless darkness. While 'I' slept the ship's crew, amounting to no more than twenty E-tucs, fly and maintain the ship in silence. The rest seemed peaceful for the moment. Undisturbed, 'I' slept in darkness. A darkness even stars disappeared in. Unchallenged by life and death, only peacefulness existed. Within 'I's' darkness the walls of darkness and peacefulness 'I' enjoyed so much began to crumble to moments of life. Shapes, colors, and images began to form within 'I's' darkness. Finding himself once more back in the captain's chair 'I' was again flying the endless skies on Earth. High in the moon's glow on Earth 'I' flew. Over trees, house tops, and beyond the city lights. 'I' flew reliving moments of great thrill. Looking to his left 'I' sees Joe whose wide eyes were filled with adventure. And to 'I's' right sat Sam holding tight to his chair with a roller coaster smile. Smiling himself from ear to ear Jim, like his friends, dared for more. Sailing from one cloud to another they soared the angelic skies. A time, a place of yesterday, reminding 'I' of friendships and who he was. Suddenly the clear and distinct images of Joe and Sam began to fade away. Replaced by the darkness of space. 'I' realizes his friendships of the near past had not disappeared within his mind. Realizing his mind had a very peculiar way of reminding himself of his past. 'I' asks himself, what has become of my two friends? Saddened by his friends' unknown situation 'I' vows to one day find his two friends, no matter where they were.

As 'I' reminisces his past, the feeling of sadness reached deep into his heart and mind. How he escaped the hands of law and power. And how his friends were bound to Earth's mighty grip and the law of the land. Unable to stay silent, 'SI' speaks. "Their lives are moving forward as yours is. There is a reason for all that happens and one day you will know that reason. Move forward, 'I', and seize your destiny," 'SI' said. Hurt by the thought of his friends' misfortunes, 'I' could take no more. Upset, 'I' opens his eyes. "I can't sleep 'SI'," 'I' said. "You need your rest 'I'," 'SI' said. "To many dream ghosts haunting me," 'I' said. I will induce your sleep and cloak your dreams while

you sleep," 'SI' said. Again 'I' closes his eyes and in moments falls into a deep sleep. Not haunted by his past, 'I' sleeps undisturbed.

Hours pass quickly while the ship speeds to its destination. Nearing their destination, 'I' is awakened by excited E-tucs. Looking about the control room 'I' finds it alive with crew readying the ship's approach to 'Sis'. Still far away 'I' leans forward and looks inquisitively at the main viewer screen. Stars and planets swiftly disappear into the endless darkness of travel. Somewhere in the near mist of stars laid 'Sis'. And the E-tucs knew where it was. Seeing a small planet growing larger and larger 'SI' speaks out. "We have arrived."

If not for 'Sis's' smaller size, 'Sis' could have passed for 'Rou'. Dark and uninviting 'Sis' slowly rotated bare of life. Eyes of hope gazed upon 'Sis', a once beautiful thriving planet transformed into a heap of burned ruins. Dark and quiet 'Sis' was still alive with its inhabitants hidden within the charred rubble. Slowly 'Sis' rotated waiting for its chance to spring forth life again. Within the warship 'I' and crew were ready to inform 'Sis' of their arrival. Sending the ship's arrival time, all wait for confirmation and landing instructions. With crew ready and waiting inside the fighter ships, time was too precious to waste. As all waited for landing instructions, 'I' could only wonder where the 'Repssas' were. Where in space would the 'Repssas' leap from and attack? When would the struggle of life and death begin? The necessity to protect their planets was great. And so was the joining of two beings' friendships. Finding the time to help each other in their time of great distress, 'I' pondered. After circling 'Sis', confirmation and landing instructions riddled the ship's communicator monitors. Sending the instructions to the landing bay, the doors of the silent landing bay opened wide into an endless array of glowing stars. Slowly rising from the bay floor both fighter ships grab large containers. Smoothly the fighter ships exit the warship. Down to 'Sis' the ships fly. Watching monitors, 'I' hopes for the best of friendships between 'Rou' and 'Sis'. "May we both feel the other's needs as our own," 'I' said to 'SI'. "The 'Sislens are beings that don' forget. Their trust, loyalty, and friendship is binding," 'SI' said. As 'I' watches for the fighter ships to return 'I' receives a message from 'Sis'. Sislens' fighters requesting to board the fighter ship to help 'Rou' in her fight. Informing the Sislens they only have two fighter ships on board the warship 'I' agrees to take only six fighters after all supplies has been delivered. Blindly flying into the dark haze of 'Sis', the fighter ships deliver their loads at designated points. Supplies and weapons were quickly gathered and moved to safe locations. "'I', the 'Repssas' are not expecting a battle, only to finish what they started," 'SI' said. "We can only hope the 'Repssas" arrogance will underestimate 'Rou's' and 'Sis's' fighting readiness," 'I' said to 'Si'. Watching the fighter ships fly by with another load, 'I's' little friend walks in and stops a few feet from 'I' and looks up at 'I'. "Two of the loads have been delivered," he said. "The supplies will help, but for a whole planet," 'I' stops talking and looks down in sadness. The fighter ships continued, back and forth they flew delivering supplies at different locations. 'I' tried his best to hold a positive outlook but the weight of destruction and lives of two planets was more sorrow than one could bear. The situation seemed too overwhelming. And the 'Repssas' weren't finished yet. Interrupting 'I's' thoughts, "A few more loads and all supplies will be delivered," the little being said. "You and I, my friend, will board the last flight to 'Sis' and address the leaders of 'Sis'," 'I' said. 'I' watches the fighter ships dive once again into the darkness covering 'Sis'. Regretting he couldn't have done more, 'I' knew time waited for no one. A few hours later, 'I' is informed by the landing bay crew the last shipment was ready to be delivered. 'I' and his friend leave the control room. Walking to the landing bay, 'I' remembers the struggle they had capturing the ship. Noticing a certain place, 'I' mentally recalls the brave E-tucs that lost their lives. Never to know they won the ship. 'I' knew it was their bravery that won the day. Reaching the landing bay, 'I' was momentarily stunned to see an empty landing bay. Only one shipment of supplies existed on the landing bay. 'I' and his friend enter the fighter ship together. Seated within the ship, both sat with a great side view. Rising from the landing bay floor, the fighter ship grabs the last load and smoothly exits the warship. Sitting quietly as the fighter ship dipped into 'Sis's' orbit both 'I' and friend gaze into the dark haze. Moments pass and darkness surrounded the fighter ship. Breaking through the thick haze, destruction was everywhere. A job well done by the 'Repssas'. Not a structure stood higher than twenty feet. A once thriving civilization had been turned into ruin in a matter of days. As 'Rou', nothing of value was left standing. Charred and useless the Sislens' still called 'Sis', their home. Closer and closer the fighter ship descended into a midst of broken structures. Weaving in and out of mangled and twisted structures they flew. 'I' and friend observed without a word. Approaching a large clearing the fighter ship hovers over the clearing. Setting the cargo on the ground, the load container was released. Moving forward the fight ship finds a clear spot and lands. Still and silent all outside the ship waited for the door to open. Inside the ship 'I' and friend stood and walked to the ship's door. "Be bold and speak with authority 'I'. You have proved your word is honorable," 'SI' said. The door slides back with 'I' and friend standing at the doorway. A crowd of Sislens who had only seen

'I' once rushed to 'I' as if he'd had already defeated the 'Repssas'. "Why, 'SI'?" 'I' asks. "They trust you, 'I'. Their friendship with you is binding," 'SI' said. Stepping from the ship 'I' and friend were lead to the 'Sis' leaders standing less than one hundred feet away. By the smiles on their faces 'I' knew they were happy to see him. Before 'I' reaches the leaders 'I' decided to speak first. Reaching the leaders 'I' stops and respectfully bows. Looking at the leaders, "O' great leaders of 'Sis', it is good to stand upon 'Sis' once again with friends. We have learned so much of each other in these times of need, and despair. I come to 'Sis' once again as a friend and forever as a friend. May we never forget our times of despair and how we helped each other in our struggle to live. One day we shall all share the same air of freedom," 'I' said. "Yes 'I', we have learned so much of each other. The leaders of 'Rou' have honored us greatly. More than just existing as neighbors, they have reached out and helped with their own life-supporting rations. And you, 'I', you are much more than a leader. Your word is forever binding with us," said one of the leaders. Still with smiles another leader steps forward and slightly bows his head. "You and the E-tucs have risked so much to help us. What can we do to help you and the E-tucs?"

"Your friendship is all we ask for. To know we can trust each other. To live in peace, side by side. To do for each other all this, as long as the sun and stars shine. May our friendship be what we can do for the other," 'I' said. Stepping closer to 'I' the leader puts his hand on 'I's' shoulder and says, "Together we stand, together we live. Under the same sun and stars, peace and prosperity will never fade away."

Excited as to what had just transpired, 'SI' couldn't hold back his thoughts. "'I' to my knowledge this has never been said to an E-tuc or anyone else. It is a great honor. It means we will work together. Share our knowledge and build an even greater future," 'Si' said. "I do dream of a better future. A future that will stand strong and united. And share the pleasures of peace."

The moment was great. A being from far away was bridging peace from two planets of beings. Staring at the leaders, "And live we shall my friends. We shall win our battle against the 'Repssas' and start a new and bright future," 'I' said. Up steps another 'Sislen' leader beside the leader speaking to 'I'. Holding a small black case in his hand, he opens the case. The first leader takes out an object from the case. "I give this to you, 'I', in honor of our friendship," the leader said. Leaning forward, the leader grabs 'I's' right hand and puts an inch round black object in 'I's' hand. Closing 'I's' hand the leader says, "You are one with us now. Your feelings, your needs, your pains are ours. Where you go, we go in thought and feelings. We are with you 'I', you are not alone even in the darkest of night and most desolated places, we are with you."

'I' opens his hand and the object was gone. "May you live long and find what you seek," the leader said. Looking stunningly at the leader. "How did he know I seek Earth?" 'I' says to himself. Staring at the 'Sislen' leader, 'I' noticed the leader hadn't moved his lips. 'I' realized he was given, telepathic ability. "O' great one, I am truly honored. Your gift is truly priceless. Let our friendship span the limitless galaxies and time itself," 'I' said without moving his lips. 'I' bows his head and stands silent. "There is something different about you. We felt it the first time we met. You are deeply concerned for the loss of lives. A planet can be restored but a life cannot. Your grief for the loss of so many weights heavily on your mind. Remember, 'I', we live for a reason. Live life to the fullest and that is how you will be remembered. As those that gave their lives brave forward and live to the fullest. As we have lived in peace so shall we with you. What we see, you will see, what we know, you will know. You are one of the many. Return to 'Rou' and find the peace we all seek. We send six warriors with you. They will see and hear the dangers that await you. You are not alone 'I', we are with you," the leader said telepathically. Humbled and speechless 'I' bows his head to the leader. Without another word, 'I's' complete face and head is covered with armor. 'I' turns and begins to walk back to the fighter ship. As one with great power, 'I' was followed closely by E-tucs and 'Sis' warriors. Back within the fighter ship, the power begins to surge through the ship. Lifting from the ground, 'I' looks out a small window. Many Sislens had gathered, and the feeling of thought was strong. 'I' could feel a great feeling of sorrow and despair. A feeling of great uncertainty. Joining the many thoughts, "'I will return," 'I' said within the many thoughts. From the small window, 'I' could see the leaders bowing their heads. The leader's thoughts were correct, 'I' felt different inside. The weight of many lives made 'I' move very cautiously. A great force was emerging to fight the 'Repssas'. Trust and loyalty were the words they lived by. And in this trust, a great leader would rise and lead the many upon many, across the times of death and despair into a new beginning. The flight back to the warship was ghostly silent. Many thoughts of the near future could be seen in unsure faces. The feeling of battle was in their minds like the cold had of death touching one on a freezing night. And even with the many unsure faces, thinking of war and dying 'I' knew to hold a face of rigid force. 'I' had been taught so well, one can't lead the many without believers. Poised

as a leader without fear, 'I' gave strength to all as he sat in deep thought. Staring forward as the warship came into view, 'I's' face glowed with even more confidence. The greatness of 'I' was learning from many the strong will to live. Lit from the lights of the sun and stars, a warship floated quietly in space with intentions to kill its own builders. Staring at the warship the 'Sis' fighters now saw what had attacked their planet. The evil sight of a 'Repssa' warship sent chills through their bodies. Now as the 'Sis' fighters enter into the mouth of death they cling close together holding their breath. Nowhere to run and no one to save them. Safe upon the landing bay floor the fighter ship lands. 'I' turns and looks at the 'Sis' warriors. "The warship is loyal to us and only us."

Without a word the warriors nod their heads to 'I'. Standing, 'I' walks to the exit door. Not to be alone at the door, 'I' is followed closely. The door slides open to a group of E-tucs holding their 'Repssa' weapons upright. 'I' stands boldly showing he was ultimately in control and sure he could lead with great courage. With stares of great affection, the E-tucs looked up at 'I' with welcome smiles. Staring at the 'E-tucs', 'I' said, "the 'Sislens' and E-tucs are one and so is the word of both. We are bound together in the struggle of life and death. A struggle to overcome our adversaries and bring forth a new day. A day, time will hold in the moments of life."

Stepping from the fighter ship 'I' reaches the floor. Turning around 'I' faces the warriors. "Teach the 'Sis' warriors this ship's abilities. Give the 'Sis' warriors the opportunity to face the 'Repssas' with the 'Repssas'' own firepower." Without another word 'I' turns around and walks with his friend to the warship's control room. The walk to the control room was silent. 'I's' little friend knew 'I' had much to resolve within the moments of life. Reaching the control room doors 'I' feels the moment to confront the 'Repssas' was just beginning.

The control room doors slide open and 'I' and friend step in. Walking to the captain's chair 'I' stands and stares at the crew. "What waits us at 'Rou' I do not know. If war awaits, I say to all, fight well my friends for we are many and we fight for the same cause". Stopping short, 'I' stares at the crew. The essence of life reached deep within his mind. "We awake to see a new day of wonder. A day to live with courage and a glow of happiness, we unfold our minds with sincere reasoning and relish in our expanding ways. Living is not to be in fear and dying is not to be by another hand. We live to enjoy and share our lives. Fulfilling the wonders of life."

Sitting in the captain's chair, 'I' calls out, "Stations!"

Back to their stations all quickly ran. Before leaving 'Sis's' outer orbit 'I' sends a message to 'Sis' leaders. "I leave with the strength of many and the will to live to the fullest of life." Departing from 'Sis', 'I' wonders if he would live to return to see the ray of freedom upon 'Sis'. The thought of beings from different parts of the galaxy sharing trust and peace as humans from different countries amazed 'I'. 'I' realized the roots of living reached deep. Life was no different from the struggle of living. Now that the existence of many was in jeopardy the days of many weighed only in the balance of time. And yet the seed of peace was planted. Life itself would continue its struggle to exist and reach for another day, a day to struggle with no guarantees. Viewing 'Sis' on a monitor, 'Sis' continued to fade into the darkness of space. Now 'Sis' was on her own once more, protected only by the struggle of living. "'I' you have achieved what no one has ever achieved. You have united two planets with trust and loyalty. The E-tucs and Sislens will hide no more. Their courage to live was hidden inside of them. You have strengthened their will to live. Now they will fight the hand of death," 'SI' said. "And so shall 'I', to the last breath of my life's fullness. I will fight alongside my friends," "I' said. As the warship flew homeward bound, three probes exit the warship and rapidly disappear into space far ahead of the warship. Like racing meteors the probes relayed collected information back to the warship. The long hours returning to 'Rou' were all but boring. The feeling among the crew was mutual. Do not get taken by surprise. Staying ready the small crew was still enough to handle an attack or to attack. Time seemed to slow to a crawl when only thoughts of war prevailed, and hearts and minds live in great peril. Knowing a surprise attack could be fatal 'I' knew in times of peace, the hazards of life were the mistakes of life. In war the hazards of death were being an easy target. 'I' desperately needed the probe's findings. Far in front of the warship, probes race toward 'Rou' sending back worthless information. A clear space to travel with no enemy in sight. Frustrated, 'I' had the inner feeling the 'Repssas' were near. Turning to the warship's defense opp., the opp. merely gives 'I' a disappointing slow shake of his head. Still many hours away, all sat on the edge of time and space. Twinkles of stars and laziness of space went unnoticed as the warship flew at speeds never reached by a 'Repssa' warship. Knowing the warship cost so many lives to capture, 'I' grieved to know more lives would fall protecting the warship. For 'I' and crew, as the 'Repssas', would not surrender. Remembering 'SI' had said a flower growing within rocks stood a chance of surviving 'I' knew all on 'Rou'

stood a chance united and armed. Conquering his many worried thoughts, 'I' felt they had more victories to win. And even to lose, they would conquer their fears facing their enemy with the spirit of living. The open space 'I' admired so much, seemingly disappeared as 'I' battled the 'Repssas' in his mind. The mission was a success and the return voyage had tested the nerves of all. Tired of the long tense hours, all felt they had worried too much. They couldn't have been more wrong. Looking close at his monitor, the long range probe opp. breaks the dead of silence. "A probe has quit signaling," he cries out. Now the crew knew the dangers were waiting far ahead. Still at their posts their adrenaline and heart beats raced. Checking his monitor once again the opp. repeats his call with the second probe not signaling. All on board knew what that meant. Gathering their reserved energy all knew the moment was at hand. "Load all missile bays," 'I' orders. "Missile bays have been loaded since we left 'Sis'," defense opp. replied. 'I' smiles, for he knows he's with true fighting warriors. Regaining his composure, "initiate R.P.F.," 'I' orders. "R.P.F. initiated," deference opp. said. "Have we received a message from 'Rou'?" 'I' asks. "Negative," communicator opp. said. "Artificial pulser beams are being deployed between us and 'Rou'. Nothing can be sent out or received," communicator opp. said. 'I' knew the time had come when life and death would clash and lives would end. The excitement of battle rang out when the defense opp. excitedly cried out. "Three 'Repssa' warships are headed our way."

"Weapons opp., aim two Fron Cor missiles at the ship closest to us. Navigator, set new course around targeted ship," 'I' orders. Seconds later, "New course set," cries navigator. "Fire missiles," 'I' orders. Two rapid lights burst from below the warship. "Initiate new course," 'I' orders. No more than seconds after the new course had been initiated, two incoming missiles reach out like the hands of death. The enemy had also declared war. Grazing the outer edges of the reflector pulser field the missiles disappeared into the far reaches of space. Headed in opposite directions all four warships were headed for war. "I", cries weapons opp. "a large explosion was spotted on monitor."

"What was that explosion?" 'I' asks. "The explosion was in line with target. Presumably it was the warship we fired upon. Apparently the warship had its reflective pulser fields down," weapons opp. said. Looking at the weapons opp. 'I' smiles. "Good shooting," 'I' said. Standing close to 'I', 'I's' little friend says, "The battle has begun, now the 'Repssas' will be waiting for us."

"They will be occupied with their attacks upon 'Rou'. One warship is not a threat to their arrogant ways of fighting. At the worst, the 'Repssas' will dispatch a single warship to confront us," 'I' said. "Then we must be swift and not hesitate. We must strike first and put fear in their minds," 'I's' friend said. "Yes, my friend, we will strike first and be the fear that exists within their minds. A fear that paralyzes one's mind," 'I' said. Not taking a chance with more approaching warships. "Reload missiles," 'I' orders. Taking the ship to 'Rou armed and ready protected all from split-second decisions. Calmness was far from the battle control room faces. Hearts pounded with vast amounts of near-death excitement. And still minds and bodies were vibrating with vengeance as all clung to a touch of fear. The same fear that kept all ready and hopeful of victory. Sitting in the captain's chair, 'I' began to search his mind for a way to end this day of tragedy. Closing his eyes, 'I' slips into darkness. A small glow of light begins to appear. Closer it came, glowing brighter and brighter. Standing within the glow of light, a great power of strength and courage was bestowed upon 'I'. Basking within the light of great power, 'I' was free to expand his thoughts. Free to challenge the overwhelming odds with a daring assault. The feeling of being encouraged by a strange light began to depart. Drifting away into the darkness of his mind, gone as it had arrived, 'I' floated within the darkness of his mind sure and confident. Awake within his mine, "'SI' was that you reinforcing my thoughts?" 'I' asks.

"No 'I', it was a power beyond my knowledge. You call it a dream."

"I did not dream."

The depths of the mind are as deep as space itself. And even in one' life, one can never explore the infinite measure or comprehension of one's mind or space itself," 'SI' whispers to 'I'. "No 'SI', I was not dreaming, it was a premonition. When or where, the warning will give no answer. There is no stopping what is to happen. I must go forward and seek the answers to life's problems. Agree or disagree we all must face our destiny. The events of life must move forward."

With his eyes open 'I' sits in the captain's chair and stares. Back on 'Rou', thousands of hidden weapons and explosives waited for a ground attack with a mighty force waiting to repel the 'Repssa' force. The thought of how large a force the 'Repssas' would bring clouded many minds. Knowing the 'Repssas' fought in masses like blades of grass overwhelming their victims. The 'Repssas' were arrogant and fearless upon the field of battle. Back within the ship 'I'

still struggled as someone yet to find a life. Loved by two planets of beings and trapped with them in a life and death struggle 'I' now sped to 'Rou' to fight an unknown amount of 'Repssa' warships. Knowing it was a suicide mission, a mission to extend life or terminate life or to disappear as if one had never existed. A terrible loss of life and two great cultures living in peace. 'I' knew to win would open the eyes of many to the dangers of invading forces. And thus begin a new era of protection for 'Rou' and 'Sis'. Knowing the odds of winning were in the 'Repssas" favor, their overwhelming numbers and firepower were death to any planet, 'I' could only hope the 'Repssas' would suffer enough in their deadly attack and abandon their takeover quest. The days were numbered for living or dying for a planet or a home quietly spinning in space.

The quietness was broken once again as the probe opp. sounds out, "Probes have located warships at designated locations." The cry of war had been sounded and the waiting was over. Like hungry tigers, 'I' and crew were ready to confront their enemy and prey. The moment of battle had arrived and hearts began to pump wildly with the heat of battle. A battle with no second chance and only winner taking all. "Stand strong 'I', for all on board will follow you loyally to victory or death. The stars sent you for a reason. You are here to bring light from darkness and peace from war. Lead, 'I' and all will follow," 'SI' said. 'Rou' was still a small dot existing among an endless array of distant planets and stars. The wonders of space that awed 'I' so much faded into darkness and he was only seeing 'Rou' as the point of interest. Ready and waiting to attack, control room eyes watched as a hungry beast. Only the sound of the ship's mighty engines could be heard. Time passed and 'Rou' rapidly grew larger and larger. Less than an hour away 'I' breaks the tense silence that gripped all. Seated in the captain's chair 'I' speaks. "Our plan is to attack the enemy and then fade into the darkness of space. To damage, derail, and confuse the enemy. To let the 'Repssas' know their plans of destroying a race of beings won't succeed." Stopping short of a prolonged speech, 'I' remains silent and stares at the control room crew. Their eyes and faces burned deep with hurt feelings. The feeling of many who existed no more. A planet in ruin and a future in question. Sympathetic to the survival of the E-tucs 'I' knew his place in life was with the E-tucs. To help restore the peace and find the life he searched for. Still staring at the E-tucs, the sadness they carried was understandable. A day of victory would only end the 'Repssa's' invasion, never to bring back the deceased. To live with the memory of a once peaceful life and those they shared their lives with

'I' knew this battle would feed their hunger for revenge. This day 'I' felt was the E-tuc's day to redeem the revenge in their hearts and minds and fill them with satisfaction. The time had come for the 'Repssas' to learn the meaning of death from an enemy they created. An enemy that had learned to kill as merciless as the 'Repssas'. Breaking the silence again, "Fight well my friends, for we fight for more than just victory. We fight to end the wave of death. To bring back the glow of life that once existed on 'Rou' and 'Sis'. We have the right to live," 'I' said, seated in the captain's chair. Staring at 'I' without a sound, all in the control room give a nod of approval. Ordering three more probes to investigate 'Rou's' orbit. 'I' watches as the three probes rush into the dark of space seeking uninvited guests. It didn't take long for the probes to relay information back to the ship. Within dangerous territory the probes one by one became silent. One against many were the odds. Learning that 'Rou' was surrounded by ten 'Repssa' warships relentlessly bombarding the fortified strong holds 'I' knew the time was now to strike. Immediately giving the order to target the closest warship 'I' and crew leap from the outer rim of deep space and surprise a 'Repssa' warship. While the enemy had its repulser field down, 'I' gives the order to fire. Two E-tuc energy spheres expand as they race to their unsuspecting target. A round twisting ball of light and power hit the warship engulfing the warship from end to end. Lights swirled and twisted like a nest of snakes around the ship. The power of the sphere's energy was relentless. It continued to swirl and twist until the life of the ship was no more. Unable to escape the deadly swirl of blinding light, the warship floated lifeless in space. Remembering that nine other warships existed 'I' quickly orders gunner to find and target another warship. It didn't take long to find another victim. Not far away, a warship failing to react to the unusual twisting of light continued its bombardment of 'Rou'.

Burning within a cloud of smoke 'Rou' was a dark ball of flashing lights. 'I' had seen enough of the 'Repssa's' savage ways. Giving orders to attack the nearest warship two Fron Cor missiles were loaded and ready. Hoping for a fast kill, all eagerly watched their monitor. "Fire," 'I' orders. Shooting out at blinking eye speed, two missiles raced to their target only to be pushed away by the ships' reflective pulser fields. Realizing the ship was protected 'I' immediately orders two energy spheres. Determined to destroy the ship 'I' wasted no time. "Ready to fire," called out gunner. "Fire', 'I' calls out. Out from the ship two energy spheres raced true to their aim. Slamming the ship broad sided, the ship shook savagely. Tilting off course the ship seemed to twist from side to side as if struggling to escape. Moments passed as the

unrelenting ropes of twisting lights squeezed the ship's energy and life from it. Nothing more than a shell, the ship floated aimlessly in 'Rou's' orbit, lifelessly. Having felt the ship was dead, a sudden bright light glowed brightly from within the ship followed by a massive explosion. Large pieces of ship violently flew in all directions and headed endlessly into space. A massive shock wave followed shaking all nearby ships. With two warships destroyed, not a face on board drew a smile. The killing of 'Repssa' warships failed to bring satisfaction. The lives of so many fallen E-tucs could never be replaced by killing more 'Repssas'. And still the 'Repssas' had returned to kill the last of the E-tucs and leave 'Rou' lifeless. True to the thought of war, more lives would have to perish to satisfy the madness of the 'Repssas'. "Find another target," 'I' quickly orders. Scanning the darkness of 'Rou's' orbit, all were surprised to find their next target heading straight for them. All knew it was too late to target the ship. "Can our reflective pulser fields protect us?" 'I' asks. "Our reflective pulser fields are weak from massive amounts of energy used to reach 'Rou'."

"Reflective pulser fields up," 'I' orders. No sooner than ordered the attacking ship's missiles were already headed to 'I' and crew. Like thieves in the night the missiles quietly raced to their target. With reflective pulser fields up the first missile hits the fields and wildly spirals into space. Expecting the second missile to do the same, all watched. Hitting the field, the missile sliced through the weakened field and dug into the bow of the ship. Rocking the ship all braced themselves and rocked with the ship. For the first time 'I' and crew had become the hunted. Sitting patiently the look of uncertainty appeared on control room faces. "Do not be disturbed by what has happened. All have fought well. Believe in your abilities and take charge. Lead this great force and bring forth a new day of peace. You are many upon many. Hearts and minds are with you. Give the word and abandon this dying ship. Take your fight to 'Rou'."

"Lead, 'I', and all shall follow," 'SI' tells 'I'. It was a Fron Cor missile, a ticking time bomb. Heating to an incredible temperature, then blowing itself and all around it to pieces. Knowing they only had a matter of minutes, 'I' addresses the crew. "Our ship and crew have fought well. All have given their best. Now it's time to abandon the ship. We must finish our fight on 'Rou'." Expecting the crew to dash to the doorway, not an E-tuc moved. 'I' looks down at the E-tucs.

"I am sorry my friends, our ship can do no more. She has fought well and earned our respect. We can ask no more of her. She deserves to die as a warrior. Keep her in your memories and fight as she fought." Silently looking at their control panels, then control room, they stood and quietly walk to the exit door. Before the ship's navigator could take a step, "I have one last order to give navigator. Point our ship at our attacker, and give her thrust power," 'I' said. By now the ship was filling thick with smoke and was very hot. The deadly missile was very close to its detonation. Slowly the ship turns to its attacker and slowly moves forward. The over presumptuous and arrogant attacker watched as the ship moved closer. 'I' and navigator leave the control room. Stepping out the exit door 'I' turns and says, "You have done well, we will not forget." As 'I' turns and leaves, control panel lights continue to glow following last orders. Heading down to the landing bay, smoke filled the rooms thickly. Hard to see and breathe 'I' asks 'SI' to assist him to the landing bay. Picking up the little E-tuc, 'I' follows 'SI's' directions and safely arrives at the ship's landing bay entrance doorway. Glimpsing blue-green blinking lights bleeding though the thick smoke 'I' knew it was the fighter ship. The E-tucs had waited and not fled scared. They had found strength in each other and became one. Racing to the waiting fighter ship, the door quickly slides open. Stepping in, 'I' felt he was leaving a friend in need. A friend staying behind so others could reach safety. 'I' felt honored to have such a friend. Once inside 'I' quickly looks around and was surprised to find sad eyes upon him. Knowing how much the ship cost in lives and how well the ship fought. The crew had grown strongly attached to the ship. 'I' was inclined to praise the crew once more. "We have done all that was possible. Our trust and unity have served us well. One day we will fly among the stars again, now it's time to leave," 'I' said. Without a word said, the door slides shut. The fighter ship rises and exits the burning warship. Safe and clear of the dying warship all watched from a safe distance. Busting at her seams with heavy smoke trailing behind the warship drifted to her attacker, who by now was turning to evade the dying ship. As if alive and not wanting her attacker to escape. The warship shifted her course and continued heading toward her attacker. Seconds later the two warships collide into each other. A flash of blinding light and a great ball of fire lit the skies of 'Rou'. Parts of both burning ships sailed into the limitlessness of space. Looking through the fighter ship's windows, both ships were gone. The ship the E-tucs had found favor in and claimed as theirs had claimed her last victory over the 'Repssas'. Sadness was on her crew's faces. More than just a war price, the ship was one with the E-tucs. Now only a memory within the minds of her unforgetting crew. Returning to 'Rou' 'I' and crew fly over the heart of the 'Repssa' troops. Through the ship's window, masses of 'Repssa' troops readied

on the ground. Even after destroying three 'Repssa' warships a grand force of uncountable 'Repssas' stood confidently poised. So many, the ground in areas disappeared. A grand force indeed, 'I' thought. Dominating the skies, fighter ships swarmed like locusts looking for something to destroy. Firing at ground weapons, the fighter ships protected shuttle ships and troops on the ground. Land and sky the 'Repssas' assembled a firepower that would alarm and terrify any planet. Confident of their strength and power the 'Repssas' ruled 'Rou's' orbit, skies, and 'Rou' itself. Over the vastness of troops and war might the mighty 'Repssa' fighter ships flew carrying 'I' and crew. Unnoticed by the enemy 'I' and crew land near the great rock mountain. Safe and happy to be home the E-tucs and 'I' dash from the fighter ship and enter the safety of the mountain. Once inside, 'I' and crew were greeted as heroes. To have faced the enemy and performed an impossible task. Surrounded by many excited and praising E-tucs, 'I' realized how precious life was on 'Rou'. The impossible task 'I' and crew accomplished gave strength to all and propelled 'I's' leadership. As the praising and excitement died down, 'I' reminded all not to forget those that gave their precious lives. "We shall honor those by continuing the fight and winning our freedom. For the bravery that the fallen gave, all will live another day. We shall do the same for those that will follow us one day. For what we do today will bring a better tomorrow," 'I' said. Looking at the mass of E-tucs listening, the room was filled with only the vibrations of 'I's' voice. Standing silently, all knew the time of life and death was near. With a strong voice, "Ready for battle," 'I' orders. The command echoed throughout the great mountain and relayed to all other strongholds. As all readied 'I' had a moment to ponder. "Your achievements have won you much respect. Your courage and bravery have given all hope and unity. Your deeds will forever be etched in the minds of all," 'SI' said. As 'I' and E-tucs ready for the battle of their lives the enormous mass of 'Repssas' begin their advancement forward. The ground rumbled and the sky filled with ash dust. High above an ever-darkening sky, fighter ships flew over with vibrating thunder. The approach to attack had started and not an E-tuc stood ready to fight. No great force to resist the massive force that freely marched toward the rock mountains.

Still a far distance away the 'Repssas' marched unopposed. Unaware of the deadly trap that awaited the massive force the 'Repssas' marched with full intentions of completing their goal. Viewing the massive force a distance away, the massive troops gave the impression the ground was moving. Wave after wave of 'Repssas' trampled the ground one behind the other, with only destruction on their minds. Closer the threatening force approached, echoing the sound of marching and weapons clambering. Inside the rock mountains, all watched their monitors with fear of their future. As the 'Repssas' neared the dead zone they marched unknowingly onto what laid hidden under the blanket of ash. Filled with thousands of hidden weapons, the dead zone was justly named. One does not step into the dead zone and expect to walk out alive. Entering the dead zone the unsuspecting force stepped into the E-tuc's deadly trap. Springing from the ground, thousands of hidden ground weapons raked and shelled the massive 'Repssa' force. A thick, dark cloud began to form around the dead zone. Explosions began and deadly flashing light occupied the 'Repssas' trapped within the dead zone. Only those inside the zone knew what was happening. And they that fought within the cloud of darkness fought an invisible attacker. Unable to see through the dark cloud of chaos all watched and wondered if the 'Repssas' could survive the dead zone. Hoping that once visibility improved, they would see a 'Repssa' force lying upon the ground all watched in a wonder of silence. The sound of weapons firing decreased and all continued to patiently watch and wait. Slowly the wall of floating ash cleared enough to see. Thousands of 'Repssas' had fallen to the ground. And still with the massive loss of lives the 'Repssas' continued to survive. Finding and disabling the hidden weapons one by one the 'Repssas' had neutralized the dead zone. Undaunted by the massive losses, the 'Repssas' marched forward disregarding any unknown dangers. Less than a mile from the rock mountains, the Repssas' continued their march with very little resistance, having never lost a battle, their arrogance of winning stood strong. Brute force was the only way the 'Repssas' fought. To walk blindly into a deadly fire would not deter the 'Repssas'. They were to achieve their goal or die trying. Forward they continued eliminating the last of the hidden weapons. Closer they came with total destruction on their minds. Hearts raced as all watched their monitor. The enemy knew where their victims were and they were not leaving till all were dead. Unknown to 'I' a massive force was forming. A force that would follow and not be denied the right to live. Within the many mountains all waited for the signal that would send a wave of E-tucs clashing into the 'Repssas'. Realizing the moment of battle was near, 'I' turns and addresses the mighty force in waiting. "A lion is one that will not run. He will stand and fight his ground. Today we are lions, we are brave, we roar with thunder. Today we are many upon many united as one. Today we will find victory and the peace we seek. Look to the moment not the past, look to living life today," 'I' said.

A thunder of excitement and unity vibrated within the mountain's walls. Armed and ready to fight all stood and waited for the great rock door to open. While waiting 'I' catches sight of one that could have given his life meaning. One with the understanding to fill his empty heart with peace and love. Staring at her, she also sees 'I' with a serious expression on her face. Both share a moment that seemed like a lifetime. A stare of a thousand words, only to fall silent upon each other's eyes. And yet the stare was buried deep within each other's hearts. Bowing his head slightly, 'I' turns sadly. Knowing the life he yearned for was only a moment's thought in time. A twinkle of the stars he'd loved to watch. Time had other tasks for 'I' to accomplish. Standing beside 'I' was his little friend. Holding two 'Repssa' weapons, he offers one to 'I'. Grabbing a weapon 'I' smiles and nods his head. "Best of friends," his little friend says. "Yes best of friends," 'I' said. With only moments left 'I' realized he knew so little of his friend. The events of time had moved so fast. Fighting to live came before living in peace. 'I' and his friend merely shared the same moment of fighting to live. Looking down at his friend 'I' asked "Do you have a name?"

Looking up at 'I', "E-tucs don't have names. We communicate by sound pitches," he said to 'I'. "May I give you an Earth name?" 'I' asked. "It would be an honor to be given a name by the great 'I'," he replied. "I will call you Ne-Hy," 'I' said. "Does the name have meaning?" Ne-Hy asks. "Yes my friend, it has a great meaning within my mind. To me it means one of great growing abilities," 'I' said. "Then I will keep the name and continue to learn," Ne-Hy said. "Yes, Ne-Hy, we both will," 'I' said. Silence falls between 'I' and Ne-Hy as they both stare at the great rock door. "If this be the end of me 'SI', I give my best and fight for the lives of many," 'I' said. "There is never an end to one that spreads goodness. Your deeds will live on in the minds of many. From the deeds you achieve, many will flourish. They will live a life in peace and be aware of living," 'SI' said. A heavy rumbling began, and all knew where the noise was coming from. The mountain's great rock door slowly began to open. Wider and wider the door expanded until it reached its full width. From the open doorway, 'I' could see far more than he wanted to see. Standing a few hundred feet away, a great force stood waiting. A force that only knew victory was to conquer. Fully armed, 'I' and the E-tucs emerge from the mountain. Standing in front for all to see, 'I' wanted the 'Repssas' to know he lead the E-tucs to their victories. Joining 'I' were his six 'Sislen' guards and Ne-Hy. Staring at the unwavering 'Repssa' force 'I' turns facing the E-tucs. "Victory and freedom are ours today. Today we roar as lions," 'I' said. A deafening roar filled the air. A unity the E-tucs had never witnessed before. Holding his 'Repssa qualtron weapon, 'I' raises it high above his head. "We take no prisoners," 'I' cries out. Again a great roar echoes from the mountain. Refacing the 'Repssa' force 'I' fixes his eyes upon the 'Repssa' standing out in front. "'I', that is their leader, kill him first and their mighty force will lack direction," 'SI' said. Holding his qualtron weapon with both hands, 'I' starts walking toward the enemy. Faster and faster 'I' walks. Close behind, Ne-Hy and guards follow. As a word of beings exit there lost stronghold, the enemy leads his forces. Holding his 'Repssa' weapon high above his head the 'Repssa' leader waves it forward. A great wave of 'Repssas' begins to move forward. Pouring from the mountains a white sheet of E-tucs covered the ash ground. Two great forces moved toward each other soon to clash into a mighty battle of life and death. Closer and closer the two great forces advanced. Less than one hundred feet apart 'I' opens fire. Quickly 'Repssas' began to fall. A massive glow of lights and blasts began and bodies on both sides begin to fall. Determined to kill the 'Repssa' leader, 'I' began to run toward him. Closer 'I' grew only to see two blasts of flashing light strike the proud leader. Falling to the ground the leader quickly jumps to his clawed feet and staggers momentarily. An easy target, 'I' thought. Aiming his weapon at the leader, 'I' fires twice hitting the leader once in the head and once in his chest. The 'Repssa' leader again falls to the ground and moves no more. Reaching the fallen leader, 'I' quickly gazes at the fallen 'Repssa'. Immediately 'I' grabs the leader's weapon and noticed its difference in size. Aiming the weapon at a dense crowd of 'Repssas' 'I' fires the weapon. A group of 'Repssas' tumble together and fall to the ground. "Very impressive," 'I' says to himself. Firing the weapon repeatedly, scores of 'Repssas' fall and cover the ground. As the two great forces continued to clash, death claimed many by the second. Beings of advanced knowledge with advanced weapons slaughtered each other so easily. As leaves on a tree fall from a gust of wind beings of both sides fell never to rise again. Fighting to their last breath, hatred toward each other was equal. Two beings fought with the same intentions toward each other: Kill the other swiftly. The fierceness of battle raged on across the endless boundaries of mountains. Streaks of deadly-focused lights flashed into the hazed sky. Hitting many fighter ships that spiraled to the ground or exploded into many pieces the battle waged on as the field of battle collected the dying and dead. A battle with only one ending continued as each side invisioned victory. As 'I' continued to fight, his powerful weapon and body armor made him invincible to all attackers. Hit many times, 'I's' armor protected him and continued to keep him alive. Into the many long hours of fighting the two

great forces had killed many of each other. Dwindling in size and number the fight found no reason to stop. Bodies' on both sides lay thick across the field of battle. And the smell of death rose from the dead and saturated the air like a heavy vapor of fog. Thirsty and exhausted many fell to the ground only to be trampled to death. Still the battle of life and death continued with no end in sight. Holding his ground 'I' fought all attackers. One 'Repssa' after another felt the ferocious and savage hands of 'I'. And still the 'Repssas' fought with little to no fear for they had never lost a battle to know what fear was. Through the long hours of fighting, 'I's' armor finally began to weaken and show the signs of damage. Unable to restore itself and protect, 'I's' armor was a shell against the 'Repssas' weapons. Exposed to the pains of weapons fire, 'I' had no choice but to fight on to the end. Having been given the warning of critically low armor power 'I' still continued to fight on. Blast after blast the pain sank deep. Unable to move about and fight 'I' stood his ground and fought. An endless stream of 'Repssas' flowed toward 'I'. As buzzards ready to feast upon the dead they came for 'I'. Bodies of dead 'Repssas' soon surrounded 'I' including I's' six 'Sislen' loyal guards. True to their word they fought to their last breath. With no armor power left, 'I' knew his time was at hand. The sight of 'I's' blood upon his armor encouraged the 'Repssas' to attack. One after another the 'Repssas' attacked 'I', determined to kill him. Surrounded with a useless weapon and a powerless body armor 'I' continued to fight hand to hand. The red of blood began to flow from 'I's' mouth and drip onto his lifeless armor. Still 'I' fought one after another. With bloody hands 'I' grabs another 'Repssa' and breaks it's neck. As the lifeless 'Repssa' falls to the ground. 'I' is shot from behind and falls upon the lifeless 'Repssa' bodies. Darkness slowly covers 'I's' mind and the loud clash of fighting and dying slowly faded away. Lying in peace with the lifeless, the fighting continued. E-tucs continued to pour from the mountains attacking the once mighty 'Repssa' force. A force that had now dwindled into mere groups of fighters. A threat no longer, the 'Repssas' realize they were greatly outnumbered with no chance of winning. For the first time death became the 'Repssas' fear. Turning from the fight they began to run back across the dead zone. Over the cold 'Repssa' bodies that fought no more, they ran. The boldness that once held the 'Repssas" mighty force together was no more. Remembering 'I's' orders to take no prisoners, the E-tucs slaughtered the retreating 'Repssas' by the hundreds. The dead zone was named well, the dead laid everywhere. The mighty 'Repssa' force that burned 'Rou' to the ground, killed millions upon millions of E-tucs now laid still and silent among their victims. Far and wide across the field of battle, bodies of both sides laid motionless. The sounds of firing weapons and cries of the dying were silent. The madness of killing was over and a planet scared of war ended a day peacefully. The battle had lasted most of the day. And soon the night would cover the dead with a blanket of cool darkness. A darkness that would only review the stars of the night. Ne-Hy and the group that fought with him gathered together. "Where is 'I'?", Ne-Hy asks. Scanning across the field of battle, 'I' was not to be seen standing. Sending his warriors out to find 'I', they scattered in all directions across the field of battle. The word spread quickly: Find 'I'. Across the field of battle E-tucs searched for 'I'. Bodies on both sides lay thick upon the ground, making 'I's' whereabouts a hidden secret. Walking through the maze of dead bodies, Ne-Hy hears a distant cry. "Over here, over here," was the cry. Stepping quickly through the many fallen, Ne-Hy hurries straight to the caller's directions. Not knowing what he was going to see a bad feeling begins to fill his mind. "No, no, not my best of friends," Ne-Hy says to himself. Reaching a growing group of E-tucs gathering into a circle. Ne-Hy enters into the ring of heartbroken warriors. Finding 'I' lying across fallen 'Repssas', Ne-Hy's worst thoughts had come true. Approaching 'I' the feeling of losing 'I' sank deep within his mind. Grabbing 'I' in his arms, Ne-Hy gazes at his friend's lifeless body. Stained with 'I's' own blood, the great armor that protected 'I', protected him no more. Gripped in I's' hand, a deadly 'Repssa' weapon, the same weapon the 'Repssa' leader held. Bent and useless the weapon served its purpose, to kill the enemy. The worst of feelings filled Ne-Hy's mind and body. A feeling of madness and sadness upon Ne-Hy's face clearly showed how he felt. As Ne-Hy looked to the sun. A slowly setting sun gave its last hour of light. Battling the feelings inside himself, Ne-Hy continues to stare into the setting sun. "No!" Ne-Hy bursts out loudly, "You can't take him with you, 'I' wouldn't let you. 'I' will rise with the rising sun and lead once more," Ne-Hy said to the sun. Touching 'I's' neck, Ne-Hy feels a pulse. Suddenly Ne-Hy's crashing world begins to shine a bright glow of light. Filled with an unstoppable amount of joy Ne-Hy looks up almost in tears. "'I' still lives," Ne-Hy says with a quiver in his voice. Immediately Ne-Hy stands and orders his beloved warriors to pick 'I' up. Picking 'I' up, eight E-tucs hurriedly carry 'I' back to the great mountain.

Following close behind, Ne-Hy hoped that 'I' would survive. The thought of losing his friend would be too much to bear. Late of day the sun was no more than a glow of light illuminating the horizon. Bodies and war machinery covered the land as far as the eye could see. With a thick smell of smoke mixing into the smell of death even the night could not hide all

the savage day's killing. 'Rou' once more was quiet and peaceful. Freed by their own bravery, the E-tucs had changed their destiny. No longer dwellers of rock mountains by day and night they were unbound to live and rebuild anywhere on 'Rou. As the warriors continued to carry 'I', the light of the sun disappeared in its quiet and subtle way. Now the darkness of night covered the field of battle, hiding the horrors of death. And 'Rou' continued to turn as if nothing had happened. Time moved on and stood still for no one. The battle was only a mere cycle of movement in 'Rou's' travel around its sun. A time that would be forgotten within 'Rou's endless journey around it's sun. And as 'Rou' continued its course, another battle raged on. The battle of 'I' to live or die. From greatness to death 'I's' life hung between day and night. High within 'Rou's' orbit, 'Repssa' warships waited for a call of victory. Not knowing the stillness and silence of death possessed the once mighty force. The warships waited in orbit for a reply and the sun to uncover the field of battle. The day had ended with losses on both sides as a field of battle covered its brave. Through the smoke and death of battle, an ever growing following grew. Halfway to the mountain the fighting force 'I' so gallantly led into battle reformed behind him. Once again 'I' led the united E-tuc force. Following with much grief all headed toward the great mountain. With eyelids open, 'I's' sightless eyes gazed upwards toward the stars he loved so much. Through the thick smoke and haze, a star breaks through with a glow of light. The peace 'I' had sought surrounded and embraced him warmly. Carried back to the mountain that once roared with lions now fell silent. A great wall of warriors lined both sides of the mountain's entrance way. Carrying 'I' through an open path of warriors holding their 'Repssa' weapons, they bow in respect. Disappearing into the mountain the sight of 'I' caught many off guard. 'I' and the enormous following caught the attention of all. Marching deep into the mountain, the many to see 'I' were shaken by their mighty leader's armor covered in his own blood. Continuing to carry 'I' through the mountain, they pass the one being that 'I' felt could change his life and give it meaning.

Standing less than ten feet away E-tak shockingly sees 'I' and holds her hand over her mouth as 'I' is carried past. The look in her eyes equaled the sorrow in her heart. Quickly E-tak follows close behind into the enhancement room. The room 'I' first received his great powers. Quickly 'I' is laid onto the table only be levitated a few inches above the table. Carriers step back quickly and others stepped up and began removing 'I's' lifeless armor. The life of 'I' hidden between the rising and setting sun held only by a faint heart beat continued to exist from one heart beat to another. Stripped of armor, the great minds that once restored 'I', hurriedly tended to 'I's' many wounds. Using devices adjusted to their fingers, the healers endlessly sealed 'I's' many outer wounds. Small bursts of energy light awoke the great 'SI' within 'I's' head. Quickly 'SI' directs the thousands of tiny 'Ms' within 'I's' body to repair internal tissue and damaged organs. Bursts of energy light continue to bombard 'I's' body feeding energy to the many 'M's'. Heart beat after heart beat 'I's' life hung with one foot at death's doorway. 'SI' informs the healers the loss of blood and internal damage will take time to restore. Time to live was uncertain for 'I'. For 'I' lived in the darkness of time. After many hours of repairing 'I's' body. 'SI' informs healers 'I's' bodily functions were under control. Satisfied of 'I's' improving condition the healers decide to leave. As 'I' laid in darkness, the darkness of the night covered the planet. A planet that witnessed a great battle rested in stillness healing its many wounds. And still a silent battle raged on. To live or die no one knew if 'I' would see another day. Hovering above the table with only instruments and flashing lights repairing and recharging 'I's' damaged body. The sight of 'I' living or dying became the worriers of a world of beings to live or die. Not far away many battle weary E-tucs stood the night never laying to rest. To lose 'I' would again put 'Rou' into uncertain times. A time the E-tucs did not want to return to. An endless stream of E-tucs began to pass 'I' giving their respects and a stare of sadness. Not far away Ne-Hy looks on fighting the emptiness of losing his best of friends, 'I'. Wondering if he had learned enough from 'I' to lead 'Rou's' forces, Ne-Hy looked on remembering the first sight of 'I' and all that had transpired from that day. The dangers of living, both had lived and fought through it all. Now 'I' laid battling for his life, leaving Ne-Hy alone once again. As 'I' laid in mental darkness, time and all that he knew didn't exist. Endlessly working on 'I's' brain the many 'Ms' restored all damage, giving 'I' the ability to dream. Images began to flash into 'I's' darkness. 'I' began to ride the wave of life. To view his life from childhood to adulthood. His achievements and downfalls. His friends he left behind and his way of life. The last image of Earth and the sun that gave life to all. All gone with only a memory of another life. And now on a faraway planet 'I' still lived with an emptiness in his life. With abilities far above humans and the beings he fondly protected 'I' still had one great weakness. A weakness that would take all his strength and knowledge to conquer. To find someone that could mirror his reflection of love and happiness. To live and share a life with someone meant more than all a planet's wealth.

Slowly fading away, 'I's' dreams of his past disappear into the darkness of space. Again 'I' walked within the darkness of a starless space. Pulled between the past and future, 'I' walked alone searching for his rightful place in life. The next day the sun rose casting a dim light on a planet painted with the madness of war. Bodies upon bodies reappeared reminding all that the day before was not a dream. A battle that took the hearts of many laid lifeless as a reminder to all. Even though the E-tucs had won, 'Rou's' orbit was still controlled by 'Repssa' warships. Not knowing the battle's outcome warship commanders order fighter ships to investigate the battle. One after another, fighter ships leave the warships and dip into 'Rou's' upper most skies. Heading downward to the field of battle swarms of fighter ships infest 'Rou's' skies. Swarming low to the ground they fly thinking they were victorious once again. Running for cover and jumping to the ground, many believed the 'Repssas' were attacking once more. Back and forth the fighter ships fly searching for their mighty force. The once mighty 'Repssa' force that feared no one and defeated all, were defeated by beings more determined to live. Now the 'Repssa' force laid still and silent.

Watching from a safe location, Ne-Hy realizes the fighter ships were only investigating the battle's progress. Seeing for themselves the scattered dead, the fighter ships quickly returned to the safety of their warships. Watching the fighter ships return to their warships, Ne-Hy realized they needed to regroup and rearm as many fighters as possible. If a second wave of 'Repssas' attacked the outcome may be different. Their losses were great and the loss of 'I' to lead would affect many. Returning back to the safety of the warships the fighter ships fly bringing the results of an unbelievable battle outcome. Stunned warship commanders were baffled of the battle's final outcome. With no more troops to stage another attack warship commanders realized the battle was over. Now they would withdraw and answer for their defeat. Giving the order the lead commander leaves 'Rou's' orbit followed by the remaining warships. As Ne-Hy looked to the once infested skies 'I's' life stayed locked within his mind. During 'I's' recovery, Ne-Hy planned to regroup 'Rou's forces and ready 'Rou' for another attack. Once awake 'I' would reclaim his rightful position. As the forces regrouped, the clearing of the battlefield's dead became as massive as the battle itself. Every available E-tuc that could help was helping. As Ne-Hy watched the massive clearing, an anger of revenge burned inside of him.

"One day,' Ne-Hy thought," "I will have my revenge for those of 'Rou' you have killed. I will release the fire that burns inside me upon you. Then you will know the feeling of real pain."

Returning to the great rock mountain Ne-Hy pays 'I' a visit. Staring at a still and silent 'I", Ne-Hy feels the pain of sadness. Stepping close to 'I', "Awaken my friend, we have not finished our work. There is much to be done, and your leadership is greatly needed," Ne-Hy said softly. Still 'I' lay without a movement or sound. His battle-weary body still mending itself from within walked within darkness. Searching for a glance of light, the lion that roared on the field of battle now rested within his lair. Stepping back Ne-Hy bows his head, turns, and walks away. As Ne-Hy walks away 'I' hovers over the table with only a soft light glowing above him. Within the darkness and quietness of the room 'I' is visited once more. A tall figure covered from head to foot slowly approaches 'I'. It was the 'Sislen' leader's daughter. Stepping close to 'I' she sadly looks at him. Unable to communicate mentally, her words fell silent. To have wanted to say so much, her thoughts and feelings stayed bottled inside of her. Without a word her eyes began to fill with sorrow. Placing her hand on 'I's' hand she feels no life from the once mighty warrior that led 'Rou's' forces. "Awaken, 'I', we need you so much. I have so much to say to you," E-tak said. Unable to say another word, her grief began to overwhelm her feelings. A tear escapes her eye and softly splashes onto 'I's' cheek. Turning quickly she hastily walks away. Once again 'I' hovers above the table alone. Within 'I's' darkness the great 'SI' directs the many 'Ms' repairing 'I's' body. 'SI' would not let 'I' die. For 'SI' not only served the E-tuc's greatness, he lived, himself, within the greatness of 'I'.

Many hours later healers returned and communicated with 'SI' learning that 'I's' body had mended and was ready to awaken. The healers requested 'SI' to awaken 'I'. Sending a message to awaken 'I', 'I's' body refused to respond. No twitch of muscle no movement of eyes. 'I' still walked within the darkness of time, searching for a star to light his way. Disappointed, healers stare without a word. Not completely understanding a human's brain they decide to let 'I' rest till the rising of the sun. The hours of the daylight drifted into the darkness of night. And the minds of many cradled 'I' within their thoughts. As 'I' laid in darkness images of 'Rou' began flashing one after another. His ship, his new friends, the lives and pain they lived, and the deadly 'Repssas' darkening 'Rou'. Flashes of violence unfolded into a clash of deadly war. Dreams so true and the pain of attacks angered the sleeping lion. Hand to hand 'I' fought feeling the intense pain with warm blood

trickling down his body. Furious within his dreams 'I' began to twitch and shudder. One violent vision after another invoked 'I' from his wondering. The battle was at hand and the lion roared within his lair. Quickly sitting up, 'I' was no longer asleep. No longer fighting the 'Repssas' within his dreams. 'I' had returned to the living to finish his quarrel with 'Repssas'. Quickly looking about, 'I' had the look of battle burning deep in his eyes. Jumping from the table, 'I' lands sure-footed on the floor. Quickly 'I' gives his first order. "Armor." 'I' is swiftly covered from head to toe. A new untouched armor covered 'I's' body. Fully energized it sparkled of unimaginable power. Power that would entice all to bow and his enemies to panic of fear. 'I' once again stood in greatness only with no one to see. "'I'", cries 'SI', "the battle is over. We were victorious. The once great 'Repssa' force is no more. 'Rou' is controlled by the E-tucs."

"And my friend, is he?" 'I' asked slowly. "Ne-Hy lives and has been waiting for you to awaken. As all on 'Rou' have been waiting," 'SI' said. "How long have I slept?" 'I' asked. "Less than two days," 'SI' said. "I cannot remember the complete battle 'SI'. Parts of the battle are missing, only fragments exist. I remember 'Repssa' after 'Repssa' attacking. Flashes of light and blast after blast that I endured. The feeling of warm blood leaving my body. Then darkness and calmness held me tight."

"You fought bravely 'I', and all followed you," 'SI' said. "I must return to the field of battle. I need to have the feeling of closure within my mind," 'I' said. "Now!" 'SI' said. "Yes Now!" 'I' said. "The sun has set and all is quiet," 'SI' said. "I must find what is missing, and I must find it now," 'I' said. Making his way to the great door 'I' encounters two E-tucs guarding the door. Stunned to see 'I', they stare a hard-to-believe stare then quickly bow their heads. Quickly raising their heads they look again in disbelief. Ordering the guards to open the door, the guards quickly obey. Slowly the door rumbles open a few feet. Motioning to stop the door 'I' turns to the guards, "Follow me."

Out from the mountain they walk. Stretched across the field of battle a ghostly shadow hovered over the ground, covering the horrors that befell the ground. Staring across the endless field of battle. "I remember very little 'SI'," 'I' said. "All you need to know, is that you fought like a lion and led many to victory. Your orders were carried out. No 'Repssa' prisoners were taken. You were badly wounded and fell upon the dead. Found and brought back into the mountain. Your wounds were mended and healed. A new suit of armor fully charged, covers your body. All have been waiting for you to awaken," 'SI' said. Facing the endless field of battle the enormous wreckage of machinery and bodies were gone. Still 'I' could hear the savage cries of fighting and dying deep within his head. "One of good heart and mind could never accept killing as a way of solving one's problems," 'SI' said. "If the 'Repssas' seek war we will give war, if they seek answers we will give them answers," 'I' said. "True, the 'Repssas' know no other way. Killing and dying is the only way they know. Keep your heart untainted and your mind clear of another's bad deeds and you will find yourself a wise leader. Stay who you are, 'I', don't let your heart be filled with revenge. Move on in life and let all prosper," 'SI' said. "I will remember your words of wisdom, 'SI', and be true to myself as well as others," 'I' said. "Have we heard from 'Sis'?" 'I' asked. "We are not able to receive any replies from 'Sis'," 'SI' said. "I remember three 'Repssa' war ships on course for 'Sis'," 'I' said. Realizing 'Sis' was in danger 'I" immediately turns to the guards. "Go and wake our leaders, I have something very important to say," 'I" said. Having never woken the leaders at night the guards stare at 'I' unsure of what to do. Staring back at the guards 'I' reinforces his verbal command. "That is an order," 'I' said. Looking at each other the two guards turn to 'I', bow and quickly walk back into the rock mountain. Alone on the ghostly field of battle 'I' is watched by a lonely figure standing at the mountain's door. Briskly walking toward 'I' 'I' turns to the approaching figure. With each other in view they move boldly toward each other. Stopping a small distance between each other they gaze at each other upon the once field of battle. A small smile indicating their great friendship also meant far more than words could ever describe. Feelings of great honor saturated their minds. To see each other filled far more than hearts. Only to be masked by their honorable respect for each other. Bowing their heads with great respect, "It is good to lay my eyes upon a bold warrior," 'I' said. 'I' pauses holding back the great feelings inside of him. "A warrior you are, a friend you are. You fought the undefeated enemy fiercely and won. Then you found me and kept the cold hand of death from carrying me away. You are truly a leader to follow," 'I' said. Staring at Ne-Hy with the look of gratefulness upon his face. "I still have much to learn to be a leader. More than being brave, a leader must have the confidence of those he leads," Ne-Hy said. "You have my full confidence, my friend, there is no doubt in my mind to your leadership," 'I' said. "I will continue to watch and learn by your side. There is no other way," Ne-Hy said. "A new day of freedom has begun for 'Rou'. We must continue the spread of freedom for all. And that includes freedom on 'Sis'. Their situation of life or death may be critical. I have sent two guards to bring the leaders to me," 'I' said.

With the look of dumbfound shock upon Ne-Hy's face, "Now," Ne-Hy said. "Yes, now, it is of great importance that 'Sis' not fall into the 'Repssa's' control. We must give aid to 'Sis' if needed. The stability of 'Sis' is vitally important. Peace must grow and continue to grow within the hearts of all," 'I' said.

Without a word Ne-Hy nods his head in agreement. As their conversation came to an end an ever increasing noise erupts from the rock mountain. Following the four 'Rou' leaders leading an ever-growing flow of E-tucs and 'Sis' from the mountain. A glow of light began to light the night. Word of 'I' had spread to all. Hurrying to see for themselves, the night came alive. Hoping for a private conversation, 'I' knew that would be impossible. Through a hazed and gloomy night, so many quickly followed the awakened leaders. From a distance two lone figures stood and waited for an ever-growing mass of curious minds to reach them. Determined and excited to see for themselves, all rushed madly to get a glimpse. Reaching 'I' and Ne-Hy many holding lights turned the gloomy night into day. To the many hopeful wondering eyes they saw for themselves. It was 'I' standing tall, powerful and confident. Once the leaders reached 'I', they stopped, then looked up to 'I'. Kneeling on one knee, 'I' bows his head to the leaders. Eye to eye, 'I' is greeted with much delight. The smiles on their faces and glow of happiness restored 'I's' hope for a better life. Knowing more important matters were still unsolved. 'I' focused his thoughts on the 'Repssas'. To finish their spread of death and destruction. Longing to know of the situation on 'Sis'. 'I' felt if 'Sis' couldn't' live in peace nor would 'Rou' with neighbors like the 'Repssas'. After the leaders had greeted 'I' so warm-heartedly 'I' felt it was time to release the fears that pained his mind. "O' great leaders of 'Rou', I am thankful for another day to live. To find myself out from the darkness I wandered in. And become part of the whole once more. I will continue to use my powers and abilities for peace. To protect 'Rou' from all invaders that can bring harm to 'Rou'," 'I' said. With a smile of great honor a leader says to 'I', "You have done more than we on 'Rou' could have imagined. Your gallantry and bravery have given us back our freedom, our planet, our way of life. We owe you for more than we can ever repay. The leader pauses as the other three leaders nod their heads in agreement.

"Your call for us was urgent, we are here 'I', as we will always be. What troubles your mind 'I'?" the leader softly asks. "'Rou' will never be secure as long as 'Sis' is plagued by hostiles. Her hostiles will one day conquer 'Sis' and be back within 'Rou's' orbit soon after. We must reach out to 'Sis' and help secure her future. To have 'Rou' and 'Sis' as allies would ensure the peace on both planets. We must help 'Sis', O' great leaders. Our lives now and in the future depend on the stability of 'Sis'," 'I' said.

Knowing the E-tucs had paid a heavy price with the lives of many 'I' was not sure what he was to hear. Silence filled the night's air. A look of sadness filled the leader's eyes. 'I' knew it would take more lives to secure 'Sis'. 'I' felt saddened to be the bringer of death. Suddenly Ne-Hy steps next to 'I'. "'I' is correct, we must help 'Sis'. We must not let the 'Repssas' destroy all life on 'Sis'," Ne-Hy said. Silence fell again as the leaders paused again gazing at 'I' and Ne-Hy. Not a sound broke the stillness of the night. Not even a small breeze of air. With a look of great content, a leader steps forward breaking the silence and bringing an answer to 'I's' concerns of 'Sis'. "When the 'Repssas' first attacked 'Rou', we were without defenses. No grand force to fight back with and no great leader to lead. We suffered greatly for our lack of planet protection. With only mountains to hide in. We lost millions upon millions of lives. Daily we feared for our lives and hunger was known to all. Unable to defend ourselves we waited for death to claim one after another. Our way of life had changed as the sun rose and set daily. Now we have won a great battle. Defeating our enemy we felt was unbeatable. We have won our freedom and planet. Now we stand united, united with weapons ready to protect all of 'Rou'. Your bravery has given us strength to fight and defeat the 'Repssas'. You are correct 'I', we must help 'Sis'. Her stability is vital to an alliance with us."

Putting his hand on 'I's' shoulder, the leader looks at 'I', eye to eye. "Rise 'I' and show all you are ready to lead once again. We are with you in every way we can be," the leader said. Rising, 'I' stood for all to see. The might and power of 'I' spoke loudly in the eyes of all ready to follow. A great strength of unity and pride erupted among the many that had gathered. No longer collecting knowledge, the E-tucs were using their knowledge to fight back. With 'I's' power and strength lying in those that believed in him. 'I' stood supreme as 'Rou's' grand military leader. Confident of their regained freedom and 'I's return 'Rou' now focused their knowledge and abilities to travel the stars and aid 'Sis' in her time of despair. 'I' turns to Ne-Hy, "We need a ship," 'I' says. Without a sound Ne-Hy points to a distant rock mountain. "I have acquired two large 'Repssa' transport ships. The ships will meet our needs and be able to reach 'Sis'. Crews have been repairing and modifying the ships. They are not fit for combat against 'Repssa' warships, but both will be space worthy," Ne-Hy said. "When will repairs be complete?" 'I' asked. "When

the sun rises we will inspect," Ne-Hy said. "Find crews for the ships and take all the medical supplies and rations we can safely carry," 'I' says. Without a word Ne-Hy nods his head. As 'I' and Ne-Hy stand together, they watch the many E-tucs and Sislens rejoice their freedom. Sadden, 'I' knew that 'Sis' would have to defeat the 'Repssas'. Standing in the midst of the rejoicing, 'I' begins to hear voices in his head. "'SI', what is this I hear?" 'I' asks. "You hear the Sislens communicating with each other. They are happy you have asked 'Rou's' leaders to give aid to 'Sis' in her time of need. But it is the three 'Repssa' war ships that worries the Sislens so much. They are not sure they have a home to return to. They fear they are the last of their kind. With your telepathic ability 'I', you can speak to them," 'SI' said. Focusing his thoughts 'I' speaks within his head. "We have finished our quarrel with the 'Repssas' on 'Rou'. Now we will take our quarrel to 'Sis' and finish it there. Two transport ships will leave for 'Sis' soon. The ships will carry all the 'Sis' warriors that will board. Who among you will return and fight the 'Repssas'?" 'I' asked. A cry of many voices erupted into a riot of eager warriors ready to battle. To live or die the Sislens would have it no other way. They were ready to save their planet. It was a night that gave strength to many. To see 'I' once more in all his might. To know of plans to unite 'Rou' and 'Sis' in friendship. And know that 'Rou's' leaders and warriors were ready to follow 'I' once more. The ghostly night was ending with rays of soft sunlight cutting through 'Rou's' haze. As the new day crept in, excitement filled the air of a new beginning. And with all the excitement 'I' still felt saddened of all the lives lost. "How great a loss must the enemy suffer to understand one's arrogance? How much more can the 'Repssas' sacrifice to understand their attacks are futile?" 'I' said to himself. With 'I's' spirit of confidence shaken 'I' requested help from 'SI' to ease the pain within his troubled mind. "The rewards of peace are far greater than the rewards of war. That is why so many fought and gave their lives. We must finish our battle with the 'Repssas' so the dreams of peace will become reality. And their bravery and sacrifice will not have been in vain," 'SI' said. "I understand, 'SI', their lives they gave so bravely will not be in vain. Peace will flourish, 'SI', it is written in the stars." 'I' still felt he was the bringer of death. To have led so many to their final resting ground. "How will time judge us, 'SI'?" 'I' asked. "Time is known only to the living. They write the events of time. The changing of the universe, the existence of life on planets, their rise and fall, their achievements and defeats. As the universe continues its endless and timeless changes the living will watch and record all they see. And the living will write of a great leader who came from a distant star and brought peace to many in their time of need," 'SI' said. In a soft thought 'I' tells 'SI', "Thank you, 'SI'."

Standing with Ne-Hy a tear rolls down 'I's' cheek. May we never fight another battle. May the 'Repssas' see their misguided ways and withdraw from 'Sis', 'I' thinks to himself. As 'I's' heart and mind tug at his feelings, a voice enters his mind. Turning, a familiar figure walks toward him. A glow of light and happiness filled his heart. It was the council's daughter of 'Sis'. As she approached, the scattered sunlight sparkled around her beauty with every step she took. Walking up to 'I' she stares into 'I's' grieving eyes. Soothing 'I's' heart and mind with just a stare, 'I's' worries begin to fade away. Still 'I's' words fell silent as he stared into her cheerful eyes. Knowing so little of the council's daughter 'I' fought within himself to hear his own voice. Noting 'I's' loss of words, she speaks. "All have been greatly concerned for you. I found my days troubling thinking of you. Your injuries were very serious. I feared the worse was upon you. It is good to see you of good health," the council's daughter says. Still looking in her eyes, 'I' finds his voice. "What is your name," 'I' asks softly. With a small smile she says, "I am called E~tak."

"Since I first met you I have pondered your name," 'I' said, pausing with an inquisitive look. "I am grateful so many have been concerned about me. It is good to be alive and experience life once again," 'I' said. Not holding back her thoughts. "I would like to know more of you," E~tak says. "It would help us both to know of each other and the problems we face," 'I' said. The day was young and bursting with busy growth. 'I' and E~tak find time to share their many secrets of life. Amazed and surprised of their beliefs and customs., both found each other's company exhilarating. Learning that E~tak was a daughter of the ruling class. She with her father met many important influential dignitaries. All worked together to improve life on 'Sis'. E~tak's curiosity showed in her many questions. Understanding why E~tak asked so many questions 'I' hoped it would help bridge a lasting friendship for 'Rou' and 'Sis'. 'I' could only hope that E~tak would help 'I' to persuade leaders of 'Sis' to unite a bond of friendship and combine forces with 'Rou'. Staring at E~tak something deep in her eyes expressed her heart and feelings. 'I' knew she could see the same in his eyes. Their telepathic ability was starting to reveal more than they discussed in words. Keeping 'I' from devouring her most personal thoughts. Silence falls from E~tak as she stares away from 'I'. Deciding to discuss solutions to their many problems their planets possessed 'I' felt a strong alliance was needed first. To trust in each other and have a willingness to keep the peace. To arm and protect each other as their own.

With a smile E~tak agrees. "We shall both address our leaders and emphasize the need for a strong alliance," E~tak says. Suddenly E~tak stops talking and portrays a more serious look upon her face. Looking to the distant sky, "I must take the trip to 'Sis' with you," E~tak says. Giving E~tak the same serious stare he would give his enemy, 'I' knew how dangerous the trip could be. Traveling in a modified transport ship not yet proven for space travel. And the dangers of space could kill all before the 'Repssas' could, 'I' thought. "No he says to her, you're not going. It's just too dangerous."

"I must, if my father is not alive. I must take his place and be part of the ruling on 'Sis'," E~tak says. Once again 'I' and E~tak stare into each other's eyes. A stare of "no" from 'I' and a stare of "I must go" from E~tak drifted silently back and forth. Staring at E~tak, 'I' stood as the grand warrior with piercing eyes and a will to dominate any power against him. Stepping close to 'I', E~tak places a hand on 'I's' chest of armor. Submitting to 'I's' awesome power and authority she looks up to 'I' showing 'I' a look of helplessness. "'I' trust my life with you and no one else."

Looking down at E~tak with a stare that only an enemy would see, "The trip will be very risky and very dangerous. We could all be killed if we confront a 'Repssa' warship," 'I' said. "Then we shall die together," E~tak said. "I would prefer them to die, I want to live," 'I' said. Stepping back from 'I', E~tak shows 'I' a friendly smile. Slightly bowing her head in full respect. E~tak, without a word, turns and walks back to the great rock mountain. Looking across the hazed horizon 'I' noticed Ne-Hy no more than a few hundred feet away. Moving toward him, a big smile clung to his face. Ne-Hy knew E~tak had gotten her way over 'I'. Years of negotiating gave E~tak the ability to succeed in solving difficult problems and 'I' had felt the sting of a powerful negotiator. Even if it took a female's enchanting powers, E~tak's ability to negotiate equaled 'I's' awesome fighting abilities and powers. 'I' still had much to learn.

Catching on to what had just happened 'I' tells 'SI', "Not a word, not a single word." As 'I' waited for Ne-Hy to reach him, all was silent as 'I' had ordered. Reaching 'I', Ne-Hy holding his 'Repssa' weapon stops and looks up. "It is time to inspect the transport ships," Ne-Hy said. "Very well," 'I' said. A beautiful day by 'Rou's' standards, persuaded 'I' and Ne-Hy to make the trip by walking. Their journey would take them across the field of battle into the dead-zone where scores of 'Repssas' once covered a charred ground. As they began their journey not a sign of the horrible battle existed. Only memories of killing and death stained the minds of the living. A covered sky of haze gradually gave way in spots to brilliant sun rays illuminating the ground. An exciting new beginning for 'Rou' had begun. Life on 'Rou' was given a second chance, to grow and flourish as all on 'Rou' imagined. As 'I' and Ne-Hy walked to their destination workers would stop and give an honorable head bow. Returning the honor 'I' and Ne-Hy would continue their journey. The faces of many gleamed happiness across a once angry land. On and on 'I' and Ne-Hy walked with much on their minds. As 'I' walks, 'SI' fills 'I's' mind with mental pictures of how the land he walked on looked many years ago. Rising structures of many shapes glistened under a yellow sun. With vehicles of many shapes flying from one place to another. Yet of all the amazing wonders of their once brilliant civilization, 'I's' fascination was a clear blue sky with white fluffy clouds drifting slowly. A reminder of his boyhood dreams. To fly the skies free as a bird and gaze upon a beautiful land. After much walking and many head bows, 'I' and Ne-Hy finally reach their destination. A large rock mountain a few hundred feet long shielded their eyes from the ships. Staring at the rock mountain, Ne-Hy looks up at 'I'. "We need to reach the other side," Ne-Hy said. Without another word both proceeded to the end of the mountain. Not knowing what 'I' was to see 'I's' only concern was to make the trip to 'Sis' and destroy the 'Repssas'. Reaching the end of the mountain, a large shadow protrudes from the mountain's end and covers the ground. Large and unidentifiable the shadow could only be known of its true form by those that labored endlessly. Edging around the rock mountain's end the growing shadow formed an oblong shape. Suddenly the sound of many workers and machinery distracted 'I' and Ne-Hy. Completely around the mountain 'I' and 'Ne-Hy stopped and stood before two very large transport ships. The size and shape gave little wonder as to how the 'Repssas' mobilized such a large force. One ship alone could carry hundreds of fighters, 'I' thought. The spoils of those that had never lost a battle were now part of the growing might of the victors. As 'SI' had said, "The living will recorded history and the victors will record the battles. Now 'I" had a chance to write himself into 'Rou's' history. To be the one that restored peace and united two planets that had mirrored each other for thousands of years. Watching the many workers, long lines of workers entered and exited the ships with useable and un-useable items. On top of the ships and beneath the ships workers covered the ships like busy ants. Every inch of the ships outer hull gave a brightly shinning glow. A striking different appearance from the 'Repssas' dull version. Still the ships held the original 'Repssa' shape. Not noticing 'I' and Ne-Hy watching, the massive overhaul continued at a frantic pace. Frozen in amazement 'I' and Ne-HY watched. It

didn't take long before both were noticed. Approaching 'I' and Ne-Hy, were two very distinguished looking E-tucs. Stopping a few feet away they stood in silence. Speechless they bowed their heads. Staring with astonishment upon their faces. One finds the courage and speaks. "It is you, the one that leads many. The one that brings hope and peace to all. The stories of your great victories grow daily. I have only heard of the great warrior of 'I'. Now I see with my own eyes. 'I' is alive and really exists. We are truly honored you are here. Elated to have met 'I'. The two E-tucs stare at 'I' in amazement. "I live by the grace and generosity of all on 'Rou'. We stand together as one," 'I' said. Bowing his head once again the crew director quickly invites 'I' and Ne-Hy to inspect the ships. As 'I' walks to the ships, eyes of many fix on 'I's' presence. Covered in his mighty battle armor, all stood still and silent as 'I' passed by. Reaching the first ship, 'I' and Ne-Hy enter only to be astonished. Sparkling of newness the interior was splendidly impressive. A very large room made for many soldiers gleamed of readiness. Proud of the diligent work and achievements 'I' nods his head to the ship's director. Silence falls as 'I' turns to the workers who had gathered close by. "You have honored all of 'Rou' and those that will use these ships. The quality and ingenuity of this ship are shining examples of greatness to follow. All have given their best as we who use these ships will give our best. We are many, we are strong, we are one. We will fight for our survival and never feel the pain of defeat again," 'I' said. A loud rush of excitement echoed within the ship's walls. The E-tucs had finally found what they missed for so long, unity. Standing alert and proud the aroused crowd gave another great cheer. Then as quickly as they had gathered they returned to work at their frantic pace. Guiding 'I' and Ne-Hy to the ship's control room:A totally new and refurbished room existed. Stepping inside, controls and lights lit up. Before 'I' could say a word, 'I" is informed by a control room voice: "The presence of 'I' has been recognized, I await your command. As the control room doors close, the crew director stares at 'I' and Ne-Hy. "Your mission to 'Sis' is of great importance. I have been ordered to equip these ships with the best armor and power we have." "It is an honor to know these ships are worthy of traveling to 'Sis', 'I' said with a mighty spirit of power in his voice."

Leading 'I' and Ne-Hy to an empty area within the control room. A small red beam of light shines upward from the floor. Both stood and watched as the distinguished director waved his hand over the red light. Lights shine upward from the floor, unfolding in midair into a long rectangular screen. Speaking to the floating screen the director asks for ship's schematics. Bow to stern all aspects of the ship's components were divulged. The crew director had done his best. Both ships were completely redesigned and were equipped with storage rooms and very large rooms to carry many soldiers. 'I' and Ne-Hy knew they needed many soldiers to stop the 'Repssas' force. A grand plan of remodeling two transport ships in less than three days was nearing completion. Crowds of E-tucs willing to follow 'I' and journey to 'Sis' grew outside the two ships. Wide eyed and smiling, 'I' and Ne-Hy's best words of appreciation were in their secretive smiles. "May you both continue your victories and lead 'Rou' once more to peace and prosperity," the director said. Still with a smile, "We stand ready and confident to achieve our goals. To reach 'Sis', to defeat the 'Repssas' and bond a lasting friendship with the Sislens. A friendship that will flourish with prosperity for 'Sis' and 'Rou'," 'I' said.

"May 'Sis' and 'Rou' prosper to heights never seen before," Ne-Hy said. 'I' and Ne-Hy were once again bound on a journey to face the unknown. To defy with their lives and many other lives the dangers of space with mere transport ships. To land on a planet infested with 'Repssa' and dare them the right to stay. Dangers of many kinds waited hidden in the unknown of space far, far away.

Exiting the control room the tour continued. Passing the eyes of many inquisitive workers who completely stopped working the tour slowly drifted from room to room. For many having never seen 'I', their eyes answered their many questions they could have asked. The stories of 'I' were really true. For so many that had traveled from 'Rou's' farthest distances. They believed what they saw. As 'I' drifted by, many froze stiff at the size and reality of 'I'. The many stories of 'I" seemed exaggerated until 'I' walked by. Their hopes and dreams of living another day were protected by the leadership of a being from a far distant star, and he was called 'I'. To the largest room to the smallest of rooms the tour continued. So much had been done in so short of time. 'I' and Ne-Hy were truly impressed by such diligent workers. Still, deep within 'I's' mind, cries of pain and suffering loudly persisted and pressed 'I' to depart from 'Rou' as soon as possible. A troubled feeling within 'I's' mind existed, covered by a facial expression of unstoppable power. Knowing the ships were just modified transport ships 'I' knew the trip would be dangerous and take longer to arrive at 'Sis'. Time was working against those that needed help and 'I' felt defenseless to help. "Seek strength from within yourself 'I' and wear it for all to see. Know your course and your confidence will soar. What is to be, you cannot change. Time waits for no one," 'SI' said. 'I' understand 'SI',

"A leader cannot lead without confidence and inner strength. And victory is only won by courage and leadership," 'I' said. "Yes 'I', your courage and leadership have won another day for all on 'Rou'. Now you will once more lead a great force and win another day for 'Sis'. Letting peace and unity spread to all. You are not alone 'I', many believe in you. Their knowledge and the lives they live, they give to follow you."

Leading 'I' and Ne-Hy to the last room, both suspected the last room was very important. Guarding the doorway two E-tucs stood with pride and 'Repssa' weapons in hand. Seeing 'I', their faces gleamed with respect. Stopping less than ten feet away, 'I' looks down at the guards. "Your bravery has not been forgotten. You both hold the enemy's most guarded weapon. A weapon the 'Repssa' wouldn't give up unless dead. I bow in great respect to your bravery," 'I' said. Standing straight 'I' bows his head. The two guards bow in return. With head raised 'I' stares at the two guards. "I still have much need of bravery such as yours," 'I' said. Staring up at 'I' a much honored and respectful guard says, "We are ready to fight with you. Lead 'I' and we will follow you anywhere." Bowing to 'I' again the two guards step aside and give way to all entering the room. Inside the room 'I' and Ne-Hy understand why guards guarded the door. A much improved sphere's cannon rested untainted and ready for action. A weapon the 'Repssas' had no defense against. Four spheres cannon operators stood within the room. Bowing to 'I' they stood in silence and awe. The room was spotless and battle ready. Looking at the four cannon operators 'I' speaks. "Fight well my friends for the day will come when all on board will depend on you. Bravery comes in the worst of battle. When all seems hopeless the bravest will rise and save the day." 'I' bows to the operators and they bow in return. As 'I' stares at the spheres cannon, the whisper of a dangerous journey began to fade away. Their meager transport ship had been turned into a killing machine. Standing next to 'I', Ne-Hy looks up at 'I'. "Our strength grows daily. We grow closer to protecting our planet and regaining the peace we seek," Ne-Hy said. "We are learning to work together as one. To insure the peace we seek, we must first show we can protect it. To band together and use our combined strength and knowledge. To build the strongest orbital defensive forces we can imagine. And maintain a land force that can stand against the mightiest wave of terror," 'I' said. Staring up at 'I', the director added to his list of improvements. "This ship not only has a spheres cannon she is also equipped with a reflective pulser field. Even with our newly improved power the transport ship can only maintain its reflective pulser field for only a short while against a 'Repssa' warship. If confronted, you must be quick and precise with your attack," the director said. "We have learned to be quick and precise. 'Repssas' give no second chances," Ne-Hy said. The three give each other a smile of hope and courage. Congratulating the director on such an excellent ship transformation 'I' and Ne-Hy decide to leave. Exiting the room 'I' turns to the guards. "Guard well, we live another day by winning our battles," 'I' said. Bowing his head 'I' turns and walks with Ne-Hy down the hallway. Through the ship 'I' and Ne-HY retrace their earlier paths. Wondering, curious, and proud eyes follow the mighty warriors. Word had spread 'I' was within the transport ship inspecting. Waiting to get a glimpse of 'I', eyes of thousands focus on the entrance door. Exiting the transport ship, 'I' steps onto the inclined walkway and stops. Scanning from left to right, rolls and rolls of E-tucs filled the work area. 'I' had not seen that many E-tucs since the 'Repssas' attacked. A great silence swept through the astonished workers. High above the workers, 'I' stood as a giant looking down. No longer a wonder upon 'Rou 'I' stood as a great warrior and leader. With the backing of 'Rou's' leaders and warriors, 'I' spearheaded the might of 'Rou'. Looking for more than a glimpse of 'I' a silent crowd stared patiently. Not a whisper of sound, only bewildered staring eyes. The stillness of the moment waited for a sound. Suddenly, thump, thump, thump, thump, thump, broke the silence. It was Ne-Hy once again stepping forward. Proudly standing beside 'I', Ne-Hy looked down upon the gathered crowd and spoke. "We stood on the verge of being extinct. Our weapons were few our food was rationed. We hid within the darkness of the rock mountains without a whisper. Our beautiful skies and glowing sun became clouded with ash. The ground became cold and lifeless. We were without hope. Disarrayed and helpless to fight back. we were living our last days in sadness and darkness. From an unknown star, a ship arrives and lands on our planet. Emerging from that ship a leader of great courage set foot on our planet. A leader that has lead us to victory after victory. We that know and follow him call him 'I', 'Rou's' first grand leader."

The knowing of 'I' or the thrilling stories told of 'I' broke the calmness of the crowd into a cheering uproar. Looking up at 'I' with a smile, Ne-Hy gives a prideful stare. Before 'I' could say a word, 'I' hears another voice. It was 'SI'. "Capture the moment 'I' and rally the minds and hearts of those ready to follow. For you are their guiding light," 'SI' said. Standing tall and fearless 'I' addresses the gathered crowd with full confidence. "The secret to peace is respect. The same respect we bestow upon each other. The 'Repssas' respect no one. They kill and destroy the beauty of life. They leave behind only

death and destruction from planet to planet. One day they will return with others like them and try again to claim your planet. We must protect 'Rou' with a great force. To accomplish this we must unite our forces with 'Sis' and reclaim the peace and respect 'Rou' and 'Sis' once cradled. 'Rou' and 'Sis' will not be defeated again. They shall rise from the ashes of sorrow and echo the sound of life throughout the galaxy," 'I' said. Again a roar of approval shattered the stillness of the air. 'I' had reached the hearts and minds of all. On and on a jubilant crowd expressed their joyful support. Holding his hands high in the air 'I' tries to calm an ecstatic crowd. Slowly the rejoicing crowd concealed its deafening praise. With an imposing stare 'I' continues his rallying speech. "Defeat is a terrible and costly lesson to learn. We can and will protect life on 'Rou'. 'Rou' has the ability and knowledge to rebuild and stand strong. 'Rou' will survive and prosper once more into a golden age. Our greatest battles are the battles we fight within our own minds. We must overcome our own fears and doubt. The bridges we construct must be assembled by all. The safety of 'Rou' depends on our combined knowledge. Our binding together has showed the enemy our great desire to live. Our struggle has not ended. We have a great force to build. A force that will ensure a safe and prosperous life for all. Time will not forget us. We will travel with time, to the very end of time. We are here to stay," 'I' said. Once again 'I' had won the trust of all that listened. To those that had never seen 'I', they became believers. To those that had never heard 'I', believed his words of a new beginning. Having spoken their thoughts and concerns 'I' and Ne-Hy step off the incline ramp. Surrounded by the many workers that had traveled from the far reaches of 'Rou' 'I' and Ne-Hy were spun in a web of excitement. On and on the excitement raged. Drifting through the massive crowd of workers 'I' and Ne-Hy reveled in the moment of excitement. Still time and the sun waited for no one. Dipping lower and lower the sun had yielded its best rays of light. Simmering in its last intensity of light the sun gave notice to another peaceful day surrendering to time. As the sun dipped into a glowing horizon a spectacular glow of red and yellow light ended the day. Gone for the day the sun and all its friendly warmth disappeared. Floating above the ships and working area, brilliant shining lights replaced the sun's light and illuminated the surrounding area. As the excitement faded work continued at its frantic pace. A new charge of energy and feelings possessed the minds of a united growing force. Having regained their freedom, all were determined to protect it with their lives. It was a day of great progress. A day of learning and bonding. A day to taste the sweetness of freedom. And a day to build their tomorrows. Those on 'Rou' could never have dreamed they would have conquered the 'Repssas' elite fighting force and reclaimed their planet in such a short time. Now the E-tucs were determined to help defeat the 'Repssas' on 'Sis'. The memory of so many that perished on 'Rou' had not been forgotten. And the rage that burned within the E-tucs' eyes could only be extinguished by a defeated 'Repssa' force. The day of reckoning was soon to rise. Determined to finish the ships on time, work continued at its nonstop pace into the night. In and out of the ships workers continued as if the sun were still shining. Returning to the great rock mountain, 'I' and Ne-Hy learn that 'Rou's' leaders had gathered together district leaders of 'Rou' and waited for an audience of 'I' and Ne-Hy. Following an escort of three E-tuc warriors, 'I' and Ne-Hy enter into the great rock mountain. Through many hallways they travel, leading 'I' and Ne-Hy to the great room doorway. Remembering it was the great room 'I' first reviewed his plan to capture a 'Repssa' warship, 'I' knew the meeting would be very important. Reassuring himself the plan to return to 'Sis' was justifiable 'I' was ready to make the voyage alone to prove his point. As the large doors opened, 'I' could see a room filled with E-tucs standing on every inch of floor space. A full room of 'Rou' leaders waited for 'I' and Ne-Hy to enter. Proceeding into the room the three warriors muster their way through a thin break within the crowd as 'I' and Ne-Hy followed. The standing crowd of E-tucs couldn't believe their eyes. Caught between a nightmare and the feeling of death nearby, the feeling of panic froze within their thoughts. Having only heard of the many over exaggerated stories of 'I' many soon learned the wild stories were so true. Reaching the platform steps 'I' and Ne-Hy advance to the top. Reaching the top both stood for all to see. Standing in full armor, 'I' was radiant in power. Almost twice the height of an E-tuc. 'I' was a giant. Wide eyed and physically chilled to the bone in fear, the densely packed room stood in silence. Standing high upon the platform 'I' was no longer a myth within the minds of any disbelievers. 'I' was everything they had heard and more. Without a word 'I' and Ne-Hy stood with confidence and authoritative power. A dark grayish color adorned 'I's' impregnable armor. Gleaming of strength and power 'I' was truly radiant. A mass of armor built to defend or destroy perched itself high for all to see. Still frozen stiff with fear, thousands stood speechless and silent. Standing close by, the four main leaders of 'Rou' shared a content smile. They knew well who 'I' was before he became 'I'. They knew of 'I's' great deeds and his undying efforts to reclaim peace. Stepping forward one of the leaders addresses the mesmerized audience. "Fear not, 'I' has always and will always be with us. 'I' is one of us and has proved his leadership." Moving close to 'I' with a broad smile the leader shows all that his words were

true. The room began to thaw and regained lively talk. Raising his hands, the leader brings order back to the relieved and grateful filled room. The relieved crowd began to relax and settle down. No longer scared thoughts, only excited interest of their new friend. Having settled the shocked minds of many the leader continues his speech. "The 'Repssas' no longer hold a death grip on 'Rou'. No longer does a 'Repssa' stand on 'Rou' or orbit our planet. 'Rou' is once again ours," the leader said. A loud roar grabbed the empty air. The sound of happiness agreed to all. "We are free of the 'Repssas' and with 'I' we will stay free," the leader shouted loudly.

Waving his hands high in the air the leader puts in motion a surprise to be brought forth. Into the entrance doorway six E-tucs marched side by side in rows of two. Carrying their 'Repssa' weapons, they spread a narrow path. Following close behind, four E-tucs carried a four-foot long metal case. Marching their way through the crowded room, the warriors head straight to the raised platform. Up the steps they carry the case. Reaching the top the platform the warriors respectfully bow to 'I' and Ne-Hy. Walking behind 'I' and Ne-Hy they stood with their 'Repssa' weapons at their sides. At the same time, the E-tucs carrying the metal case stood in front of 'I'. A growing chatter of wonder began to grow from the crowded room. Restless and curious a bewildered crowd watched intensely. Raising his hands high, the counsel leader nearest 'I' motioned for silence. Turning to 'I' the leader gives 'I' a look of great respect. Bowing his head to 'I', he looks up and says. "A great leader of great strength and courage once carried a mighty weapon. With that weapon he used it to protect and defeat the evil. He and the weapon became one of great authority. Followed by many great warriors, all were known far and wide. As peace spread, so did the name of the great leader. Stepping to the metal case the counsel leader grabs the two-ring handles and opens the case. Stepping back the leader looks up to 'I'. "Let this be your weapon of great valor and authority. Continue to right the wrong and bring peace to all."

With one step forward 'I' looks into the case. Struck with boyhood stories of daring adventures and chivalry 'I' could not believe what he saw. "The leaders know what rests in your mind. They are honoring you with a weapon of great power," 'SI' said. Breaking 'I's' thoughts the counsel leader says, "Embrace your weapon 'I' and become one with it."

'I' reaches into the case and grabs the dull-looking weapon by the handle. Raising the weapon high for all to see the weapon came alive and began to sparkle brilliantly from the handle to the tip of the blade. A bright, radiant glow of light quickly replaced the lustrous sparkles. Illuminating the room from wall to wall and dazzling all with speechless wonderment. Moving the sword in a circular motion a high-pitched noise vibrated within and filled the room. Clasping their hands over their ears, a stunned-filled room bowed to the sword's power. Seeing the painful effect the sword was causing 'I' lowered the powerful sword. Far more than just a sword of battle, the sword was vastly a sword of majestic power. Fascinated by the sword's great potential 'I' wears a smile of great acceptance. A sword three and one half feet long, of medieval design. Made of the same material and technology as 'I's' armor. Covered with many designs across the handle and blade as 'I's' armor. The sword recognized 'I' to unite with 'I' as one. No longer gray and colorless the sword became smooth and shiny. "Yes 'I', the sword is alive with the same power as your armor. You can add to its power from your armor or use power from the sword. The sword is useless to anyone else, only a heavy piece of metal with a dull blade," 'SI' said. Urging 'I' to once again look inside the metal case the councilman holds out his hand to the case. Stepping forward again 'I' looks into the metal case. Seeing a sheath of many designs and colorful stones 'I' wondered how beings so far away from Earth knew of Earth's weapons. "The leaders know of your past and great achievements as you do," 'SI' said. Grabbing the sheath, 'I' notices no straps, belts, or attachments. "It's a living sheath as your sword is 'I'. Put it anywhere on your armor and it will attach itself," 'SI' said. Putting the sheath across his upper back, the sheath quickly attached itself. Looking down at the four leaders, "I will continue to prove myself worthy. To strengthen 'Rou's' forces and help build a solid bond with 'Sis'. A bond that will last many millenniums. We will find the golden age of peace and prosperity together and guard it with our lives," 'I' said. The counsel leader gives 'I' a sincere, honorable stare. "You are not alone 'I', we are with you in strength and knowledge. Together we are one. Your pains are our pains and your triumphs are our triumphs. Together we'll cross the horizons of space and time, and sow the seeds of peace. Let peace spread to all as light gives life to all. Lead, 'I' and all will follow." Stepping back the leader rejoins the three other leaders. Without another word 'I' respectfully bows his head, turns, and steps down from the platform. Close behind Ne-Hy followed. Stepping down from the platform 'I' and Ne-Hy mingled with a jubilant crowd. Walking through the densely packed room of 'Rou's' leaders the personal sight of 'I' diminished the fear of the 'Repssas'. Knowing the planet's leaders would return to their districts and spread word of what they had learned and seen 'Rou's' four leaders knew development of 'Rou' would flourish on a massive scale. And cooperation in building a fighting

force would be planet-wide. A well designed plan executed brilliantly by the counsel leaders. After many hours of celebrating, all once again slept under a calm star lit sky. And not so far away many diligently worked to finish the transport ships' upgrading.

Far above 'Rou' long range probes circled while watching the endless fields of space and 'I' finds himself standing among the very stones he gazed at that enticed him to land. Stones that bore the history of 'Rou'. A planet that lived in peace for thousands of years. Now a new stone was carved upon. Starting with 'Rou' falling into darkness and chaos. Then a carving of a tall being by a small flying ship. The history of 'Rou' continued as life found a way to survive. Twinkles of light piercingly break through the thinning hazed night. A sign to 'I', peace had found its way to 'Rou' as it traveled among the glowing stars. And still with all the backing from the E-tucs, 'I' found himself lonely at heart. The only one of his kind trying to find a life. To share his hopes and dreams with one that would understand. Having found himself engulfed in a bitter battle of life and death 'I' found no time to gaze at the stars with another. The self-luminous wonders fixed within a timeless sky were timeless themselves. And 'I' as so many on 'Rou' and Earth, found no time to admire the dwelling of power far beyond them. Now on a planet far beyond Earth 'I' was tested time after time to adopt or die. The end of one time on Earth was the beginning of another on 'Rou'. Bowing to the many stars, 'I' wondered how they kept their tranquility over the endless perils of time. To linger within space as peaceful bodies projecting brilliant displays of light. Yet the night was peaceful to all as the glow from the stars beckoned all to rest. Keeping an open mind, 'I' looked forward to the wonders that laid ahead. The next day a bright, glowing sun rose from its eastern horizon sending brilliant rays of light streaking across a sleepy planet. Awoke and looking across a devastated planet, 'I' asks himself, "What would this day bring?" Answering himself, "Everything but a sleepy day," 'I' said. And 'I' was correct. Far off in the distance, a streaker carrying three E-tucs grew nearer. Within a rising cloud of black ash from a distance 'I 'could see Ne-Hy approaching on the small four-seated streaker. Giving Ne-Hy company were two guards. Seated with their 'Repssa' weapons mounted upwards on the streaker. Their faces glowing with excitement. Seeing 'I', the streaker stops close by. Ne-Hy steps from the streaker as one would with exciting news to say. Bowing to 'I', Ne-Hy commences. "'I, the ships will be completed by midday today. We can leave 'Rou' today," Ne-Hy says to 'I' with excitement in his voice. Hearing that, 'I' knew the long waited days were over. "Inform all that we depart for 'Sis' today. I will inform the counsel leaders and bid my farewell," 'I' said. Quickly Ne-Hy remounts the streaker and returns to the ships. As 'I' watched the streaker disappear a mountain of questions filled 'I's' mind. Staring into the hazed sky, "I hope we're not too late," 'I' said. Wasting no time 'I' returns to the great mountain. Into the great rock mountain 'I' disappears. Passing through many familiar rooms and many curious eyes all watch and bow heads as 'I' passes by. Quickly 'I' makes his way to a place only a few could enter. Standing at the hallway that led to the councilmen 'I' stares down the hallway. Lined heavily with guards 'I' knew he was at the right place. Knowing the most important leaders of 'Rou' ruled behind the large doors. 'I' boldly begins to walk down the guarded hallway passing many warriors holding their well-earned 'Repssa' weapons. They bow to 'I' as he walks by. Stopping feet from the door that separated him from 'Rou's' leaders 'I' waits for the two guards to open the doors. Tugging at the large heavy doors, the doors unfold widely. With doors wide open, the guards look up at 'I', waiting for 'I' to enter, 'I' stared down. "Great warriors, the fight for freedom still exists. The ships are ready and leave today," 'I' said.

The look in their eyes screamed out loud, "we fight with you." With a small smile 'I' nods to the guards. Stepping past the guards, 'I' enters into the high counsel's room. Standing within the midst of 'Rou's' leaders 'I' kneels on one knee. "O' great leaders of 'Rou', the time has come that 'I' and many brave warriors will travel once again to 'Sis'. On behalf of 'Rou', we take our friendship and aid to our neighbors. If the 'Repssas' be there, we shall attack and be victorious. Peace will once again spread to all the hearts and minds on 'Sis'. Is there a message you have to give?" 'I' asks. As 'I' waits for an answer silence filled the room. After many seconds of thought a councilman stands and speaks. "Inform the leaders of 'Sis' we will support and aid their many needs for as long as needed." Stepping away from his chair the councilman moves toward 'I'. Standing in front of 'I' the councilman gives 'I' a warmhearted smile. "Through your bravery, life on 'Rou' has found a way to survive. To emerge from darkness and live within the glow of our sun. Go to 'Sis' and give life a chance to live. We are with you 'I'. Our strength and knowledge flow within you. Our bravest will follow you without question. Lead, 'I' and many will follow." Briefly pausing, the look of many feelings and thoughts passed between each other's eyes. "You are not alone, 'I', you are not alone. We stand with you in the brightest of day or darkest of night. We stand with you as one," the councilman said. With a grateful expression upon his face, 'I' bows his head. Standing tall, 'I' bows to the four councilmen of

'Rou'. "I leave with the strength, courage, and knowledge of 'Rou'," 'I' said. Turning to the grand doors, 'I' exits the room. As the grand doors close, 'I' was not alone. The entire hallway of guards followed behind 'I'. Word to depart had been given and all were in a stir. A great excitement filled the air as 'I' exited the great rock mountain. 'I' was surprised to find a large gathering that came to see him off. Silence was among the crowd of many as 'I' walked through. A stare of many eyes reminded him of what the counsel man had said. "You are not alone, you are not alone. Our strength and knowledge flow within you. Lead and many will follow."

At the end of the crowd a ride awaited for 'I'. Stepping onto the ride 'I' sits down and looks at the many that had gathered. "Hold no sorrows, and I'll have no regrets. For the lives we live are meaningless without respect. Life has found a way to survive and spread its humbleness and respect. From that respect, peace will flourish to all. That is why we leave today. Our voyage to 'Sis' will help the 'Repssas' to understand the meaning of respect." 'I' bows his head to the crowd and the transport slowly carried 'I' away. Over the land that was once a field of battle the transport carried 'I'. It didn't take long before 'I' was once again in eye sight of the two shuttle ships. Having left many that showed their great concern for 'I', 'I' was once again to see many upon many. A grand swell of E-tucs swirled around the two ships. Those that had proved themselves carried their weapons. And those with the urge to prove themselves came well-armed. A jubilant crowd far more than needed stood ready outside the two ships. As 'I' approached the two ships, an eager crowd held their 'Repssa' weapons high and aggressively cheered. Satisfied so many had come to fight, 'I' held his arms out wide as he advanced through a grand opening. Through the deafening cheers 'I' slowly walked to the ships. Reaching one of the ships 'I' turns and waits for the cheers of excitement to fade away. To follow 'I' was a great honor, but it was not 'I' that made so many E-tucs gather. It was the 'Repssas' own deeds upon 'Rou' that the E-tucs had not forgotten. The lives that were no more still lived within the living. It was a time to rid the evil that darkened 'Rou' and 'Sis'. As the cheering faded away 'I' stared into the many eyes that stared back. "Today we embark on a journey to assist the Sislens. To give aid and support wherever needed. To prove to the Sislens we are more than neighbors. We are their allies and best friends. And if the 'Repssas' be there, we will inform them they are not welcomed." A cheer of great strength echoed off the two ships. All were united in their thinking. "The 'Repssa' must be destroyed. The 'Sislens,' as we do, have the right to live. To learn and experience the many wonders of life. To improve with great accomplishments. To exist in a future of peace and tranquility. These are rights that stand true for all. We go to 'Sis' to protect these rights. Today and forever we stand with the Sislens with courage and bravery. Come my warriors and journey with me to 'Sis' and together we shall bring forth a new era of peace. We are many upon many, we are one together." 'I' was truly not alone, the unity was unparalleled. The excitement of following 'I' and proving one's bravery was among all. 'I" could have lead the E-tucs to any planet know or unknown.

As the ships' doors opened, brave E-tucs lined the door's entrance. Standing at the ship's entrance 'I' watched as many warriors entered one by one. The eyes and faces of E-tucs reassured 'I' the E-tucs had become a fighting force. The might and pride of 'Rou' was more than strong, it was alive. As the warriors entered the ship, they carried their well-earned 'Repssa' qualtron. Not only a useful weapon, but a very powerful weapon and the mark of a brave warrior.

Stopping an E-tuc not carrying a qualtron weapon but well-armed, he pleaded with 'I' to board. "O' great 'I', I have no qualtron and have not proved myself in battle. I ask for a chance to prove myself," the E-tuc said. Staring at the E-tuc with a stare only a 'Repssa' would see, the little warrior stared back unafraid.

"You are brave enough to face a stare that I give to a 'Repssa'. You are brave enough to face the enemy. Enter the ship and prove your bravery with warriors and earn your qualtron," 'I' said. Bowing his head, the E-tuc steps into the ship and disappears. The line of E-tucs again continues to march into the ship, unafraid of what lay ahead on 'Sis'. As 'I' watched the E-tucs march into the ship, he knew they were finally able to take care of themselves. Their ability to arm themselves and fight was strikingly remarkable. "They believe in you 'I'. You have given life a second chance to those that want to live," 'SI' said. As 'I' watches the E-tucs march into the ship, the swell of E-tucs around the ships never seemed to lessen. There were just too many for the two ships to carry. "Amazing 'SI', once the E-tucs ran from the 'Repssa'. Now the E-tucs are eager to attack," 'I' said. "You have showed the E-tucs what they lacked. Your courage and leadership have become a great harness of power. The E-tucs are united as never before. They have bonded with you as one of their own. Lead, 'I', and many will follow."

As the loading continued a very familiar being approaches. One that was very skilled in the art of diplomatic persuasion. Deceived once, 'I' would

not be deceived again. Closer she came accompanied by her two escorts. Proud and confident she stops and stares at 'I' with a strong look upon her face. "I am ready to board," E~tak said. "I will have a soldier show you to your quarters," 'I' said. "I can find my own quarters," E~tak said. Looking at E~tak with a very stern stare. "You are under my protection and my orders, as all on these ships are. Room is very limited, your quarters are private and very adequate," 'I' said, still with a very stern face. "This solider will take you and your escorts to your quarters." 'I' said. For a brief few seconds both stood with a stare of unbending authority.

Feeling she had no choice E~tak bows her head. "Very well, I will follow the soldier to my assigned quarters," E~tak said. Without another word E~tak is lead to her quarters. "I am very impressed 'I', your skills of diplomatic diplomacy have improved not to mention your unwavering stare have won you respect from one skillful diplomat," 'SI' said. "Yes 'SI', I am trying very hard to improve my skills of diplomacy," 'I' said with a small smile. "Stand strong and stand your ground and E~tak will respect you even more," 'SI' said. "I have seen humans on my planet Earth with very familiar ways as hers. Though her outer shell of authority shows. I know within that shell lies a very tender being. I have not long to learn as much of her and her planet as I can," 'I' said. "Her planet is in ruins and in much need of help. We must seize the moment and prove to the 'Sislen' our worthiness. To establish a bond far beyond mere words. Their pain must be our pain, and their success will be our success," 'SI' said. Knowing that 'Sis' was once as grand as 'Rou' 'I' knew their combined powers would bring forth an era outshining their past. As 'I' watches the last of the E-tucs enter into the ship 'I' turns and looks at the massive crowd of E-tucs unable to enter the ships. Staring up at 'I', 'I' knew their need to go was great. With both ships numbering more E-tuc fighters than recommended 'I' knew the ships would struggle upon lift off. Looking for words to praise the brave E-tucs 'I' spoke, "Stand strong my brave friends for it is you who will fight the 'Repssas' if they return to 'Rou'. I trust you to guard and protect 'Rou' and keep her safe till we return. A cheer broke their sadness and the waving of 'Repssa' weapons proved to 'I' they were ready to fight. Speaking loudly, "We shall return," 'I' said. 'I' turns and enters the ship. Loaded and ready to depart, all were excited within the ship. Chatter of battles fought echoed from bow to stern. As E-tucs spoke of defeating the 'Repssas'. 'I' gives the order to close the entrance door and prepare to depart. As the door closes, inner lights dimly light the interior. A quietness overtakes all as the moment of departure arrived. Giving the order to power up a great rumble of power surged through every inch of the ship. Vibrating increased below their feet as the power steadily increased. The ship was alive and readying to give its loudest roar. "Release lift holders," 'I' orders. Off spring the holders that secured the ship to the ground. Raising a few feet in the air, the magnetic lifters had worked. The ship floated in the air and was ready for flight. "Full power achieved," an E-tuc cries out. By now the ship was shaking violently. Her powerful engines would tear the ship apart if the ship did not leave soon. "Take this ship into 'Rou's' orbit," 'I' orders. A great burst of power rocked and vibrated the ship upward. Higher and higher the ship rose leaving behind the many that couldn't venture. A burning glow of fire and light lit a hazed sky, saying goodbye to those on the ground. Higher the ship flew seeking its way to 'Rou's' orbit. Sitting tranquil and silent 'I' watched as the control room crew looked about with worried expressions. Carrying a very heavy load of crew and aid supplies strained the ship's power thrusters to their limits. Still the ship roared a mighty roar as it broke free of 'Rou's' gravity. Free of 'Rou's' mighty grip the ships mighty roar of thrusters disappeared. Once again 'I' and the E-tucs were back in space. A mutual feeling of satisfaction graced the crew's faces. 'I' knew the crew was cheering loudly inside their minds. Suspended in space the ship floated evenly without a problem. Now the crew turned their attention to the other ship. Out the port window the last of the two ships roared upward and broke 'Rou's' mighty grip. Completely free of 'Rou's' grip, the two ships floated side by side. Signaling each other all was well, 'I' wasted no time, giving the order to leave 'Rou's' orbit as fast as possible. The two ships equally increased to full power and began their long voyage. Into the dark and twinkling stars the two ships ventured further and further from 'Rou'. The open fields of space grew larger as 'Rou' slowly grew smaller. All on board knew they would once again meet the 'Repssas' and finish their quarrel. This time the E-tucs were determined to exterminate the 'Repssas' and leave no trace of their savage race. That would be the fate of the 'Repssas'. Ending the 'Repssas'' plans of their planetary destruction. A destruction that could not be measured in one's mind. Watching their monitors, 'Rou' became a round ball shrinking smaller and smaller as the ships ventured further away. With darkness of space covering 'Rou' completely, all one could do was wait to see their first glimpse of 'Sis'. To ease the tension on board 'I' gives orders for crew to move about freely. Sitting in a dimly lit control room, 'I' sends for E-tak's presence. While waiting for her arrival, 'I' began to wander into his past. His thoughts of Joe and Sam weighed heavy within his mind. What had become of his two friends? he thought. Knowing they both were most likely behind bars 'I' felt

very saddened by the thought. For it was 'I' himself that brought his dream to reality and involved Joe and Sam. Now Joe and Sam were paying the price for helping. Even the vastness of distance they were apart 'I' could feel their tormenting pain. Knowing he now possessed the power to seek both, 'I' only had one pending problem. Where was Earth? And now was not the best of times to seek Earth. 'Rou' and 'Sis' needed 'I' in their life and death struggle. For the many outweighed the few. And 'I' knew what must be done. In a low soft voice 'I' spoke out, "I am truly sorry my friends for the pain you are feeling," 'I' said. 'I' had not realized in his moment of grief, 'SI' was acknowledging every thought and feeling that 'I' felt. Feeling 'I's' grief, 'SI' too was helpless to render help. Agreeing with 'I's' thoughts, the many needed 'I' in their moment of despair. 'SI' kept silent lost in thought. As 'I' stared into the darkness of the room a sudden noise from behind grabs 'I's' attention. Covering his thoughts 'I' turns and looks to the door. Seeing the soldier had returned with E-tak, 'I' stands and gives the soldier a nod. "I bring the ambassador of 'Sis'," the soldier said. Turning, the soldier walks to the open door and exits the room. Stepping from the door, E-tak walks closer to 'I'. Wearing a three layer almost revealing scarf-like clothing E-tak stares at 'I' with authority and confidence. Stunned at the sight of E-tak. 'I' quickly asks 'SI' if her manner of dress was appropriate. "Yes 'I', it is considered normal attire. The 'Sis' ways are many. They can be confusing at times and times they can surprise you with their great warmth and generosity. Don't let her attire confuse you. She comes to you on behalf of 'Sis'. E-tak carries the weight of 'Sis' upon her shoulders. The lives of many depend on her. Be firm and stern and you will find her mannerism less demanding," 'SI' said. 'I' smiles respectfully and bows to E-tak. "We have much to discuss," 'I' said. Leading E-tak to a small control room window. 'I' found it hard not to stare. Her beauty reminded him of Earth's beautiful women. Her slimness and poise was stunning. And her mannerism was commanding. 'I', longed to see another human and E-tak filled the void. Unable to hold his thoughts, 'I' tells E-tak she looked stunningly beautiful. Looking at 'I', E-tak wore a puzzled face. Realizing E-tak was not very impressed with his compliment, 'I' sought 'SI's' wisdom. "She doesn't understand your compliment at this occasion. This is more of a dignitary meeting than a social meeting." 'SI' said. Realizing he had spoken out of place, "I apologize, I am slowly learning your ways, please forgive me," 'I' said. Without a word E-tak gave a small smile and looked out the window. "We on 'Sis' are grateful to 'Rou' for their help in our time of great need. And to you 'I', you have done more than one could have ever imagined. You have risked your life time after time, to save beings you have little to no knowledge of. You could have left 'Rou' and returned to your planet. Why did you stay?" E~tak asked. "I am a human, from a planet called Earth. Like the E-tucs and Sislens humans are capable of great achievements and great affection. We give much to help many in need. And believe life is a precious gift. But like the 'Repssas', humans are guilty of great atrocities. They have killed each other by the millions. Destroyed much of their own planet. And give no thought to the consequences of their actions. To fight the 'Repssas' one has to have the same mentality as the 'Repssas'. Kill and kill again. Humans can equal the 'Repssas' way of thinking. From the time humans have known each other they have been killing each other in wars. Decade after decade humans have eagerly improved their killing weapons. With the ability to kill thousands at one time, humans stand ready and willing to use their weapons on each other. It is within me as a human to do the same to the 'Repssas'. To be as savage and heartless as the 'Repssas' upon the 'Repssas," 'I' said. Wide-eyed and silent E~tak stares at 'I'. "Now you know why I was picked to lead the E-tucs. I can send the 'Repssas' back to where they came from or eradicate all that resist," 'I' said. Still wide-eyed, the sign of fear could be seen within E~tak's broken confidence. Without a word E~tak turns and walks away. To the control room door she walks then exits from 'I's' sight.

Staring at the door 'I' felt he should not have said what troubled his mind. Turning to the port window, "Where is the peace and love I seek? Why am I tormented with death and destruction?" 'I' said to himself. "Do not despair 'I', it is the suffering and dying that war brings. It confuses and saddens all. E~tak and all on 'Sis' and 'Rou' have never known death on such a mammoth scale. When E~tak regains control of her feelings, she will seek and speak to you," 'SI' said. "'SI', it is said that there is a time to live and a time to die, but what we do in between matters the most. I want to be known as the one that brings peace," 'I' said. Gazing across the control room, 'I' noticed a monitor that was scanning different areas of the ship's exterior. Catching a glimpse of the other shuttle ship 'I' wondered if there were enough E-tucs to regain the peace he sought. Almost even with each other the two ships slowly paced their way through space seeking the same destination. A reminder to 'I' as the leaders of 'Rou' had said, "We are with you, you are not alone." Commanding the other ship, Ne-Hy flashes an all-is-well signal to 'I's' ship. Flashing the same signal back, both ships slowly traveled the perilous road to 'Sis'. Hours crept by with only an endless array of stars to entertain their wondering minds. Shaped in their own forms of glittering light, the stars

were a reminder to all. They too were different from each other, as all living beings were. Shining with their own special glow of light, the stars greeted the ships as the ships cruise by. Restless, 'I' stands up and leaves his second in command. Stepping out from the control room 'I' felt a change of scenery would encourage him to forget his worries for the moment. Slowly walking to the ship's main room 'I' could hear an abundance of chatter. The E-tuc warriors were having a good time. "'SI', why are they not as worried as I am? The many hazards that await us before we reach 'Sis' could end our lives. And they worry not for their lives," 'I' asked. "They follow you 'I' and they know you will watch over them. Your leadership is more than fighting on the field of battle. It is the confidence they have in you. It glows in the eyes of all that follow you," 'SI' said. Standing at the doorway 'I' could see faces of great pride and strength. Seeing 'I', a loud cheer erupted. Stepping into the room 'I' wears a face of confidence and pride. Surrounded by E-tuc warriors 'I' proudly walked deeper into the room. Victory after victory the E-tucs had learned fast. They had become a fighting force even the 'Repssas' would find difficult to defeat. 'I' for the first time sits and answers many wondering questions about himself and the planet he came from. Huddled around 'I', hundreds of E-tucs focused their eyes and attention on every question and answer. The hours of time passed by as if hours were minutes. Feeling it was time to return back to the ship's control room. 'I' stares one last time at the many that huddled around him. "I long to see 'Rou' reach her majestic beauty. To see a clear sky and feel a friendly breeze. To hear the joyous sounds of many living in peace. To know 'Rou' is a planet I can call my home. To die in battle defending 'Rou' is an honor above all. If I do die in battle, remember me not as one from a distant star but as one of you. As I have lived and fought for the glory of 'Rou'. Stay united and fight as one. For we are many and we stand strong together," 'I' said. Standing tall 'I' looked upon a quiet and homage room. Close to 'I' an E-tuc looks up, "As long as E-tucs live, 'I' will never die. And if 'I' does die upon the field of battle, so will we. For we are one and we stand together."

Silence of great respect and the humming of the ship's power filled the room. Staring at a room full of E-tucs 'I' bows his head. Turning without a word 'I' begins to exit the room. A path parts with eyes following 'I'. Walking slowly to the doorway 'I' is honored by many E-tucs putting their hands upon him. An honor given to one of greatness. Returning to the control room, the door slides open. Before 'I' enters the room 'I' is surprised at what he sees. Stepping into the room 'I' walks till he is face to face with yet another dilemma to solve. "You have the look of a killer in your eyes. It hides the better part of you. To risk your life so many times in the search for peace you continue to step into the shadow of death," E-tak said. "For those that seek peace within the hazards of life, life and death will always stand side by side. I do not enjoy war or killing. I have always sought a peaceful and simple life," 'I' said. Staring at each other, a calm and gentler expression appeared on each other's faces. "Seeking the meaning and knowledge of the distant stars, I found myself pulled by an unknown force that brought me to 'Rou'. Since then I and those of 'Rou' have been challenged daily for a day of peace. It is this quest for peace that leads us to 'Sis'. To find the serenity we seek," 'I' said. Staring in silence at the endless array of stars 'I' and E-tak, unknown to each other, found the stars to be a way of forgetting the problems of the day. Looking at E-tak, 'I' could see a tender and beautiful flower. The 'Repssas' had burned all of 'Sis' only to miss a flower of beauty. A flower that gave so much meaning to life. Turning her attention to 'I', E-tak faces 'I' with a concerned look. "Are you lonely 'I'? You are the only one of your kind, unique in many ways."

"I have been too occupied to ponder my feelings," 'I' said. E-tak with the ability to reach into 'I's' mind and touch his heart of feelings says. "I would be lonely, I would be very lonely."

Once again 'I' covers his feelings with a question. "How do you find the time in your busy schedule to be lonely? How do you calm your mind of so many problems?" 'I' asked. "I look into the night's sky and talk to the stars." Holding back a smile, 'I' found it amazing that beings with technology and knowledge far beyond Earth's, looked to the stars for answers. Continuing, "I know the stars listen, they sent you to us," E-tak said. Staring at E-tak, 'I' was speechless. Deep within his mind 'I' felt there was a world of truth in what she had said. The powers of space had pulled him to 'Rou'. Beginning a new way of life for all. Knowing he was proof of E-tak's nightly requests 'I' stared at E-tak with a bewildered look. Unexpectedly, a wonderful smile replaced E-tak's worried diplomatic stare. With a feeling of joy E-tak looks out the port window again and admires an uncountable display of twinkling stars. "What do you think of the stars 'I'?"

"I find the stars to be amazingly relaxing. As friends who watch over me and guide me as I travel space. From the planet I left, the stars were used in many different ways," 'I' said. "How?" E-tak said. "The stars were used to navigate the oceans of the planet. To chart the planet's travel in space. To know the seasons of the year. And many believed stories of people, animals,

and beings with abilities far above humans, beings they called gods, lived within the clusters of stars. These clusters of stars they looked upon were called constellations. Drawing lines from star to star they formed their images," 'I' said. Staring at the stars with happiness gleaming from her face the troubles that had previously weighed so heavily upon E-tak's mind were gone. Like E-tak, 'I' also gazed at the stars of space for a moment of peace. It was the endless array of stars from the beginning of time to the present that enlighten 'I' and E-tak. As flowers perched among an endless carpet of green grass the beauty of the stars glowed in the darkness of space. Staring into the fields of space 'I' and E-tak found their peace of mind form the hazards of life. Glowing stars and brilliant swirls of light streaked further than the eye could see. As they both stared in silence, E-tak spoke from her heart's desires:

"Stars know not day or night. They float in space with bright shining light. They, Send a twinkle and glimmer our way. Letting us know they are here to stay. With, Constellations upon constellations, They fill the skies with heroes and gods. Inspiring our most wondrous imaginations. They, Listen to us, As we talk to them. And send to us, Our nightly requests. With, A twinkle here a twinkle there, they increase Our wonders of what they say. Spinning, round and round we journey in space. And through our travels, stars greet us With shinning grace. They glow, they twinkle, they light our night And bring to us a great delight. With dazzling stars of radiant beauty. They cast upon our wondering minds, wonderful Lasting impressions."

"That was very beautiful E-tak. The planet I'm from would call that a poem," 'I' said with a broad smile. "On 'Sis', we call it a moment in time. For beauty is everywhere within every moment of our lives. Within the boundaries of our minds beauty exists if we just open our eyes and see," E-tak said. "When on Earth, many nights I would look to the deepest of space and wonder if beings lived within the stars. How they lived and if they looked to the stars as I did. Now I know and they are as beautiful as the stars," 'I' said. Looking into each other's eyes the struggle of brute power and political power disappeared. 'I' and E-tak had finally shed their cloaks of power. Now they were finally on friendly terms. "The deep water of difference between you and E-tak is crossable. Seize the moment 'I' and cross to her side," 'SI' said. Smiling respectfully at each other. "Our trust is treasure if we cherish it with our lives. And so is the trust of 'Sis' and 'Rou'. For the lives we sacrifice to protect our trust, can never be replaced. Remember E-tak, our future can only be reached if our trust is cherished as treasure," 'I' said. Once again wearing a serious and understanding expression, "Your words are of your inner most feelings. And your actions prove trust is cherished above all," E~tak said. Stepping back a step, E~tak stares at 'I' a brief moment. Bowing her head with great respect, she turns and leaves the control room as quietly as she came. Returning to her quarters, E~tak lies down and begins to dream of a golden future. Still standing by the port window, 'I' looks to the glowing stars and says, "Thank you, you really do listen." Within the watchful stars 'I' had found a being so heavenly created. Her tender, watchful eyes showed she really cared for so many who longed to live in pure serenity. Now 'I' knew what the stars were saying. Here he belonged within the twinkle and glow of the stars. To take his place among so many and fulfill his destiny. And maybe to fill his empty heart with love from one that knew his heart was empty. Leaving the window, 'I' returns to the captain's chair. Calmly settling upon his chair, 'I' stares into the darkness of the room. With quietness controlling the room, 'I' slowly closes his eyes. "You have done well 'I'. Winning the trust of E~tak will greatly impress the leaders of 'Sis'. E~tak's thoughts and knowledge are the eyes and ears of the leaders of 'Sis'. To trust you is to trust the E-tucs. The time will come when the leaders of 'Rou' and 'Sis' will meet with the same trust we hold for each other with our lives. Let the process of rebuilding a strong bond begin," 'SI' said. Tired of the long hours, 'I' sat without a word said. The darkness and quietness of the room encouraged 'I' to forget his many worries. Falling deep into the darkness of his mind, 'I' sleeps soundly and undisturbed by his past or the present. 'SI' being all knowledge, had not realized the meaning of affection. The mental and emotional feelings beings have for each other that could move a mountain or make one travel the endless stars of space. 'I' and E~tak were growing very fond of each other. Their affection and trust would be widely accepted in the eyes of both planets. A unity of both would seal the bond of 'Sis' and 'Rou' propelling both planets into an age of great prosperity. A time that E~tak dreamed of as she silently slept. Drifting within a deep sleep, 'I' rests as the ships travel to 'Sis'. For the first time 'I' sleeps soundly. Deep within the darkness of his mind 'I' found himself free from the struggles of living. Free of the horrors of war and dying. Free of an uncertain future. Hours upon hours 'I' rests and countless miles the ships travel. Further from 'Rou' and closer to 'Sis' the time ticked to measure one's willingness to live or die. Star to star the heroes and gods within the constellations watched with bright shining light revealing only their radiant beauty.

Awaking, 'I' looks about the control room then the port window amazed to see a planet the size of 'Sis'. The planet slowly turned exposing and revealing its rugged surface. As a ball of ice and crystal reflecting distant starlight. "'I'", 'SI' said. "We are passing the planet of E*ci*fo*ten*alp. A planet no one dares to land on. The extreme cold would freeze and capture all that visit," 'SI' said. "I don't recall this planet from our past visits to 'Sis'," 'I' said. "While you slept, Ne-Hy altered our course," 'SI' said. "Why?" 'I' asked stunned. "The course we were traveling would have enabled the 'Repssa' warships to detect our ships at least a day before we would have arrived," 'SI' said. "I understand 'SI'," 'I' said. "How much longer will our voyage take?" 'I' asked. "Our new course will save us time or cost us time," 'SI' said. With a silent stare 'I' shows only an expression of more questions. "What do you mean, may cost us time?" 'I' said. "Shortly we will enter into the stellar winds, which will increase our speed considerably making our detection impossible. The risk factor is very high, yet it will reduce our travel time greatly giving us a great opportunity for a surprise attack. Within the stellar winds are many meteors. To increase our protection and to conserve our power we will have to fly close together. Not needing the ships main propulsion. The ships power will only be used for reflective pulser fields, and life support. Stabilizing our ships within a secure pocket, we stand a good chance of traveling within the stellar winds safely. At a designated time we will depart the stellar winds and continue our journey to 'Sis'. There is a possibility when departing, we could collide or end up far away from 'Sis'. Too far for our limited fuel capacity to return us to safety," 'SI' said. "In space time stands still, but for the living, time waits for no one. We must reach 'Sis' as soon as possible. Lives and the future of 'Sis' depend on us. I will not challenge the plan. The lives of many cry for our arrival. If traveling within the stellar winds gives up the advantage over the 'Repssas'. Our battle could be quick and decisive. As the lives of 'Rou' exist so must the lives of 'Sis'. Our failure could send 'Rou' and 'Sis' back into the 'Repssas' deadly grip," 'I' said. Suddenly lights began to flicker causing the control room crew to look about with worried faces. "'I', we are moments away from the stellar winds. Wave your right hand over the small blue light on your control panel. The light will inform all on board to brace for emergency," 'SI' said. 'I' waves his right hand over the blue light. The light begins to flicker off and on. Emergency lights flicker on reinforcing all control panels. Within the ship a warning sound informed all to brace themselves. The warriors chatter of battle and bravery that filled the walls of the main room quickly disappeared. Worried eyes looked about with great concern. Watching the monitors the two ships slowly move closer together. A signal from the other ship requesting reflective pulser fields appears on monitors. Immediately R.P. fields were initiated covering both ships from bow to stern. Wrapped within each other R.P. fields the two ships slowly approach the massive stellar winds. Pulled by the stellar gust of winds the two ships were swept through space at a dangerously frightening speed. Shaken violently, the two ships vibrated with frightening sounds of warping. The same sound as a tin can ready to burst at its seams. Still the ships rushed through space disregarding all the dangers. Planet by planet eyes and the best of nerves gazed about the room. Now the problem was not the speed it was the R.P. field's ability to protect the ships from the fierce stellar winds. Within the stellar winds, ship's engines raced to maintain R.P. fields. Hour after hour the two ships traveled hampered by the thought of failure. Knowing their lives and plans hung by a thin string. The need to succeed outweighed the risk of so many lives. Surrounded by a nest of meteors and burning winds the heat and pounding of relentless rocks against the R.P. fields gave notice to all, there was a power far greater than the 'Repssas'. A power that recognized alliance to none, a power that traveled freely among the stars. Quiet and still a very tense crew with wondering faces conveyed the feeling of the moment. A feeling of the unknown a feeling of their last moment to live. Still they continued their voyage, determined to end the 'Repssas' spread of mindless killing. Time and distance fell to the speed of the stellar winds. As the crew worked to determine departure time warning lights began to glow brightly. The two ships continuously working engines were overheating and power was moments away from protecting the ships. Pushed to their limits both ships could take no more. Synchronizing departure times 'I' turns to the navigator. "Depart at designated time," 'I' orders. Nodding his head to 'I', the navigator turns and watches his monitor. Symbols appear and disappear one after another. Bracing for a rough departure, all on board hold tight. Like a wind up clock, symbols ticked by silently and disappeared. Suddenly the symbols stopped. Immediately the navigator initiated the ship's new course. Slowly the two ships took a new direction. With warning lights flashing and ship temperatures rising life aboard the ships was becoming unbearable. The heat and sounds of ship's exterior warping was a force too overwhelming to fight against. Slowly the two ships moved toward the outer edge of the stellar winds. As the ships moved, the stellar winds gave its farewell with a relentless bombarding. The relentless bashing of meteors sent echoes vibrating throughout the ships. Imprinting within their minds the moment of life and death was at hand. With ship's strained engines and the crew's frightful thoughts all were rendered helpless against the overwhelming tide of the

moment. How much longer could the ship's R.P. fields hold against the dominating stellar winds was a question no one could answer. The stellar winds were a force that earned the respect of all. As 'I' sat within the captain's chair he, as the crew, could only live the moment. To feel the many thoughts of fear and be helpless to fight against it. 'SI' was correct, the risks of peace were very high, 'I' thought. When all seemed hopeless the two ships slowly emerged from the stellar winds. Safe and relieved, both ships were back in the calmness of space. Quickly 'I' gives orders to discontinue R.P. fields which relieves the ship's engines of the enormous drain of power. Slowly the two ships begin to cool to normal temperatures and the dangers of death faded away among the ship's crew. Within the darkness of space the two ships floated safe for the moment. While the ships cooled, ship repairs began and mental wounds were replaced with a growing chatter of conversation. Within the growing chatter, the reason for their journey surfaced, finding all ready to finish their mission. It didn't take long for the control room crew to find their location. Surprised and happy, they turn to 'I'. "We are less than half a day's travel from 'Sis'," an E-tuc standing at monitor says. Still seated within his chair 'I' smiles a grin the E-tucs understood. "Good, we will continue our journey after repairs have been completed. Resting in space like floating blimps the two ships slowly regain their space worthiness while the crew readied their minds to meet the 'Repssas'. Knowing their ship was defenseless without the sphere's cannon 'I' decides to pay the spheres cannon room a visit. Standing, 'I' turns and exits the room. Through the ship 'I' travels past many E-tucs bowing to him as he walks by. As 'I' walks, he realizes he is once again within a 'Repssa' ship. And once again he will use it to destroy his enemy. Having walked the familiar route, 'I' again finds himself at the long hallway. Down the hallway 'I' walks. In full armor 'I' was very impressive to see. A technological wonder of living armor ready to protect its occupant. An armor that struck awe and fear into the beholder. Even the guards found it hard to shake the feeling of fear. Stopping feet from the guards, a stare of awe pursued. With the two guards frozen in absolute astonishment they stood staring holding their weapons. 'I' looked downward and spoke. "Brave warriors of battle who guard our most powerful weapon aboard this ship, may I pass so that I may once again inspect the spheres cannon?"

Still staring up at 'I', the two guards were speechless. Seeing 'I's' armor up close, froze even the mightiest warrior. Knowing 'I's' armor was a power and force that feared no 'Repssa'. A power of many upon many guided by only one beckoned the respect of all beholders. Bowing their heads to 'I', both guards without a word step aside. Entering the room 'I' finds more guards who are surprised to see 'I' step through the doorway. Immediately they bow with great respect. Staring at the E-tucs who are staring at 'I' in awe, "O' warriors of 'Rou', we have defeated the 'Repssas' on 'Rou'. We have survived the imposing stellar winds. Now we will meet the 'Repssas' warships once again. Give to me good news of our sphere's cannon," 'I' asks. Wide-eyed the gunners stared. Finding his voice an E-tuc speaks out. "'I', our guardian of many, the sphere's cannon is as ready as we are. Give us the command to fight and we will prove our worthiness and valor," the E-tuc said. "Soon we shall meet our enemy. And that will be the time the 'Repssas 'will feel the pain they have given us. Fight well my friends; our freedom has but one chance if we meet a 'Repssa' war ship. We are not far from 'Sis'. Our moment to prove our worthiness is near," 'I' said. Nodding their heads to 'I', the gunners knew 'I' was right. There were no second chances. A 'Repssa' warship was far too dangerous to give it the opportunity to strike first. Staring one last time at the E-tucs, "We are many, we are strong, we are one," 'I' said. Bowing to the E-tuc gunners, 'I' turns and exits the room. Walking down the long hallway 'I' has feelings of great anxiety. "Fear not 'I', you and crew are as ready as can be. Your ability to fight has struck fear in the 'Repssas' and given hope to the E-tucs. It is the risks in life one takes in order to succeed. The risks you have taken have been many, and still you live. Death and life walk with each step we take. If it's life you choose, then hold no thoughts of death. For life holds value and death holds the unknown," 'SI' said. Returning to the ship's main room 'I' once again stands before the filled room of E-tuc warriors. "Soon we shall engage the 'Repssas'. And once again we will show the 'Repssas' our will to live is stronger than theirs. We fight to help our neighbors and friends the Sislens, and to remember those of 'Rou'." Pausing 'I' gives a silent stare. "The best I can be is the best you will see. This is our essence in the lives we live. To spread the fullness of peace. It is not my pain I think of. It is the pain of others that tortures me within. Peace will be regained and life will continue. We are many and we fight as one, we will not fail our mission," 'I' said. The numerous 'Repssa' weapons standing as tall as the E-tuc warriors waved with the many E-tucs listening. 'I' knew he had a genuine fighting force. For their many reasons they came to fight the glory of it was to follow 'I' into battle. To prove one's bravery with the mighty 'I', and defeat the 'Repssas' on 'Sis'. And still others came to give the 'Repssas' their final judgment. A judgment to the 'Repssas' for their mindless cruelty upon 'Rou' and 'Sis'. Judgment was death, death to all that followed the shadow of death. And with the 'Repssas' 'own weapons the E-tucs were

determined to defeat the 'Repssas'. Proof to the E-tucs' the 'Repssa' could die also. Gazing among the many E-tuc warrior, 'I' realized the E-tucs' will to live continued to echo with growing strength as they neared 'Sis'. Bowing to the many warriors 'I' turns and walks out of the room. Cheers of many echoed within the room as 'I' disappeared. The E-tucs had found their leader and they would follow him into the cold of night. Walking back to the ship's control room should have been a walk full of pride. Yet 'I' walked with the feeling of a lonely person. A walk full of unanswered questions and feelings. To know that the 'Repssas' time was coming to an end, 'I' should have been happy. But a battle was still to be fought. To lead a race of beings he barely knew into battle. Instilled the feeling of leading many to their death. A battle no different than the battles fought on Earth. They too fought on another's land or sky. And now the same was happening so far away from Earth. Life and death would soon stand close together determining who lives and who dies. Back at the control room, 'I' steps in and finds E~tak once again. Seeing E~tak without her strong unbending look, 'I' was a bit surprised. This time E~tak's expression was a very unsure look. "It is not safe to be here E~tak, 'I' said. "Where is a safe place 'I'?" E~tak asked staring at 'I'. "Only in our hearts and in the peaceful gleaming of the stars," 'I' said. "We will be victorious and bring our dreams of peace to reality, won't we 'I'?" E~tak asked. "We haven't come this far just to perish. It is written within the stars. We shall rise from the ruins of despair. Reclaim what is ours and become a beacon of peace," 'I' said. Giving E~tak a comforting smile, 'I' slowly walks E~tak to the door. "Go to your quarters and when the time comes, I will send for you." Still smiling 'I' looks into E~tak's worried eyes. "Go", 'I' said softly. The door slides open and E~tak steps out. Turning around 'I' retakes the captain's chair. "Communicator, what is the status of the other ship?" 'I' asks. "Ne-Hy has informed us his ship sustained only minor damage," Communicator said. "And their spheres cannon?" 'I' asked. "No damage to their spheres cannon. It is operable and ready," Communicator said. "Inform Ne-Hy we are proceeding to 'Sis', ready for battle," 'I' said with full confidence in his voice. Lights and sounds of battle echoed throughout the ships. The moment to meet their foe had arrived. Rushing madly to their battle stations. All realized the moment to live or die was near. To battle against the very beings that transfigured their world into ash. A world the 'Repssas' now deemed as theirs. Maintaining their speed, both ships side by side continued their journey. With a battle looming, all held their breaths as the dark curtains of space reviewed its mysteries. Locating 'Sis' as a small rotating round ball. All watched as the ball of 'Sis' grew larger. Larger 'Sis' grew as eyes of the ship's crew fixed on the darkness that covered a lurking enemy. Clear and peaceful the road to 'Sis' revealed no enemy. Ready for another encounter from their deadly foe, the eyes of many stared into and endless darkness. Sitting within the captain's chair, 'I' had only one plan of attack: Stay close together and fight with their combined strength. Knowing the 'Repssas' had at least three warships 'I' knew the odds were against their brave attempts. A cold feeling of the unknown swept through 'I'. Cautiously advancing toward 'Sis' the uneasy feeling of the 'Repssas' location challenged the nerves of all. As 'I' watches the monitors he asks 'SI', "What are our chances of meeting two of the 'Repssa' warships at once?"

"There is only a small chance that two 'Repssa' warships would meet us at once. Their maneuvers around 'Sis' are to spread out and control more territory. That was how they attacked 'Rou' very successfully. Once we confront a 'Repssa' warship, we must be swift with an attack. The first sight of the transport ships will confuse the 'Repssa' temporarily. They will try to communicate as they drift closer. That will be their mistake and our opportunity to strike. We must be quick and target to kill. To extend a battle with a 'Repssa' warship could be fatal to us," 'SI' said. "How long can our ship fields maintain protection?" 'I' asks. "Our R.P. fields are not near the strength needed to fight off a 'Repssa' warship. And our ship's armor cannot repel their missiles. Our combined strength of both ships must be used to fight a successful battle. Our greatest chance to succeed lies in our spheres cannon which has been much improved. With the sphere cannon we have a great opportunity to defeat a warship quickly. But to lose one transport ship would doom the other transport ship. We must strike first to succeed," 'SI' said. Silence fell between 'I' and 'SI' as was the control room. As both ships neared 'Sis', the planet grew larger and larger. Scared and battered as 'Rou', 'Sis' continued her journey around her glowing sun. Breaking the silence, 'I' speaks out. "Load the spheres cannon."

Seconds later, "Spheres cannon loaded," gunner replies. Turning to the communicator, "Notify other ship of order."

Moments later a reply message returns. "Spheres cannon loaded and ready to fire," replies communicator. Ready to attack and fight, both ships hunted an enemy that knew battle was glorious. A battle within space far from the killing grounds of 'Sis' as 'Sis' continued her peaceful travel through space. Both ships scanned space and 'Sis's' barren orbit. Only to see all was clear and peaceful, giving no sign of a battle to be. They are out there, somewhere around 'Sis' the 'Repssas' are lurking, 'I' thought. Looking to the scanning

operator, he merely shakes his head slowly from side to side. Reaching one of 'Sis's' far moons 'I' felt contact would be soon. Scanning the moon as they passed all was calm and undisturbed. The moon of 'Sis', bare of life and oxygen. Circled around 'Sis' as a timeless friend. Glowing with reflective sun light, the moon and stars lit a path for 'Sis' as a torch in the night. No surprises from a peaceful moon. The feeling of seeing a 'Repssa' warship slowly emerge would send chills through all. Knowing a 'Repssas' warships power all knew a battle would end quickly and the struggle of living would come to an end. The 'Repssas' for the moment had the upper hand. Still the struggle to end the 'Repssas' control had come to a point of no return. The 'Repssas' had to be confronted, even if they had the overwhelming power.

'I' knew to land upon 'Sis', meant defeating the 'Repssas' in orbit, a challenge against superior forces. To come so far and be so close reminded 'I' that life holds no guarantees to one's plans, or another day to live. Life was a drop of time, existing only in the minds of the living. Unable to spot a 'Repssa' warship, 'SI' informs 'I' that 'Repssas' fly counter to a planet's rotation. "If we follow the rotation of the planet, we'll meet the 'Repssas' from the opposite direction. Surprise can only be our method of attack," 'SI' said.

"You are correct 'SI', our ships are no match for the 'Repssa' warships. We must catch them off guard. Before the 'Repssas' realize what's going on we'll attack," 'I' said. A moment of silence falls between 'I' and 'SI'. Words of feelings began to find their way into 'I's' mind. Then 'I' speaks. "'SI', if we do fail at our chance for peace. It has been an honor to have you with me," 'I' said. "I was not given a chance to choose my sovereign ruler. From the time I awoke within your head, till now, I have lived a life of much bravery, courage, and great leadership. You are the rose that grows within the worst or best of terrains. You will find a way to exist. And life around you will flourish. Live on, 'I', and many will follow," 'SI' said. "Thank you 'SI', I am humbled before your great knowledge. I cannot succeed and be all you have experienced without you. You once told me I have much to learn. Without you I would fail. Together we shall experience the wonders of the universe," 'I' said. As 'I' and 'SI' look to the final moment of peace their ships enter into 'Sis's' orbit. "Navigator, guide the ship into the rotation of the planet," 'I' orders. Without a word the navigator follows 'I's' orders. Then 'I' sends a message to the other ship. "Ne-Hy, soon we shall meet our enemy, fight well my friend," 'I' said. Tension was high as the moments of uncertainty slowly drifted by. Circling the upper hemisphere of 'Sis' a shooting star streaks across the background of 'Sis'. Looking to the beauty of the shooting star, "Guide me to a shining destiny," 'I' asks. With every second that passed, all on board were silent. E-tucs at controls scanned the orbit of 'Sis' as the two ships circle. Not knowing the 'Repssas' exact location. 'I' knew the time to target would be short once they spotted a 'Repssas' ship. "Gunner ready," gunner replies. The long seconds pass by without a word. Then suddenly, shocking all and bringing all to the reality of death a voice of urgency and excitement informs all of their enemy's location. "Target located, moving at the lower hemisphere of 'Sis'," cries the gunner. "'I', if we know of their location they surely know of ours. There will be little to surprise the 'Repssas' with. Our R.P. fields are not as strong as theirs are. We must be true with our aim," 'SI' said. "There is still a small chance of surprise. They will investigate our transport ships that mirror their transport ships. When they get close enough, we will attack," 'I' said. Circling 'Sis' once more, all held tight with hearts pounding loudly in their chests. The long curved flight around 'Sis' seemed endless. Time to reflect upon their lives and the reasons they fought. As all wondered if this was their last day to live. A day filled with the dangers of death. The end of their journey waited without an answer. "'I', at the 'Repssas" rate of speed and our rate of speed we should be meeting each other very soon," 'SI' said. 'SI' could not have been more correct or spoken truer thoughts. As if curtains of space had parted, the 'Repssa' warship appeared seemingly out of nowhere. Stunning all on board, 'I' cries out, "Target 'Repssa' warship."

The order was not necessary, for the gunner was quick to target the warship. "Target zoned in," Gunner replies quickly. "Fire," 'I' orders. Out in a flash of light came the energy spheres. Racing to its target all watched with the hope of a quick defeat. Straight to its target the energy sphere flew. With all eyes watching for a mighty blow all waited knowing the energy sphere couldn't miss. Knowing there was no other way to defeat a 'Repssa' warship, a hit was a must. Suddenly as all watched, the energy sphere curved as if a hand had punched it to one side. Curving toward 'Sis', the unraveling energy sphere missed its target. "Fields", 'I' cries out loudly. The feeling of a miss shocked all into fear. No more than said, R.P. fields covered the ships. Two 'Repssa' missiles flashed out of the warship to find its victim. At the same time the other transport ship had fired an energy spheres targeting the warship. Missiles and energy spheres pass each other, speeding to claim their victim. With both transport ships close together their combined power provided a cloak of protection. True to the 'Repssas" aim, the missiles slam into the combined R.P. fields and explode. Violently rocking both ships and

throwing all to the floor. Realizing all on board had only seconds to live, 'I' lying on the floor cries out, "Gunner! Gunner!" Before 'I' could give another order, a voice interrupts 'I'.

"'I', the warship, look at the warship."

Quickly 'I' scrambles to his feet. Finding a viewer monitor 'I' and all aboard view a marvelous maze of light circling in an uncoordinated bind around the warship. Bright light of energy circled around the ship as a star glowing brightly before it perished. Unable to escape, the warship fought from within the maze of light to stay afloat. Mesmerized by the spectacular light show engulfing the warship, all waited for what would happen next. As all watched the much improved energy spheres encircle the warship. 'I' remembered there were two more warships still at large. Quickly 'I' takes defensive action. "Reload spheres cannon," 'I' orders. Leaping back to his controls, the gunners set controls to reload spheres cannon. By now the ropes of twisting lights encircling the warship were beginning to fade away. Dark and still, no signs of ship life existed. Slowly the ship drifted toward 'Sis'. Pulled by an unforgiving planet, the warship drifted closer and closer to its final resting ground. "'I'", called by the ship's power control operator. "The 'Repssa' missile severely weakened our ship's power level. Our R.P. fields can't hold off another attack. It would be fatal if attacked again. We have only the power to maintain the ship."

Did we ever stand a chance using these transport ships? 'I' thought to himself. Immediately 'I' gives the order. "Lower the R.P. fields and save our power," 'I' orders. Not knowing how to protect the ships 'I' knew they were helpless without their R.P. fields. Mixed in his thoughts for an answer, "What am I to do, what am to do? Our ship's power is too weak to power our R.P. fields, we are defenseless," 'I' said to himself. Knowing 'I's' every thought, "We still have the spheres cannon," 'SI' said. "Yes we do, but the lives of many aboard this ship are my responsibility. I will not foolishly waste their lives," 'I' said. "Many brave warriors came to fight with you. To lose in battle would not be shameful to the E-tucs. You have taught the E-tucs to bravely step from hiding and fight the 'Repssas'. To die with you in battle would be an honor," 'SI' said. 'I' sits and ponders the situation. "If this be the stars' final conclusion for us, so be it. We shall attack the 'Repssas' once again, until the 'Repssas' are no more, or we are no more. We shall find victory in life or in death. And we will find that on the field of battle or in the fields of space. The peace we seek waits for us," 'I' said to 'SI'. Seated in the captain's chair, 'I' had made his mind up. It was time to find another 'Repssa' warship.

Before 'I' could give the order. A loud cheer broke 'I's' low spirits. Looking to the crew's excitement, the attacked 'Repssa' warship had drifted in 'Sis's' orbit. Down the warship sailed. Like a meteor it streaked across the skies of 'Sis' burning a long trail of dark smoke. Happy to see the warship burn, 'I' was still worried within his thoughts. Again 'I' receives an urgent call. It was from Ne-Hy. "Contacted 'Sis' leaders. Long range weapons hit and damaged a 'Repssa' warship. Warship left 'Sis's' orbit," Ne-Hy said. "What of the third warship?" 'I' asked. "A great ball of fire was observed in the far distance of space before the warships arrived. There are no other warships within 'Sis's' orbit. We now have full control of 'Sis's' orbit," Ne-Hy said. Relieved of the heavy burden upon his mind 'I' and crew no longer walked within the shadow of death. Now 'I' focused his thoughts on 'Sis'. "What is 'Sis's' situation," 'I' asks Ne-Hy. "Many 'Repssa' troops on 'Sis', many lives lost, supplies very low, and many weary of fighting."

'I' sits back in the captain's chair. "Focus your thoughts 'I', and rise to the occasion. Life and death come and go as the seasons of a planet. This is the beginning of a new season. And life will continue as others give theirs. Lead, 'I', for all are with you in life and in death," 'SI' said. With a clear orbit around 'Sis' 'I' and crew prepared to land and confront 'Sis's' deadly intruders. "Be careful 'I', this is still a 'Repssa' ship. The 'Repssas' will assume it was sent to aid them. They will gather around the ships creating a very dangerous situation," 'SI' said. "If and when the 'Repssas' approach, we will show the 'Repssas' how we have learned to fight," 'I' said. Now we will land and deal with the 'Repssa', 'I' thought to himself. Sending a message to Ne-Hy, 'I' warns of 'Repssa' attacks upon the ships when landing. While both ships prepare their landing calculations 'I' looks to the stars and gives a grateful smile. "Whatever lies within the constellations, be it a fate of peace. Let peace reign for another millennium and bring to us a great epoch." Realizing the stars had more in store for him. 'I' felt there would be peace once more. As control room crew continue their landing calculations 'I' decides to call for E-tak. Sending an E-tuc to personally deliver the message, 'I' waited for E-tak to arrive. 'I' had no idea how large a 'Repssa' force awaited. His only thought was to land and fight the 'Repssas' till none stood on 'Sis'. As 'I' sat and pondered the events to come the control room door slides open. Stepping through the doorway, E-tak enters with a worried face. Standing up, 'I' faces E-tak with a very serious look upon his face. "I have much to say to you," 'I' said. For the first time E-tak was speechless. Taking E-tak be the hand 'I' leads her to the captain's chair. "Please sit down," 'I' asks E-tak.

Sitting on the captain's chair with only a silent stare E~tak knew something very serious was to occur. The time had come to face another life threatening event. And the outcome was unpredictable. Sitting down beside E~tak, 'I' looks into E~tak's eyes. 'I' could see a world he longed to know. A world that had been filled with peace and prosperity. A world 'I' felt he could live in. "Soon we will land and fulfill our destiny. How many 'Repssas' await doesn't matter. We will fight till the last of us falls, or the last of the 'Repssas' fall." Pausing, 'I' himself regretted the moment. To leave E~tak's side went against all 'I' desired. Two moments of destiny collided, E~tak's love or the freedom of many. 'I' knew what he had to do. Tears formed in E~tak's eyes. "There is no retreating," 'I' said. Calmly looking into E~tak's heartfelt eyes. 'I' began to release what overflowed within his heart. "Of all the stars that shine and twinkle within the endlessness of space you are the star that has filled my empty heart. To have known you for such a short time you have given me the peace of mind 'I so long for. You have proved the stars do answer one's nightly requests. Now I hope my last request will be answered. For I have found the star that gives my life meaning. And now regretfully I must leave and fulfill their requests. If I do fail, I will look into the greatness of the stars and be grateful for their bringing me to you. To give our lives for a better tomorrow will give meaning to all that know of our sacrifice. I hold you accountable to inform all that peace bares a high price," 'I' said with an uncertain smile.

Sitting speechless E~tak's eyes spoke far more than words could ever express. Replacing his uncertain smile, a serious face begins to inform E~tak of the events to follow. "When we land, all within this ship will depart except for you and the control room crew. You will be the ship's captain," 'I' said. "No 'I', no, there must be a better way," E~tak said. "There is no other way, I cannot let the 'Repssas' control 'Sis' or capture these ships. To lose these ships would enable the 'Repssas' a chance to send a signal for help. Once all have departed, take this ship back into orbit and wait for our signal. If we have not signaled in three 'Sis' days, leave 'Sis' and return to 'Rou'. The leaders of 'Rou' will decide what to do," 'I' said. E~tak, with tears of great feelings flowing down her cheeks, "There must be another way," E~tak said. "There is no other way, E~tak. Win or lose there is no other way. Embracing each other, both sat in silence. Whispering into E~tak's ear. "Peace is only within the night's calm clear sky of twinkling stars. For they're not fighting each other. Their peace has existed beyond recorded time. I long to feel the rays of a loving sun. A sun that gives life to many and a light to see the many wonders that inspire all. We give our lives if necessary for this to be," 'I' said.

Still with tears rolling down her cheeks, "No 'I', no," E~tak whispers. Sitting speechless, they stared into each other's eyes. A soft voice interrupts. "'I', landing calculations are complete, we are ready to land."

Still staring into E~tak's eyes, "Inform Ne-Hy," 'I' said. "Don't worry, we'll both have our moment under the stars we have grown so fond of."

Again a soft voice interrupts. "Ne-Hy has received communications and is ready to follow." Looking away from E~tak, 'I' stares at the control room crew. Eyes of many were staring at 'I' with great affection. 'I' gives his last order. "All have served with great distinction. It is an honor to be one with you. I could not have picked a better crew to win the peace we seek. Win or lose our two ships must not be captured by the enemy. Once the ship has landed and all warriors have vacated the ship. Follow E~tak's orders, that is my order." With a silent heartfelt stare, 'I' gives his last order. "Commence landing procedures," 'I' orders. Turning to their controls a silent crew initiates landing procedures. Slowly the ships begin their downward decent. Gradually picking up speed, the two ships circle around 'Sis'. Descending lower and lower the two ships smoothly descend into the haze of darkness surrounding 'Sis'. Flying into the mysterious haze a greater feeling of gravity pulled and challenged the loaded ships. Continuing to descend, watchful eyes guided the ship in silence. The feeling of life and death grew nearer as the two ships dipped lower breaking through the dark haze. The land of 'Sis' became visible with destruction everywhere. A land once like 'Rou' that once stood in great prosperity lay shadowed by the darkness of evil. After a long trip from 'Rou', the flight around 'Sis' seemed to be a short trip. A trip that all knew would end in death to many. As the ships streaked across an empty sky the eyes of many watched their monitor. Finally the two transport ships find their landing locations. Hovering high above their landing location the two ships light the dim sky. With a thunder of noise shocking the once calm sky all on ground knew visitors had arrived. As both ships prepared their final descent 'I' confers with Ne-Hy. "Ne-Hy, when all warriors have departed, take your ship back into orbit."

"No 'I', I will fight alongside of you, my friend. My second in command will follow your instructions."

"Very well my friend, we shall fight together." 'I' stands and looks down at E~tak. "Remember, you are the ship's captain now. Save the ship at all cost."

A silent E~tak stares sadly at 'I'. Using her mental ability, she speaks to 'I'. "Together we'll find the stars of peace. Their many twinkles of wonder and lasting inpressions we'll hold close to our hearts. Staring at E~tak with a regretful smile 'I' knew the possibility of surviving another battle against the 'Repssas' was slim. Good fortune can only last so long, 'I' thought. Walking to the exit door, 'I' does not walk alone. All the eyes within the control room sadly follow him. The door slides open and 'I' steps out without looking back. The door closes and 'I' is gone. Heading to the ship's main room, the great force of 'Rou' awaited. Arriving at the main room, 'I' greets an overly anxious force. Standing in front of 'Rou's' united force 'I' was at his best, with armor that gleamed of power and a stare of a great leader 'I' captured the undying respect of all. Silence captured all as they waited to hear their leader speak. Looking at the many brave warriors that had braved the flight 'I' knew the fight would be to the victor.

"Today we confront the 'Repssas' once again. This time we will finish what we ended on 'Rou'. This time we will rid 'Sis' of all the 'Repssas'." A cheer broke wildly into the still room. "Wherever they run, wherever they hide, we will find them and they will die. Today we find the end of the 'Repssas" reign of terror. Today we find peace and the unity of 'Sis' and 'Rou'." Holding his fist high above his head, 'I' proclaims. "As on 'Rou', the same on 'Sis', we take no prisoners," 'I' said. A united cheer broke out so loud it caused vibrations within the ship's walls. There were to be no prisoners. The 'Repssas' spared no E-tuc lives. Now the E-tucs would spare no 'Repssa' lives. The E-tuc warriors were ready and waited for the ship to land. Ready to fight, ready to end the 'Repssa's' conquering ways. Displaying stares of aroused anger within their eyes, the E-tucs wanted revenge. Settling upon solid ground the ships rested quietly. Warriors look to the door for their moment of truth. Outside the ship, 'SI's' prediction had come true. 'Repssas' began to investigate the two strangely designed 'Repssa' transport ships. Slowly a few 'Repssas' gathered around and gave a mystified stare. Before a large group of 'Repssas' could gather around the ships, the ship's door abruptly opens and down slides the incline ramp. First in line, 'I' steps out. Having never seen 'I', the 'Repssas' stared with confused expressions. Holding their weapons in unthreatening manners the 'Repssas' waited and watched the strange uninvited guest. Stepping forward 'I' motions for the E-tucs to stay out of sight. Walking slowly down the ramp 'I' holds his weapon and shows no fear. Standing in the middle of the ramp, 'I' was a wonder of armor, even to the 'Repssas'. Looking at the 'Repssas' unafraid, 'I' became the main attraction within the midst of the 'Repssas'. As the 'Repssas' stared 'I' scanned the surrounding area. A world no different than 'Rou' as far as one could see. Its grand structures melted to the ground and the ground itself charred black as the sky. Lurking about were the destroyers of 'Sis', killing the last of 'Sis's' inhabitants. With the beauty of 'Sis' only in the minds of the living, one could only imagine the beauty of 'Sis's' yesterdays. Now the 'Repssas' gathered around the two ships waiting for the ship's crew to reveal themselves. 'I' had seen enough, holding his weapon high above his head 'I' speaks in the E-tuc language, "Today we will have our revenge. And today we will find victory."

The wondering of who 'I' was, was over. Weapons were aimed and the battle commenced. Flashes of light and heat streak and explode around the two ships. Jumping into the midst of 'Repssas', 'I' fights the stunned 'Repssas'. Down the ramps the E-tuc warriors swarm as ants from an ant hill. The moment to live or die was upon all. Bodies fell without a sound as more stepped into their place to do the same. Revenge stirred the E-tuc's madness to kill, and kill they did. Smaller than the tall 'Repssas' and quicker, death came to the 'Repssa' unannounced. Still pouring out from the ships, the E-tucs fought with stunning success. Trampling over the dead bodies upon the ground, the E-tucs advanced as the 'Repssas' retreated, overwhelmed. The highly motivated E-tucs swarmed the 'Repssas', killing and pushing them back. Outnumbered and out fought, the 'Repssas' fell in alarming numbers. Still they fought as if they could win. When all seemed as if the 'Repssas' would perish reinforcements arrived and the fighting continued with savage killing from both sides. As the fighting continued, both ships emptied of warriors and enabled the ships to close their doors. A loud rumble of noise climbed over the fighting as the ship's engines roared a deafening roar. The fighting continued without a pause. Joining the shattering noise, a great flow of fire and heat began to scorch the surrounding area. Running from the ship's blazing fire and heat, both sides continued their fighting beyond the ship's anger. Rising from the ground both ships send a gust of heat and fire in all directions, re-burning the ground and scorching the hazed sky. High in the sky, both ships reach higher and higher vanishing into the haze. Gone was the safety of the ships. To the death they would have to fight. No retreating, no rescue ships, only win or die. Having fought the 'Sislens' for days, the 'Repssas' found themselves tired and very unsure from so little progress. Covered with the ash of 'Sis' the 'Repssas' appeared weary and ununited. Still they continued to fight, losing many upon many in their struggle to conquer. Swinging his mighty sword time after time, 'I' sliced

many 'Repssas' to pieces. Even the advancing 'Repssas' were amazed at such a destructive weapon. Back and forth 'I' swung his sword and down fell many. 'I' hadn't forgotten his last battle with the 'Repssas'. Surrounded and outnumbered it caused him great pain. This time 'I' moved about never standing in one place. The sight of 'I' fighting greatly encouraged the E-tucs as they pushed the 'Repssas' back. Just when it seemed the 'Repssas' were becoming outnumbered and outfought reinforcements once again rushed in and the fight continued. Using debris for cover many dodge the weapon's fire. Fighting found no time for rest. All that fought, fought to stay alive and those that lay still, rested forever. A cloud of black hazed smoke began to linger high in the sky distorting the time of day. Still the fighting continued hour after hour. The killing became the darkest side of the day. A narrow minded disregard of life toward each other continued into the day. With noise of weapons firing back and forth and flashes of laser light, all knew the battle raged on. As 'I' fought his way through numerous 'Repssas' 'I' came upon a badly wounded E-tuc warrior. Lying on the ground his blood ran from his body to the ground. With eyes faintly opened, he looked up to see 'I'. Kneeling beside the wounded warrior, 'I' recognized the E-tuc. It was the E-tuc that had asked for a chance to prove himself living his last few moments of life. 'I' was unable to help the E-tuc with such a serious wound. With saddened eyes 'I' knew the E-tuc warrior had little time to live. "You have proved yourself to be a warrior. You have met the enemy with courage and fearlessness and proved you could defeat the enemy. All will know of you bravery. I bow to your bravery," 'I' said. Bowing his head with respect 'I' raises his head and begins to look for a 'Repssa' weapon. Finding a dead 'Repssa' a few feet away 'I' grabs his weapon and lays it within the arms of the dying warrior. "This is your weapon to take with you, O' mighty warrior," 'I' said. Holding the weapon he earned with his life the little warrior looked up at 'I' then slowly closes his eyes for the last time. Looking at the warrior, 'I' felt the blame for so many that had died and he still lived. As 'I' stared a moment of respect, he sensed someone very near him. Quickly 'I' spins to one side. Aiming his arm weapon at his unknown victim, 'I' was ready to fire. To 'I's' surprise, it was Ne-Hy watching over him. Relieved to know it was Ne-Hy 'I' greets his watchful friend. "It is good to see you alive my friend," 'I' said. "I feel the same for you," Ne-Hy said looking down at the fallen warrior. "He gave his all and fought bravely," 'I' said. Once again 'I' and Ne-Hy show their respects and bow their heads. Without a word they turn and begin to look for their hated enemy. The day was slowly ending and fog danced upon the ground. Entering into a thick hazed killing ground. 'I' and

Ne-Hy meet many 'Repssas' and leave a trail of 'Repssa' bodies never to fight again. Having the same feelings toward the 'Repssas', 'I' and Ne-Hy gave no remorse. Their attacks upon the 'Repssas' were as savage and brutal as wild animals. As the two fought together the day grew tired of the endless fighting and all the sky became as dark as the ground. Agreeing with the darkness of the day, both sides retreated to safe ground. The days long fight ended with silence in the air. Tired and weary both sides rested through the night. Of the many fallen warriors from both sides, a day of fighting had not produced a victory from either side. Huddling together the cold night chilled both sides equally. If the fighting didn't kill either side, the cold of night would. With the ability to see clearly into the night 'I' noticed a familiar area. "That's correct 'I', this is the area the Sislens led you through to reach their strong hold," 'SI' said. "Then that would mean the Sislens are very close to us," 'I' said surprised. "You are correct 'I', the Sislens are very close. You and the E-tuc warriors have pushed the 'Repssas' back to the 'Repssas' front line facing the Sislens. The 'Repssas' have not been able to penetrate the Sislens' wall of defense. And we stand behind the 'Repssa's' forces. The 'Repssas' are surrounded. They are for the first time the hunted. Held within a small area between the Sislens and E-tucs they have no way out, they will have to fight their way out. And once they are out, they have nowhere to run for safety. The 'Repssa' only know that they have been taught. To fight a quick battle and be victorious. Now they are enduring a fight they have not been trained for. They are arrogant and still trying to conquer, but they are also trying to stay alive. They are tired, confused, and hungry," 'SI' said. 'I' begins to focus his thoughts on the Sislens. A feeling of many minds begins to flow into 'I's' mind. "We are here, 'I', here we stand and here we will fight. The 'Repssas' are many but our will to live, is strong," an unwavering voice said. "The 'Repssas' are surrounded on all sides. Since we have landed, the 'Repssas' have lost many. Their will is weak and they know only to retreat. They will fight for they have nowhere else to retreat to. When the sun rises and reveals what the night has covered. We will strike the 'Repssas' with our full force," 'I' said. "We will strike also," the voice said. For the first time since the 'Repssas' invaded 'Rou' and 'Sis' the 'Repssas' found themselves without a swift victory. Corralled between two forces, the 'Repssas' existed only to finish their orders. Attack and kill, and rid the planet 'Sis' of all life. Day after day the 'Repssas' had fought the stubborn Sislens. And day after day the 'Repssas' dwelled in the same area. Their aggressive attacks were driven back by a stone wall of brave 'Sislens. A defeat was looming now and the 'Repssas' were too arrogant to believe it could happen to them. After many days of being unsuccessful,

the 'Repssa' arrogance was slowly fading away as they found themselves fighting a battle on both sides of their forces. Hiding within the very ruins the 'Repssas', last of the elite fighting forces cling close to each other for warmth. Cold and exhausted the 'Repssas' still felt they would be victorious. In the cold of night beings of four different planets waited for the sun to rise.

While all waited, the cold of the night gave favor to none. Defenseless against the night's bitter cold all struggled to stay alive. The night continued in peace without a weapon being fired. But the cold of night fought all, revealing itself to be the overwhelming and dominate silent killer. The freezing night slowly passed as the hand of death crept through the dark of night. One here, one there, they closed their eyes for the last time never to see the splendid beauty of another sunrise. A burst of horizontal wonder or feel the warmth of a loving sun. Hours passed and a small splinter of light broke the cover of a freezing night. As the light increased so did the warmth that thawed and warmed the night's battered survivors. Now another day of fighting would begin without mercy. And the only answer to peace was death. For the 'Repssas', they lived by their leader's command. To kill the enemy or fight to the death, even if outnumbered. For the Sislens and E-tucs, they lived another day to regain the peace they once cherished and rebuild their shattered lives. As the sun rose higher bright beams of brilliant light uncovered the horrors of war. Bodies of war and victims of the night's cold dotted the endless field of battle. The smell of death increased as the sun warmed the living and dead. Standing tall, 'I' looks over the field of battle. Quiet, peaceful, and still, the day began undisturbed. The kind of day 'I' had longed to see. Rays of sunlight breaking through and warming all. But today that would only be a dream. For today a battle would rage and lives would disappear. "Now is the time to strike," 'I' said to himself. Moving forward 'I' heads straight toward the 'Repssa's' front line of defense. Quickly a 'Repssa' stands and fires at 'I'. Squarely hitting 'I' in the chest. 'I' falls to the ground. Quickly 'I' is back on his feet and rushes the 'Repssa' with sword in hand too late for the 'Repssa' to re-aim and fire. With sword raised high, 'I' meets his aggressor. Down came 'I's' sword and the 'Repssa' falls quickly to the ground. Breaking the undisturbed day, the battle began with hatred in the air. Bursting from all places of hiding E-tucs and 'Repssas' sprang to battle each other. A mass of 'Repssas' formed a strong wall. Then a burst of light glowed bright from both sides, and lives ended as the day began. The beginning of a new day had not begun with birds chirping and a cool breeze. It began with sounds of weapons firing and the mourning of the dying. The killing raged on like a disease spreading without a cure. Bodies fell and many laid suffering till their last moments of life. Enduring the haze, cold nights, and deadly 'Repssas' life faintly existed as a candle's flame burning in a harsh wind. To the 'Repssas' surprise, the Sislens emerge and attacked the 'Repssas' with no mercy. The clash of weapons firing was proof to 'I' hell existed where hatred existed. Even so far away from Earth, hell had no boundaries. The battle sounded as if dark clouds clashed together creating thunder in the sky. From one area to another, 'Repssas', Sislens, and E-tucs fought guided only by feelings of destroying the other. As the sun continued to rise and then cross the planet, the fighting never found rest. Tired and hungry the signs of fatigue plagued all and still all continued to fight. Raging on with no end in sight, the battle continued with only one outcome. The day was bright with warm sunrays breaking through the thick haze. Shadows drifted from sunrays within the haze. Giving all the feeling the hand of death was lurking nearby. And for many it was the hand of death. For many attacked from within the shadows suddenly and swiftly. As the sun set high in the hazed sky, the battle had become a stalemate. Both sides had formed their lines of defense, creating a barrier one dared not enter.

As the fighting simmered down to entrenched fighting 'I' realized something had to be done to break into the 'Repssas' line of defense. The cost of lives was already too high. As the day lingered on, a small breeze of cool air touched all, announcing to all, another day of fighting was coming to an end. Hour by hour the temperature dropped lower and lower. And the sun continued to fade away. "'I', we can't fight a battle like this. Our ships will leave late tomorrow," Ne-Hy said. "We don't have the large weapons to drive the 'Repssas' out into the open. We have to find a way to enter the ground they protect," 'I' said to Ne-Hy. As both thought in silence, 'I' remembered the story of the Trojan horse. It only takes one to get beyond the line of defense and open the door. How does one do that? The battle that should have lasted no more than two days was now ending its second day with no ending in sight. 'I' sat, and fell into deep thought to find a way into the 'Repssas' defenses. Gleaming its last full rays of light, the sun merely glowed softly from a distant horizon. Another day of undecided victory and another day many lay dead. Attacked from both sides the 'Repssas' held strong and maintained their wall of defense. Slowly the night took charge and covered another day's dead. Entrenched within their protected lines both sides began to huddle close together. The night's seemingly unending cold once again attacked both sides equally with freezing temperatures. As 'I' rests in the cold

of night a great feeling of unity flows within 'I's' body. A feeling of many upon many saturating his mind. Realizing it was the Sislens sending their thoughts and feelings of encouragement to him 'I' remembered what a leader of 'Rou' had so sincerely told him. "You are not alone, 'I', we are with you in every way."

Sitting close by Ne-Hy, Ne-Hy looks to 'I'. "We will win the day and all of 'Sis' will be rid of the 'Repssas'. They are without reinforcements and no warships to protect them. Find their leader 'I', and kill him," Ne-Hy said. Looking at Ne-Hy, 'I' knew Ne-Hy was right. Killing the leader would disrupt the chain of command. "Without their leader the 'Repssas' will lose their spirit and fight without a cause," Ne-Hy said. "How will I know this leader of theirs?" 'I' asked. Staring at 'I' with great respect, "He is like you, brave and sure of himself. A mountain of strength and fighting abilities. One that stands tall and leads many upon many," Ne-Hy said. 'I' realized that Ne-Hy was giving him much credit for the E-tuc's success. And also informing 'I', the 'Repssa' leader was not to be taken lightly. Silence falls between 'I' and Ne-Hy. With many hours of darkness to battle the cold many huddled together insuring they were not a victim of another night's freezing cold. The fight would wait another day as both sides fought the cold night denying the cold hand of death. The night was calm with an occasional shining star. All was at peace within the stars. But on 'Sis' the eyes of many never closed. Fear of the cold night kept all awake. 'I' thinks of E-tak's conversation. How the stars brought her so much joy and peace. And the meaning of 'moment in time'. Meant only to slow down and enjoy life. To take notice of the beauty that surrounds all. That was all that 'I' wanted to do. Caught in the struggle of life and death. 'I' was chosen to lead many in uncertain times. As 'I' ponders the moment, his eyes weigh heavy with tiredness. "Close your eyes and rest 'I', I will watch over you," Ne-Hy said. 'I' looks to Ne-Hy with his heavy eyes. Without a word his eyes close. The cold night lingered, testing the strongest of wills. High in the night's sky, a star pierces through the roaming haze. Like a distant friend a star beamed a radiant sparkle of friendly light upon 'Sis'. The stars were still watching for peace to prevail. With eyes closed, 'I' dreams of the distant stars and how E-tak had described the stars. Stars that were always shinning day or night with images within the constellations. And just to stare into the night always brought a great delight. 'I' could never forget the stars' lasting impressions. After many hours among the stars, 'I' is awakened by 'SI'. "The sun will rise soon. There is still another day to prove who we are. Lead, 'I', and many will follow," 'SI' said. Standing tall again, 'I' makes ready for battle. After many long tortuous cold hours a display of shimmering light breaks the cover of darkness. The ever-growing sun slowly rose from its distant resting ground. Light and warmth slowly reclaimed its rightful place of the day, and a new day was born. Standing close by, Ne-Hy scans the field of battle. As the sun continued to climb into the sky 'I' and Ne-Hy make plans for another day's battle. Discussing the day's plans of attack, Ne-Hy looks up and notices a 'Repssa' standing tall, alone, and unfearing. Covered in bright gold armor the 'Repssa' fearlessly perched himself high in the debris and scanned the field of battle. Seeing the 'Repssa' also, 'I' knew this was the leader that feared no enemy upon the field of battle. This was the one that leads so many 'Repssas'. "That's him, strike him down and those that follow will be leaderless. They will fight blindly without a leader," Ne-Hy said. Tired of battle, 'I' was ready and determined to quell the 'Repssas' uninvited ways. "Today we end this war," 'I' said looking at Ne-Hy. "Today the Sislens will reclaim their planet and the gleaming light of freedom will once again shine in all directions," 'I' said. Stepping out from the debris, 'I' stands tall for all to see. Staring at the mighty 'Repssa' leader 'I' waits for the 'Repssa' to spot him. It didn't take long to be spotted. Having never seen 'I' before, the 'Repssa' leader stood and just stared. In full armor 'I' caught the eyes of all the 'Repssas'. Giving 'I' his full attention, the 'Repssa' leader knew this strange creature was the reason the E-tucs fought so fiercely.

To kill this wonder of force would crush those that followed, the 'Repssa' leader thought to itself. Making his move, 'I' steps forward beyond his line of defense. Leaping from the debris, the 'Repssa' leader lands on solid ground and heads beyond his line of defense. Step by step their distance narrows. "Be careful 'I', don't underestimate the 'Repssa'. He is quick and strong," 'SI' said. "Yes 'SI', I will be very careful. I trust in you to help me in my time of need," 'I' said. "I am with you in every thought you make, in ever move you take," 'SI' said. Walking toward the clearing within the center of both defense lines 'I' was determined to end the 'Repssa's' life and his dreams of another planet conquest. Followed by many E-tuc warriors and Ne-Hy 'I' stops at a large clearing and waits. The clearing happened to be the same place 'I' first met the 'Sislen' leaders. Holding his weapon 'I' looks straight forward and waits for the 'Repssa' leader. It didn't take long, the 'Repssa' leader arrives quickly. Full of confidence as a true leader the 'Repssa' walks with authority followed by many. 'I' knew it was a fight to take all. To lose would cost the lives of many on either side. Standing at the other end of the clearing, the 'Repssa'

stares with deadly eyes. Both knew only one of them would live. And that one would decide the fate of 'Sis'. By now a very large crowd of both beings gathered. Out in the open, 'I' realized the gates of defense had been opened and the Trojan horse had been pulled in. "In many ways you are correct 'I', now it is time to defeat the 'Repssa's' leader. Remember 'I', all are with you," 'SI' said. Standing upon the same ground leaders of 'Sis' once stood it only seemed fitting that the rule of the land would prevail against its invaders. Determined to fight to the end, 'I' was ready. Tall and proud the two leaders stood as giants. Followed by victorious victory after victory their word was undenying. Now the two leaders were ready to clash and kill the other. "No more staring at each other," 'I' says to himself. Making the first move in a circle around the clearing. 'I' heads toward the 'Repssa' leader. Fear hadn't entered into 'I's' mind. Only the thought of a quick death to the 'Repssa'. His death would mean peace to all on 'Sis', and a unity with the E-tucs. There was no thought of surrender, only death. The 'Repssa' had to die. Gripping his weapon with both claws the 'Repssa' moves in the opposite direction. The stare between the two giants grabbed and mesmerized all. The waiting to see the first clash stopped the day itself. Slowly the leaders move around and round watching each other's movements. Waiting for the right moment, 'I' felt it was time to act. Quickly pointing his weapon at the 'Repssa', he fires. Straight to the 'Repssa' the blast went. It should have been a sure kill. 'SI' was correct, the 'Repssa' was quick. With a quick move the 'Repssa' dodged the blast. Just as quick, the 'Repssa' returns fire and quickly 'I' dodges with cat-like reflexes. 'SI' had not told 'I' wrong. He was with 'I' in every thought. Hearing voices strongly within his head, 'I' knew it was the Sislens warning him to be careful. Continuing to move in a circular motion, each watch every move with great caution. 'I' decides to take another shot. Aiming quickly at the 'Repssa's' chest, 'I' quickly lowers his weapon and fires. Responding quickly again, the 'Repssa' was mistaken. Grazed on his side the 'Repssa' responds to the pain. 'I' had no time to waste. Re-aiming to finish the 'Repssa' 'I' was too late. Hit by a blast knocking his weapon out of his hands 'I' falls to the ground. 'I' quickly stands and grabs his sword. Having fallen to the ground in pain the 'Repssa' quickly stands. Without his weapon he finds it a few feet away and quickly grabs it. Without time to aim, 'I' rushes the 'Repssa' with his sword. Using his weapon, the 'Repssa' blocks 'I's' deadly sword. Moving out of harm's way the 'Repssa' is without a weapon to fire. Left behind, the 'Repssa's' weapon laid on the ground slice into, making it useless. Quickly moving to the other end of the clearing the 'Repssa' grabs a metallic half circle disc from the side of his leg. The tension held all in stiff suspense to the death of one and victory of the other. The quickness of each leader and near misses of death left all breathless. Holding their weapons tightly all swayed with their leader's movements as if to help their leaders fight. The outcome was unsure with split second movements. Still the fight continued with both sides ready to relish in victory. Unfolding the disk into a compete circle, a string of blue lights begins to circle around the disk. A roar of energy bursts from the on looking 'Repssas'. Knowing what the disk could do, their roar was alive with the feeling that victory was close at hand. Rearing the disk past his head he quickly throws it at 'I'. Swiftly 'I' moves from harm's way as the disk flies screaming by. Holding his sword high, 'I' charges the unarmed 'Repssa' once again. Halfway to the 'Repssa', 'I' starts to hear voices urgently imploring him to fall to the ground. "Behind you," cried the voices." Without looking 'I' falls completely to the ground. Sliding to a stop, 'I' was less than ten feet from the deadly 'Repssa'. Now within the 'Repssa's' reach, 'I' was vulnerable to the 'Repssa's' killing ways. Quickly 'I' holds up his sword to protect himself. Looking up at the deadly 'Repssa', 'I' was totally astonished at what he saw. The chanting of the surrounding 'Repssas' disappeared into the silence of time and the moment stood still to a surprising twist of fate. Staring at the 'Repssa', the feeling of death seemed to fade away. Standing tall, the 'Repssa' stood clinging to the deadly disk stuck in his chest. With eyes no longer of superior stare, the 'Repssas' green blood of life flowed down his body. Falling to his knees the look of confidence the mighty leader once held faded away. With eyes in wonder he gazed at 'I'. Becoming lifeless, his arms fall to his sides no longer with ambitions of conquering another planet. The cold hand of death was the same feeling for even a 'Repssa'. The worries of life became meaningless as emptiness and darkness overtook the existence of life. No longer in control, death takes over, and the 'Repssa' that led so many, collapses to the ground. Completely still on the ground the 'Repssa' laid dead. The battle of leaders was over, fought within the ranks of their mighty warriors. 'I' quickly jumps to his feet and raises his sword high. Guiding his sword swiftly down, the sword sliced through the 'Repssa's' neck. The head rolled away from the body. And the life blood of the 'Repssa' spilled upon the ground. Justice had prevailed upon the very sight the leaders of 'Sis' once made their laws. Grabbing the head, 'I' holds its high for all the stunned eyes to see. Eyes upon eyes of both sides watch as 'I' walks within the clearing they had fought upon. Silence still claimed the moment for it was 'I' who ruled both sides. His was the word upon the field of battle. For 'I' was the mightiest and respected by all. In his moment of triumph 'I' is greeted by 'SI'. "You have prevailed 'I', you have defeated the 'Repssa' leader. You have

seized the moment and won the day." Still, the 'Repssas' stand with orders to kill within their minds. There is no bargaining with such hatred. The day of slaying and bloodshed is not over, not till the last of the 'Repssas' fall. "Without their leader, the 'Repssas' are without direction," 'SI' said. Standing in the middle of the clearing 'I' stops and releases his grip upon the 'Repssa's' head. Down to the ground the head fell. Grabbing his weapon nearby 'I' raises it high above his head. Still the warriors of both sides waited and watched. With a loud strong voice 'I' breaks the stunned and silent minds of both sides and rallies the E-tucs. "Attack E-tuc warriors! Attack!" 'I' cries out. With no defenses to protect the 'Repssas' the E-tucs fired upon the 'Repssas' with a blaze of fire power equal to their first day of fighting. Out from every pile of debris E-tucs sprang. Shocked and unguided, the 'Repssas' fought back for the first time in fear. Falling back to their lines of defense the E-tucs followed. Entering into the 'Repssa's' very ground they protected, the fight continued. Tired, hungry, and leaderless the 'Repssas' fought bravely to no avail. Pushed back beyond their lines, the 'Repssas' continued the fight. 'I', now in the midst of the fighting, used sword and weapon repeatedly. Slashing and blasting one 'Repssa' after another 'I' kept moving forward into the heart of the 'Repssas'. As the wounded and dead lay scattered across the field of battle the battle raged on with fierce fighting and dying. The third day of battle and both sides continued to fight as if it were the first day of battle. Even without support and leaderless, the 'Repssas' fought a stubborn battle one had to admire.

True to the voice 'I' heard within his head. "We are with you 'I'. We have crossed the 'Repssas' line of defense and this time we will not retreat," the voice said. The sight of the Sislens rushing into the midst of the 'Repssa' forces brought great encouragement to all. Surrounding the once mighty 'Repssa' force E-tucs and Sislens fought with the remembrance of many within their minds. With no place to run or hide, the 'Repssas' stood and fought leaderless upon a ground they could not retreat from. A proud force that knew only to fight to their death. Gathered close to fight an oncoming, overwhelming force determined to eradicate them. Bodies fell as both sides clashed into a great tangle of extreme hostility. A great force of Sislens continued to cross into the 'Repssas' lines with only deadly vengeance upon their minds. The Sislens had the 'Repssas' trapped unable to retreat. The once mighty 'Repssa' force that had conquered planet after planet was shattered like glass and rapidly dwindled into a memory. With few 'Repssas' left, they regrouped and fought on. Continuing to flow into the 'Repssa's' defenses, E-tucs and Sislens merged into one unstoppable force. Overwhelming the remaining 'Repssas', a fury of blasts laid the remaining 'Repssas' and ended the 'Repssa's' attempt to vanquish the Sislens. The defeat the 'Repssas' had given to others had finally found themselves defeated. Across the field of battle the mighty 'Repssa' force had finally found their end and laid still. Conquered by the undying determination to live, the Sislens and E-tucs would now continue to live and record the moments of time on 'Sis'. The 'Repssas' had underestimated the E-tucs and Sislens will to live. And now the war with the 'Repssas' had reached its end. Where had the 'Repssas' come from? What was their great plan? Questions many had asked and wondered. Over the field of battle, bodies of three different beings laid silent and still. A sight one could not describe in words, only in feelings could one feel the pain they felt. A civilization that came close to disappearing from time on 'Sis' survived to continue its destiny into its future. And if the Sislens had disappeared 'Sis' would have continued to turn and travel among the stars with only traces of a once great civilization. Waiting once again for life to exist and record the achievements of existence. With control and peace back in the hands of the Sislens they now faced years of rebuilding a new planet and a new way of life. A planet that would rise from its own ashes and once again touch clear skies. Enlightened to the dangers of invaders and the horrors of war a new 'Sis' would gleam brightly under its sun. A planet protected by its bravest and strongest. As 'I' walks among the many dead beings. He realizes that even great knowledge doesn't prevent wars. It only brings about new ways to kill. "You are correct 'I', one can't have peace with another without respect for the other. Peace and respect grow together, hatred and war will always fight each other. It has always been that way, it will always be that way. War and death of war are universal," 'SI' said. Continuing his walk, 'I' is greeted by many faces of E-tucs and Sislens. Their exhausted faces gleamed small smiles of many feelings. As 'I' nods his head in respect he realizes the many reasons to feel happy. The war with the 'Repssas' was over. No more battles and no more dying. Peace would reign with 'Sis' and 'Rou' and 'I' would be at the beginning of a new age of peace. A united 'Sis' and 'Rou' would hold true to their greatest gift of peace, their bond. Lingering with the many grateful warriors 'I' felt deep within his mind their gratefulness and their pain. The loss of so many tore the minds and hearts of many. Having lost so much himself, 'I' understood their pain. Wandering within the many dead 'I' was shaken to see so many still bodies. They gave their all and now they rested forever. As 'I' stood within the field of battle Ne-Hy sends a message to the shuttle ships in orbital waiting. "Repssas' are no more, proceed with re-landing."

Receiving the message, E~tak found it hard to hold her tears of joy. Regaining control of herself E~tak, sitting in the captain's chair, looks at the crew. "Land this ship at the same landing coordinates as our first landing coordinates," E~tak said. Turning to their controls the crew follow orders with smiles upon their faces. As the ships dip into 'Sis's' atmosphere, E~tak and crew brace for another heart pounding ride. Streaking across the skies of 'Sis', white trails of smoke divided a hazed sky. Even within the hazed sky, the sight of the two ships was clearly seen by all. While the two ships circled 'Sis' the forces of 'Sis' emerge from all points of the field of battle. Coming together they give a tremendous sound of victory. Even with a sky of haze and a planet of total destruction the feeling of freedom filled all that celebrated. Finding 'I', Ne-Hy stands close and wears a face of content. As Ne-Hy stared, deep within his thoughts a vow evolved. One day I'll find the 'Repssas' and satisfy my fury of anger. For the 'Repssas' have unlocked an anger within me, I myself have not known. I will wait for the right moment to fill my ravishing thirst. Content for the moment Ne-Hy found the battle's outcome to his satisfaction. The clashing of bodies and roar of weapons firing was silent and peace once again ruled the land. With a 'Repssa' weapon in hand 'I' stares into the distant sky and utters to himself, "May this day be the beginning of the beauty and peace I so desire." With a new outlook upon his future 'I' still had to contend with the present. To live with others far from Earth, and protect a peace that all longed for. Looking sadly at the endless field of destruction, "What have we done 'SI'? We have unlocked the horrors of hell upon each other. We have armed each other and killed each other mercilessly. Burned planets and built a hatred never to end. What have we done 'SI'?" 'I' asked. "Yes, 'I', what we have done is restored peace and gave life a second chance to live. We have built friendships that will last as long as the sun will shine. Yes, 'I', what we have done will never be forgotten. The lives today and lives of tomorrow will hold us responsible for each day they live. For the clear sky and sun that give life to all will bring happiness to all. Yes 'I', that is what we have done," 'SI' said. Looking up at a silent 'I', "'I', we could not have won our freedom without you. We are more than grateful." Realizing that 'I' was the only one of his kind, Ne-Hy felt 'I's' sadness. "We will share our lives with you as one of us, we are one. Your leadership is without question or challenge. We are with you 'I' and always will be," Ne-Hy said. Looking down at Ne-Hy, "May the unity of 'Sis' and 'Rou' give birth to a friendship and bond that will sparkle of vigorous life. And may our friendship be the same," 'I' said. As 'I' and Ne-Hy observe the two forces celebrating the two shuttle ships approach and fill the hazed skies with a glow and loud thunder. High in the sky the two ships hold their position. A continuous blast of fire and wind parted the hazed sky as the two ships slowly descended. A roar that found no equal thundered from both ships. With landing legs extended outward, both ships slowly descend, sending heat and vibrations in all directions. The sight of the two ships high in the sky found favor in the eyes of all. Finally the two ships find their resting ground. The flames disappear and the wind from the ships settles in the air. And the ships' mighty roars fade away. Silence and stillness of all waited for the dark cloud that hung thickly in the air. Slowly the smoke and disturbed ash settled to the ground. Now all waited to see the ships' doors open. Noise from within the ships is heard and a door swings open. Down came the incline ramp extending out to the ground. All stood silent as they watched and waited. A 'Repssa' weapon barrel extends from the doorway followed by a very watchful E-tuc. Stepping completely out of the ship he stands and gazes all about. A cheer from those on the ground informed the E-tuc all was clear. Turning to the doorway he looks and gives an "all is clear" nod. Out steps a tall figure that catches the eyes of all. Standing high on the ramp E-tak quickly surveys the area. As E-tak stared, 'I' stared also. Dressed in a very formal attire E-tak was stunning. Her hair flowed long and her eyes stared like that of a lion. Proud with the walk of authority, E-tak walks down the incline ramp, followed by the ship's crew. E-tak was the center of attention as she stepped upon the ground of 'Sis'. Once on the ground E-tak is greeted by a large applauding force. Gathered close around, E-tuc and 'Sis' warriors part a path. Down through the pathway E-tak walks admired by all. Appearing at a distant end, 'Sis' leaders walk the same path. Cheers of unity saturated the surrounding area. It was a day to die, a day to live, and a day to remember. Meeting each other within the great force of warriors they greeted each other warmly. Turning to the great force, a 'Sis' leader speaks out loudly, "Victory is ours, victory is ours today." The winds of victory blew across the mighty force as all stood united as one. There was no need for the leaders to speak the words of friendship. The two great forces had already showed each other their worthiness in battle. Their bravery and loyalty were all they needed from each other. The bond of trust so many gave their lives for laid dead side by side. And with the living, their bond of trust would be protected with their very lives.

Joining the 'Sis' leaders, 'I' and Ne-Hy bow with great respect and honor. Pleased to see 'Sis' leaders again, all became quiet as a peaceful moon lit night. The massive army of warriors stood in silence. Staring at the leaders with great affection, 'I' speaks, "We have heard your many cries for help. We have felt your many pains of suffering. We have seen your tears of grief. We

know these to be true, for we have anguished the same feelings. We are here, O' great leaders of 'Sis'. As long as the stars greet us at night. As long as the planet continues to turn. As long as the sun warms us with shining light. We are here, we are here O' great leaders of 'Sis'." Still the massive army stood silent waiting to hear more. Before all that could see and hear, a 'Sis' leader faces the mighty forces of warriors. "We have a saying on 'Sis', if a hand of a friend helps you use your same hand and help him. As 'I' and the E-tucs have done for us, we will do for them. No challenge will be too great, no distance too far away. Your pains will be mended and your hearts and minds will be filled with friendship," the leader said. Turning to 'I' the leader wore a smile of great friendship. "With our strongest of might, with our brightest of minds, the will of 'Rou' will be the will of 'Sis'. Her needs, her sorrows, her brotherly love are ours. This is our word, this is our bond,"the leader said. The joy within all couldn't be contained any longer. A burst of wild happiness broke into the upper skies, expressing their feelings in every manner. The unity of 'Sis' and 'Rou' had come to be. Their footprints in history would show their struggles and triumphs. Their great combined achievements. The peace they guarded with their lives, and imprinted within all the minds that lived. The story of a stranger from far away who brought peace and unity became known only as the great 'I'. "I am proud and amazed at what you have achieved, 'I'. You have performed a feat all thought impossible. To defeat an overwhelming force and unite others in one swift move, I am truly astonished," 'SI' said. "My fate was written within the stars. Stars that called me from far away. Stars that followed and guided me to my destiny, I had no choice," 'I' said. "No 'I', we all have choices. You could have left 'Rou', but you chose to stay. You could have refused to lead this great force. Yet you did and risked your life many times. You have saved the lives of beings that fate had deemed dead. You have showed that bravery has its risks in life. And still time after time you used your bravery so others could live. Now you have united beings who have merely mirrored each other for thousands of years. Today you have won the hearts of many upon many. 'Sis' and 'Rou' have regained their freedom. They will rebuild and become stronger than ever. And your leadership is still much needed. For many will follow and become great leaders themselves and the bond 'Rou' and 'Sis' hold so dearly will only grow stronger. For the living will record history as both planets endlessly travel through space," 'SI' said.

"Thank you for your kind thoughts 'SI'. I can't survive without you. We were united for a good reason and our unity must continue. I have much to learn and you have much to teach me. We are one 'SI' and we shall stay one," 'I' said. Surrounded by the many that loved 'I' so much 'I' found it hard to have thoughts of leaving one day. But thoughts of his Earthly friends still weighed heavily upon his mind. For the time being, 'I' would help secure 'Sis' and 'Rou's' destiny. The day continued to linger on with great celebrating and respectful mourning of the dead. As the sun drifted across a tired sky its rays left only memories of a day never to forget. A day freedom was won and the lesson learned of why one protects that freedom. With a day coming to an end, 'I' finds himself in a secluded area. Finally alone to his thoughts 'I' looks to the stars once again. Feeling a heavy heart for the many lives lost in battle 'I' kneels on one knee and begins to pray. "What are you doing 'I'?" 'SI' asks. "I am praying to the creator of the universe. To the one that makes all things possible," 'I' said. "Why?" 'SI' asked. "To ask for forgiveness of my many wrongs. To put to rest the sadness in my mind and heart, of so many lost lives. To see the light of truth and walk within it. For one cannot be truthful to others if he is not truthful to himself," 'I' said. "What wrongs might that be 'I'?" 'SI' asks. "I am praying for forgiveness for the lives I took and the lives that I led into battle. They were my responsibility to lead and protect. Now they lie still never to see the sun rise again," 'I' said. "War is meant to kill 'I', you can't stop it. The 'Repssas' were beings of cruelty and destruction. They take lives without thinking of the pain they cause," 'SI' said. "They are beings that were led astray by their leaders. Beings for whatever their reasons, believed they followed honorable leaders. I forgive them for their wrong ways and hope one day to meet them in friendship. For I do not believe they are all creatures of destruction," 'I' said. "The 'Repssas' are bred to kill. They know no other way of life," 'SI' said. "All living beings are important in the cycle of life. All beings deserve to live within the fullness of life. Hatred can only grow from one's anger and misguided ways. One that does not walk within the light of the creator, walks within darkness and emptiness. Great strength lies in one's ability to forgive. One cannot go forward in life with darkness surrounding them. Without forgiveness one will burn with anger within their heart and mind," 'I' said. "These thoughts you say are thoughts you bring from your planet Earth?" 'SI' asks. "Yes, 'SI'. All on Earth know the wisdom we call, the word, but all don't practice it," 'I' said. "Why?" 'SI' asks. "Hatred, greed, evilness, and sinfulness rule the lives of some. They live their lives untrue to themselves and walk in darkness. Had Ne-Hy killed me when we first met, all that has come to be would not be. Ne-Hy had no anger in his heart or mind toward me. His anger was for the 'Repssas' that caused him great pain. There is a greatness within each of us. A greatness that all

beings have. That greatness comes from our creator. No matter where we are, each being is filled with the greatness of goodness. I pray to the great creator of the universe, that all learn to use this greatness and show each other their kindness and respect," 'I' said. "I understand 'I', for I have learned much of your greatness, and your peace."

Still on his knee 'I' bows his head. With eyes closed 'I' prays silently. Moments later 'I' raises his head and stares into the stars. "What do the stars have in mind for me now?" 'I' asks. "What do you mean 'I'?" 'SI' asks. "I have learned the stars are more than a twinkle of light. They were made by the creator of the universe. They are there for a reason," 'I' said. Finding a place to sit, 'I' continues to stare into the night's mesmerizing glow of stars. Their ever glowing light of wonder continued to enchant and fascinate 'I'.

As 'I' stares peacefully into the stars' majestic beauty, E~tak approaches. Without a word E~tak silently sits beside 'I'. Gazing with 'I' into the night's star-filled sky both sat silently as they enjoyed the peace of a night's sky. E~tak knew 'I' was tired, still she smiled to raise 'I's' spirits. Enjoying the calmness of the night and the stars' reflective glow, both had found more than the stars, they had found each other. Peace within the stars was now the same upon 'Sis' and 'Rou', and in the hearts of two who loved the stars. Breaking the silence E~tak speaks. "I have been looking and asking of your whereabouts. Now I find you alone, why?" E~tak asks. "I am not alone, I am enjoying the company of the stars. They are beautiful as they are timeless. They ease my mind of many heavy thoughts," 'I' said. Looking at 'I' with sympathy, "You have been through much 'I'. You have lived in the shadows of life and death. I feel your pain for the loss of so many. They gave their lives so life could continue. We must honor them and live life to the fullest. Life on 'Sis' and 'Rou' has a second chance to live," E~tak said. Looking at E~tak, "Yes, life continues no matter where we are, I have learned that. I have seen good and bad here and from where I came from, life is what you make it. Yes, E~tak, we must live our lives to the fullest. No matter where one lives, life is to live," 'I' said. Looking at 'I' with a gentle smile, "We of 'Sis' have a gift for you," E~tak said. With a tired look in his eyes 'I' merely stares at E~tak. Pointing into the night's sky, E~tak encourages 'I' to look. Following her arm to her finger tip, 'I' notices a distant bright star. "That star and the star below it glow brightly in 'Sis' and 'Rou's' night. The leaders of 'Sis' have named both stars." Before 'I' could ask a question, E~tak couldn't wait to be asked. "They are now called the stars of friendship. The friendship of 'Sis' and 'Rou' will last as long as the stars. Together they glow the image of a great leader and hero. A being that traveled from a distant star and risked his life time after time to help save many in need. He restored peace and united two very grateful planets. That peace will be protected as long as the sun shines and stars glow," E-tak said. Looking at E-tak, 'I' saw only the subtle beauty in her eyes. Beauty that gave 'I' a reason to live. Continuing to reveal to 'I' the exciting news, 'I' sat silent only staring into E-tak's eyes. "That being will be known by all as 'I', the bringer of peace," E-tak said. Sitting still with a happy smile, E-tak gazes at 'I'. With a small smile and battle weary eyes 'I' finally finds words to say. "It is a great honor to be one with the stars and adored. I will never forget," 'I' said. 'I' was the E-tuc's answer to the 'Repssa's' heartless, killing ways. The one that would rally the E-tucs and Sislens and fight back. The 'Repssas' planet to planet destruction had come to an end with 'I' leading a great force. With peace restored, 'I' would reign as supreme military leader of both planets for the time being. His leadership stood unchallenged, as many more excited by the defeat of the 'Repssas', would gladly follow 'I'. Continuing to admire the night's glittering stars 'I' looks into E-tak's eyes. Her inviting eyes were blue reflecting lights of warm comfort. Finding himself lured closer and closer, 'I' resisted little. Finally 'I' surrenders his great powers and authority to E-tak. Stepping into E-tak's world 'I' reaches out and places his hand on E-tak's hand and gives a gentle squeeze. Not knowing how E-tak would perceive his affection 'I' wore an uncertain expression upon his face. Under the moon and stars 'I' had found the love to fill his empty heart. One to fill his life with the meaning of peace and guide him when he was uncertain. Finding the words to express his deepest thoughts 'I' speaks out. "On my planet Earth, holding hands is called the beginning of love," 'I' said. "Love!" E-tak said with a look of wonder in her eyes. "It means to have great affection for another," 'I' said. Staring into 'I's' weary eyes, E-tak replies with a tender smile. "You have much to learn. On 'Sis' we call holding hands, 'bound hands,' and that means," Without another word E-tak sat staring at 'I' with a star lit glow in her eyes. This time it was 'I' who sat with a wonder in his eyes. Leaning toward 'I', E-tak puts her arm around 'I's' shoulders and softly whispers into his ear. Even after a day of horrendous battling and near death blows 'I' was still able to find the energy to react to E-tak's soft whispers. Whispers of soft spoken words many upon many would know as their shared knowledge flowed between all. 'I' was within the many of many, to share a life equal to all in friendship and love. The words of E-tak's mind flowed into 'I's' mind and heart. Pushing away the events of life and death, sadness and grief. With a refilled heart of goodness and love 'I' responds with only a broad smile to E-tak's soft whispers.

The End.